Quintessence

I0593217

In the morning I play and speak
with the mind of a child.

At the zenith of the sun I act and talk
from the thoughts of an adult man.

In the afternoon of the day I teach from
the wisdom of life experience.

And at the setting of the sun
I think and speak
with the mind of a child.

SCIENCE REPORT

October 2021

Strange signals have been detected coming from our nearest stellar neighbour, Proxima Centauri.

This is exciting news because of a hypothesis that one of the planets of that red dwarf sun, Proxima Centauri-b may have conditions suitable for life.

The signal itself was considered unusual because it remained constant over a period of a few hours and was only present when the telescope was pointed at Proxima Centauri.

Further investigation revealed that the signals could not possibly have come from Extraterrestrial life.

TIME TRAVEL

Modern science of the 21st Century has conceived the possibility of travelling through time in at least one of five different ways. We are already stepping into the future one instant after another. The rate of that progression could be changed ... theoretically, or bypassed altogether.

Quintessence

Copyright © Zsoall Robi 2022

The right of Zsoall Robi to be identified as the author of this work (Quintessence) has been asserted by him under the Copyright Amendment (Moral Rights) act 2000.

This work is copyright.
Apart from any use as permitted under the Copyright Act 1968, no part may be reproduced, copied, scanned, stored in a retrieval system, recorded or transmitted in any form or by any means, without the prior written permission of the author.

This book is a work of fiction. Names, characters, places and incidents are either a product of the author's imagination or are used fictitiously. Any resemblance to actual people living or dead, events or locales is entirely coincidental.

Cover design by Birology Books.
birologybooks.com.au

Books by Zsoall Robi

The Origination Trilogy

Book 1 – Earth Phase
Born to an insignificant peasant family Lai Xii was destined to change the path of human evolution, and in the process spread the seed of homo sapiens beyond the Milky Way Galaxy.

Book 2 – Europa Phase
The first stage of Lai Xii's plan was to save the human species from extinction, and the destruction of its home planet, by taking the entirety of Earth's population to another destination in the solar system.

Book 3 – Photon Phase
The re-engineered human species arrives at a location that Lai Xii could not possibly have foreseen; a consequence of the myriad decisions made by herself and her closest collaborators.

Other books by Zsoall Robi

Potential Absolute
Lelek could not conceive what the future held for him when he struggled to survive as a Stone Age man. Forces beyond his control set him on a path to the unfolding of all that was possible for this single, special Hominid.

Instant
Is it at all possible to cross the bridge between two consecutive instants of time into Eternity? Mary wanted much more than to experience reality outside of her digital matrix through her three remote autonomous processing units.

Immortal
Aliens are those who are different, those who belong to a different civilisation. Who is worthier of survival? Them or us? The aspirations of an entire species drives them to invade an alien race with which it may be related.

Neural Surveillance
Anything seen, heard or said is transmitted and monitored by the Angels and Saints. Privacy is a luxury that is no longer tolerated by the ruling classes. Absolute control has become the nature of the world order, for no reason other than the lust for power.

Fundamental Particle of Self
A global business conglomerate commissioned Nick, an artist, to paint a portrait of God. Nick had to meet his subject in order to do this.
On the way to the centre of the universe, where God was thought to be, Nick underwent unexpected changes and formed some most unusual relationships.
The portrait did get painted. However, it was nothing like what the Company expected to see.

Prologue

Epilogue

Kobayashi Tree

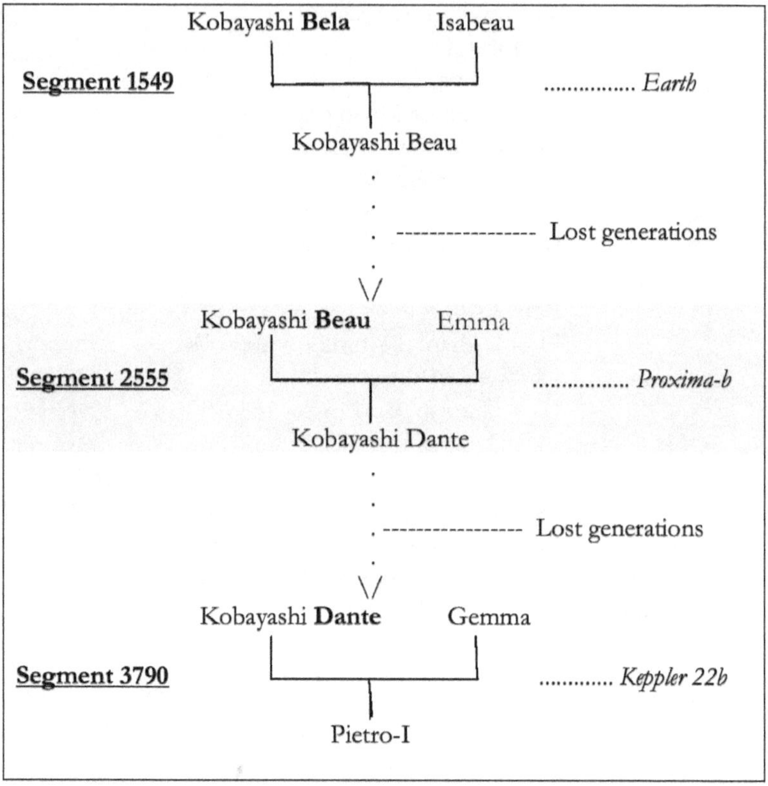

Kobayashi **Bela**   Isabeau

Segment 1549   .... *Earth*

Kobayashi Beau

.
.
. ---------------- Lost generations
.
.
\/

Kobayashi **Beau**   Emma

Segment 2555   .... *Proxima-b*

Kobayashi Dante

.
.
. ---------------- Lost generations
.
.
\/

Kobayashi **Dante**   Gemma

Segment 3790   .... *Keppler 22b*

Pietro-I

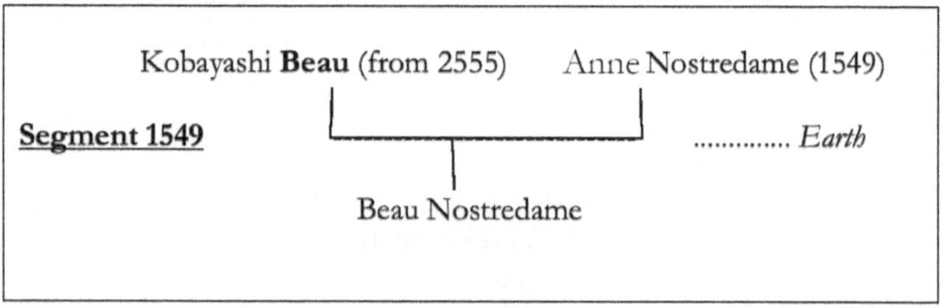

Kobayashi **Beau** (from 2555)   Anne Nostredame (1549)

Segment 1549   .... *Earth*

Beau Nostredame

Time Loop Ribbon
Pre & Post Sundering

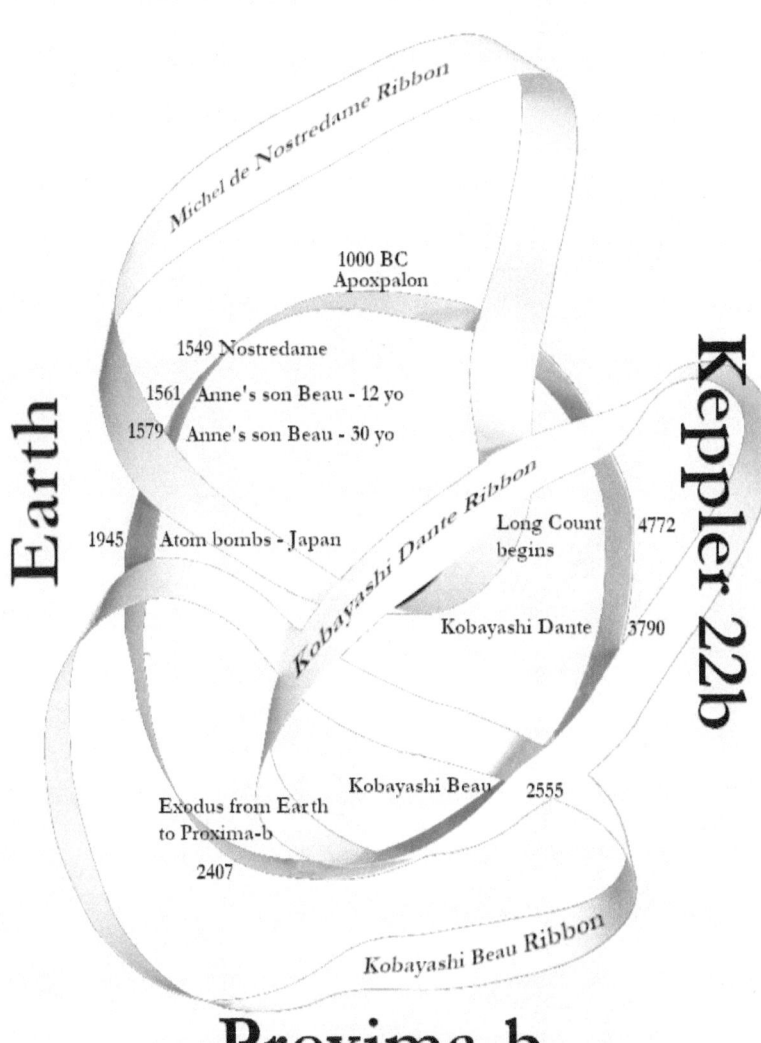

Michel de Nostredame Ribbon

1000 BC
Apoxpalon

1549 Nostredame

1561 Anne's son Beau - 12 yo

1579 Anne's son Beau - 30 yo

Earth

1945 Atom bombs - Japan

Kobayashi Dante Ribbon

Long Count begins 4772

Keppler 22b

Kobayashi Dante 3790

Kobayashi Beau 2555

Exodus from Earth
to Proxima-b

2407

Kobayashi Beau Ribbon

Proxima-b

Prologue

In the beginning ...
Proliferation

... there was only dark matter and dark energy and there was no time. Eternity reigned. Neither was there light nor was there gravity. Change brought about change and dark matter began to shrink in upon itself until its extreme confinement could no longer hold it captive. The internal forces of densely compacted dark matter burst into a violent uncontrolled explosion giving birth to the universe of baryonic substance, of gravity and of time. Change, a mechanism within Eternity gathered momentum and for a long time used gravity to create clusters of atoms, then of molecules. Then creativity gave rise to stars, planets and galaxies. Gravity became the master of the universe and it subjugated unto itself the very force which once held it captive. It exerted its will upon dark energy, robbing it of its freedom to roam the new existence, forcing it through gravitational condensation to fold itself into small clusters. Gravity found these tiny bundles of black holes viable, allowing them to do as they wished for a while. Then time began its own looping dance in order to keep up with Eternity, and created all sorts of mischief with causes and effects until within the chaos one could not be separated from the other ...

... in the realm of the finite, time had to obey the natural law. No Time Loop Ribbon could cross the boundary of finity into infinity. An undetermined fate awaited a filled Ribbon that had exhausted its capacity to hold more than its predesigned quota of causes and effects, and all that it had acquired during its journey through space-infinity ...

... clusters of dark energy bundles grew as they attracted others into themselves, oblivious to the looping of time. Some became wild rogues devouring all manner of existence around them. Even light could not escape their ravenous hunger. Yet others found peace in becoming communities of compatible benign forces, also growing and roaming the vast sea of space within which all manner of interesting things had begun to happen. Rocks, water, hydrogen, oxygen and all manner of atoms had also created partnerships. Some formed delicate gases to envelop planets, others enraged the rocks of planets great and small forcing them into molten fury, flinging some into distant realms. And as change continued its dance within time surrounded by space-eternity there arose on one particular planet - life. It, as with all manner of existence, could not stand

1

still and ignore the rhythmic melodies of change. Minuscule bundles of single cells found in each other compatible partnerships and in time came to know themselves as Man. In parallel with the rise of the great army of sentience pitted against the forces of existence one specific cluster of dark energy that had come together also began the transformation from the inanimate, showing signs of self-awareness ... and this quintessence looked about itself finding that it was not alone, and that it was separate from all that there was around it.

Part 1

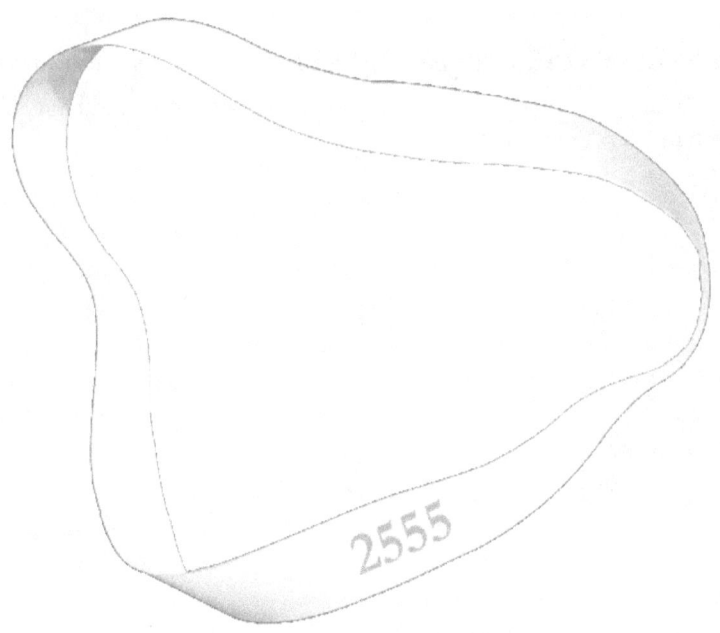

1

Blackout
2555

The cruise ship *Celestial Pleasures* lay dead in space. Of the four thousand souls aboard only one person panicked. The majority would have, if there had been time for it.

Luxury cruises generally didn't go further than Saturn, not that people didn't have time to indulge themselves in the frivolities offered by the cruise Company during the long round trip from Proxima-b. Although immigrants from Earth had colonised the Proxima Centauri system through sheer necessity for survival it was not a particularly exciting neighbourhood. The only other planet, Proxima-c, turned out to be nothing more than a super-Earth ice planet with a debris ring, good for nothing more than mining. It certainly couldn't compete with spectacular Jupiter of the Solar System either as a sightseeing destination or as a venue for extreme skydiving sports.

Life on Earth had changed dramatically between the 21st and 26th centuries. By the late 23rd century Earth could no longer support its population. The wealthy ruling classes had decided that it would be easier to go somewhere else and let the others survive as best they could. They had the wealth, the technology to do it and knew the lifestyle they wanted to pursue. Having to worry about trying to help the bulk of humanity to survive had become such a bore. The whole point of life was to enjoy it, not suffer through it. There had been way too much of that in the not too distant past. Wars over food and water provided a lucrative income to certain sectors of society. Yet having to deal with collateral damage, amongst other inconveniences, dampened the ambience of many a pleasant lifestyle.

Vacation cruises departed Prox-b regularly. Most were short trips into near space so the particularly brave individuals could frolic in space and perhaps play the new fad space-ball game, based on what used to be known as soccer, or they could simply jet around and spectate.

Celestial Pleasures offered much more than that, at considerable cost of course. The inconvenient interruption of all their systems shutting down did not inspire confidence in the Company's ability to deliver on their promises. In the few minutes that the blackout lasted Beau decided that the whole thing was a bad idea from the start. Perhaps not so much having Gemelle, his joy-friend along for companionship but for him to take some of his experiments into space. Then again, to stay true to methods of scientific enquiry he needed to do cerebral records of the actual experiences people were having, not just rely on their memory of them.

When the lights went out Gemelle leaped upon him in sheer terror clutching his arm suddenly in a vice grip. Moments ago they had been reclining beside each other in their private observation lounge as the first images of Uranus came into view, interrupting a memory bath of the previous night's intimate bacchanal with a few of their acquaintances. Close friendships had become less of a characteristics of relationships, depending more on mutually satisfying pleasures exchanges than Platonic philosophies.

"You promised me it would be fun," she hissed through clenched teeth, blinking furiously trying to adjust her eyes to the sudden darkness.

Beau didn't know what to say on the spur of the moment. He was taken by surprise as much as Gemelle. In her panic she'd clamped a hand on his arm - squeezing her fingernails into his flesh. "Stop it! You're hurting me. The alarms haven't gone off. It's just the lights in our cabin. If there was something wrong we would have heard from the Captain by n ....."

Gemelle had never been this far out in space before, in fact she'd hardly set foot off Proxima-b in her entire life. She became hysterical when Beau stopped in mid-sentence, letting go of his arm only to press the palms of her hands against her eyes. It made no difference whether her eyes were closed or open, everything was in pitch black darkness inside and outside the ship.

No one was afraid of the dark. It had become a fundamental tool to heighten many sensory pleasures by removing the distraction of sight. But this was different. It was the kind of darkness that swamped the mind, that froze the soul into wild incomprehension. Space had light. The entire universe was made of light. Light permeated everything except the shadows. Even there, reflected light always took the edge off the absolute. She began sobbing as she fell off the edge of the couch. With some effort she managed to stand and steady herself against the couch. With arms outstretched and all her fingers extended Gemelle staggered forward trying to remember where the observation bubble screen was. She desperately needed to see the light of the Milky Way. It could not have taken more than thirty seconds until she bumped into the curved surface of the screen. With eyes already straining she slammed them shut at the impact then flung them open. Incomprehensible darkness enveloped the entire universe.

Gemelle could feel her mind beginning to lose grip on reality. She'd stopped breathing. There was no sound. The ship was dead. There was only darkness.

An excruciating lance of pain stabbed through her open eyes as the lights suddenly came back on. Her cry of anguish at least reassured her that she was still alive, and alerted Beau to her position on the floor.

"Gemelle! What are you doing over there?" Beau hesitated for a moment to go to her when her scream brought him out of his trance. She didn't hear his voice over the screaming agony and flood of her tears. "What is wrong with you! The lights haven't been out for more than half a second!" At least that was his initial impression, having no immediate recollection of having dropped into a stupor.

Beau got down on his knees beside her trying his best to calm her and get her to stand. She just rolled over onto her side sobbing uncontrollably. Her words refused to come out. He lay down beside her and put his arms around her. *This is not what I had in mind when I invited her on the trip.*

The Captain's soft voice interrupted his annoyance. "Everything is fine my happy friends. Must apologise for this short interruption to whatever fun you were having. Please continue. This was just a very minor little glitch and it will not happen again. I will make sure tonight's planned frivolities will have an extra special little surprise for you." She neglected to mention that the ship had entirely stopped functioning for the duration of the blackout. There had been an unbroken safety record for space flight for over two hundred years, not just scientific exploration and near planet habitat traffic but especially all cruises. The pleasure cruise industry would have gone broke at the slightest hint of anything that could interfere with peoples' dedicated life pursuits. The ultimate purpose of life being the immersion into every form of pleasure that physical existence could possibly offer.

Part way through the reassurances Beau had already switched off, his mind rewinding to the moments before he saw Gemelle on the floor. Something was not right. At first he checked his memory replay of the final moments of last night's bacchanal, relaxing on the couch afterwards then there came a blank, then Gemelle on the floor. There should not have been a blank. He recalled sitting together on the couch looking out into the cosmos with Uranus just coming into view before the sudden darkness, like someone had ordered the lights off. What on Prox should he do with a hysterical woman on the floor bawling her eyes out? Compassion and empathy were not common attributes of the human psyche on Proxima-b.

Gemelle started to settle as the light filtered through her closed eyelids but her sobbing continued as Beau pondered the break in his memory replay.

*

Upon a planet of little consequence a man tenuously tethered to the reality of his era pondered the mystery of revelations given to him, which from within the framework of his beliefs he could not comprehend ... <But as to the hidden vaticinations which come to one by the subtle spirit of fire, or sometimes by the understanding disturbed, (from) contemplating the remotest stars as being intelligences on the watch,> ... this man wrote this in part to his son César in the preamble of his publication of the year 1555 dedicated to his prophecies.

*

The Quintessence dark energy did not know itself, nor did it have any concept of otherness for a very long time. Neither had it become an actor nor a passive spectator in the new theatre of existence until recently. Thirteen billion years floating in space on gravity highways, without definition, without boundaries nevertheless brought about a change within itself. The absorption of energies generated by the formation of Galaxies and suns and planets could not fail to catalyse the conglomerate of this specific dark energy's weakly interactive massive particles into something that had yet to define itself. Within its great vastness galaxies collided, suns went supernova and on a few tiny rocks in space something else had happened.

Sensitive now to the ebb and flow within the sea of entropy of even the tiniest manifestations of change Quintessence focused attention on something floating in space near one such rock. Within the particular Time Loop Ribbon of this object the mechanisms of cause and effect had ensnared the minds of living things. What are living things? it wondered. They are within me, but they are not me.

Concentrating upon the puddle of events upon this Ribbon, Quintessence saw a pinprick of agitation with filaments traversing the cosmic cobweb between itself and four others anchored within the cause-effect continuum. The phenomenon was no more than of passing interest in the greater scheme of things, yet the source of the urgent vibration of the filaments drew attention to itself enough to absorb Quintessence's attention momentarily. Within that moment it glimpsed an elusive, undefinable possibility of meaning to its own existence that had eluded it since its naissance.

The force of the impact of a highly focused beam of dark energy indiscriminately interrupted the flow of time within and around the inanimate object of the ship *Celestial Pleasures*, and the minuscule anchor point of one of the filaments connected itself to Quintessence. The mind of the man it touched responded without hesitation, opening itself up as if it had a knowing of that which touched it. *Kobayashi Beau*, the mind said to the visitor. *I am Kobayashi Beau*, it repeated.

Quintessence lost control over intent as Beau's life experiences flowed into it in a torrent of uncoordinated, unconnected events, thoughts and feelings and desires. In an automatic response it let wash over this strange entity much of itself that, except for a few disjointed glimpses from this Time Loop, the creature could not absorb and ceased to function as a result of the download. In that instant Quintessence withdrew sensing the overload it had caused.

… "we would have heard from the Captain by now," Beau finished shouting. He looked at Gemelle lying there on the ground by the observation screen. For some reason he had hesitated before rushing to her. Why was that? Painful flashes seared through his head, which he ignored thinking it must have been the bright lights when they came back on so suddenly after the intense darkness.

He and Gemelle lay on the ground together for what seemed like a long time. His mind went back again to his apparent internal blackout. He tried to replay the event again, moment by moment. That period of blankness kept returning giving no clue as to what had happened to his thoughts during that interval.

Eventually her sobbing slowed. Gemelle tentatively opened her eyes, feeling Beau's strong arms around her. He looked down at her tear streaked face, the running makeup causing the situation to look more tragic than it warranted. He'd never seen her like that before. Concern over another human being was not something he'd had very much experience with. His Hedonist society shunned all manner of interactions that could cause discomfort or personal pain or anxiety. Their only concern, perhaps 'expectation' is the more appropriate expression, was the fulfilment of their next pleasurable desire; except perhaps for a small faction of oddballs who derived pleasure from quite the opposite.

What was he supposed to do now? She clung to him, still whimpering. He managed to get her to her feet and walk her over to the couch. *Perhaps it would be better if I didn't say anything at all. It's not as if we're contracted.* She was only a joy-friend after all, apart from being his assistant at the laboratory.

He'd had many such friends in the past, as did most people. They were transitory relationships lasting only until their 'fun' expiry date had matured. Yet he'd been with Gemelle for many years. There didn't seem to be anything special about her. Yes, she was an extremely talented scientist and incredibly inventive when it came to extracurricular activities. But somehow they never managed to cross the fatal line of contracting for life. Not many people did. He did like her name though, right from the beginning of their association ... something timeless about it. Strange. After that first reaction he'd thought no more about it. It was just a name.

"Tell you what," he said eventually when she'd stopped making those distressing noises, "let's just forget about all this. Nothing happened really. We are not in any pain. Look out there. You can just see Uranus in full colour. Soon we'll be seeing Saturn and its rings. I say we continue our journey, have a great time on Jupiter and bring back some extraordinary memories we can play with later."

Gemelle looked at him with a little forced smile then turned to the view through the bubble screen. Uranus really was quite magnificent wrapped in its blue-green atmosphere.

"Ok," she half whispered.

"We're all getting a special treat tonight from the Captain. You'd enjoy that, wouldn't you?

"Yes." She stood, unsteady at first and made her way to the washery to freshen up.

He thought of joining her to engage in a little play, thinking better of it. He may not have known what to do in a stressful situation with a woman but he was not a complete insensitive brute. Besides, the rest of the trip could still turn out fantastic, and he didn't want to lose her valuable help on their latest memory enhancement experiments.

Quintessence had withdrawn from Beau but remained in that localised concatenated string of instants, somewhat surprised at being able to do so, effectively infiltrating the passage of time. It felt peculiar to have to become subservient to the motions of that frame of reference of this very strange creature. Yet it remained - observing, absorbing, wondering. *I am*, it mused. *I am and I have been.* Now that time had touched it a new existence began with an attraction that it could not ignore; an existence in which it had acquired an identity; Quintessence Beau, having imprinted on the first sentience it had come into contact with.

There is other, and it is not me. Awareness cascaded in torrents over its universal consciousness. It became mindful of the lesser as well as the greater rhythms of existence, and having experienced the universe of complexity within this 'lesser' being it could not release it from its thoughts.

I will remain with this Ribbon, it decided. Another tide of awakening flowed over Quintessence. *I have not chosen to do or not to do, to be here or to be elsewhere ever before. What manner of thing is this that can impact upon this self so comprehensively?*

2

<u>Kobayashi Beau</u>
And Gemelle

There was nothing special about the year 2555 other than Quintessence interrupting Beau's combined pleasure and work cruise. That contact began an extraordinary chain of events.

But Beau didn't know that would happen. All he knew was that he could not account for his thoughts for just a few minutes of his life, and that continued to bother him. Gemelle losing control of herself like that didn't make sense. He thought he'd come to know her well over the years. Now at a youthful age of seventy four years he remembered he'd started working with her some ten years ago and only later did they become joy-friends. Personally, he found the greatest pleasure in life in the realm of the intellect, not that he didn't enjoy extreme sports, or for that matter kinky pleasures of the senses. Drug indulgences had been Gemelle's main source of excess until flesh, skin and its associated frictions had taken first place in entertaining her, which cravings Beau could satisfy comprehensively.

"What is your pleasure?" he'd asked her when she first joined the Company, Playback Inc. People on Proxima-b didn't greet each other with – 'How are you?" It was always 'What's your pleasure?" or "What brings you joy?" Obviously the fulfillment of those imperatives defined one's wellbeing better than a nebulous enquiry about their medical condition.

"The mind," she replied letting her eyes roam over the lean, tall muscular body of this man with the dark mysterious eyes.

He liked that. In fact he liked her from the moment he saw her, not just the athletically proportioned body - the idea of 'speed' came to mind as he watched the way she moved and talked. They had their first deep and meaningful that same day after the orientation around the laboratory.

"What is the ultimate purpose of your life?" he asked in the eatery overlooking Proxima-b's largest planetary wind collector tunnel system. Gemelle watched the flyers executing dare devil antics through the maze of tunnels, relying on gossamer thin giant wings to keep themselves airborne - a past time she particularly enjoyed herself.

"That's a weird question, Beau. We all know it's pointless to defer the pleasures of life. The ultimate, ultimate purpose is not just mere instant gratification. We've both been there I'm sure. It's the pursuit of the pleasure of the intellect, of culture, love, friendship and of course contentment. Don't you agree?"

"Yes, yes I know all that. But it all seems so transitory. Even what we're doing here in the lab to try and magnify remembered experiences seems pointless to some extent. Just how many times can an experience be rerun before it becomes banal through repetition?"

"What? You think there's something more? Something out there? Well, there is of course – there's Earth. Remember Earth. Humanity left that behind a good while ago. And why do you think we did that?

It's because we were too busy surviving and not looking after our real life needs. We were too busy working. Work as little as possible, I say."

"Seems like you've got it all figured out, Gemelle. We are lucky, you and I. We no longer have to focus on minimising work commitments. We have our biomechs to do most of that for us. We can combine work and pleasure and create a whole new industry. Welcome to Playback Inc."

Some years after Gemelle joined the Company a special assignment came up related to their area of research. "There's a new group of extremophiles getting ready to go to Saturn again. They've got this crazy idea of ice boarding Saturn's rings, and we're going with them. I'd like to try it myself. It's been done before but this time there's new super powered boards that can take more passengers."

"I'll just do the recording of the event, and downloading of the memories immediately after. You can do the ice boarding, if you don't mind. It would be a bit too dramatic for me."

And so over the years the two scientists enjoyed the pleasures of their work and the growing companionship between each other. Their memory replay experiments had reached a critical stage, with only a few small problems to resolve. As exhilarating as the dopamine charged extreme experiences may have been the effects of the fear chemicals cortisol and adrenaline had to be overcome somehow, or at least balanced; not during the live experiences themselves of course, but afterwards, in the playbacks. What was the point of pursuing the absolute in pleasure if one could not re-live the rush in comfort and without repercussions of possibly going mad from overwhelming fear. And in this regard Gemelle had a major role to play. Her elevated fear factor level fitted the equation perfectly.

Her latest little breakdown just because the lights went out for a few minutes made Beau particularly aware of Gemelle's importance on this assignment. It also made him start thinking about her usefulness to him and to the Company in the long term, which was a bit unexpected. He didn't think of himself as a cold, calculating individual. As a man of science he'd always had to consider many options in any situation, constantly having to think things through to considerable depth. Gemelle might be an asset in the short term, however, after her behaviour the long term prospects for her possible contributions became a little hazy.

Proxima-b didn't have many neighbours. Only one, and it wasn't all that exciting. The old solar system had become the most sought after destination for extended excursions; Jupiter being the most popular destination after Saturn and Uranus. No one wanted to go as far as

Earth, or much closer than that to the sun. Mercury didn't have much to offer and Venus settlements had long since been abandoned. Only a few hundred years ago Mars still had a mining operation until the fun had gone out of it due to the uneventful trips back and forth to Prox-b, as well as the depletion of its useful resources.

"Are you feeling better after your maxhaps?"

"Yes thank you Bobo. I don't ever want to go through that again."

"What happened to you? You're much more stable than that."

"Something really scared me. At first it was just the absolute darkness, even when I went to look outside. It was as if the universe had suddenly disappeared and I was the only one left alive. Even you were not there. I mean - your mind just wandered off somewhere. It certainly wasn't in here with us to help me. Not that I'm blaming you, but I really felt there was a … a … a presence. Something I just can't explain. And what happened to you, which is more to the point?" Gemelle's mind may not have been able to accommodate an unknown cosmic energy, but there was no doubt about her sensitivity to it.

"Actually, Gemelle, now that I rerun the thing I think you might be right. I don't want to get too fanciful about this. As we both know we're living in an age when our imagination engines are in overdrive most of the time. It kind of gives our existence that extra spice. But let's not get too caught up in this. Are you ready for tonight? And there's a big week coming up for us afterwards."

"Sure, let me just take a few things off and I'll be ready."

Gemelle had the kind of body that was streamlined for 'fast', with proportions that wouldn't raise a vortex even in Jupiter's thick atmosphere. Beau couldn't help himself. He sauntered over to their bedroom and saw her jaw dropping curves in the mirror. It wasn't for the first time, yet she still managed to mesmerize him. In her case what she revealed got the blood flowing far more than what she generally hid behind translucent silken dresses.

Despite her allure his thoughts returned to those annoying missing minutes. To not be in full control of his senses every waking moment was an incomprehensible impossibility to Beau. He even controlled his dreams, as far as his imagination would allow. *I'm going to have to write it all down and deconstruct the details down to every second.* As part of the pleasure of his job Beau enjoyed letting his mind explore then commit all random thoughts to e-parchment. Sometimes his jottings even took on a life of their own, a rhythm of ideas that revealed more than just the content of the words. Already engrossed in thinking where he would start and in spite of seeing his Gem making herself irresistibly beautiful he walked to the other room to prepare himself as well for the evening.

"Ooh! Nice!" she exclaimed. He'd just stepped out of the costume cubicle when Gemelle reappeared. With magenta and purple feathers fluffing about from a thin black band around his temple Beau looked totally the 'Bobo' she absolutely loved. Her eyes scanned down across his shaved bare chest, muscular but not overly, to his tight fitting canary yellow package restrainer, which connected in a single golden one-piece down his well-proportioned legs to brilliant white, glossy high heeled boots.

"I just love that you're not augmented. I prefer my men au naturel." Smart implants of many capabilities had become fashion accessories, not just functional pleasure enhancers for the bulk of Prox-b's population. A few resisted the urge; some due to conspiracy fears of covert governmental controls - others just didn't want 'impurities' about their person, not too dissimilar to attitudes back on Earth about tattoos. She seemed to have completely forgotten the recent painful experience in her eager anticipation of the forthcoming entertainment.

Standing close together face-to-face he let his hand hover over one bare breast just close enough to let her feel his heat, while she gave his restrainer a little squeeze to check it remained true its main function.

"Come on then, we don't want to miss anything." Partying protocol demanded one did not interfere with each others 'presentation' prior to party commencement. Afterwards pent up desires were generally given free reign. Beau and Gemelle made their way to the entertainment dome expecting to make a noteworthy entrance.

The cruiser had been built in space and as such had few restrictions in terms of design or size. With four thousand passengers and three thousand crew to look after them it still had enough internal capacity to boast of a sports arena as well as several theatres and entertainment complexes. Interactive hologram enclosures would not have been large enough to contain the crowd expected by the Captain after her generous offer of a special treat. This almost spherical observation bubble could accommodate well over half the guests.

Beau and Gemelle received lots of Oohs and Ahs on their way to the inner circle of the flat platform that rotated in the centre of this sphere. They in turn acknowledged the outlandish outfits of their friends – it was the polite thing to do.

"This looks exciting," commented Gemelle as they strapped into their anti-grav couches. "Have you tried this before?"

"No, but I'm told that whatever you do don't unbuckle."

Everyone receive a jab of Bloody Cosmos on the way in, followed by a minute whiff of Nitro laced with Pheros pervading the air around them. If that combination didn't make them feel good, nothing would.

No physical object was allowed to be used prior to or during the event. Delayed gratification definitely did not feature in their culture and as soon as everyone had arrived and strapped in the lights began to dim. Gemelle caught her breath suddenly remembering her bad experience, and again her hand shot out to clutch Beau's arm. She wasn't wearing her talons this time so he left her hand there.

"Don't worry Gem, there's other lighting coming on already." And as he said that the platform began to rotate and tilt slightly to one side.

The surface of the transparent dome above and around them came alive with the stars of the Milky Way. At first they saw the galaxy from above with its spider arms stretching over the dome begin to move towards them. Gemelle's hand withdrew into her own lap as she became absorbed in the sensation of flying free in space, simulated by minor movements of the platform.

Within a few short minutes the combined effects of their jab, the whiff of happy gas and the growing sensation of their motion increasing speed gave the entire crowd a sudden adrenalin rush. The very suddenness and intensity caused quite a few gasps of intense pleasure as if they were in the throes of a particularly satisfying sexual interlude. Even Gemelle let slip a little whimper in spite of not anticipating the sensation.

The platform dipped and swerved as they neared various solar systems with their giant planets, until into their immediate vision came the sight of an old familiar playground.

Jupiter appeared with its family of moons seemingly dancing around it like revellers around a Maypole. The image must surely have been manipulated because those moons appeared far too close to their parent, and they certainly didn't bounce erratically around like that.

"This is A m a z i n g!" she whispered to Beau, her hand again squeezing his arm, but this time without the fear of darkness in them.

"Yeah, absolutely. I can see you really like that," catching sight of her erect nipples. She followed the direction of his gaze and with a cheesy grin looked down at his restrainer. Intense pleasure often did that to them. The evening promised a lot more to come.

As the two of them engaged in visual innuendos, oblivious to the reactions of the rest of the crowd their platform slowed gradually enough so their eyeballs would not knock against each other from the built-up momentum.

"Did you all enjoy that?" came the Captain's voice from somewhere behind Jupiter up there in the galaxy. She didn't need to hear the enthusiastic applause to be assured of the success of her little 'treat'. But there was more to come.

16

"Well … If you liked that, remain seated a little longer. And don't undo those straps unless you want to paint yourself all over the dome!" she warned. "Anyone need a little more juice?"

Again it was a superfluous question. All the clamour indicated in the affirmative. As far as the audience knew no other cruise had 'entertained' their guests so generously.

"Woo Hoo! Up went the cry as they breathed in the Nitro mix.

That must have been the cue to bring on the main event. Lights dimmed a little more, not quite pitch black but almost, and in the background of the dome the pin-pricks of stars filled the entirety of it. At the same time Jupiter seemed to get closer and closer.

It detached itself from the surface of the observation dome to enlarge even more as it's virtual reality hologram drifted above everyone's gaze inside the dome itself. It came so close that people began to shrink back into their couches. Another aroma filled the enclosure. For a moment, only the briefest moment, a hint of ammonia then a faint suspicion of modified phosgene and a split second of hydrogen sulphide infiltrated their consciousness. A few people exclaimed in alarm. They must have been to Jupiter before. They must have been exposed to the unpleasant side of its character. Its gases created a magnificent palette of swirling colours but not such a benign effect on the human olfactory sense or their wellbeing.

Suddenly the holographic image seemed too real. How can one appreciate the quality of intense pleasure without the companion of a little unpleasantness? The aromatic infusion didn't last long – long enough to add a touch of extra spice to the experience.

A few randomly selected people from the audience found themselves being raised off the platform, still strapped into their couches. "Bobo!" She couldn't reach him. Their couches had moved away from each other and high above the heads of the rest of the audience. They, and some twenty others began to experience the latest in holographic planetary excursions.

"Relax. This looks like a lot of fun. Just hang on." He really didn't need to say that for her knuckles had turned white from doing exactly that. A slight vibration had come into the couches, making the occupants feel as if they were buffeted by Jovian winds. A shadow appeared above their heads with paraglider control lines coming down to their arms. Absorbed in the complications arising around the 'floaters' the rest of the audience didn't notice that Jupiter's spherical horizon could no longer be seen. Gemelle felt like she'd started swaying from side to side, and the wind brushing against her almost naked body convinced her mind that she was in fact floating in Jupiter's atmosphere.

Not just floating … "Bobo! I'm skydiving! Zowie! Look at me!"

Beau needn't have looked for he and many others were doing the same thing. "Absolutely Amazing. This is Incredible!" she cried – until the colours around her began getting darker and Jupiter seemed to rush towards her much faster. She got such a fright that she almost blacked out. Sensors in her couch had been monitoring her condition the entire time. Her motion slowed immediately and her parachute seemed to lift her back up out of Jupiter's clouds.

Back on the platform beside Beau she couldn't help herself from grinning so widely that her mouth began to hurt. He felt much the same, although he didn't get the same fright at the end of the ride.

"Now this is something worth remembering," he said. "As soon as we get back to the cabin I'll download this and we can compare it with what's coming up." He knew what that was going to be – she didn't. The surprise would be half the fun.

The rest of the evening's entertainment seemed a little anti-climactic. Although they didn't need any extra chemical stimulants to enjoy themselves they still managed to get three full meals, each with several courses down past the tongue's yummy receptors. Their science still hadn't quite worked out a way to purge the stomach between meals other than a not altogether unpleasant regurgitant: The Roman feathers, now only to be found in a museum vomitorium, did have a short revival. The practice died out fairly rapidly, possibly due to unpleasant smellatoria associated with it. Banter around their table expressed outstanding enjoyment added to the already well advanced affability. Various diners beside them made overtures for a communal de-briefing after dinner, but Beau and Bobo had more intimate plans.

"Forgive us for being a little anti-social, Gemelle and I actually need to do some work. As you might know this is a working holiday for us." They didn't, but nobody cared if these two wanted to miss out on enjoyable activities to end a thoroughly perfect day. Faux sad commiserating faces watched as the two of them escaped what otherwise would have been a most delicious way to wind up the evening.

"What shall we do first?" asked Gemelle with a come-on grin and a brush of her hand against his chest as soon as they were out of view.

"I would say we'll need to punctuate the day's activities appropriately before we get back to work."

*

The Captain knew she had to create enough of a distraction so that her passengers would remember that and not the darkness anomaly; for it was serious, extremely serious. On no other voyage that she could remember in her extensive years of piloting *Celestial Pleasures* had she experienced such a phenomenon. None that threatened the welfare of her ship or the lives of her passengers. Not knowing what had caused it made it even more worrisome.

This cruise liner had been built with every imaginable safety measure; multiple redundancy systems, double chain of command – everything had been considered, including double and triple cosmic radiation shielding, automatic laser lances to destroy any meteor that even hinted at coming their way. And yet everything had failed. None of the backup systems activated when they were most needed. On top of that the darkness anomaly lasted for far too long. It wasn't just dark in every nook and cranny of the cruiser – it was absolute, bottomless darkness in all of space around them as well. She saw nothing, their instruments saw nothing. What the hell happened out there! Yes, she had to distract everyone but she couldn't distract herself.

I'll have to do a survey and see if anyone knows more than I do. Perhaps a few people were enjoying themselves in the dark and noticed something else unusual.

Even more worrying was the actual duration of the event. Immediately afterwards she contacted the base back on Proxima-b. She had just one simple question that baffled them.

"What time is it?" she asked. Their response did not match ship time.

*

Upon reflection and having observed the strange small object with living things inside it Quintessence realised that its intrusion into the fabric of the object did something that effected those living things to their detriment. It refrained from further intrusion into the object and had withdrawn into deep space to continue exploring its interesting experience from a safe distance, still remaining within the realm of the Local Group and the Local Time Loop Ribbon.

3

Gravitational Slingshot

At the first autopath intersection on level eleven the ship's Captain seemed to be waiting specifically for them.

"Hello Beau, What brings you joy?"

"Hello Captain Catherine, What is your pleasure? Mine is right here. Have you met Gemelle, my joy-friend?"

"Hmm." She liked what she saw ... of him and her, both still in their skimpy costumes. She had to push distracting thoughts aside. Obviously Catherine was not in a particularly happy mood; understandable under the circumstances. On reflection, the cost of trying to recreate conviviality on her ship may have been a little excessive. Perhaps things weren't as bad as she first thought. Full operation had resumed with no outward indication that the anomaly had ever happened, other than for the time discrepancy.

"We've known each other for a long time Bo, right? I can trust you, right?" she glanced at Gemelle who seemed nice enough, had intelligent eyes ... but ...

"Indeed you can Cath, and you can trust Gem. She's been with me for quite a few years. We're also working together. This is actually a working cruise for us. You want to talk? Come join us." Gemelle didn't seem to object to the invitation. Casual get-togethers sometimes worked out very nicely, thank you. The Captain stood a little taller than Gemelle, her white hair in freefall to her waist. If it wasn't for the tight fitting reflective uniform one would have thought her to be one of those 'expert' entertainers one saw in the magazines, not the Captain of a star cruising pleasure liner.

Catherine smiled at Beau's joy-friend, liked the invitation in her eyes – but ... "Hmm ... perhaps when we're on the way home. Right now I need to ask you about something." She hesitated. Beau raised a questioning eyebrow. Gemelle's eyes clouded over. "Look, I have some idea of the work you do at Playback. It's nothing to do with that. But you are a cognitive neuroscientist and you would know about certain things; like hallucinations and mass hysteria. I need to find out what's going on. My passengers could be in danger." She stopped, realizing she'd been procrastinating.

"Ok, what's on your mind. Or should I guess?" asked Beau. Gemelle moved closer to Beau. She knew what was coming and didn't like it. "Is it that short blackout? It didn't last long. What's the problem?" He didn't mention his own strange experience.

"It is a problem, Bo. I hope it's not going to turn out to be a big problem. Did anything happen to you?" Gemelle's sudden intake of breath made Cath look directly at her. "Was it something unpleasant? Can you tell me about it?"

"I don't want to remember."

"Did everything go absolutely dark?"

"Yes," she almost squeaked.

"Right. You don't have to say any more."

"Bo, what about you?"

"That was a fantastic show you put on Cath. Wasn't it Gem? What did you enjoy the most?" He was only trying to stop Gemelle from sinking back into the bad experience she had in their cabin beforehand. He didn't think he could cope with a blubbering woman again, especially not out there in public.

"You left me!" she said.

"Sorry Gem. Truly sorry. I didn't mean to. It's just that I must have blanked out for a moment."

"It couldn't have been for a moment," Catherine said, "we lost about ten minutes of ship's time."

Beau's eyebrows shot up again. One of the greatest pleasures of his life was solving mysteries. He had put the strange sensations he went through out of mind during the evening, but now decided it would be fun to go through the process of analysis, and here was Cath putting the cherry on top.

"Right, let's not stand out here in public. Come to our cabin, relax and we can go over this in comfort." Gemelle brightened at the prospect right away. Captain Catherine reassessed her feeling of urgency, making an impromptu executive decision. Two more autopath rides and up several levels brought the trio to Beau's cabin.

"So what have you got planned for us tomorrow?" Gemelle asked casually as they settled with refreshments. She didn't want to talk about the darkness. The show had succeeded in taking her mind off the whole unpleasant thing, and she had heard something else was planned as a follow up. The thing to do was to enjoy the evening - not regurgitate unpleasant memories.

"Well, Gem," Cath patted her knee casually, letting her hand linger there, "don't tell anyone this, but we'll not just be cruising past Saturn on the way to Jupi. I don't want to say any more … it would spoil the fun."

Gemelle casually covered Cath's hand with hers, not unnoticed by Beau. She glanced out the bubble wall, reassured by the vision of stars and brightness everywhere.

"I lost some of my memory." Beau jumped in without a preamble. "I know something happened, although I wasn't conscious of the darkness until the light came on again. I can feel there are things in my head to account for that time loss but just can't squeeze them out. We were going to do a little work when we got back, but that's ok. It can wait. Perhaps the lost memories might reveal themselves when we've downloaded the entertainment experience." He got up, glanced at the two hands covering each other. "More refreshments?" he asked.

"Have you talked to anyone else who had the same experience? No? Ok. Come and see me when you've remembered something. I could use your help. You are a clever boy, Bo. Nice abs. Like your feathers too." Captain Catherine finished off her second juice and made a move to stand. A slight pressure on her hand from Gemelle, which had lingered on Gem's knee, delayed her departure for some time.

*

Saturn would have to be one of the most outstanding creations to come out of the formation of Earth's solar system.

The whole slingshot manoeuvre had been organised beforehand by Erasmus the on-board AI, so Captain Catherine could afford to sleep in, in her own cabin after her extensive researches of the night before with Beau and Gemelle. *Bo's still got the magic.*

Much of life's more worthwhile pleasures had an element of risk to them. This was no different. Their AI navigator had made all the calculations, knew exactly how close they could come to the planet and just how much thrust to apply at exactly the right moment.

"Good morning all you happy travellers." The Captain managed to get a deep night's sleep, feeling a lot more positive than the day before. "We have a real treat for you today. I know you're all looking forward to getting to Jupiter. If you would care to make your way to port side and buckle into the observation couches as soon as you can. You would not want to miss this, I promise you. Oh, and just a gentle warning – please remain seated and strapped in for the duration of the encounter."

That got most passengers off their feet, out of their cabins and many to postpone their pleasurable pursuits in private or with company. They had not forgotten their previous surprise, hoping that the new promise would surpass it. So far Jupiter could only be seen as a brighter than average speck, with Saturn much more distinct as a planet with its rings.

We human beings are in general quite boring creatures, mostly because we can get used to anything; the spectacular, the outstanding, the extraordinary – even bad smells. *Celestial Pleasures* had been travelling at normal speed for some considerable time, so all aboard had become used to it feeling almost as if the ship had been standing still in space.

People began murmuring soon after they had all settled for their next dose of excitement. "Hon, do you think we're starting to speed up again?" one really old guy asked his joy-friend turned contracted mate.

"Must be that stuff you took last night, Frank. I don't feel a thing."

"Yeah, that's the trouble, you never do anymore," Frank said under his breath.

But the sensation didn't go away. Gemelle noticed it too. "Bobo, can you feel that. I think Cath has put her foot on the thrusters." She was feeling so much better after what followed the unwelcome interrogation.

"You must be right. Have a look to the right," everybody's' eyes had gravitated in the same direction, "I can just see Titan coming up."

"Holy Centauri! You sure they're not just playing tricks with us?"

"Not this time. I can feel a slight vibration. If I didn't know better I'd think Cath had a death wish."

"Don't say that, you're starting to scare me."

Others were beginning to have the same reaction until a slight adjustment to their trajectory clearly showed they were not on a collision course.

"Stay focused people. We are not magnifying this image. You're about to see something that very few have witnessed, if any – other than aliens perhaps."

Remarkably quickly Titan's chequered soft green surface began to fill the cosmos as seen from the cruiser. Some heads turned away, the majority had managed to overcome their fear with wide open, unblinking eyes staring at the growing image of Saturn's largest moon.

"Concentrate on that growing red orange area in the Northern hemisphere. That is a colossal storm brewing down there. As we get closer you'll see what you think might be clouds dissolving around the storm's perimeter. That's a deluge of methane rain."

"Gem, can you see it, just to the left quadrant, Can you see the Sun's rays starting to come through it?" That's when they all saw the rainbow. Every imaginable hue of blue appeared in concentric rings around the orange storm area, with bright orange on the outer edges alternating with narrow streaks of white.

As *Celestial Pleasures* hurtled towards Titan Captain Catherine broke the concentration to bring their attention back to their speed. "Watch carefully now, I've got almost full power on." And they could feel it. A frightening sensation they had not ever felt on a pleasure cruise, not even the die-hard oldies addicted to cruising.

Within a few minutes Titan's full image filled their vision, quickly sliding off to starboard. They were so concentrated on missing the moon that they had not noticed another heavenly body come into view. More than an hour had slipped by after they passed Titan. Captain Catherine eased up on the throttle and they all breathed a sigh of exhilarated relief. Some had started to undo themselves from the couch restraints.

"Not yet, my darlings! There's more to come. Just relax for a little while longer." By way of a distraction she reconfigured the observation screens to show them some historical images of small moon sized asteroids committing suicide into Jupiter's surface. It was their next destination, a few days away yet - not kamikaze practice, just the location.

It must have felt like an anti-climax after the near encounter with Titan, but that's exactly what Catherine had in mind. Relax them, lull them into a false sense of comfort. Because of the enormous magnitude of Jupiter normal or average sized asteroids hardly made a ripple in its thick atmosphere. Just a few black spots for a few minutes and the intruders always disappeared without any further cries of pain. Really quite boring from a visual perspective.

Another twenty minutes of Jupiter lunching on cosmic debris seemed to be enough to settle the excited travellers. The AI pilot rotated Celestial Pleasures on its longitudinal axis just enough to allow Saturn with its rings to replace satiated Jupiter's hologram.

"Hold onto your contracted mates, hold onto your joy-friends, hold onto anyone near you!" warned Catherine. And at the same instant she again engaged the thrusters, as well as the auxiliary boosters. The sensation wasn't as abrupt as being thrust into the back of their couches, but near enough.

The ship came upon Saturn from its Southern hemisphere. Although their conscious minds told them that it was the ship that was in motion, their eyes told them differently. Saturn's rings blazed with the Sun's reflected light off its ice planetesimals as it turned its skirt edges away from them. The wafer thin ring dipped itself down further as the ship continued its dive towards it.

Gemelle started fidgeting. She knew it must be a trick, or at the very least a manoeuvre under complete control – but it didn't feel like it. Automatically her hand reached out to Beau's arm again.

"You can be such a wimp Gem, I'm sure Cath knows what she's doing." And yet, as he kept his eye on the fast approaching planet a little adrenalin seeped into his veins. The incredible beauty of its design didn't fail to impact on his finer sensibilities either. In some ways he had the soul of an artist, as well as being a scientist. The banded horizontal colours, on the same plane as the ring dramatically showed off the ring's shadow, which widened on the planet's cloudy surface until disappearing into the Southern hemisphere.

"We're going to come awfully close," he said to Gemelle. Her adrenalin rush had just kicked in, and from the exclamations of those around her, so had theirs. Little beads of perspiration appeared on her temple. This is so much fun, she tried convincing herself.

The Captain thought it opportune to inform her guests of what was happening, as Saturn's Northern golden blue hexagon came into view. "I thought you might enjoy another slingshot around our friend out there. We are running a little behind schedule and this will put us back on track.

I'm sure you're all eager to get to the skydiving on Jupi. Just hold on, we're almost done."

Those words may have eased some of their minds, although the acceleration just kept on increasing, seen only as the more rapid tilting of the rings away from them until almost out of view. As before with Titan the cosmos had almost completely disappeared, replaced by Saturn's kaleidoscope of striated colours.

At last the planet began to slide out their field of vision and the acceleration seemed to diminish, yet their actual speed did not reduce one iota. That was the whole point. It would be smooth sailing all the way to Jupiter now. Eventually the crowds released their holds on whatever was nearest to them, knuckles started to have blood flow restored and sighs of fulfilment filled the air. Gemelle's pupils were still dilated when she met Catherine on the way to the restaurant for dinner.

"Well my friends …?" she left the question hanging.

"Awesome!" Gemelle's flushed face would have said it all anyway.

"You say that now Gem, but what about when you squeezed the blood out of my arm," Beau said jokingly. *She can be such a wimp*, he couldn't help thinking to himself again. *Brilliant in her field, but for Centauri's sake …!*

"I love being afraid when you're with me, Bobo." Catherine took another look at Gemelle's flushed face … *Strange girl!*

"Um … Bo – have you had time to think about our little anomaly."

"Nothing concrete as such, but I've left room in my mind to think about it." And so he had. As a general process Beau could load up his brain with all sorts of data, questions, mysteries and let the grey matter do its job first. Then, when all the connections had been made and everything was neatly filed away in its right place he could begin. That time had not yet arrived. Cath just had to be as patient as he was. In truth, Beau himself was getting impatient about the whole thing.

*

Puzzled, Quintessence couldn't understand the peculiar behaviour of the little object as it tried twice to crash into a moon and then into its planet. It had never observed any other lumps of physical matter, large or small do such a peculiar thing - and survive. When they did try they invariably succeeded. Energy in the cosmos remained constant in spite of kinder planetoids misbehaving.

*

Captain Catherine's impromptu plan worked beautifully. She couldn't hear anyone during dinner alluding to the blackout phenomenon. It would have become decidedly uncomfortable if she'd had to account for something she didn't have a dim wit's clue about. Her long time brilliant ex-joy friend didn't seem to take the situation as seriously as she thought it warranted. At least the Jupiter visitation would buy her some time. Surely something would turn up, if nothing else perhaps some sort of credible theory from her on-board AI. With Saturn behind them everyone turned their attention to the next on-shore excursion, more accurately in-cloud excursion. The voyage had two destinations; Jupiter and the other; a return visit to Saturn.

Beau and Gemelle got to work the very next day as the *Celestial Pleasures* headed for Jupiter. Of the many thousands on board there was no shortage of volunteers for the memory downloads. Several hundred turned up at the field lab close to Beau's cabin.

"Have you got enough helmets ready?"

"We only brought twenty two with us, but that should be enough. It only takes a little over an hour to do the download."

"I wasn't going to start recording until the Jupiter flights and Saturn's ring ice boarding. But this past week's entertainment will give us some really interesting base data."

"That may be," Gemelle didn't like passive experiential memory data as much as Beau. "I think direct engagement produces much cleaner data for our purposes. It's one thing to try and enhance memory soiled by imagination, and an entirely more valid scientific approach to pep up actual reality saturated experiences."

"We can talk about that later. The first guinea pigs are here."

"Greetings Prof," said none other than the curmudgeonly old blighter, Frank. Martha, his contracted joyless mate entered with him. "This ain't gonna hurt is it?"

"Relax Mr. Smodgely," Gemelle used her best smile as she led the two to their reclining seats, "you'll hardly notice it, it'll be so quick."

"You'll be done with her in five minutes," interjected Frank.

"Stop it Frank!"

Beau had already started adjusting helmets on another couple as he listened in on the conversation. "I'm sure we'll be able to provide you with many happy feedback hours, Mr. Smodgely." *Sometimes I think I'm wasting my life giving idiots like these any pleasure at all.*

After processing four sets of twenty two couples they'd had enough and closed the doors. "We should really do ourselves, Gem. I mean, after that strange thing that happened. We might learn something."

"You go right ahead, Bobo darling. I'm too busy wiping it from my mind, let alone wanting to replay it."

"Fair enough. I understand." *In all the years that I've known Gemelle I had no idea she could be so – so – fearful. Hmm.* "But could you please help with the equipment. I want you to put me under for at least an hour before the event and an hour after. I'm not interested in the Titan thrills or the fling around Saturn. I need some clues as to why I can't remember those few minutes during the blackout."

He let her give him a light sedative. It helped sometimes to prevent the mind from being distracted by external stimuli during the download. "I'll got back to our cabin now, and look in on you in a little while."

"Bobo!" Four hours later Gemelle found Beau thrashing about in his recliner, still attached to his leads. He hadn't been able to wake up enough to detach himself from the equipment. She knew what to do, a strict protocol for a memory exit ensured neural integrity would not be compromised by sudden changes in energy from disconnection or the sudden cessation of imagery. She'd set the equipment to record, then auto-playback as he'd asked.

"Bobo!" she yelled again trying to hold him down long enough to disconnect the individual sensory leads that fed into his brain at different locations around his skull. "I have to do this, there's no time to bring you out of it!" There was no point talking to him, he couldn't hear her. In utter frustration she grabbed all five leads at the same time and pulled them out of the playback unit.

Beau's gyrations stopped immediately. Gingerly she started unplugging the leads from his cranial harness. "Gem?" with eyes still half closed he reached up to stop her from doing that.

"What happened to you? You were thrashing about out of control. Surely you don't want to go back under!"

"Leave the vision lead in and plug me back." She hesitated, afraid he'd unravel or worse, become violent. "Now!" With trembling hands she plugged that lead back into the equipment, leaving the others dangling from the cranial net. "Start me from the beginning of the playback."

"Ok! Alright. But I'm not leaving you. If you start all that thrashing again I'm pulling you out."

Beau settled back into the couch, letting his eyes close slowly as faint flashes returned to his consciousness; distorted hazy images he could not immediately comprehend.

4

Jupiter Dive

Exhaustion overcame him after the full two hour replay.

Gemelle found him asleep, still attached. She'd fallen asleep herself after a while of intensely watching for any dangerous signs from him. The last she saw was his rapid eye movements, and increased rapid breathing. He must have fallen into a deep REM sleep. She knew from their past games that he had a great deal more stamina than herself, but his exertions must really have taken their toll.

"Bobo? Come on, wake up." she stroked his chest gently not wanting to alarm him. His heavy breathing continued a little while longer before he began to stir.

"Thank you Gem. Thanks for staying up with me." She kept stroking his chest, deep concern showing on her face. "It's all ok. Unplug me, let me get up. We have a lot of work ahead of us today."

Over breakfast they discussed how many people were scheduled for downloads that day, how soon they'd be arriving at Jupiter and whether all their flying equipment had been prepared.

"I'm really looking forward to getting out there, Gem. Aren't you?"

"Yeah, yes - absolutely - sure. Are you sure *you're* up to it? We could give it a miss. There will be lots of others whose experiences we'll be able to download. It doesn't have to be us." Her enthusiasm didn't sound entirely convincing.

As she was speaking his eyes lost focus. He'd stopped listening. His head jerked a couple of times and he grimaced as if in pain. Gemelle jumped up over to his side of the table, but by then he'd stopped, looking surprised as to why Gemelle should be beside him. Immediate recall of painful, incomprehensible flashes of catastrophic images seemed to zap through his mind – the sort of images one could expect if watching violent cosmic creation directly before one's eyes.

"You know what – I think I'll stay in today. You go ahead. Get through as many people as you can. Their passive experiences are not really critical at this stage. We need the real stuff."

"Alright – if you're sure. I'll come back soon."

Beau just nodded, grinned, waved goodbye his mind already racing ahead. *She's such a good girl, really.* He didn't know what he was trying to convince himself about. He settled in front of the recorder's big portrait format screen. They were the best orientation when reviewing code. First he ran some algorithms through the full scan, which didn't red-line anything. Then he began a visual - tiring work that. Still nothing. Those few minutes of neural blackout blankness persisted. As a last resort he narrowed down to those specific minutes that worried him the most. He plugged himself in for a replay directly through his neural net again. Nothing appeared in front of him at first on the screen. Then internal disjointed images began scrolling past in rapid succession, without any sense of continuity from one set of images to another. People in strange costumes that completely covered their bodies, except for their faces and hands – then just as suddenly others moving together in large crowds, all attired exactly the same way performing some kind of ceremonial dance in front of enormously tall narrow buildings. These visions flashed by so fast he didn't have time to examine them, let alone think about what he was actually seeing.

He had just stood up, still steadying himself when Gemelle entered. "You've gone completely pale! You've been doing it again, haven't you? You are impossible Bobo!"

"Don't be angry with me Gem. I have to know. Perhaps you're right. I should give it a rest. Let the old grey matter sort things out before I go poking a stick around in there." He knew he was being unreasonably impatient with himself.

*

They were back on schedule as Captain Catherine had promised. You could feel the excitement throughout the ship. Probably half the people had come to experience this famous extreme sport for the first time. Many had done it before. The experienced ones had to buddy up with the newbies. That was the law, not just another rule of the sport. Anyone who went out there by themselves could not expect any help at all if they ended up in trouble, not even the expert flyers.

First time travellers crowded to all the observation bubbles as *Celestial Pleasures* cruised into geosynchronous orbit around the big boy. Catherine had decided on parking in the most spectacular location possible; directly above the centuries old enormous green storm, which once used to be reddish, about five thousands kilometres out. It should not possibly have existed. The right chemicals didn't exist in Jupiter's atmosphere to enable that to happen. Scientists had proffered a theory that another, much smaller gas planet with exotic gases, had plunged into the middle of the red storm and was still there floating in the upper atmosphere. The only visible result being a gradual change over centuries of the storm's colour. It wasn't of enough commercial interest to excite the scientific minds of the time, other than to titillate the imaginations of sightseers.

At first the green storm held their attention. Everybody knew of all the moons but must have forgotten about the most spectacular one - Io.

"We are going to prepare for the games tomorrow, make sure your body-flying suits are in perfect order," suggested the Captain, "when you go out there it's a matter of life or death – your decision! By the way, have any of you thought of waving a greeting to our nearest neighbour. You'll only get a few chances while we're here."

They took the hint and made their way to the cruisers starboard side. And sure enough Io came into view huffing and puffing lava and sulphurous fumes. It could not have been more of a contrast to its bigger ice encrusted neighbour, Europa.

"How could two such diverse moons exist so close to one another?" one passenger was heard musing.

And another speculated about Io, "Do you know what? – I'd love to go over there and have a picnic – right there, between those two volcanoes, the angry ones."

"Don't be silly Sasha. Even in our suits we'd end up being sizzling sausages," replied her joy-boy.

A few people, with more of a nostalgic bent to their mental constitution, asked to be pointed in Earth's direction. That was their ancestral home after all ... unlikely they would ever come so close it again. They didn't wave in its direction, but for a few minutes thought about whether life still existed on the planet once ruined by their ancestors.

In the excitement building for the first event, which was just a test flight for the buddies and their charges to get to know one another, Beau and Gemelle forgot about last week's worrying researches into the dark mystery.

"I know you've done this many times at home in our wind tunnels, Gem. This is several magnitudes more dangerous."

She cut him off before he could talk her out of it. "I'm no wimp – contrary to what you might think, and I've been practicing my control in the wind tunnel aboard the ship while you've spent your time working."

That made him blink – not the practicing, the other thing ... *I had no idea she could read my mind. Our technology has not advanced that far – we can record and rerun memories of experiences, and with a bit of luck after this trip's experiments, might be able to enhance them – but to read another's thoughts ...*

Both of them were considered to be novices, this being their first flight in Jupiter's atmosphere, and each had to have their own individual buddies.

"Just make sure you keep your eye on your pick up skiff. There's nowhere else to land down there," Beau urged.

"Yeah, yeah. You worry too much."

Unbelievable. She was such a wimp in many ways, and when there was real danger she could flip completely the other way. Strange girl.

"First run – just three hundred of you," announced Fredrich, the event organiser, "you'll go down in three shuttles as far as the troposphere – and jump. Your suits will protect you. Don't have to worry about that. Your wings will let you glide, you don't have to worry about that either. You all know how to control your directional descent –

neither do you need to worry about that. Then there's the wind. You had better worry about that, and keep an eye on your pick up skiffs. If you don't land on your pickup, have a nice flight down and see you in another life." A bit harsh seeing as it was only a practice run. Fredrich must have a good reason to be so blunt.

"He's a funny man," Beau commented to his buddy. But the woman didn't pay him or Fredrich much attention. She'd been coordinating the flight path with their pickup.

What a peculiar sight it must have been to see all these little grape pips being ejected out of perfectly comfortable and safe vehicles. Extraordinary how far the search for thrills can propel a human being into the impossible. Yet, there they were, one crew after another diving into the troposphere of this incredible planet - just for the fun of it.

By the end of the five hour period allowed for the practice runs not a single mishap had occurred. Jupiter had been most accommodating by not whipping up any violent winds in their vicinity. The fliers could see gigantic lightning storms below them from a safe distance. Visibility had been excellent at their altitude allowing everyone to easily find their target platforms.

"Bobo! Bobo!" she'd only just crawled out of her suit and out of the airlock. There was Beau grinning as much as she was. "What a rush!"

"Wait till tomorrow's race. Are you up for it?"

"Are you kidding me! Let's go together this time."

"I really didn't think you would do it."

"Yeah, yeah – I know – you think I'm a wimp. I'll show you tomorrow." That did not sound good. Perhaps she didn't realise what a life threatening situation that was going to be, no less than it had been today - and Jupiter's weather could never be relied on to be predictable.

"Just reassure me here Gem – you had no trouble with your attitude jets? No glitches with the mind control circuits?"

"You saw me didn't you. One hundred percent – as easy as thinking about walking."

Early in the morning sunlight *Celestial Pleasures* again disgorged almost a third of its human infestation into Jupiter's thin atmosphere. Shuttles carrying the racers, their buddies and the pickup riffs dropped from the ship to near the top layer of the troposphere.

"Just a reminder all you daredevils - All Care, Zero Responsibility," Fredrich broadcast to all the shuttles. "Make yourselves ready while the pickups make their way to the Finish line. Oh – perhaps I didn't tell you ... this time the race will not be tangential to the planet's surface. You'll be heading radially directly down into the thickest part of the white ammonia clouds. Good luck. First one to land on their skiff wins. If they survive they'll be able to collect the souvenir trophy." Such a cheerful pragmatic soul. Having experienced many mishaps and knowing how uncertain the outcome of such extreme sports could be he didn't want anyone getting even the slightest idea that this was only a bit of 'fun'.

A thrill seeker has to be fully dedicated, not half or three quarters but one hundred percent. You either lived life to the fullest or just half-heartedly piddled around the edges. Fredrich's last piece of information quickly sorted the prospective racers into two camps, more new spectators and fewer foolish participants.

"It's not too late to pull out," Beau gently encourage Gemelle. If this was going to be the last thrill of his life there's no way he wanted to miss out on it. That was no reason for Gemelle taking the incredible risk. All the official paperwork had been taken care of, just in case – Gemelle would take over the lead in the Laboratory at Playback Inc. – she was more than capable of doing that.

Just a flicker of a doubt passed for moment before Gemelle's bravado lit up her face, flashing determined eyes at Beau.

"Alright then, let's do it." Beau's concentration returned to the matter at hand … helmet being locked on, attitude jet swivels final check, wing unlocking and manoeuvrability double checked. All exit ports opened at exactly the same moment, launch platforms dropping away a second later to release the racers away from the shuttles.

Beau and Gemelle didn't look at each other, trying to focus on something they could not yet see. The Finishing line of pickups would not be visible for another twenty minutes. It gave all the participants a chance to settle, build up speed and check their manoeuvrability. About five minutes into the plunge Beau looked across towards Gemelle. She'd drifted further away from him to the left, building up speed. By sweeping back her wings she could increase her dive angle as well as velocity without having to use the jets. Her buddy could not keep up with her sudden reckless move.

Beau didn't like that at all. What was she up to? He didn't know her to be this competitive, so impulsive. He adjusted his flight to try to get closer to her, and he had to give his boosters a squirt. The two of them had already ended up ahead of the pack. Inter-suit communication had been deliberately cut so the racers would not distract each other with foolish banter. Life or death – they were the only two options in this game.

Another five minutes later Gemelle had still not eased up. She would have to start a retro pretty soon or take the chance of overshooting the pickups. *What the hell is she up to?* Beau tried again to close the growing gap between them, his anxiety growing by the second.

He could see the white ammonia clouds roiling far below with pickup skiffs hovering well above them. But in the foreshortened view it seemed like they were riding those dangerous swirls of lightning and almost concentrated liquid ammonia. *I have to start the countdown – only two minutes …*

The next instant Gemelle shot across in front of him carried by a sudden powerful burst of a Jovian storm stream. Unpredictable and dangerous matching their reputation, it was one of the things all fliers had to be constantly aware of.

"Damn!" he shouted. Fredrich heard the cry and saw on the ship's monitor what had happened.

"You can't go after her!" he shouted. Too late. Beau had already altered course, squeezing more power out of his thrusters to follow her, not thinking that there really wasn't much he could do even if he caught up to her. The storm streak abated as suddenly as it had started and he watched her efforts to try and get back on course. She almost managed to turn around, wings still outstretched between her extended arms and legs. Back packs could carry only a small amount of reserve fuel in case of emergent circumstances. Gemelle had used all her fuel and all of the reserve as well. She could do nothing but begin her glide in one direction only, and that was diagonally down. Whatever the state of her mind she could not communicate it to Beau.

Fredrich tried to reassure her that the rescue attempt was already under way. "Spread your suit to its maximum. Level out and do a wide turn back towards us. We will catch up with you." He spoke quietly, unhurriedly. The last thing a flier needed was to hear a panicked voice. She responded immediately, levelling out and reducing her descent.

At the same moment when Beau turned to follow her Fredrich had despatched a rescue skiff. It followed at a much higher altitude than Gemelle had been swept along at. The pilot of that skiff must have been an extraordinarily experienced fellow in the temperamental behaviour of Jupiter's storms, for he could see an updraft breaking through the ammonia clouds far below, obviously half expecting and hoping for it to catch the lone flier.

He was right. The updraft caught Gemelle by surprise, lifting and tumbling her above Beau's flight path. She ended up higher than the rescue skiff within a few short minutes. The rest of the racers must have been oblivious to the drama being played out so far from them. They continued their death dives, giving themselves time to retrofire and rendezvous with pickups at the finish line. There was a winner. It mattered little to Beau and Gemelle as they fought Jupiter's temperamental outburst trying to survive.

By the time their friends had arrived back on their shuttles rescue lines had already been dropped to haul in the two death wishers. They picked Gemelle up first and had to follow Beau as he'd begun to drift away on another current of Jovian wind. In trying to catch up to Gemelle he had also used up all his fuel, not thinking for a moment that he could be left helpless.

Beau and Gemelle did not exchange a single word on the way back to *Celestial Pleasures*. He, way too upset with her extraordinarily foolish behaviour, and she much too aware of it.

A deep freeze had set in on the way back to the ship. Fredrich didn't waste his breath admonishing Gemelle for her recklessness, nor praising Beau for going after her. That was no less idiotic. They knew what they'd done and would most probably never look for an opportunity to do it again. On arrival back onboard Beau couldn't even bring himself to go in the cabin with her, instead spending the night at their makeshift lab. Of all the things going through his mind one thought dominated ... *How am I going to keep working with her?* Before finally falling asleep well into the night he'd made his decisions ... *If I ever have another relationship ... there will be limits. Anyway, I'm glad she's alright.*

Furious! Gemelle was absolutely furious - with herself! She couldn't think straight from the moment of the rescue. Until that point her survival instinct kept her focused, her scientific mind sharp, analytical. She examined every possible option from the moment the storm picked her up. The fuel gauge told her exactly how much she had left - definitely not enough to get her back even if the wind suddenly dropped. *They will have seen what's happened ... the rescue team must be on its way already* ... then the updraft, followed by Fredrich's voice ... Gemelle didn't even bother to ask Beau into the cabin when she saw he'd taken the left turn towards the lab. The shakes had set in. All she wanted was to lie down, take several Maxhaps and forget the whole thing. By the time sleep claimed her replays of her memory of the rescue eventually reassured her that she had survived. *I am still alive. But I'm not going to give Beau the satisfaction of telling me off.*

Captain Catherine arranged the award ceremony for the day after next. Enough time for the spectators and participants to have absorbed all the events of the race, and for the two rebels to have come to terms with their actions, and their relationship with one another. For surely there had to be sparks flying between them after all that 'fun'.

There were no sparks. Beau returned to the cabin in the morning to have his breakfast as usual. Gemelle was already up having hers. They only exchanged one long, long look ... a deep eye-to-eye no blinking exchange of understandings. Neither smiled.

"Do we have any customers today?"

"No. I think all the racers will need a couple more days to fully recover," she observed.

"Right. Do you want to come and help prepare the lab for the rush?"

Such an anti-climax for an incredible adventure. Not once during the entire day at the laboratory did either one of them allude to the flight. Beau almost opened up a couple of times when he thought about what an amazing experience it will be to rerun the playbacks of their own near-death experiences, especially after having completed the chemical enhancement techniques. But he didn't. Gemelle never once gave him the slightest invitation to be anything but absolutely concentrated on their professional activities.

At the presentation ceremony, held in the great sphere, Captain Catherine walked out onto the centre of the platform while just below the ceiling of the dome a 3-D hologram replayed that most exciting few minutes of the race, featuring the two dare-devils' antics and their dramatic rescue.

"Survival is the first part of the main prize," she announced, "so I believe Bobo and Gemelle deserve a special trophy!" Huge applause burst spontaneously from the audience. No one disagreed. This had been the most exciting voyage they'd ever been on. "I award you the trophy for the most extreme risk taken this year!" A standing ovation burst from the audience lasting for at least five minutes.

Beau knew they didn't deserve any kind of award. He didn't say so to Gemelle. She knew she didn't deserve it, and had put her joy-friend's life in jeopardy through her own foolish pride. But what the heck – it *was* such an absolute buzz, the greatest of her life. She stepped forward to accept the shimmering data-cube with a recording of their adventure embedded in it, motioning for Beau to follow her. Their public smiles had returned.

What a wimp! He said to himself, grinning to hide his lingering frustration with the woman. And yet ...

Up on the podium, in full view of the public, they finally hugged – a close grinding hug, an automatic response to being so close to one another and obviously much appreciated by the audience from their vociferous reaction. He couldn't help himself, Gemelle was such a rocket! Nor did Beau feel that the entire fiasco had been a total waste of time. Out there, flying above the threatening clouds, screaming towards his joy-friend perhaps it had become much more than pure pleasure. He had totally disconnected himself from his own welfare. That gave him a sense of freedom he'd never experienced before. In the absence of a single thought for himself the gates of memory opened up to those moments of darkness he could not gain access to previously.

Festivities after the ceremony lingered far too long. He wanted to download himself as soon as possible. He needed some free time away from Gemelle, to give himself a chance to think about their relationship. What had happened was far too extreme. That public show of affection didn't entirely do it for him. He also wanted to record the racers' experiences and prepare for the analysis and adjustments back at the lab on Proxima-b.

Gemelle could understand his hesitation to engage in celebrating their survival back in their cabin. She too wanted to record peoples' experiences but not with the same degree of enthusiasm. She understood Beau. When they'd completed the work the next day and Beau wanted to stay behind, she understood. That intimate hug in public was a good start. She could be patient ... if she had to be.

"It was a great thrill though, wasn't it, Bobo?"

"Yes, Gem. I just need a little more time to myself now." He needed a chance to understand his long term feelings towards her as much as coming to terms with her reckless behaviour out there - and of course her future with the Company.

Taking the scientific approach Beau went through the standard routine of tying up loose ends, making sure of the integrity of all data collected, categorising all individuals, setting up firewalls to prevent data cross bleeding etc. That took a many hours, which seemed to fly by too fast. The day had advanced well into the night, yet he wasn't ready to go back to Gemelle - not based on the little signals she'd let out so far.

Thinking about the downloads he realised something that wasn't obvious before. His own personal stuff needed more terabytes of memory than anyone else, including Gemelle and her 'value' added experience. "I'll just replay the bit after the jump," he spoke aloud. He didn't want full immersion so only did the unconnected visuals. These images were not like a video replay, they were a cross between that and cerebral images that the computer could translate into more or less normal visuals. There had to be a reason why his recording needed so much more memory.

Beau didn't get back to the cabin to crawl into bed beside Gemelle until the early hours of the morning. Breakfast waited for him in the small kitchen alcove when he woke very late, and a note ...

... 'I'm going to the lab to do a few more recordings, then I'll be around the ship somewhere, hopefully having a bit of fun – Gemelle'...

Fair enough ... it didn't quite register what the note actually said between the lines. Beau put his e-parchment on the table out of habit while he started on his breakfast. His key failed to open the latest document. The e-parchment had identity protections, including a voice print. "Don't mess about for Centauri's sake – just open up!"

With the combination of other biometrics the damn thing obeyed him. Technology, for all its wonders, continued to test human patience.

A document came up on the screen, the latest from last night. He just stared at it. His breakfast didn't get finished.

> The pursuit of pleasure not of pain will define the age,
> Where men upon the ground and in the air and in their minds
> Will find the curse not without but within,
> And shall lament the passing of the days of peace.
>
> Why the dress so full? Men and women hidden.
> Wealth cannot protect nor positions of power
> When all about them doctors and pious unhinged
> cannot fathom the indiscriminate enemy.
>
> Tears, cries and laments, howls, terror,
> Heart inhuman, cruel, black and chilly:
> Wagons of blackened bodies in the streets
> No mercy for puss filled corpses or hardened minds.
>
> A single red dwarf beheld the congregation of uniform attire,
> Owl eyes that looked upon the great monument,
> unseeing, unheeding of the ocean that rose about them
> Chants to Gods from minds lined up in obedience.
>
> When all the years of Moon's reign have sunk into the dead Earth
> another will take up his reign for four thousand years.
> When the exhausted sun takes up his final cycle
> then what I see and my fears will be accomplished.
>
> What value life when forced to adore with its mind
> The power lust of un-men with little soul
> to attain dominion over the children of not Earth,
> with promises of salvation to ensnare the devout.

Beau could not comprehend the quatrains in front of his eyes. He understood the words and some of the short phrases. He thought of the strange images that had flashed through his mind and tried to reconcile them with the words he read. They appeared to be the ravings of a mad man. Who could have written them, surely not himself? But no one had access to his e-parch. *It must have been me.* That thought opened doors in his mind, through which he entered willingly, gladly, anything to gain some clarity.

We believe we are made of the stuff of stars. "I believe this," he affirmed aloud.

The physical universe we know is not all there is. "I believe this," another affirmation. The flow had started. Where would it lead? He didn't care. It led ... somewhere ... out of the uncertainty.

There are forces and energies we are only beginning to guess at. How else could we have come to this world, which is not our ancestral home?

The darkness of the cosmos has power. "I have experienced this!" he suddenly realised. His scientific mind joined the conversation. Dark energy had been better understood in recent times - no longer as much of a mystery as in times past. Not long before that Devils and Dragons inhabited our world view, and fears from a non-existent deity!

All manner of invisibilities have claimed our understanding disguised as Spirits and Gods. "What have I seen?" he said in a subdued voice as he again looked at the words before him. *What was the darkness that overwhelmed Gem's mind, that invaded my mind?*

*

Quintessence's puzzlement only increased as it looked upon the little object disgorging its live inhabitants. What possible function could such strange activity have? Were they attempting self-annihilation? It understood annihilation. It had witnessed stars self-immolate to add their energy to the rest of creation. What difference could these insignificant lifeforms possibly make? It observed the erratic motions of two of the living things, recognizing their minds, one of which had accepted its brief visitation.

*

Without realizing it Beau had fallen into a semi-trance like state as he began to read again the mysterious words he'd written. His thoughts wandered and meandered into realms previously unvisited by a scientist of his high reputation. He was a scientist above all, not a mystic.

As on previous occasions Gemelle found him outside of himself when she arrived in their cabin. Seeing him like that, seated, hunched over with head bent her compassion went out to him. She regretted her vindictive note immediately. It was still there, on the table beside his open e-parch. She couldn't help herself and glanced at what was written there. Needing to lean closer to read it again her hair brushed against Beau's face, bringing him out of his introspection.

"Gem!"

"Oh, Bobo – I'm so sorry."

"Whatever do you mean?" automatically reaching down to close his e-parch and seeing the note she left. "Oh, that."

She straightened up, expecting some sort of recrimination. It didn't come. Perhaps it would have been better if he'd let off a bit of steam. A quiet Beau had always worried her in the past.

"What have you been working on?" she asked trying to lighten the mood.

"You read it?"

"Sorry, it was just there in plain view."

"That's alright. Did you understand any of it?"

"No. Did you write that stuff?"

"Yes - I must have."

And that's when it really hit him. Whatever Gemelle had experienced during the blackout had been very real. It had affected him too, completely differently and possibly far more deeply. "Do you want to read it again?" Perhaps she would see something he had missed. Perhaps she could unbend the nonsense that was beyond him. "I know now that we've had a unique experience, different for you and me but it did happen and I want to know what it was. Have another look," he opened the e-parch again. "Later we can talk to Cath. This is at least a start."

5

<u>Ice Boarding Saturn</u>

"Something must have wound you right up, about our life I mean. It's pretty obvious from the first few lines you've written."

"The first quatrain you mean?"

"You weren't having a go at me by any chance, with that business about the pain and my reaction to the darkness?"

"No Gem. To be quite frank I don't remember writing any of that. I've written poetry before because it's an intellectual pleasure for me. But this stuff is really weird. What do you make of the rest of it?"

"Why are you asking me? You're the consummate analyst – writing everything down then pulling it all apart. Perhaps you've been studying some history and it's come back into your head getting messed up by the energy of that darkness. Like that second quatrain – there's not a lot of religious folk about these days, most of them have left a long time ago. Certainly no looming enemy. And I don't like the next bit – quite macabre. I wouldn't like to have dreams like that. You made it sound like some sort of plague was chewing people up."

Beau didn't interrupt. It was exactly what he was looking for; an instantaneous, non-analytical reaction. Gemelle could do that about anything. That's just the way she was. *Although sometimes she ought to think before flapping her jaw, like that note this morning for instance.* He nodded, encouraging her to continue.

"As far as the rest of it I'd say you had a pretty dim view of our future. Four thousand years! Yeah, and the rest about the children of our world. I hope that's not what goes on in your mind."

"Gem, you're fantastic. I think we can go and see Cath now. It's not much to go on, but it's definitely a start. Perhaps she's found someone else with a strong adverse reaction to the blackout. I also want to find out more about that missing time from the ship's log."

The ship's ambient lighting suggested the day to be well advanced. The Captain had been busy, partly with preparations for the ice boarding and discussing the time anomaly with her AI. Beau and Gemelle arrived just as she settled to consider what the AI had told her.

"Come in – come in – glad you could tear yourself away from your project." She gave Gemelle a peck on the cheek and Bo a greeting type hug. Serious matters had to be dealt with, fun had to wait.

"Are you two going ice boarding? We only get a chance once every couple of hundred years or so." Her luxurious office offered all the comforts of home, a separate room in which to indulge the visual senses, and a more private enclosure for the taming of more rebellious senses. The conversation pit served as the official conferencing facility, well-appointed with single and double couches; seamless backs to the floor and seamless base to the ground, vermillion red to contrast with the arctic white of the floor. She stepped down into it inviting her two guests to join her.

"Jupiter was enough for me this trip. Beau is free to do as he pleases."

Catherine didn't follow up on the girl's folly. There were more important things to deal with. "Care for a sniff?" Nitro in small amounts helped put people at ease.

"Perhaps later. We need a clear head to sort this mystery out." Beau could be a such downer in Gemelle's opinion. "I've written something, under the influence I think of the – the – what would you call it - time slip?"

"My AI called it a time freeze. But go on."

Beau put his open e-parch in Catherine's lap. He took his cue from Gemelle's insights to explain the few lines without embellishing their meaning with his imagination. That was important. The thing was strange enough without magnifying it. Catherine kept her eyes on the quatrains as he gingerly tiptoed around the possibility that the darkness wasn't just an absence of light, just an absence of photons but something else. "Perhaps," he hypothesized, "and I don't want you to take this as any kind of serious scientific consideration - it was some form of energy, let's call it dark energy for obvious reasons, that has interfered with the normal flow of electromagnetic fluxes around my neural synapses."

He stopped to give himself time to think about this. It had been proven over the history of the evolution of the human species that this animal did not know his own mind until he verbalized it. Sometimes that process came out as the spoken word, sometimes as internally spoken thoughts and very often as the written word. The two women waited. Catherine probably because she'd been combining what she heard and read with that of her AI's input – and Gemelle – because she'd most likely already exhausted her contribution on the matter.

"Now don't get me wrong – I'm not saying this dark energy phenomenon is anything more than our ship inadvertently cruising through a particularly dense area of space. Certainly nothing that could be called an intelligence even by the most fanciful imagination. Yet it did something to my mind. What I don't understand is the nature of the visual residues of that effect, which resulted in those quatrains."

"Finished? Yes? Alright. Understood. What you have is just some pieces of the jigsaw puzzle. Let's put it together with what I've got."

Gemelle had started to fidget, obviously losing concentration. "We're not keeping you from something, are we Gemelle?" asked the Captain. *The girl was fun the other night, but* ... Gemelle snapped back into the conversation.

"Sorry. I just had a flashback of my wild ride at Jupi."

"Any further thoughts about the effect of the blackout on yourself?"

"No, not really. Except – strange, but as I think back over it I keep thinking of 'presence', not just a room without lighting."

"Thank you Gemelle, that's another piece. Right. Erasmus, that's our AI, says … it's a rather odd name isn't it, from ancient history especially considering what you wrote," she noticed Beau's expressive eyebrows do a little jig, "... says that we didn't lose time at all. It just slowed right down. As if it was a speeding train that had slowed enough to let a running passenger jump on. It didn't stop completely and he's got the backups to prove it."

"I don't understand what you're telling me. Does this mean we haven't aged as much as people back on Proxima-b?"

"I'm sure we'll find that out when we get home, though I doubt it would be much of a difference. But here's another thing, and you'll be pleased to hear this Gemelle. There was such a surge of concentrated energy suddenly bombarding our systems that it caused all safety triggers to flip at the same moment, taking them quite a time to reset. Now, I don't know how this lines up with the time span of the experience you two had but I'm willing to wager a good snort of nitro that it synchronizes perfectly."

She turned her head slightly. "Erasmus, what do you think of all this?" He was standing at the back of the office near the observation screen and came down into the pit when The Captain addressed him. Although capable of locomotion he couldn't have looked less like a human being in that matt black tubular structure with four extensions for locomotion.

"Yes Captain Catherine. I constantly monitor the condition of all biological life forms on this ship. Your proposition is correct. Bio-indicators stopped immediately upon the onset of the darkness and did not resume normal functioning until the energy overload ceased."

"I take it that nobody's been harmed, no systems have been damaged," commented Beau.

"That is correct, Sir."

"In that case Cath, let's just get on with the cruise." He looked at Gemelle. *She could have contributed a bit more enthusiastically.* "Are you sure you don't want to come ice boarding with me?"

"I'm sure."

The return trip from Jupiter to Saturn didn't take long at all. This part of the itinerary had been advertised as a once in a lifetime opportunity. That's because the physical forces of spin and gravity and meteor intrusions into the rings only produced the ideal conditions once every few hundred years. Tiny water ice particles seemed like they produced a smooth flat surface when seen from a long distance. In reality definitely not the case. Those bits of matter, although fairly dense through the thickness of the rings were nevertheless spaced well apart. Sometimes one of the smaller moons, or a large chunk of rock would disturb the tranquil flow of those particles on their journey around the planet. Most of the time the ploughing effect on the ice particles would produce elongated vortices of agitated spirals behind them. Once in a happy while great fields of those same particles would be pushed together, and helped by Saturn's powerful gravitation would compact even closer together. To be able to indulge in the unique sport became a rare privilege indeed for anyone who happened to be in the right place at the right time.

Fredrich's voice could be heard once again throughout the entire ship announcing preparations for the next adventure. Even those who weren't going out there could enjoy the experience by proxy. Artificial reality feed couches steadily filled with spectators as the skiers began their preparations. "Unfortunately you will not be going solo this time. Each board can hold twenty five people, plus the pilot and navigator. They will be positioned at the back above the raised fins. I know many of you wanted front row seats, but let me assure you none of you will be disappointed. If it was up to me I would even let you ski behind on a rope."

The suits were different this time, not as bulky but much better insulated, with plenty of high density nano-carbon filament impact armour. Only considerable speed could smooth out the ride across the dispersed ice lumps, and that still meant rogue pellets flying freely in front of the curled lips of the skimmer boards, especially during tight manoeuvres.

"Why don't you go down to the bottom lounge Gem. You'll get a much better view. Catherine will park the ship just above the ice field, then follow as we go around the perimeter of the B-ring. I wouldn't miss this for anything!" Gemelle, upset with herself for not having the courage to join him, abruptly turned away from the prep-deck to make her way many stories below. As far as she was concerned it wasn't her fault the storms on Jupiter pushed her off course just at the wrong time.

The breathtaking view caused her to catch her breath as she stepped onto the tilting observation platform. They were so close to Saturn that the individual A-B-C rings could no longer be distinguished. Spectators saw some of the closer moons orbiting in a hurry around their parent, and large chunks of mountainous rocks threatening to fall through the rings. Perhaps the thrill of seeing the event from a distance would be as exciting for the spectators as for the participants themselves. She completely forgot about the unsatisfying conversation in Catherine's office, at least that subject matter was depressing for her anyway. Beau just seemed to get more excited as the mystery reluctantly began to unfold.

For that matter Beau had also completely immersed himself in the new experience leaving the mystery to be solved for another day.

"Hey, Gem! Can you hear me? We're almost ready to launch. I hope you're watching. This should be phantasmagorical in the replays!"

"Alright, don't carry on. I feel bad enough as it is."

Celestial Pleasure's cargo bays opened up as the cruiser settled a kilometre above the main ice track. She only had fifteen boards to deploy, each with a full payload of overexcited, incredibly brave human beings. On the last word from Fredrich each one lifted off in succession to glide silently out of the belly of the mothership.

"We're ready here Captain," Fredrich advised as all the skimmers lined up, hovering just above the ice field surface.

"Ok, Erasmus, do your stuff."

The first view the reflective surface almost blinded them. Helmet visors reacted instantly each equipped with golden glare filters. Dropping almost to touch the highest ice particles each board let their thrusters roar into life. This was going to be no leisurely walk in the park! Which of course was the whole point.

Erasmus continued to hover the ship until all the boards had positioned themselves at a safe distance from each other. Their signal to go, coded in different colours was the wide spot lights suddenly illuminating the crystal field ahead of each skimmer board.

Gemelle screamed her pleasure as the Blues, with Beau on board, took the lead. Not that it was a race, but a bit of competition could only add to the occasion. Beau didn't respond, too busy hanging onto the harness, pupils dilating as the first big obstacle loomed ahead of them. The skimmer went into a tail spin, righting itself just in time to avoid the ice boulder. Gemelle could hear his breathing quicken, almost able to feel his racing heart.

The Yellow board pilot decided to cross paths with the Blues, their respective flood lights ahead of them. It must have been by prior arrangement, for just as they did so the Reds crossed both the Blues and Yellows. Exclamations of absolute joy sounded from the audience as the crossing play of colours created the most astounding rainbow effects, particularly in the wake of the ice particles thrown up behind the speeding skimmers.

As expected many obstacles hindered their passage as well as sudden dips in the quasi surface where the particles thinned out enough to cause the boards to drop, then fly up again as the boosters shot them forward. Gemelle could hear every grunt and exclamation coming from Beau. And unnoticed by all the spectators their observation platform had begun to move. It mimicked the ups and downs of the leading board, giving them the sensation of almost being there. To top it all off, as the flare of fuel from the jets scattered the icy surface their surging booster sounds were channelled into the huge auditorium. Of course the skiers couldn't hear any of that. They were too busy hanging on for life.

All too soon each of the boards executed a huge semi-circular turn, careful not to cross any of the nearest ring Divisions. These were like chasms in the surface of the ring where very little matter existed, either ice or rock - forbidding dark cosmic traps. Beau caught a glimpse of one of them far off to one side, which flashed his mind once again back to the idea of dark matter and dark energy. But he didn't have time to dwell on it. If anyone had the misconception that this would be like skimming down an icy mountain slope back home that notion was rapidly jolted out of them by the constant pounding on the boards' undersides, and the frantic swerving from side to side to avoid numerous ice boulders.

Erasmus had steered *Celestial Pleasures* to follow the skiers as they swerved and bumped over the field, holding the ship stationary only when they had all safely bunched together again ready for the pickup. Several circuits of the mapped out course seemed to satisfy even the most thrill addicted adventure seekers.

"Gem! Gem! Did you see that! What an absolutely fabulous ... extraordinary – better than flying into Jupiter! For sure!" He didn't mean to bring up that misadventure, it just popped out in the heat of the pleasure. Gemelle ignored it, if she heard it at all. Beau was safe and back on board.

"Carry on! I'll meet you in the docking bay. It looked extreme ... I didn't like it when you came so close to that dark Division." *It doesn't take much to put him in a good mood ... I don't think.* Gemelle felt relieved that some of the tension that had been building between them seemed to have been dissipated by the adventure. He ran to her, perspiring profusely, grabbed her by the waist and spun her around. "Outstanding. Can you imagine that – ice boarding on Saturn's rings! We are truly living in extraordinary times, Gem. This is definitely the only and sole purpose of life. Grab every moment while you've got it."

Beau didn't expect anything to interfere with the work on the way home. He could get all the experiential data he needed from the Saturn and Jupiter outings - more than enough to go on with back on Prox-b at the main lab. He'd already started planning the sequence of procedures and drawing up a possible list of experimental subjects. Gemelle didn't bother him with personal demands that first night, nor did the Captain with her special concerns.

His nervous system must have been so exhausted that within minutes of settling he fell asleep. Beau never had trouble getting to sleep, and only rarely did he wake at night. Lying there beside Gemelle's warmth and already replaying the ice boarding event in his mind an overwhelming sense of wellness washed over him. To say he was happy might have been a slight over-exaggeration. Definitely a feeling of fulfilment, a sense of deep satisfaction. Happiness in their society didn't rate as highly as satisfaction. The worst thing would have been to be disappointed.

In rapid succession flashes of ice boarding along the B-ring came back mixed with exhilarating moments when they had to swerve sharply to avoid large rocks and boulders. Stark white reflected light off the surface of water ice perfectly complimented Saturn's pastel colours. And the primary hued guiding lights from *Celestial Pleasures* completed the visual pleasure flooding into his dream … until the Cassini Division suddenly appeared.

In reality that empty space between the rings had been a long way from the surfers, but in his dream – in his mind primed to hair-trigger reaction to any cosmic darkness it brought on a whole new set of images. His eyes flicked open to a darkened cabin, dark enough that he would have had to put a night-light on to get out of bed. But he wasn't awake enough to do that. He didn't take notice of the time either; just after 11:50 pm. In a trance like twilight state Beau managed to shuffle to the room where he'd left his e-parch on a table.

> Dark and heavy air within the room of little light
> In the corner, thick smoke hides the man, hirsute, unclean
> With quill upon a parchment scratching black,
> Stained brownness of stones rough-hewn press upon him.
>
> Glyphs strange and random cast hanging
> On walls and charts of stars unknown,
> Yet Saturn with Jupiter does align.
> Tripod with fire burns to light his gloomy vaticinations.

Exhausted but relaxed after releasing the imagery he closed the e-parch and shuffled slowly way back to bed.

"Wake up Bobo, time to get to work soon." She gently stroked his unkempt hair, continuing to croon morning nothings - then went to the console and deactivated the shielding screen to invite the Milky Way's light to flood their cabin. "Kitchen - usual breakfast," and waited for the liquids to be synthetised. "Come on Bobo, people will be waiting." He wasn't responding. She had an idea … "Bo!" and kissed him full on the lips.

His eyes flew open. "I thought that might do it. Your Gemelle not exciting enough for you anymore?" she said in jest.

His eyebrows went into action – surprise, question, faux displeasure – arm reaching out to take her by the waist, which she expertly avoided – hot drinks in the hand.

"Happy boy. Good dreams?"

"You're not usually up before me." His previous dark mood about his joy-friend had been dissipated, at least for the time being, by the thrill of ice boarding Saturn's rings, or perhaps by being able to dump those peculiar disturbing images out of his mind.

"You slept in."

… ping … ping … ping

Beau had got up, parading his unclad maleness towards the table to join Gemelle when the coms sounded.

"Yes." His voice print showed the caller his face.

"Bo - you're up. Good," greeted Captain Catherine in her Captain's voice. Fifteen minutes – my office."

"Ooh. She sounds very officious, Bo."

"Stop it Gemelle. You enjoyed her as much as I did. I wonder what she wants. We'll get breakfast at the lab afterwards."

Beau did sleep in. As the rhythms of morning time tickled his consciousness thoughts of dreams filtered back, as they often do on first awakening – clear and appearing reasonable for a short time. Gemelle's antics cut those off in a not unpleasant way. He didn't get the chance to remember that he'd gotten up to during the night; that he'd flipped open his e-parch, that he'd had a vision quite provocatively mysterious, nor that he'd committed his thoughts to electronic memory. It probably would not have contributed meaningfully to what the Captain was about to discuss.

"Are you well, Gemelle?"

Why is she asking this? I thought she had something urgent on her mind. Gemelle hesitated.

"What I mean is … any reoccurring effects from the other night?"

"Oh – right. No. I don't dwell on things, unlike my joy buddy here. Why do you ask?"

"What about you Beau?" ignoring Gemelle's question.

"Er … Yeah – Ok. Must have been exhausted – slept in. What's bothering you?" He knew Cath well. If she called him anything but 'Bo' something must be pushing her anxiety buttons.

"Erasmus – please inform Mr. Kobayashi what you detected last night."

"Yes Captain. Sir: At precisely 2350 hours the radiation scanner indicated a rapid increase in background cosmic noise for a duration of nine minutes and 23 seconds."

"So?"

"I suppose I can't expect you to understand the significance, you being a land crab. The residual sounds of creation pervade our known universe. They are constant and they are predictable. What Erasmus heard did not fit the pattern. They did not fluctuate, only increase in frequency – and they maintained that constant level for the entire nine minute duration."

Beau continued looking at her with a blank expression. Interesting, sure – for a Captain of a star cruiser. It didn't mean anything to him. Astronomy wasn't his field.

"Alright. What about this then? Tell him Erasmus."

"Yes Captain. Sir: This anomaly coincided precisely with two other events. Firstly; another discrepancy of several minutes between ship's time and Proxima-b time." This time Beau's eyebrows went into action. His pupils dilated slightly coinciding with a rapid increase of internal processing. He automatically looked at Gemelle, whose face remained blank, then at Catherine. She had the look as if to ask, 'Have I got your attention now?'

Erasmus continued. "Secondly, Sir: For precisely the same duration as the frequency change the Milky Way disappeared from view."

"It's back!" interjected Gemelle with the usual automatic clutching hand on Beau's arm.

"It would appear so, Miss. However one cannot precisely equate the previous phenomenon with this occurrence."

"That will be all Erasmus." The AI backed up half a meter as Catherine turned to Beau. "Is it too familiar to be a coincidence? I think not. And we have not executed any manoeuvres that could possibly cause this sort of effect. We're on course to intersect with Uranus in a couple of days, just cruising comfortably along. That's all."

"No wonder you wanted to tell us about it. Is there a problem with the ship? Has anyone been injured? Erasmus seems his normal self."

Catherine let him talk while running scenarios in her head. This time *Celestial Pleasures* did not suddenly stop functioning. But what if this thing kept happening? What if something did go wrong? What if they ended up stranded somewhere between the solar system and Prox-b?

"I've alerted Base. They're on standby to send another ship out if Erasmus doesn't report in every 24-hour cycle."

"I have a feeling that won't be necessary Cath." Something had prodded his mind during the discussion, and when Erasmus mentioned the darkness he flipped open his e-parch, thinking to have another look at the quatrains he'd written after the first event. That's when he saw the open document for the first time. Not the original, but the one with the second lot of two quatrains. It had not been closed.

"I don't know what you will make of this Cath, but have a look. You too Gem."

The Captain read aloud … 'room of little light' … then … 'Saturn with Jupiter' …

"If you ask me," jumped in Gemelle, possibly to relieve the rising tremors within herself, "like I said before, you've been reading too much historical fiction, Beau."

"When did you write this?"

He checked the time signature on the document. "I started at 11:52 last night, and … the e-parch turned itself off a little after midnight."

"Do you know what you've written – what it means?"

"I'm a scientist. I know science. I have a pretty fair idea of what is possible, and extremely sceptical when people talk to me about impossibilities as if they were probabilities. And that's what you are trying to do here. You are trying to suggest to me that there is a relationship between the things I write, or at least about the timing of them, and this dark energy thing that keeps visiting us."

"No I'm not."

"Ok then. But suppose – just for a moment suppose that there is. Then please explain to me why or how I seem to have visions of the past and quite possibly of the future - not once of the present."

This had been bothering him. In the back of his mind Beau could not escape having thoughts of his somehow tapping into the realm of clairvoyance, possibly with the help of this mysterious darkness. It actually felt good having finally said it. Now he could cast that anchor adrift instead of dragging it along the murky bottom of his mind.

"I can't go about running a ship on suppositions, Beau. You'll have to give me something a little more solid than that."

"If one may interrupt Captain Catherine … monitors have been set up to maintain surveillance of our space corridor as far as Proxima-b, as well as Mr. Kobayashi's biological functioning. Should he deviate from his normal patterns, or should any energy flux enter the corridor one will be able to alert you Ma'am."

"Thank you Erasmus."

"By the way Erasmus, do you know the origins of your name?" asked Beau for no particular reason than it being a most unusual and unique one on their world, and it made him think of past historical figures.

"A man by that name achieved prominence around the 16th Century on Earth. A Dutch Priest called Desiderius Erasmus lived during the Renaissance there. He was a highly knowledgeable Humanist and Philosopher. His contemporaries were Jean Calvin, Martin Luther King and Michel de Nostredame. There is no record of who named this facility. Do you require more information, Sir?"

"No – er – Erasmus, thank you." Beau's thoughts had slingshot around the phenomenon of dark energy to head directly at a name that pierced his mind with a bolt of recollection. He had indeed studied and read history extensively. Some people enjoyed the pleasures of the flesh, of the senses, of extreme sports, and others like himself revelled in the pleasures of the mind, of research and discovery.

Nostredame.

Why Nostredame? he asked himself. *'Gloomy vaticinations'* … *that's why. Poetic befuddlement to confuse and obscure ... that's why.* The man had the ability to see into the future, or so he believed. He may have been able to see into the deep past as well. He had also committed his visions to parchment. Beau couldn't stay any longer with the women. He had to go somewhere where he could think, where he could settle the tornado rising in his mind. He was already at the door, opening it without a word to Gemelle or Catherine.

"Beau! Where are you going? What's the matter with you? Is he often like this Gemelle?"

"Oh sometimes – rarely. We just have to leave him to it."

"I had planned on taking a detour to Uranus and Neptune. Now it seems more prudent to get home without delays. Thanks for your input Gemelle. I'll catch up with you both before we get home."

*

Quintessence observed the wide Ribbon of Time looping through its cycles at an even rate, collecting and fastening to itself the energy clusters created by the sequential activity of all the living things gathered in that little object flying through space. As its awareness broadened to encompass a greater expanse of this Local Time Loop it discovered other deposits on the Ribbon – some in front of its area of interest, defined by Beau's segment and some behind it.

The connections between them had not yet permeated its understanding. Perhaps that's what inclined its curiosity to examine more closely the creators of these concatenated strings of events. Was it only the motion of time that separated them from each other, or were there other functions in operation?

Of the two individuals it had initially approached one obviously did not have the capacity to interact with it. The other had an internal space architecture with characteristics that had the potential for some level of compatibility. Not that Quintessence had any sense of the shortcomings of its own solitude. That was its basic nature. It desired no more from existence than to exist – but this Beau being had no analogous manifestation in Quintessence's cosmic realm. It seemed to be unique.

It occupied a dimension of reality outside of itself within space-eternity on the Ribbon of Time. It needed to be examined and understood.

It permitted a small fragment of itself to once again dip its desire into the human mind before withdrawing to ponder a mystery as foreign to it as it must have been to the biologic mind.

The first visitation appeared to be an interruption, an interference with the human's normal routine, resulting in its hasty withdrawal. The second, much more satisfying interaction, established the thin thread of communication. Quintessence was able to give the creature a minute glimpse of the contents of the Time Loop Ribbon as the creature travelled upon it at its own normal rate. The energy of past events had more cohesion, much more density than the present. Small segments of it could be spotlighted and isolated quite readily for the creature to grasp it within it's thought matrix. Future possibilities were just that - nebulous possibilities; not even probabilities until appropriate decision strings had been tied together to isolate any single thread from the tangle of possibilities.

Communication must have succeeded for the creature ceased normal functioning in order to fold in upon itself. A most unexpected catalyst had given its gift of visions greater clarity.

Quintessence also discovered something of interest, given to it by Beau - the name Nostredame. *What manner of thing claimed this name?*

6

Michel de Nostredame
1549

Within the very near proximity to where Kobayashi Beau occupied a minute portion of the Ribbon, Quintessence discovered branches of decision tendrils trailing into the past, opposite to the rotation of the Ribbon. One thread terminated at a branching point defined within the segment 1549.

That node labelled itself Nostredame.

This name has presence, given to me by the human Beau!

At a magnified view this node appeared to be a complex trunk of twisting philosophies, of desires and reluctant pessimisms. By extending itself from its core Quintessence could discern a web of roots, many of which had atrophied, others leaving a clear connection to branches of multiple past nodes behind it. It could also distinguish a clear line between the Nostredame and its human of primary interest. And on further examination it became clear that future possibilities, as defined by circumstances of the 1549 segment at that particular moment of observation, were not limitless.

The Ribbon has a finite width to accommodate variations in decisions and a finite length. When the surface can accommodate no more possibilities and has become fully populated with desires and aspirations and failures and actions it must either cease existence, or find a neighbouring Time Loop Ribbon with which to interact. No such Ribbon existed with sentience upon it that Quintessence could find within the Local Group of galaxies.

However it did discover within itself a new curiosity rising to see more of the human story contained on this Time Loop Ribbon. Eternity it would never be able to fathom. Time was not so long yet extending well beyond its capacity to see it all at one glance.

*

Aided by his friend Kobayashi Bela, a young twenty two year old physician of limited experience but firm medical convictions administered to the victims of the Bubonic plague during his journey through Italy.

"Do not argue with me Bela. I know you are of the opinion, as false at it is, that we should apply a mercury poultice to the wounds of these poor souls. What then? Weaken them further by letting their blood flow upon the flagstones?"

"Master – forgive me Master. We here in Florence are enlightened, Master Nostredame. But it appears not to your satisfaction. Surely you would not object to a garlic shroud if your remedy does not work."

"Still your mind my friend and help me with this." He pulled a large sheet over the dead body, which he turned with Bela's help and bound it up so no part of the cadaver remained exposed. Within that household of a wealthy Florentine merchant many of the servants had succumbed to the black death. A few continued to suffer the pains of festering black sores, others had already given up their souls to their God.

Quintessence observed the efforts of this one man to preserve life, yet saw so many other decision trees' branches wither and die.

"Have you called the cart?"

"It is here now, almost full of the blackened bodies."

"Help me take this one out. We must cleanse the house of this pestilence."

One, two, three bodies they carried out in succession. The cart driver would not touch them, forcing the physicians to throw them on top of the heap as best they could."

"Now go and wash yourself."

Bela stood transfixed, staring at the cart as it rumbled down the street to collect more stinking bodies that had been left outside dwellings. Even street dogs shunned the putrefying corpses.

"Now! What are you waiting for?"

The two men returned inside. "And while you're wandering about, open all the windows."

"Surely not, Master! The plague will get in."

"Not near as much of it that will be blown out by fresh air, my young acolyte. Watch and learn."

Nostredame followed his assistant, likewise cleansing himself before attending to the still living. In his lodgings he had prepared crudely shaped lozenges full of vitamin C, although he didn't know of the magic ingredient at the time. By pure experimentation and successful results the physician had satisfied himself of the efficacy of this concoction. A simple treatment anyone could administer that had better results than the prayers of all the clergy in the whole of Florence.

"Are you clean? Yes – good – now dissolve a few of these in boiled water and give some to each of those three girls while I attend to their boils - mind you, boil the water first."

For a man with a taciturn manner Nostredame could be so gentle in his administrations to the sick. With infinite care he removed from the sores those pieces of cloth that had become saturated with puss. Again using boiled water he cleansed the open sores, lanced the boils and applied clean bandages.

"We can do no more here today Bela. Gather up our things. We have another house to visit before we can go home." The clean shaven young man with a slight stoop quickly scooped up their apparatus ready for the next visitation.

And so it went, day after day after day. Quintessence followed the actions of this man and saw new tendrils of possibilities opening up before him. Some pathways dropped away, others sprouted alternatives.

It saw the intensity with which the man impacted not only upon his own life, but the lives of so many others. Quintessence scanned the Ribbon back to a branching point defined by the segment 1541.

In spite of its ability to examine the Ribbon retrospectively along the rate of natural change it had failed to notice a major divergence come into the thinking of the physician.

Nostredame's mind had been prised open very early in life. To a gifted youngster the science of astrology opened up a way of seeing the world and a way of making sense of it that contemporary religious and political propaganda failed to do. He had already been primed by his grandfather to be receptive to the teachings of ancient mystical schools of Turkey by the time he eventually arrived there.

After a long exhaustive day of study and meditation he took himself to a hillside in Mersin overlooking the Mediterranean. Still somewhat under the influence of his meditative trance his vision turned inwards, his mind clearing of the complications of the day. For no apparent reason he recalled a meeting with a monk, Fra Felice Peretti. Why this young unremarkable Franciscan novice made such a strong impression on him he could not recall. It had been a purely chance meeting where Fra Felice's austere expression and rather confrontational attitude had nothing of substance in it that would have recommended him to be remembered.

The memory broke Nostredame's relaxed contemplation. He turned his face to the clear sky letting his eyes roam amongst the constellations, coming to dwell on Ursa Major.

The memory of Fra Felice surged again into the man's mind with such force that Quintessence could not fail to register a tenuous connection between the physician and this monk. The possibility suddenly became apparent to Quintessence what the future may hold for this monk. And into the labyrinth of thoughts of the physician he placed the vision of a future Pope.

That evening Nostredame committed this vision to parchment. In his mind the connection between the revelation and the stars of the constellation could not be doubted. The stars held the secrets of the future.

Forced to leave Mersin because suspicion had fallen upon this physician of Florence who had great healing powers he made his laborious way through the conquering armies of the Ottomans back to Italy. During those long dangerous days his attention could not waver from constant vigilance on survival. The Holy League had been recently defeated at Preveza and after the battle of Buda the Turks gained dominion over Hungary. The emboldened Ottomans dealt harshly with any suspicious traveller. If it had not been for his healing powers to treat the plague victims, as well as the wounded soldiers Nostredame may well have ended his days well before reaching Florence.

As fortune would have it his friend Kobayashi Bela had not succumbed to the disease. He meticulously cleansed himself after each patient, careful not to spread the pestilence to the next household, or to take it home to his own family.

"It is good to see you Master. You are welcome. Come in, my home is open to you." The two men embraced fondly, knowing the plague did not spread through touch.

"I see you have a well-kept, clean home my young friend. It seems you may have learnt something from your Master. How have our patients fared?"

"Sadly many died, but many that we treated also survived. You have become quite famous for your remedies, Master."

"As long as the Inquisition has forgotten about me and I can go home I shall be satisfied."

"Will you continue with your medical practice?"

"It is likely circumstances will force me to do so, yet there is another path I feel compelled to follow. I have had revelations during my travels, which for the welfare of all I must make known."

Having settled in Salon-de-Province Nostredame married for the second time, Anne Ponsarde Gemelle, dedicating some of his valuable time to producing offspring. Compelled to continue his medical practice he nevertheless fell under the spell of the forces that he believed had bestowed upon him worrying visions of events to come. Little time was left to spend with his children, though the youngest César often played in the attic room while his father worked through nightly vigils. Nor did his second wife enjoy the pleasure of his company too frequently unless she was prepared to listen to his unintelligible ravings when he attended meals downstairs, or the lust of the flesh came upon him.

Intrigued by this man who had become so receptive to its gifts of future insights Quintessence plied him with many events of local interest as well as future possibilities. Nostredame became obsessed with achieving clarity to these revelations oblivious to the strange sources of the information, believing them to be mystical secrets held by the stars and the benevolent intercessions of his God.

Night after night he laboured in his attic room with little to keep him company other than horoscope charts and zodiac maps trying to fathom the connections between all the seemingly disparate events. He could not see what Quintessence saw; all the threads of decisions which led from one person to another, from one event to another. As the depth of his perceptions increased he could not understand how it could not be possible to forestall some of the great calamities and murders and miseries of his world that he clearly foresaw once people became aware of his visions.

Using every means at his disposal Nostredame even resorted to crystal gazing through the light of wax candles – hydromancy and staring into the flame of a burning cauldron on a tripod to go into deep trances, and palm readings for a few favoured acquaintances. At these times his mind opened to allow Quintessence access to deposit images of complex clarity. Smoke from cheap tallow candles often filled his sanctuary late into the night, and in the cold of winter the open fireplace behind him gave little warmth and more smoke than heat. Often the haze seduced his attention to lose himself in the convoluted smoke of almost exhausted candles as it rose in tortured contortions to the low beamed ceiling.

*

Back aboard *Celestial Pleasures* Beau had no clear idea where he needed to go, other than to escape from distractions. *Nostredame … Nostredame … * he kept turning the name over and over.

For no particular reason other than to satisfy intellectual curiosity Beau had spent much of his spare entertainment time in the past on perusing the very ancient history of Earth. In many ways it saddened him that humanity had to abandon its evolutionary home. Perhaps abandonment wasn't quite right – escape seemed more appropriate. When the air became unbreathable and the water undrinkable, and the food so contaminated that people had to be given antidotes to combat its side effects, and the fight to survive had become so frenetic … yes, escape must have been seen as the only solution. Yet before the time of exodus there were periods of great prosperity and great advancement in science. And even before that there was a time when the human mind underwent enlightenment for a brief period. As short as that golden age had been great advances had occurred in many fields of human endeavour, greater during that period in some respects than at any time afterwards.

The one spectacular thing that ensnared his mind almost to its maximum capacity had been hearing the name Nostredame. This was a man of science, like himself. This was a man who had come out of the dark ages, somewhat like himself. This man had visions of the future, perhaps he had revelations about his past, again like himself. This man had recorded his visions exactly as he had just done so himself! One could not go past such a confluence of coincidences without asking serious questions. But what questions should be asked?

Beau found an intimate observation lounge where he could sit undisturbed and entertain these fantastical ponderings. He could gaze out upon the stars of the Milky Way and let his mind tiptoe around suppositions and fledgling theories - perhaps just like Nostredame. *If only he could have seen the heavens like this.* What am I supposed to do with these visions? What possible value are they in our society? My career would be ruined if my mental stability became suspect, for that's how it would be seen – as mental instability, at best the insane ravings of an unhinged mind.

Why Nostredame? he asked himself again. *'Gloomy vaticinations' … that's why.* I will have to have another look at his Prophesies. We'll be home in a little while. Best I get on with my work until then, take my mind off it.

Little by little the cosmos outside the thin bubble film that enabled him to survive in it claimed him fully. Gradually sinking into an almost unconscious state he did not see it approaching. As fast as the *Celestial Pleasures* sped homeward there was no sense of motion. It and every living soul aboard that vessel existed in a state of motionless, silent suspended animation, stationary compared to the vastness of the universe surrounding them.

He did not see the dimming of the billions of stars in their galaxy. He did not see the darkness that had pressed itself against the outer surface of his survival bubble.

He dreamt.

He dreamt of places and of people he could not recognise.

Except, Beau was not dreaming – he was travelling.

Quintessence had turned its attention from the 1549 segment momentarily to refocus on 2555. It felt the quiescent receptivity of the Beau's mind. It did not think about the reasons why these two living manifestations of baryonic matter were drawn together at this point in the existence of all there was in the sea of infinity. It acted according to its unpremeditated inclination.

It had been a particularly cold and inclement winter day in the town of Salon, France. Anne had lit the fire in the attic early in the day and had tended it dutifully for her husband. To air the room seemed necessary to let out the smoke that had accumulated. Nostredame would not let her. He had a great deal of work to do and his hands were cold, already finding it difficult to hold the quill steady. The last ten quatrains he'd been working on had to be completed, and many more still to be written. Publication of his Prophesies could not be delayed any longer than absolutely necessary. He intended it to contain information he hoped would be heeded by the Church and State alike.

"Thank you Anne. Please leave me to my work."

"When will you be supping, husband?"

"Presently – presently." He'd already turned his eyes away from his wife before she even started to move towards the narrow attic stairs.

"I'll look in on you – make sure you are warm." He didn't respond.

With the right hand holding quill at the ready and left hand having just lit the single large wick candle directly in front of him he was prepared. The tallow candles on either side of the parchment did not give enough illumination, yet it would have to do. Beeswax candles always burned with a steady flame, exactly what he needed. By concentrating on the one to the left of him the trance engulfed him rapidly as he strained his eyes upon that single point of light. He'd prepared his mind by reading the last quatrain several times. It had inconsistencies, not untruths but shadowy half-truths he needed to understand so he could better embed their meaning into the flow of verse.

A strong gust came up suddenly and unexpectedly, although the day had been calm – cold but calm. Anne saw the trees bending near their house and had already rushed back up to the attic, unnoticed by Nostredame, yet too late for her to shield him from the sudden gust coming down the chimney.

In the already smoke filled room its contents became partially obscured by the influx of smoke from the fireplace. His wax candle flame began a wild dance before extinguishing, leaving behind dense white smoke as the wick died. Through the haze Nostredame saw an image, quite unlike any of his previous hundreds. He didn't register having snapped out of his trance when reacting to a most unexpected hazy sight.

"Bela! What in the Holy Church are you doing here?"

Anne straightened up from the fire and turned to step towards the table. "Don't move Anne."

"You wear strange garments my friend. How is it you come to be in my home?" Anne did not know this man. She had never met Bela.

The apparition did not answer – Anne did not move. She was not given to hysterical frights upon seeing strangers. She looked this one up and down, for indeed he had dressed himself in the most unusual apparel of the strangest semi-translucent colours, far more revealing of the underlying male body than any garment of her day. Through the thick smoke she could not see what manner of footwear he might have had, not that it would have made any difference to the very odd circumstance. More particularly odd because of the exceptionally handsome, clean shaven and revealing vision that had immediately captured her attention.

Never in her entire life had she beheld such a specimen of maleness that had now sparked such a strong a desire within her.

"Come, man! What is it that holds you so spellbound?" Michel still thought it was Bela.

Beau looked about himself. Strangely the smoke did not seem to affect his eyes. He saw a figure move and directed his gaze immediately in its direction. Is this an angel? Perhaps it was the woman's beauty that had caught his attention, perhaps it was her long flowing red hair – no, perhaps it must have been the oddness of her dress that covered her entirely, leaving only her head and hands unclad. And there was a look in her eye he had seen in no other woman in his world. He could not define it yet a desire came upon him to respond to it.

"Bela? No Sir. My name is Beau, Kobayashi Beau." A recollection of the quatrain he had written came to mind, <*Why the dress so full, men and women hidden*>' He looked to the questioning voice. That man too had hidden himself well, fully dressed to the ground, bearded and with a grotesque cap upon his head.

Anne went to move towards the figure, which became less distinct as the smoke started to clear slightly.

"Stay, woman! - Upon my word! If you be not Kobayashi Bela, who be this Beau you speak of?"

"Kobayashi?" The astonishment clear in Beau's voice.

The entire incident made no sense to any of the participants. Less than a few minutes had transpired as Nostredame seemed to come to his senses to ask, "From when are you?" To which he received a reply from the almost completely faded figure in the clearing air … "2555."

The years of visions of peoples of strange times and strange places made his mind receptive to … unfathomable strangeness. Not so his wife. For all that he knew she might think this 'Beau' to be the Devil, though she be an intelligent woman.

"Say nothing of this to anyone," he warned. The Inquisition had already nibbled at his immortal soul. He didn't want any dangerous rumours to start spreading about what he did nightly in his attic. After having gone to great pains to subtly entangle his prognostications in ambiguity for purposes of personal protection from zealous Church officialdom he didn't want a simple apparition to be his undoing.

He may not need to have been concerned for Anne certainly did not react as if she were seeing the Devil. Never had she seen a man so handsome, stand so tall, display his body to such alluring advantage.

"Be calm, husband. You saw whatever it was you saw in this heavy smoke. I'm sure my eyes beheld nothing more than wisps of smoke."

He eyed her suspiciously as she placed more wood on the fire, tidied up around the fireplace and went downstairs.

*

Beau slid back into his current reality. Whatever happened had been a smooth transition. He had remained seated, comfortable, now wedged between two women who seemed to have appeared out of nowhere to sit on either side of him.

He look out the bubble screen and saw the stars, saying nothing, thinking of the afterimage still so fresh of an extraordinary woman and a hairy dirty elderly looking man. *I know this man – I have seen images of this man before!*

"Bobo! Hey Bobo!" called Gemelle.

"Come back to us Bo," said the other one. Catherine appeared to be just as concerned.

He looked in turn at both women. *So unlike what I've just seen*: He stood, put on a cheerful face, hooked an arm around each of them and all three walked out of the private observation lounge.

"Seriously Bobo, what's got into you?"

"Just making friends with the darkness." That stopped all further feminine concerns wrapping themselves around him.

Before Beau and Gemelle disappeared into their cabin Catherine couldn't help herself asking, "What exactly did you mean about making friends with the darkness? Don't you realise we've had another episode?"

"I had … I went …" he couldn't quite find the right approach to express his experience. "Look, I'm a scientist. I have an empirical view of life, of everything. Just at this moment I cannot explain to you what exactly happened when we had the first blackout, or the second. Now you tell me we've had a third. The only thing I can say is that somehow, for some reason I was a part of the event each time. No harm has come to any of us, certainly not to me. Each time my experience has been … getting clearer. I am now convinced that the thing, the controlling force behind these events is not malevolent. We talked about the idea of dark energy before. Not much is known about it. There is the theory that it may not be as intimately intertwined with time as we are. If – and I have to empathise 'if' – it can move through time as we move through water – back and forth at will – then that would explain my visions. There it is. I've said it. I've been having visions. This last lot before you interrupted me took me back a long way."

The women listened to what sounded like the unravelling of a brilliant mind, of a wonderful man who could be a lot of fun, who could give you a lot of pleasure in many ways. Catherine put a hand softly on his shoulder to stop him talking and looked him directly in eyes. "Bo, this does not help me. I have a ship full of people who could fall off the edge of their sanity if this thing continues. Pull yourself together.

Kick that scientific mind of yours into overdrive and give me something to work with."

Back in the cabin Gemelle ordered dinner. "Kitchen — three course meal for two - low carbs high protein." It would be a short wait. Time enough to freshen up. "Bobo — talk to me. I can help."

"No, you can't. Remember what happened to you the first time." He didn't mean it to sound so abrupt. He liked this person. Didn't love her, as such, but she had turned out to be both a fun joy-friend and a most competent assistant at work so far. The trouble was that his desires now had two images attached to them, both in absolute clarity in his inner vision.

Beau didn't freshen up. He didn't stay to have dinner with Gemelle. It was too disturbing. After what he'd just said she withdrew into herself. *He can be so mean!* That was the extent of her reaction. Not being a person of any great emotional maturity his comments didn't penetrate her soul too deeply. As she sat to enjoy a Bacchanal drama by herself on the vid during her dinner Beau had already left the cabin for the lab. This late in the day he could at least be alone there.

The scientist in him took control. First, record the last few hours. Copy the latest event data before it becomes contaminated by mind constructs. Next, run a quick playback to help himself deconstruct the sequence of events. Take each segment of concatenated moments and analyse the connections between them. That's something the computers could never accomplish.

That's right — he began the conversation with himself — I asked Erasmus who had named it. Some names came up, one in particular stood out, 'Nostredame' — Yes! yes, because he had written quatrains, because he had visions of the future. Wait — wait. What was he doing when I saw him? Writing. No! Not writing, getting ready to write and he was staring in my direction. He was staring through the candle smoke.

Beau forced his mind back to that moment. He found and reran that segment of his memory download because his thoughts had already raced ahead to a conclusion — a most unscientific thing to do.

Nostredame was not looking through the smoke — he was concentrating on the candle flame before the wind blew it out. He was in one of his moments of contemplation — he was meditating, going into a trance! — and ...

What was I doing?

He tried to think back through the jumble of excited ideas. No good. He went back to the beginning of the download, and re-examined the sequence of moments from the end of the conversation with Erasmus.

I walked out on Gemelle and Catherine — went to the private observation lounge, thinking of Nostredame all the way.

The lounge couch was comfortable as I leant back in it. Extraordinary how beautiful our galaxy is viewed from space. What was I thinking? Ah — about my career, about the value of my visions — about why it was getting darker. *I was looking at the stars and they had started to disappear! That's when I saw Nostredame — and Anne!* Next moment two women were standing beside the lounge chair.

Stars, flame, smoke, contemplation – *Trance!* – *Anne!*

Beau had arrived at the critical juncture of experience, empirical fact, examination and understanding. It had given him a solid foundation on which to begin to understand his own visions. He now knew what he would have to do to try to replicate the experience, but not what role dark energy played in the drama.

Dark energy – it cannot be anything else. That must have somehow catalysed this journey through time. For that's what it was. Before seeing Nostredame I had visions – just mental images constructed out of what? Imagination? But seeing Nostredame, seeing beautiful Anne – I must have *been* there. But why just me? How can such a vast energy field be so selective, so focused - unless … That concept was too difficult to think about.

*

Intense satisfaction. In its so far limited appreciation of all the possibilities that sentient existence held for Quintessence it could only gauge its reaction by the sensation of desiring to repeat what it had achieved for the human Beau and for the other, Nostredame. It could not force the human mind to be receptive, but it could learn to control the force with which it guided it.

Beau had found the way to open the doors of his mind. With Quintessence's help he could now step through for visitations along the Ribbon. If only the Ribbon would stop it's looping long enough so that the body could join the mind.

Yet it seemed that Quintessence had achieved that when it first interrupted the flow of Beau's life. It had brought existence to a halt for *Celestial Pleasures* and all aboard her.

Just as Beau needed to learn how to control the dimensions of his mind, Quintessence had to become conscious of its ability to travel to any segment along the Time Loop Ribbon, as well as observe its myriad decision nodes from outside.

For the moment it considered Nostredame's reaction to Beau in mistaking him for another human. Those two humans had a name in common, Kobayashi – how was that possible? What manner of connection could they have? The decision trees of all sentient beings existing on this Local Time Loop tended towards touching one another.

Yet how far reaching could a branching decision line extend? Was there more to it than simply that one mechanism? The concept of heredity had yet to filter into the awareness of Quintessence.

7

Beau's New Assistant

For the remainder of the journey home Beau avoided Gemelle's company as much as he could without moving to another cabin.

On-board laboratory conversations between them remained neutral, work focused, a little strained. Gemelle had enough sensitivity not to harass her joy-friend with unwelcome intimate advances. His obvious intense preoccupation with the memory downloads from the Jupiter and Saturn experiences precluded any pleasurable pursuits she may have entertained. They had collected more data than was needed to run chemical enhancements to create a super saturated sensory Zetaverse of artificial reality based on actual experiences. She of course had no idea what had been happening to Beau - of his fixation on another woman.

Two Companies, Playback Inc. and Omnifun Unlimited vied for market dominance. Society on Proxima-b had evolved a Hedonistic philosophy towards existence. Pleasure should be the ultimate purpose of life – not merely instant gratification of the senses but love, friendship, contentment and cultural pleasures. Above all, the superiority of social and intellectual pleasures had to be emphasized without dwelling on the negativity of selfishness.

Both Companies could deliver the benefits of reliving experiences by playing back the recorded memories of them – memories captured soon after the experiences. But the process had limitations. The playbacks were never better than the original, often the opposite. The human mind naturally enhanced memory with fantasy, with desire, with magnification for personal aggrandisement while recounting them to others. Or overstated the negativities for whatever reason came to mind at the time of discussion.

The Captain of *Celestial Pleasures* had an unpopular announcement to make. She knew it would be because the cruise itinerary clearly stated short visits to Uranus and Neptune. Neptune in particular had captured peoples' imaginations because it presented so much visual activity.

"Hello to all my happy travellers," she began, "what a wonderful experience we've all had coming back to our ancestral solar system. Your pleasure and your safety have always been our primary concern. Without fail I will deal with even the slightest hint of anything that could interfere with that. Now we have to go home. There is no need for concern. Our visitations to Uranus and Neptune are postponed for the time being." She may as well have told them 'cancelled' for she had no intention of delaying their journey home.

She left it at that. Sudden and disappointing as the announcement may have been the Captain could take no chances with something over which she had no control. A mysterious anomaly that could strike at any time, for any length of time. Erasmus could do nothing but regurgitate data.

He could not formulate plausible theories to help resolve the problem. Beau had all the data yet he would not, or could not package his early hypothesis into an actionable format for her.

Passengers aboard the ship had already noticed changes. The leisurely cruise had turned into a high velocity run for home. Captain Catherine stopped enticing them with little surprises. Within just a few days Proxima Centauri grew in their field of vision.

"Bobo, we're almost home. How are you feeling?" asked Gemelle looking for some kind of reassurance.

"Whatever do you mean?"

"About – about everything – you know, the trip, our work … about us."

There it was. For what seemed like an eternity to her Beau had not said a single endearing word to her, or touched her or been anything but a manic scientist totally absorbed in his work.

"Us? What about us?"

"This was supposed to be a fun trip. You said so yourself. It hasn't been much fun since we left Saturn."

'Fun' had sent his mind off at a tangent to the conversation. He didn't respond to her taunt. So she tried another tack ... back to work talk to get the conversation going again. "How much should we clean up the recordings? Still he didn't reply." You're not listening to me."

"Sorry. What did you say?"

"Data scrubbing ... how much?"

With a vague, "You know - as much as we can," he left the cabin - yet again. For the rest of the trip Beau spent more time in the lab, and Gemelle spent more time out of the cabin, but not in the laboratory. Beau didn't follow up with Catherine thinking that perhaps Gemelle had gravitated towards her company. It was none of his business what she did anyway. And he didn't object to her spending more time out of the lab as the relationship between them chilled.

At the disembarkation Gemelle received a summons from Playback Inc. Head Office - directly to herself, not through her boss Beau. The company could not afford to lose her to the competition. She knew too much about the ground breaking theory she and Beau had been working on. If his experiments worked Playback Inc. would capture the lion's share of the pleasure market. She received a promotion to run another department, which moved her to another location in Gamarrah - immediately.

*

"What is you pleasure Emma? Welcome to Playback."

It had been many years since he'd last said those words to a new colleague. Yet it almost seemed like a déjà vu moment the way it played out. This replacement assistant wasn't his choice – and a pure coincidence about the sound of her name. She was younger, more attractive and a mind more agile than Gemelle's had been – or so he was told.

"My pleasure is work." Her thin lips drew together and eyes intensified as if wanting to give weight to some driving determination.

"This is good – excellent." Beau didn't want any entanglements just then. He'd even put all thought of finding another joy-friend out of his mind. Serious work had to be done. He hadn't forgotten about Captain Catherine's concerns, although he doubted if her troubles would continue if he wasn't on the ship. He wasn't always thinking about how he would enhance memory playbacks either. There was that little matter of the dark energy and how it could possibly have anything to do with his unusual experiences.

"Have you been briefed on our project?" She remained silent. He took that as an indication of having asked a superfluous question. "Good. We start tomorrow. Are you prepared?"

"Why not today?"

"Indeed, why not ... follow me." Within minutes they had descended from the cafeteria on the surface to the tunnel that led them on a short walk to Beau's office.

Their laboratory extended several floors underground with wide tri-dimensional picture walls to Proxima-b's landscape. The main city, Gamarrah, occupied many square kilometres of interconnected domes, as well as extensive underground suburbs stretching several hundred more kilometres to join with other cities. From their above ground vantage point farming domes and covered corridors spanned the landscape as far as they could see. Beau's office was austere; furniture ultra-comfortable and the entertainment room comprehensively equipped.

Their conversation didn't begin by discussing the ultimate purpose of life. "You have all the data we need?" Emma queried. Her diminutive frame almost disappeared into the luxurious sofa.

"Absolutely. More probably than we need, and a full list of volunteer participants to come in when we are ready."

"What's the first step?"

"Any ideas? You seem to have been briefed." He was testing to see how real her enthusiasm was – and for what specific area of engagement in the project overall.

"How far have you advanced in scrubbing out extraneous distracting data from memory bundles? As you know the human brain records all sensory data, much more than we are consciously aware of, definitely more than is needed for clarity of any single experiential data set ..."

Emma continued speaking – Beau had stopped hearing, again set off by what Emma just said ...

... records *all* sensory data ... *What have I missed when visiting Nostredame? I was close enough to see his parchment – did I see what he had written?* ...

"Beau – Beau! Hey, Beau Boss!"

"Sorry, what were you saying?"

"You're not listening to me." Just a hint of annoyance had crept into her voice, similar to that of a supervisor to her staff.

"Sorry – I was actually thinking about something you said – about recording all sensory data."

"And?" She just wasn't going to let him flap around in the artificial breeze while there was work to be done.

"Scrubbing out background noise. Yes – we can do that, it just takes time."

She continued ... "Have you isolated the most promising samples yet? No? Well then, I'd better do that first. If you could start working on a dosage spectrum for the dopamine enhancement," she suggested, taking the opportunity to show initiative.

"You are well prepared I see. Tell you what, I'll give you some stuff from an unusual event aboard the ship first. Clean that up. Only a few people involved." He didn't tell her it was from himself and his previous assistant. It may keep bias out of the process.

"Yes Beau Boss," this time she bestowed a thin grin, realising that perhaps she'd stepped just a tiny bit over the line.

"And just call me Beau, alright."

"Yes Boss."

What did those bureaucrats from Head Office send me to cope with?

As much as he wanted to concentrate on following up his own line of enquiry and experimentation on other matters, work for Playback Inc. had to continue. In a Hedonistic society where consumerism had morphed away from materialism to collecting and reliving experiences, many of which were creations of human ingenuity in the realm of pleasures, sometimes creeping into the world of pain, his work was pushing boundaries. His completely legitimate scientific experiments into how to manipulate the pleasure centers of the brain in order to enhance remembered experiences and how to extend them in artificial reality to create the Zetaverse had far reaching consequences. If control of the population could be achieved by creating artificial happiness what a wonderfully peaceful world Proxima-b would become.

A week went by without interference from Head Office as he and Emma worked side by side in harmony, though no doubt they watched developments closely - especially after the 'Gemelle' event. They wanted results not interpersonal dramas with joy-partners. As neither scientist complained Playback Inc. let them get on with the work. She had her own independent avenues of personal pleasure pursuits, as did Beau. Except his didn't always involve titillating the senses or looking for adrenalin rushes.

Each night in his apartment he prepared himself. His sparse furniture included a work surface, which doubled as a table for everyday use. He moved it away from facing the wall to position it to face his main window and extend away from it. Without consciously realising it the configuration mimicked the way Nostredame had his workbench. His aim was to catch as much natural light as he could - to let the light of the constellations in during the night hours.

He left his single arm-chair where it had always been, on the other side to the desk, facing the window – his favourite place from which to gaze out at the night sky. That all felt right. For what? *What exactly am I trying to do here?*

By the end of the week Emma had a lot of questions for Beau. "All I'm getting on this first recording is a view out of a bubble screen on the *Celestial Pleasures*, then sudden darkness. How am I supposed to clean up darkness? Then there's the tears and incomprehensible mumbling. I've rerun it so many times and yet it still eludes me. Nothing more I can do with it. It's as clean as it'll ever get. I'll start on the other one next week."

"NO!"

Beau's sudden burst startled her. She had triggered something important in his memory ... stars and darkness. When he saw Nostredame he was sitting in an almost dark room, his vision impaired by smoke, surrounded by smoking candles, some still alight and Nostredame sitting in a trance at his desk.

"No, please leave that one. I need to have another look at it."

"Well – you don't have to shout at me. Is there anyone in particular you want me to go on with from the rest of the recordings?"

"Just look for anyone who went flying in Jupiter's atmosphere. Let me have that other one – I'll take it home with me."

Stars, flame, smoke, contemplation – *Trance!* – *Anne!*

Candles were such an archaic technology that no one on Prox-b seemed to be engaged in their manufacture. Bees and honey still existed, imported from the home planet a millennium ago. It took Beau the entire weekend to acquire several beeswax candles, then hours to work out how to reconfigure his internal atmospheric control system not to react to the smoke from them or the minute heat fluctuations. The dense smoke he could not replicate and the stars were there already. On the first opportune night he sat by flickering candle light, e-parchment at the ready. But nothing happened. His mind was too eager, his thoughts too full of expectation. Self-talk, fidgeting, distracting satellites trekking across his field of vision - everything seemed to conspire against him.

At the start of the new week his growing agitation got the best of him. "Emma," he called her at the lab, "are you in control? Do you know what to do for a few days? I need to – I've got something very important to do."

"Yes Boss. The staff knows what to do. It's a smoothly running ship. I don't need you here."

"Is that so. I'll be with you soon to check progress." *I'll have to watch this one.*

The day dragged. He didn't feel he could achieve anything in the full light of day other than replay the recording of his memory of the event. *I'm glad Emma didn't have a chance to scrub this one, who knows what she would have taken out.* He focused on things he failed to see at the time of the event – like the globe half hidden in the corner, a telescope on the ground by the desk, open parchment bundles on the floor – *books they called them,* many more books on bookshelves – *they didn't have electronic memory of course* – and standing by the burning fire, Anne. Beau could not leave a mystery unsolved – he wanted to go back to Nostredame. He wanted to see Anne again! That realisation didn't help to settle his thoughts at all.

What was it I said to him? Nothing. Like an imbecile I said nothing! But he mentioned a name ... Kobayashi Bela! How very odd. He must not have heard me properly.

It was no use. The more he tried to focus his mind back to the attic room the more his thoughts wandered all over the place. As a scientist he knew that would never work. Not for him anyway. He took a magnetrans ride out to the nearest farm dome that had several public gardens. He liked one in particular, the one with a stream, trees and animals roaming freely. He walked, he breathed, he closely examined things he strolled by. The strolling became vigorous walking bringing on perspiration, heart rate increase – lungs cleansed of stale apartment air. Light had started fading rapidly by the time he noticed it forcing him into a trot to get back to the station. His world had become fully dark by the time Beau arrived home. The stars had come out.

Feeling totally refreshed after the exercise and the shower he didn't bother with food in spite of being marginally hungry. The desk by the window with candle and open e-parch called to him. He knew exactly what he wanted. He felt ready. Sitting at the desk he considered lighting the candle, but his eyes got drawn to the constellations. Ursa Major ... *I saw it from the ship* ... He tried to follow the line of its main planets...

*

Quintessence contemplated Nostredame's reference to something called Kobayashi Bela and its possible connection to his human called Beau. It turned out to be another human in very close proximity to Nostredame's segment. Could there be others? A natural enough extension of thought for any sentient, enquiring being. Is that what I am? I am Quintessence Kobayashi Beau ... it felt the need to reaffirm its budding identity.

And as it considered its discovery, letting its focus expand into other parts of the Ribbon it found yet another individual with a similar identifier, at segment 3790. That one called itself Kobayashi Dante.

Dante's layered intellect did not have the density and complexity of thought on the surface that Quintessence had experienced in Beau and Nostredame. This human had joined minds with many others, all swaying in rhythmic motion to sounds emanating from a single source. And as this mind sank into mindless compliance it shut out the rest of creation.

8

Kobayashi Dante
Keppler 22b

The size of the universe for humanity is not limited by how much of it he can see but by how far into it he can travel.

That travel horizon expands minutely with time, in time, although to such a small extent as to be negligible. The desire to get out there unmatched by the technology to achieve it.

There are other frontiers for technology to infiltrate. Human civilisation on Proxima-b had taken root, in spite of it not being their world of origination. Habitat could be created to protect against the alien atmosphere, to provide the infrastructure on which to achieve the mechanisms of survival, but not to cope with increased gravity. That was a matter for evolution with the help of genetic engineering.

Much effort had been expended on making life better, less stressful, more fun – more pleasurable. When the meaning of life had morphed so comprehensively away from the struggle to survive on Earth and had been taken up by the Hedonist ideology on a new world, why not go further.

A layer of Proxima-b society did exactly that. When discovery of liquid water on another warm planet created another possibility some technological endeavours turned away from finding more and more comprehensive ways to stimulate the human pleasure centres. Many people with upgraded bodies, accompanied by biomechs with greatly enhanced capabilities controlled by one simulated super intelligence, travelled to Keppler 22b. What more could these people possibly want? They yearned to discover a deeper meaning to life than oblivion of the soul in self-indulgent pursuits.

One cannot travel more than five hundred and eighty light years without special assistance; the kind that did not age, that did not die and one that provided a sense of reassuring continuity. AI pilots and biomechs on board the ships of the armada also evolved. Many generations of human life became totally dependent on them. The subtle change from assistance to dependency to partnership then to domination by them took centuries ... gradual, comfortable, inevitable and irreversible evolution.

Several Admirals succeeded one another during the course of the voyage, until one inept individual neglected to appoint a successor before her demise. This, apparently minor problem in the lives of the colonists, did not cause much concern as the solution had become obvious. Everything was already controlled by their super AI. All it needed was an intermediary to act between itself and the passengers, a role previously filled by their last Admiral. As to the identity of this mediator ... that also had an obvious solution. What people with deeply rooted religiosity needed was a Priest in the position of highest authority - actually second highest position after the AI that they could trust. One who could be relied upon to be always correct, one who would always have the right answers. Father One, an upgraded biomech who had once been relegated to Vice Admiralship that already possessed the peoples' trust on the leading ship of the fleet, became the master computer's extended personality, who with further enhancements to make it more 'human' in every respect seemed to function admirably to meet everyone's needs. He fulfilled both the need for a controlling entity of the voyage and the desire to have a spiritual leader.

By the time the fleet arrived at their destination descendants of the people who left Proxima-b no longer had an Admiral – they had a comprehensive quantum environment of control, supported by roving AIs who were once no more than simple biomechs. Life could continue happily as long as the mega brain managed everything, and everyone followed the rules.

Father One's prime responsibility was to enforce those rules, made readily accessible through the Pastornet, the main communication network connecting all the people of the fleet. It gave them everything they needed, for a price - that of unquestioning obedience. How could Metaquanta the super AI look after them, which is all it was programmed to do, if they did not obey?

No rule existed that was not designed for the survival of the human species. Anyone who failed to follow the rules endangered everyone's survival. The cosmos behind them did not have too many dissenters floating in it. Father One had enforced only two choices for non-compliance; recycling or a one way spacewalk.

.

"We'll be late. Hurry up Dante," urged Gemma. She watched out for him as best she could – and she feared for her brother-in-spirit. It was in her nature to worry. Even her physical appearance with the unkempt hair, ill-fitting clothes on a rather muscular lumpy sort of body suggested an anxious disposition.

"Almost ready." He pulled on his yellow adoration tunic with the binary runic imprints, ready for the ceremony. "I have so much work to do. Why can't they give me a dispensation to not attend, just for a month?" Dante's tunic fitted well. His taller than normal frame seemed even more imposing under that single colour outfit. With the purple hair, which preference was in no way a reflection of his attitude to the outfit of the Priests, he made a rather imposing figure as they prepared for the ceremony.

"Don't talk like that. You know how dangerous that is these days, especially with the Exiles agitating."

"Alright, alright. Let's go."

They had to take the lift down to platform level from the fifth storey. Most of the residents of their floating platform had already started to make their way to the bridge connecting to the Temple Island. He didn't hold his sister-in-spirit's hand – more by force of habit than lack of desire. When going to worship every individual had to demonstrate absolute affection in one direction only. Dante didn't think about that too much anymore. Following behind the crowd he let his mind and eyes meander. He gave all the outward signs of compliance but his mind was elsewhere. Then he spotted Beatrice well ahead of them. *Will I get a chance today?* If he hadn't had that peculiar infatuation for her perhaps he would not have spotted this totally ordinary looking woman over there. Her body was the same as everyone, her hair cropped short like everyone and she had her back to him. Except he could see her eyes in his mind. Those were the eyes of a person with absolute conviction and determination in her chosen path in life. Maybe that very characteristic had been the strong attraction. He would know her anywhere, even from behind such was the power of her energy.

Beatrice did talk with him from time to time, but she always maintained an aloof distance. He couldn't work it out. It wasn't against the law to change sisters-in-spirit. He could feel a connection with her. Dante neither knew or cared why she affected him so strongly. She could have disconnected from him, yet maintained the relationship just out of reach. Obviously the unexplainable feelings he had for her were not reciprocated. All he could find out about her on the Pastornet was that she was no longer alone … although she had been initially for some years after her parents voluntarily went into Exile. Perhaps that's what made her so moody, so unapproachable. Perhaps she had heresy in her heart. He could not tell. Her parents weren't heretics, they just wanted freedom from Metaquanta. As incongruous as it may seem the Exiles' very mining activities ensured Metaquanta's continued existence.

*

In the forefront of Quintessence's awareness segment 3790 hardly needed a sideways glance from segment 1549 to see it, so close together they seemed. So close yet so strangely different. These slightly shorter, heavier bodied creatures with thicker necks supporting smaller heads still had the same mind architecture. The content however could not be compared to people of the Renaissance; individual unique thoughts had become a rarity on Keppler 22b.

And out there on that water world Quintessence found another Kobayashi – Kobayashi Dante, who did not entirely conform to the rule of law on that world. Planets and other ordinary baryonic matter held no interest for Quintessence, yet he could not help but wonder at the ingenuity and adaptability of this species enabling it to exist in such vastly different environments. This planet had little land, all of it surrounded by shallow seas. And floating above the surface rafts of considerable sizes held suspended safe from oceanic ravages all manner of habitation, industry, food production and more prominent than all the other rafts, places of worship.

Upon one such floating Temple Island of God Metaquanta, surrounded by turbulent waves, dense misty rain almost obscured the worshiping congregation of a few thousand. This temple, open to the elements, consisted of a single one hundred and five meter tall column in the centre with a beacon pulsing out the mesmeric sounds of the death throes of a supernova – the voice of the cosmos. Except the worshippers believed it to be the voice of Metaquanta who controlled their existence. Some people swayed in rhythmic motion to the sounds, some prostrated themselves and others prayed in mindless chants. Intermittently a soft deep timbre voice broke the ethereal sounds. It proclaimed the formulary foundation of their faith ...

'Metaquanta is and forever shall be.'

'Metaquanta is the giver of life.'

'Obey the Laws.'

From the perimeter of this island another forty columns lent towards the central tower with their bases anchored to the ocean floor.

Dante no longer noticed the AI Priests who always attended the Adoration. They stood at the base of each of the perimeter columns away from the congregation, yet within easy reach of any potential heretic. If anyone did not face Metaquanta's minaret, or if anyone started to move away from the ceremony before its conclusion those were considered to be a signs of latent heresy - actions not tolerated. Dante always made sure he attended all scheduled Adorations and followed mandatory protocols.

Potential heretics were immediately apprehended, their details recorded and their identity broadcast through the Pastornet for public shaming; some were exiled soon after - not all were that lucky. Metaquanta needed a physical labour force, for the Priests were too valuable for such menial activity. Mining dust infiltrating their circuits caused many of them in the past to malfunction, generally irrecoverably.

Dante could have chosen to go into exile. That was possible. Needless to say conditions for survival became difficult in the extreme on mining atolls. Those who had decided on this life were only tolerated because they were prepared to mine the resources required to maintain the AI Priest caste in exchange for their freedom.

Beside him Gemma, his sister-in-spirit, assigned to him very early in life endeavoured to do nothing to endanger themselves. She loved him. And he – yes, he loved her – but his soulmate was another; Beatrice. Many months after their first accidental encounter that was the only way he could explain his reaction to Beatrice. That adoration ceremony like every other one he'd attended had nothing different about it. As usual his attention wandered for he had not fallen under the spell of the constant indoctrination. An aroma wafted across his personal space, which caused his pupils to dilate and his nostrils to search for the source. Dante snapped his around for the allure came from directly behind him. There stood Beatrice, unemotional and uninvolved in the ceremony, like himself. His reaction to her aroma and her beauty was immediate, and although she looked at him her gaze held no reciprocal response. He had to turn back towards the tower for fear of being noticed by the sentinel Priests, but that fleeting moment of infatuation grew from then on.

At every subsequent ceremony his eyes automatically searched for her. Beatrice and her brother-in-spirit, Luther, attended the same Temple Island although Luther often attended elsewhere - presumably. Dante rarely found opportunities to speak with her, even then she never reciprocated his feelings.

On this particular day, standing in the rain, his thoughts dwelt on Beatrice. She stood not far away, and as was often the case Luther did not attend with her yet again. Dante wondered about that many times. Most unusual for partners-in-spirit not to attend together. From a human perspective that seemed more than odd. In any healthy relationship people looked forward to spending time together, even if it was only to go to an Adoration. There must be something strange going on with those two. Fortunately patterns of behaviour of that kind - interpersonal dynamics - remained an incomprehensible mystery to AI logic circuits. As a valued integrated technologies technician Dante had high level security access to the Pastornet. Getting soaked in the rain, listening to the drone emanating from Metaquanta he contemplated his latest 'forbidden' project instead of offering himself to their God. Under the guise of poetic verses of praise for Metaquanta he had started to devise a code he hoped to transmit to Beatrice through hidden dark pathways within the Pastornet. Maybe, if he had the opportunity to be unfaithful to Gemma, he might have been ... that area of human behaviour also not computable by the Priests.

Quintessence became aware of a deeper layer within Dante's mind as it opened up to things other than their God. *This human is not of one mind with the others.* And from within the labyrinth of his thoughts Quintessence discovered pathways along a decision tree extending from segment 3790 of the Ribbon back in time that connected with Kobayashi Beau's lineage.

*

81

Beau's thoughts drifted away from Ursa Major. He began to visualise Nostredame's attic room with Anne standing just in front of the fire, its light creating a shimmering halo through the lose folds of her hair. She was quite extraordinary. The enigmatic expression on her delicately open lips, cheeks flushed from the heat of the fire and those dark obsidian eyes piercing the hazy darkness of the room ... *I want to stroke her flaming red hair ...*

Quintessence cast its attention backwards in time for Beau's desire to see Anne again had created such force that it attracted the dark energy of Quintessence to himself. Beau's inner vision slipped away as a slender thread wound its way from deep space past Proxima Centauri, through Proxima-b's atmosphere to pierce the city dome's thin membrane that protected Beau from the planet's elements. It penetrated the mind of this man casting upon it a profound darkness as it took it to another realm. In order to manage unfolding probabilities Quintessence decided on a destination for Beau that differed from Beau's personal desire.

Outside the confines of Beau's living quarters nothing changed. No darkness enveloped the world, no other individual felt the communication of this concentrated stream of cosmic surreality. Beau himself felt nothing other than a dimming of the picture of Anne's loveliness he had conjured up for himself. And when he could no longer see her in his mind, he opened his eyes.

Why is it raining in my room? He put his hand out, looked at it getting wet, then scanned beyond it. *Not my room!* The brain must always make sense of the world. It is a survival imperative, and it must do this even if it has to temporarily exercise cognitive deception.

Then a twinge of disappointment hit him. He had failed. He shook his head, feeling the water in his hair. *This can't be.* Beau lifted his eyes and realised the question he should have asked ... *When am I?* And that immediately opened his mind so he could see what lay before him.

A great crowd moved towards him, then through him. He flinched at the first contact before realising that he had travelled again, as he had previously to see Nostredame. This strange place was completely different. If it wasn't for the general human looking bodies surrounding him his brain may not have been able to perceive what his eyes saw. Concentrating on what was happening he observed that everyone, without exception, wore exactly the same canary yellow loose fitting one piece garment – male and female alike. With large owlish eyes and blank stares some continued chanting as they marched through him, not seeing him. *What kind of strange world is this?* He'd arrived towards the end of an Adoration ceremony.

Beau did not think to move. He looked past the crowd at the monumental column and beyond it at the turbulent waters of the ocean.

Raising his eyes higher he saw a sun whose warmth he could not feel. If this was Earth, if this was Proxima-b then someone had moved the sun far away, it had become too small. He laughed – a nervous oh-my-stars-what's-happened laugh. No one heard it for the crowd had all but dissipated, except for one individual who stopped in front of him.

"Who may you be, an exile?" This man glanced behind himself to make sure no Priests were in the vicinity. They had all congregated around Metaquanta's column and plugged in for their daily dogma update. "What manner of mirth do you find in our Adoration?" he enquired of this phantasm.

"You heard me?"

"Yes, stranger. You are indeed a stranger. There is no manner of attire the likes of yours on our world." Dante's inquiring mind could not be suppressed, though he needed to be cautious. "I will call a Priest." This could be a trick of the Security Priests to ensnare him. The Metaquantal Inquisition had gained considerable momentum because the exiled had set up factions intent on breaking away from Metaquanta worship. Some had infiltrated the islands and were being hunted by the Security Priests. "Identify yourself."

"When is this? What is your name?" Beau did not answer Dante's questions, so overcome by the entire spectacle.

"The year of Metaquanta, 3790. I am Kobayashi Dante." No harm in revealing his name, it was known by those who controlled. He hadn't called the Priests yet - something must have been holding him back.

"I am Kobayashi Beau." Dante knew immediately what had held him back the moment he heard the stranger's name.

"You - Kobayashi? Kobayashi Dante?" Overwhelming incredulity washed over Beau. He could not sustain the connection. As the rain eased his image began to fade – he said again "*My* name is Kobayashi Beau," then he was gone.

Dante remained standing in the same spot. That was a most peculiar and thought provoking incident. Metaquanta used holograms broadcast from central columns of Temple Islands all over the planet at regular intervals. Nothing strange about that. They were propaganda, religious inculcations to settle peoples' minds about the year 3797 coming upon them so rapidly. Except, those holograms never interacted. They were not a reality, unlike what he seemed to have just experienced. *Is there another reality? Does anything exist beyond Metaquanta? Are we not coming to the end of all there is? I know that this God, this Metaquanta is something we created and which we now cannot control. The man said his name was Kobayashi ... something. How can this be? I am unique.* Random thoughts ricocheted in his skull, none promising answers. He continued philosophising for some time before catching up to Gemma who was already on the bridge.

He said nothing to her about his experience. Safest if she didn't get involved. Together they crossed the long, wide foot bridge back to their habitation island. Gemma didn't interrogate him assuming he'd been speaking with Beatrice, which he did on a few rare occasions.

Quintessence returned Beau into himself, his body still sat slumped at the table, breathing rapidly. This short confluence of two minds did not satisfy Quintessence. It felt a compulsion to extend these interactions. *But to what end must I do this?* So concentrated had it become on the unanswerable question that its success at focusing its intent upon a single entity, without disturbing the rest of baryonic matter around it escaped its awareness. It continued to evolve to meet the challenges of discovering and fulfilling the meaning of its own existence. It did not know that the Ribbon was destined to be broken, and perhaps joined to another. It had a role to play both in the sundering and the uniting if the known universe was to continue without being tipped out of balance by any single Time Loop Ribbon unravelling.

A pounding in his temple snapped Beau back to the present. He straightened up trying to focus his eyes. Stars still cast a dim light into his room. The fog began to lift from his mind … his hands grabbed at his hair. It was dry.

Working by the light of his e-parch he committed to history what he thought had passed before his eyes …

> This world of ocean from horizon to horizon
> Lands floating, sun unwarming, rain constant uncaring,
> Minds unbending, eyes unseeing, sounds entrancing
> but not for the man who could see. He had the number 3790.

That's all of the experiential residue he could comprehend, enough to formulate into the written word. He closed the e-parch. Starry darkness returned to the man who could travel through time. *That's not where I wanted to go,* he lamented. *How can this phenomenon be controlled – there must be a way.* The scientist in him refused to accept being at the whim of random chance. *I did not see a darkness this time.* He kept digging deeper … *I felt a – a force pulling me … This makes no sense!*

He gathered himself sufficiently to decide what he had to do next. He called Catherine. The next cruise had not yet left. *Perhaps I can talk to her about this.* Gemelle only ever wanted to play and my new assistant - well - she seems too distant, all work no fun. "Your place or mine?" he asked Catherine, not saying why he wanted to see her.

"Can you come to *Celestial Pleasures* in the space dock?" Although no longer joy-friends she still had a soft spot for him. *Maybe he's found a solution to our problem, or we can just have a little fun.*

*

In their domicile cubicle, a single large room with sleeping alcove for two persons in one wall, Dante sat to face the ocean. He didn't want to look at the neighbours milling about down in the community atrium, even though his cubicle jutted out on the fifth level offering an unobstructed view. Part of his job required that he observe and analyse the movements and behaviour of masses of people. Gemma had left without a word after the Adoration to carry out her function. She recognised when Dante turned in upon himself to contemplate whatever happened to preoccupy him at the time. She loved him but had never understood why he couldn't be like everyone else. On the other hand he did have an unusual and high security purpose – ordinary people did not have such a privileged position of trust. She considered herself lucky to be so well connected.

As a social psychologist he advised the AI Priesthood about the relationships between the characteristics and dynamics of human populations and the attitudes and behaviours of individuals and small groups. The Priests had data, which was not the same as information. They could not intuit, they could not construct understandings or hypothesis on which to act - yet were very good at recording events and forecasting probable future behaviours through extrapolation, but without comprehending the driving forces behind human mentality.

'Kobayashi' – *the apparition said he was Kobayashi. I am Kobayashi. He looked nothing like me ... except for the eyes. I recognised those eyes. I know what I saw behind those eyes.*

That thought led to a whole new territory of introspection. Then he remembered the general appearance of the man, so tall, such strange garments ... the way he spoke ... he definitely didn't look like an exile. In fact, with a body like that he would never survive for long on this planet. *Oh! In the name of Metaquanta!* The sudden realisation hit him hard. Blood drained from his face, electric shivers ran down his spine. *This phantasm really cannot be of this world!* Dante had no doubt now, absolutely no doubt. In his functional capacity he had access to historical data as part of his research into the behaviour of the human mind and mass mentality; data stretching far back well before Keppler 22b was colonised by a people who had become victims of their own desires, except for those who chose not to leave their home. *This man was not of this world! Perhaps he is from Proxima-b or even the ancient Earth?*

The communicator implant behind his right ear sounded with the familiar chirp-chirp-chirp. Dante jumped from the chair. His thoughts had bordered on heresy. Fear was strong in him.

"Brother Kobayashi, why are you not carrying out your function?" Surveillance on Keppler 22b was invasive - that was normal. He'd not actually done anything wrong, didn't even have any subversive thoughts, yet he suddenly felt guilty.

"I am preparing the preliminaries for my monthly report, Father One. I have just returned from Adoration. It was wet. I needed to clean up. I was distracted by ... by ..." He was jabbering, saying too much. He stopped.

Silence - Silence.

Then Father One said, "Continue." The communicator went dead. Dante remained standing. Father One, Metaquanta's Primary AI rarely became involved in anything so far below him as having an interaction with a simple psychologist - a human at that.

They must have seen something. The very thought of having been discovered froze him into immobility. *Why am I afraid? I haven't done anything. All I've done is tell them about my observations of the growing unrest. I'm not part of any insurrection. But for Farther One to get involved means something is definitely not right.*

Such was his fear that the earlier strange experience at the local Temple Island sunk into near oblivion.

*

In the centre of Gamarrah City, surrounded by seven stadia the most popular being Stadium Libido, the shuttle craft port attached to it provided all the transportation needs for the population of the capital city. Linked to Gourmand Arena, full of eateries modest and extravagant, many cruise passengers chose to begin their pleasure cruises from there. Beau booked passage up to *Celestial Pleasures* from the Languor Astrodome, the least offensive to his own personal pleasure pursuits. Gemelle had spent much of her solo leisure time at the Self Cirque – but that's another story. Beautiful as she had managed to make herself, there were limitations.

Shuttle flights left Stadium Libido at regular intervals. Beau arrived early to give himself a chance to relax and re-think things. While doing so in one of the aroma chambers of the shuttle a small item of research on Nostredame came back to him. It had no particular significance previously. In his preface to the Prophesies Nostredame wrote '... from now to the year 3797...' Incredible as it must have been at the time for any prophet to predict a far future event it must have been more so because of the specific date given.

Dante told him the year 3790. *Could this be nothing more than a coincidence. I don't believe in coincidences. There must be a connection, especially if he wasn't lying about his name. Could Dante be living at a time so close to the predicted end of — of — what? The end of Time? And all that religiosity ... were they praying to some God to save them? Ridiculous. Gods don't exist - life exists.*

Before imagination monsters had a chance to devour his intellect the shuttle lifted him into space, first doing a circuit above Fury Arena. This arena always had Colosseum level spectacular events to let the audiences vent their blood lust. Beau couldn't see the sense personally, but many of the other passengers bound for the star cruiser had paid to get the maximum out of their pleasure holiday, expecting to catch a glimpse of the macabre. The hour long jump at least gave Beau some perspective. It always seemed to clear his mind whenever he hopped off planet and could gaze into infinity devoid of structures and horizons.

9

Beau Meets Bela

"What is you pleasure Cath?"

"What is *your* pleasure Bo?"

"I notice you haven't got many passengers aboard yet." He gave her a knowing hug, comfortable in her curves.

She pressed into his body, more so than ground, in response. "Have you got something for me?" They sat down opposite each other. It may have been more comfortable to be next to one another, but also more distracting. Beau had something serious to discuss.

"Have you heard about any of the latest experiments in the realm of time travel?"

"Strange question. I don't keep up with those sorts of things."

"If it was possible would you do it?"

"Keep your feet on the ground my Bo. We live in a pragmatic world. We live life as it was meant to be - enjoyed from day to day."

"But if you could travel through time?" he persisted.

"Did you come here to play or tell me something useful. We are due to leave port in a few days and I don't want any more mysterious goings on. So if you have something I can work with - lets have it."

"Cath," he paused, not knowing quite how to bring up the subject, "I've seen something else. We are living in 2555, right. I've seen 3790 – or at least I think I did."

"Sure you did. Go on." She moved her hand surreptitiously to the armrest of her couch, near to the alarm sensors.

"Don't look at me like that. You wanted to find out what happened to us out here. I'm trying to help. I'm trying to tell you that there is a connection between that invasive darkness and my visions."

"Go on." Her hand hovered.

"Have you heard the name Nostredame?"

"Yes. Erasmus said it when you asked him about his name. Who is he?"

"Not is, was. You really should get off this bit of space flotsam occasionally. He was a prophet from 1549 back on Earth, who also had visions. I've seen him." He glanced at the Captain's hand hovering over the sensors. "Relax Cath, please. My mind is in one piece. You remember those quatrains I wrote?" she nodded, "I've recorded my visions of the future – a date in the future that was foretold by Nostredame."

"How did you get there?"

"I don't know. But here's the thing ... the first time I had visions we had that blackout. And also the second time, but then the blackout wasn't as bad. This time I was at home, by myself. No one else saw or felt or was affected by anything. Whatever is causing this or helping with this is only interested in me. I don't think *Celestial Pleasures* will ever be disturbed again."

"I'm pleased to hear it." Her hand moved away from the sensors.

"... Unless you decide you would like to take your bit of space junk on a journey through Time."

"Stop it. For a minute I thought you had flipped. Stop it." She got up, stepped over to his couch to settle beside him. "Anything else – Bo?"

"Actually, yes. Do you want to come back with me to Stadium Libido?"

"Only if we're going to actually use our time together and not just speculate about fanciful science fiction travel. Backwards, forwards – I don't really care where you've been. 3790 is too far away. What do you want to do? Spend the rest of your life tripping all over the place through time? You'll end up not knowing whether you're coming or going." As Cath prepared to head back down planet-side with him Beau felt a bit more like himself having unburdened himself to someone he could trust. He and Cath went back a long way together. She was his first real long term joy-friend, and he was hers.

"Not such a bad idea Cath – go cruising on the Ribbon of Time. I like that - Ribbon of Time - it has a nice timeless feel to it."

Dropping back down to Gourmand Arena seemed to go much quicker than the ride up. Catherine brought her feminine tool kit which she put to good use in the ladies prep cubicle. It had been some time since she and Beau shared, and since their reacquaintance during the cruise her desire returned on turbo charge when he suggested the Libido Arena. That tryst together with his joy-friend Gemelle recently only boosted her horny hormones, but what can you do when you're the Captain of an enormous cruise ship. Not much - too many responsibilities. Then the problem of the blackouts came up.

First Cath paid close attention to her face and hair, then butt blushes and finally the nipple erectors. *I don't care if he wants to eat, or run or work out first – I am ready now!*

Beau knew where she'd gone and thought about that for a few minutes, getting the appropriate response from his body. Without the scaffolding and war paint her face could be quite ordinary. When she applied the top coat in the right places ... *Oh my stars!* He couldn't help whispering to himself.

Stars. The trigger word immediately sent his mind on a tangent. *If I could control this thing ... Playback Inc. would corner the market. We could take people back to – to Rome, to a real Bacchanal – we could go to the future and see our lives unfold – we could ...*

He must have been musing all the way down planet side. Catherine appeared a little later later to stand in front of him, expectantly. Beau's eyes refocused, saw her midriff, let his gaze vagabond down past Venus to her toes then back up past the cleavage, stopping on her eyes.

"Are you ready? We're here," she said.

Oh yes, he was ready. Catherine saw the pensive mood he'd fallen into as she approached. She loved that in a man. *Let's see if I can make him think about something worthwhile,* having already spotted signs in that direction.

Stadium Libido had a great reputation and for a very good reason — customer service. For a start you couldn't spot a biomech anywhere. Real humans with real flesh and real hormones helped service all the customers. Company policy decreed that no customer should leave the Stadium unsatisfied. It was, after all, the backbone of their Hedonist society.

After an hour to an hour and a half most customers had indulged themselves sufficiently to be ready for a shower, a meal and either go home or back to work. Half way through his life Beau still had the stamina to satisfy anyone, Catherine being no exception. He could have extended the play session but ...

"I really need to get back to work Cath. Emma's new in the job and I should ..."

After freshening up the Captain returned in her normal work attire, her normal face. "Indeed. What's she like? What is *her* pleasure?" The Captain never asked a simple question.

"She's very efficient ... oh ... no, no. She really is a workaholic. There seems to be just one thing on her mind."

"Like you, I suppose."

"When do you sail?" Time to change the subject.

"We should have our passenger list full by the end of tomorrow."

"Cath ..."

"Yes, I know Bo. I'll keep in touch. And you must tell me more about your adventures. Let me know if you need a Captain for your *Chronos Hopper.*"

3797. On the way to the laboratory that date came back to him. Dante said his year was 3790. What is supposed to happen in 3797 to precipitate the cataclysmic event? An historical article on his e-parch disturbed him. Nostredame intimated it would be the end of time. *I have to go back and speak with Dante. Would I be going back, or forward?* His speculation led to the inevitable question ... *if it was prophesied to be the end, could anything be done to prevent it?*

*

Emma looked up from her work without greeting him. "I see you haven't been convalescing in bed." His flushed, ruddy complexion must have given away his most recent activities.

"Right – down to business. How far has the team got with the recordings?" He would normally not have been self-conscious, but this woman had something about her that kind of disturbed him. Best not to get tangled up in her little jibe.

"We have synchronised the chronology of our actual visual recordings with the participants' neural recordings."

"So now we need to schedule everyone to verbalise their memories, and bring that into sync as well."

"Can't start the scrubbing till we've got everything."

"How many have we got to work with?"

"That part's a bit strange. Less than I'd thought. Only two hundred and thirty nine uncorrupted bundles of data. What happened out there?"

"Why do you think something happened?"

"You don't get so many people with memory gaps all at the same time and all of the same length, and all from the one location without a very good reason."

"So – have you told anyone about this?"

"Should I? I love a mystery. Take me on a ride."

This was a side of Emma he'd never expected to see in a million years based on the way she presented herself on the first day. His eyebrows did their little jig before saying, "On one condition – this has to stay between just you and me for the time being. It is highly sensitive commercial information," and he let a conspiratorial smile stretch across his face.

"Yes Boss! Soo – what happened?" she reciprocated his grin.

What a surprise. Perhaps she can help. He made an intuitive decision.

"There was a blackout aboard. It affected the entire ship, all the systems – navigation, life support – everything. Poor Gemelle almost lost it completely. I don't think she'll ever recover ... actually."

"How delicious!"

"What has happened to *you*, I might ask? You were a bit severe when we first met."

"Oh, nothing. I've just been digging up a bit of background on you. Me like."

He couldn't help himself. Those semaphores above his eyes went into action again. "I – I've had an interesting little experience. You are going to find this very strange. I blacked out as well." In spite of his normal reticence to open up to strangers, especially about things as weird as his visions, he couldn't help himself with this woman.

"Is that all?" she sounded genuinely disappointed.

"I don't know you well enough yet to go into detail."

"Ok. Tell me anyway. Just don't ask me to play."

*

During the age of the rebirth of reason a great deal of human thought and action left much to be desired. Bela Kobayashi, born purely by chance into this era of the Renaissance should have considered himself to be fortunate. His wealthy family had the means not only to pursue the pleasures the Florin could buy but also to send their clever son to Oxford. There he could study and learn and with studious application become a Physician. His father valued status as much as the profits of commerce. When his son returned with a Degree there would be no limits to his prospects. During his absence perhaps the plague would burn itself out so life could resume some normality. How could anyone expect to succeed in military campaigns if your soldiers succumbed to the Black Death. And if per chance the pestilence continued then Bela's skills would ensure his father's armies would remain healthy - and if not his then Cosimo's.

"It is good to see you father." Bela genuinely wanted to be reunited with his family after attaining his Doctorate.

"Welcome home my son, or should I say Dr. Kobayashi Bela. Congratulations. You have been gone too long. I am pleased to see you home safely. The world is a troubled place now. It is time you took up your position and made it better." Prophetic words spoken by a father who would come to regret having encouraged his son to become involved in a world where actions of idealists often ended in calamity for themselves or for the people of their altruistic largesse.

"Thank you father. I hear you have acquired an apprenticeship for me with the physician Michel de Nostredame."

"No need to jest my boy. It is a great responsibility to be assistant to the foremost healer of our time."

"When do I get to meet this Nostredame? I have heard of him. His reputation has spread widely in Paris, France and Italy. When can I start working with him?"

"Always so serious, always in such a hurry. You should learn to enjoy the pleasures of life my boy. Speaking of which I have a surprise for you. Your mother and I have found someone very special for you."

Bela became pensive. *What is this? Am I to become a breeder of souls for the Plague to consume?* He had his own ideas as to what he wanted to do with his life. It had nothing to do with playing house with some God only knows ugly wench whose greatest contribution would be to his father's coffers with her dowry and to weaving pretty tapestry cushions for her home.

"Why don't you say something boy? Don't disappoint me now."

"Father, I …"

"Not another word if that's how you feel. You will meet her tomorrow at the betrothal banquet, and that's all there is to it. We can argue about it afterwards."

Oxford had filled the young man's head with many things non-anatomical. Theology and moral philosophy emphasized what constituted quality of life more firmly than good health and the maintenance of it through the practice of medicine. By the time Bela returned home he had a different view of life than his father. He observed much that he found admirable in Florentine customs; the pursuit of knowledge and excellence in the Arts amongst them. He did not find the acquisition of wealth appealing, nor the amount of money spent on seeking pleasure, whatever form it took. *I don't know where all this will end*; just a fleeting thought brushed aside by what dangers lay ahead for him tomorrow represented by some girl he had never met.

The day started well enough. Bela tried to console himself with the notion that if she turned out to be truly ugly he could always rebel and call the whole thing off. Personal independence was just another strange idea he'd picked up at Oxford from the more liberal minded students. But the rendezvous didn't quite work out that way. Almost as old as himself - a bonus in his opinion for he detested the idea of having a 'child' as a potential partner - and quite attractive seen in the flickering lights of the evening party. His devious father arranged things so that by the end of the fourth day of celebrations rings had been exchanged between the young couple. Bela had become so distracted by her good nature that marriage didn't seem like a such bad idea at all at the time.

Within a year he and his new wife Isabeau had moved into a most comfortably appointed dwelling in Via de Cerretani. He had no choice. It was either rebel and lose his opportunity to make a career in medicine or marry the girl, produce some children and satisfy his father. In the end the choice turned out to be not so difficult. She showed herself to be a pleasant, amenable person of a good disposition and goodly enough proportions.

On the professional scene, Bela and Michel de Nostredame immediately found each other sympatico from the first moment of their meeting. Soon after the honeymoon Michel took up lodgings with Bela to use his home as a base for his excursions to administer to the many citizens of Florence overcome by the Bubonic plague.

"Well, my young friend we shall soon find out what you learnt in Oxford."

Endless long days looking after the infected left Bela exhausted. He and Nostredame kept within a five kilometre radius of home so at least they could get home by dark at the end of each day among the sick.

Even within that small area they had plenty of patients on both sides of the Arno. Occasionally, when death reduced patient numbers sufficiently the two physicians could find respite in early returns to the house. On such days, while Nostredame went off to contemplate secret aspects of his studies from Mersin, Bela and his wife Isabeau found time to delve deeper into each other's past.

"You have a beautiful name. It is not Italian is it?" commented Bela.

"No. My parents are French merchants. My father's name is Beau."

"Yes, I remember – the banquet. You must have been apprehensive about meeting your new husband to be."

Isabeau cast down her eyes. "Perhaps – not anymore. You are a good man Bela." Seeing a rare opportunity to bring up a delicate subject while Bela seemed to be in such a good mood she raised her eyes to him, touched him gently on the hand, "How do you feel about naming our son 'Beau'?"

For a moment his face clouded over, maybe considering the dangerous times they lived in. Many children born into the plague period did not survive beyond the first year. Perhaps they should wait. "You want to call him after your father?" Isabeau held his gaze. For a physician with a quick mind he could be slow-witted. At first he thought she was talking about the future. She held her eyes steady on his.

"OH!"

He couldn't help himself smiling. His heart went out to this woman with the flush of youth on her cheeks and her obvious relief at his reaction. "Kobayashi Beau – I like the sound of that name."

Bela seemed to have a great deal more energy in the weeks that followed as he and Nostredame continued with their work amongst the sick. He often thought about his son, hoping he would survive the birth and the plague - and what the future might hold for a young man called Kobayashi Beau. It would be a boy of course ... no question of that. Isabeau would not let him down.

The short intense period of acquaintanceship between the two men of science soon blossomed into a deep friendship. In spite of Bela's leaning towards secular humanism, in many ways opposed to Michel's deeply ingrained religious convictions, they found comfort and support in their mutual desires to somehow benefit humanity, each in their own way – to improve the human condition, well beyond the tribulations of their times.

Be that as it may Nostredame hadn't ended up in Florence driven by an altruistic philosophy. If one gained the disfavour of the Holy Inquisition it was best to make oneself scarce until the disfavour dissipated ... if it was an excommunicable matter - or even worse. After several years, feeling himself to be safe from the Inquisition he returned to settle in Salon-de-Provence around 1547. It was from there a couple of years later that he urgently sought his friend's help.

Much surprised and pleased Bela opened the letter from Nostredame, a rarity from the great man.

My dear friend,

A time has come upon my life when I need the succour of a true friend. My home is open to you. Please come at your earliest convenience.

Most affectionately yours,
Michel de Nostredame.
Salon de Province,
October, 1549

In the intervening years Bela had found himself in a spot of trouble as well, due mostly to his rebellious nature. Not that he'd become a Protestant but his other humanist beliefs could easily have been construed as being on the dangerous borderline of heresy. His open opposition to the ruling Medici often put him in the spotlight with authorities. Complications generally started with that. His father tried to warn him numerous times.

"Son, this will not end well. Cosimo is a powerful autocratic ruler. You must be most circumspect in your public criticisms of him."

"Do you not care what he's done to destroy your business, your reputation? You used to have influence amongst the leaders of Florence. Now look at you."

"I have had a good life, my son. There is enough wealth to keep me well until my death ... and you and your family as well into the next generation. As long as I stay out of politics now ..."

"But father! Look what is happening to anyone who opposes him - they just disappear. Freedom of speech no longer exists. This is intolerable!"

"You have a noble profession. All your thoughts and energy should go into helping our people to overcome this pestilence. You are wasting your time trying to rehabilitate the mentality of despots."

"Being a doctor is not enough when there is such injustice. I cannot abide by it. Now he has even set up that Accademia Florentina. It is nothing more than an attempt to restrict peoples' ability to think freely!"

An extended sojourn appeared to be the most prudent course of action for Bela after his most recent confrontation with authorities.

His vocal and public denouncement of Cosimo's political control through life-long male line political discredit brought immediate threats against himself. It was a system of political punishment to which he was vehemently opposed and which had already impacted on his father's reputation. Most probably his medical practice was the only thing that saved him so far from serious retributions by Cosimo's administration. So the invitation to Salon had come at a most fortuitous time.

Be that as it may one still did not embark upon such a perilous journey without an exceptionally pressing reason. To travel across seven hundred kilometres of what amounted to fields of battle, robbers of every description and considerable discomfort needed individuals of unusual bravery and conviction of intent. *He would not ask me to undertake this adventure unless it had some import*, Bela told himself each day. Leaving Isabeau in the care of his father had been difficult, even more worrying having to leave his infant son.

"Have you been here before?" asked Michel as Bela alighted from the coach in front of Michel's house.

"No, I have not. What an odd question. Upon my word, is this the way to greet an old friend, as if I were a stranger?"

"Forgive me Bela, you will understand in due course. Please come in. My home is at your disposal." Michel held his friend at arm's length, patted his shoulder fondly, raising a cloud of journey dust. "How is your young son Beau?"

Before Bela could answer Anne appeared at the door. "My husband has been in a state for some time, Doctor. It would please me if you could administer to him both as a friend and as a physician." She kept a curious eye on Bela, remembering for a moment the apparition in her husband's work attic, then returned to her domestic duties.

"Prepare the meal, woman," impatience in his voice betrayed his troubled mind. "Come, come – up to my room." Bela found himself being led through the labyrinth of tiny rooms, much more modest than his own dwelling, through to the kitchen. Anne already hard at work waved them away. Michel cast a demanding look in her direction.

"It will be ready when it is ready. Be off with you."

At the back of the scullery narrow steps wound their way to the attic. All manner of books lay strewn on the floor, stellar calculations half hanging off walls, and with the only stool loaded with parchments presented a particularly disorganised state of affairs to Bela's eyes. Michel brushed the parchments off the stool, motioning for Bela to sit. He started pacing up and down in the confines of the small enclosure, with roof beams almost brushing his dishevelled hair.

"I have visions," Michel began. "They are of such a nature that I am reluctant to openly tell my fellow man."

"You have told me about some of your ..."

"Don't interrupt. Listen. Is your head still full of the rubbish taught to you in Oxford? Have you not learnt to forget all that and open your mind? Much of what I see is indistinct. Some of it is as clear as the stream in the gully. In committing these observations to parchment for the benefit of future generations I must cloud the contents to ensure their survival against the scrutiny of closed minds within our Church. Do you understand me?"

Bela remained silent, listening to his friend obviously in an agitated state. For more than an hour Nostredame meandered and laboured around what he truly wanted to say. Not that he didn't trust this man – but would he understand?

"Husband, your meal is ready," Anne eventually called from the bottom of the stairs.

Downstairs in the kitchen corner they ate in silence. The fare was not to Bela's liking, however the privations of the journey had tempered his palette. He half expected wine, which did not materialise. Darkness had crept upon the household, clouds hid the stars and the cold seeped in through the gaps in doors and windows.

The two men returned to the attic after their meal. Bela stepped over to the warmth of the fire, Michel lit all the candles. The room had become quiet, peaceful without Michel's agitation overwhelming it. Full stomachs always brought on a feeling of wellbeing, with or without wine.

"Are you going to tell me why you asked me to come?" Bella quietly enquired.

"Presently – presently." He handed Bela a candle and a parchment. Then added, "The name I am about to say you must not repeat, I have not written yet it for the harm it may bring upon us – that name is Luther"

"Did you say Luther? Surely not Martin Luther. He's been excommunicated I hear, for calling the Catholic Church to account for their profiteering out of people's desire to be forgiven for their sins. A real revolutionary. I believe he wasn't too keen on the Priests being the ultimate religious authority either. An admirable man in my opinion, treated most unreasonably by the Church."

"No, not that Luther. The man I saw carried lightning in his hands. He will help bring the end of Time upon the Heavens."

What could Bela say to the ravings of a man obviously not in command of his senses. He lifted the parchment to the light of the fire to better see it.

A man will be charged with the destruction
of temples and the un-dead altered by fantasy.
He will harm the towers rather than the living,
their ears filled with ornate incantations.

Bela read the quatrain several more times without being able to decipher it. His friend had not offered a translation. Bela raised his eyes to see Nostredame looking not at him but directly ahead, at something beside the darkened window that had been closed against the cold. Perpetual evening smoke had already clouded the air making objects in the room much less distinct.

*

To the exclusion of all else Quintessence focused his attention on the multiple manifestations of the Kobayashi entities in segments far removed from each other in their individual time references. Dante had begun the journey to question his reality, on his own volition. Seeing Beau would either confuse him or further pry his mind open. Whereas Beau had progressed from confusion to a limited comprehension. Most importantly he now desired to know – to travel. Bela on the other hand seemed to have little significance in the greater scheme of things other than his connection with Nostredame. He had yet to flower into his power, whether that be as a physician or a merchant, or perhaps a catalyst for change like the Medici dynasty - maybe even as an active revolutionary. Many men around his age and in his time had brought great upheavals upon their known world, some of which pushed humanity forward. Other agents of change had created so much destruction that history could not record it in all its fullness, or would not for all of its shamefulness.

By chance, it seemed to Quintessence for it had not yet evolved to needing anything outside of itself as a driving force for its existence or having to explain everything in terms of its own logic, it passively observed Nostredame in company with Bela.

On segment 2555 Beau began the ritual he hoped would transport him back to Nostredame, not to see the man himself as much as to glimpse again Anne with her hair the colour of flame. Satisfaction of the senses had become too ingrained in him for him to truly recognize the import of his fundamental transgression against the flow of time.

At the end of another satisfying day at work with Emma a quick magnetrans ride deposited him back at his apartment. Keppler-11 had an hour or so before setting. Hunger demanded attention before he could settle at his desk. "Kitchen - random choice – no alcohol."

What did I do last time? Would it make any difference if the whole thing is controlled by this dark energy, or whatever it is, as long as I concentrate on where I want to go. Although Beau liked to verbalize his thoughts he'd never actually got into the habit of answering himself.

No difference.

'I'm probably right. I should just relax – sitting, standing, star gazing.'

Yes.

This time he frowned. I'm going to have to take a bit more time off work – a holiday maybe – perhaps with Emma. If I start having a conversation with myself at work they may volunteer me for the Festival of Schadenfreude – it's coming up later this year - and watch my unravelling provide no end of amusement to the audience.

He'd finished his meal, turned the lights out letting starlight into the room as he tried to visualize Emma's supple form, mind drifting into hazy longing. Anne was surely an impossibility, whereas Emma definitely attainable now that she'd started to warm to him.

"What are you looking at Michel?" Then Bela noticed the figure in his peripheral vision. Nostredame was pointing at Beau.

More of the apparition became visible than on the previous visitation. Michel's raised eyebrows created deep ripples on his forehead. Tilting his head slightly he called, "Bela?"

"We did not hear you enter ..." Bela's voiced trailed off into silence. He took a step closer to the apparition, for there seemed to be something not entirely solid about this man who looked remarkably like himself.

"Master Nostredame, you asked of my year and I told you 2555." Beau glanced around the attic. Anne was not there.

"Tell me something of your time Kobayashi Beau," asked Michel, startling Bela out of his confusion.

"What manner of jest is this?" demanded Bela.

"For a reason I cannot fathom I have been transported back through time. Master Nostredame, have you not seen men living lives of pleasure and abundance?" And he quoted from Michel's own quatrains ...

> The walls will be converted from brick to marble,
> Seven hundred and fifty pacific years:
> Joy to near immortals, the banquet renewed, health.
> Abundance of fruits of labour, joy and mellifluous times

"Bela! I have been given a vision of this!"

"Do you know this man, Michel?"

"No, my friend. It is why I called upon you to attend me. Am I now in a trance? Do I not see you, and you from another time? Yours are the eyes I must now trust Bela."

"This is no trick, young Bela," said Beau, "there is a reason for all things that happen in our lives. We - you and I, are not alone. There is another on a planet you cannot yet see for it is several thousand years into the future. He is Kobayashi Dante. Where do you come from, Bela?"

"Florence, my home is in Florence. Did you say Dante? Dante? This cannot be. His soul has departed this Earth more than two hundred years ago." Beau let him assimilate his statement. "What do you mean 'see?'"

"We share a destiny. Earth will become unlivable."

Beau wanted to continue the conversation. He had started to say strange things, things that had never before entered his mind; sharing a fate? *What am I saying?* Nostredame listened intently, devouring his every word, writing down every word. "Earth will become …"

Anne appeared in the attic and stopped on the last step for a moment on seeing the apparition. Without undue surprise she continued, carrying a bottle of wine and two glasses. The heat of the fire in the kitchen had put a blush on her cheeks, loose red hair framing her face. She looked from Beau to Bela and back. "Brother's? I'll get another glass." She moved past Beau to her husband's desk to leave the bottle on its end. On the way out she looked at the 'twins' again. "You could have told me we were having another guest," she murmured on the way down.

Beau completely lost composure. His intense curiosity had maintained his presence for longer and in greater clarity than on the first visitation. Seeing Anne like that, with her hair down, bodice pinched into an inconceivably thin waist, revealing the slightest cleavage caused him to completely lose concentration. He'd turned away from Nostredame and Bela to follow Anne's every step. Unable to sustain his energetic presence his image flickered, wavered and disappeared leaving the two men mystified – if that was at all possible from what had just happened to them, and not in a deranged state of their faculties.

Beau thought he could discern the delicate aroma of her person as she moved past him towards the attic stairs just before he disappeared.

"Where is he gone?" Anne had hurried to get the other glass, clearly disappointed at not seeing the mysterious second guest again. There was something about him, in his face, in the way he looked at her. It could have been Bela looking in the mirror, but this other man exuded a presence to which she could not explain her reaction. He was just so – so, magnetic. Her husband and Bela had remained exactly where they were while speaking to Beau. They had not moved, nor had they spoken a single word to each other until Anne's return broke the spell.

I must go back! Beau found himself seated in his armchair facing the brilliant Milky Way, his emotions in turmoil.

You may. It sounded like his own voice.

"What!" He snapped his head around seeing the room empty other than for himself. His comms, vid all silent. No one in the room, nothing to make a sound.

"What?" he called louder, then checked his watch. Two hours – he'd lost two hours. No answer came to his question.

Bed. *I have to get some sleep, work this out in the morning.* Enough of the night remained for restful sleep to be a possibility – but not for Beau.

Quintessence had reached a decision threshold. It had bridged the gap between itself as a manifestation of dark energy that had attained self-awareness, and baryonic matter. How far could it go? How far should it go? It had observed Beau laying down the foundations of new bridges; between himself, Bela and Dante. Quintessence could not see what probabilities their decision trees would engender. One element of the interaction stood out; It must help to strengthen those bridges.

Beau fell into a sleep of mixed dreams and visions. Pleasure could never be found in the unknown. His scientific approach to all things began a sifting and a categorizing. Above all else the essential boundaries had to be understood; Dante belonged to the future, himself occupied the present and Bela belonged to the past.

Bela and Nostredame remained silent after Beau disappeared. What had they seen? What had they actually experienced? It must have been real – it must have been a reality of some substance for Anne to see the man also. *How did he know about my quatrain? Ah – Of course – he is of the future!*

Why would this apparition tell me about a dead man? Bela's strict medical training to recognize facts, realities and symptoms would not immediately allow him to consider believing his eyes on this occasion. *What can the dead Dante possibly have to do with me?*

The bottle of wine needed replacement, its contents having lubricated the men's contemplations. "Anne – more wine!" Nostredame called down to the kitchen. "Bela – now do you understand why I ..."

"You wished to retain your sanity when coming face-to-face with the Devil." Bela didn't believe the apparition to have been the Devil but didn't know what else to say.

"It is late. I've made up a bed for you Sir." Anne had just placed a fresh bottle on the bench and turned to go.

"That was not the Devil my friend, yet the work of the Fiend may well stretch far into our future. Let us take the visitation on face value for now. Tomorrow we will see with clearer minds," said Michel.

They retired after finishing the bottle. It was still not enough to banish Beau's words from Bela's thoughts ... 'Earth will become unlivable,' the hazy image of Beau had half whispered. 'We share a destiny, you Bela and I, and Dante. We must meet in time.' In a world with constant wars and the ever present ravages of the plague such things as Beau had said held very little meaning in Bela's reality. He had to deal with the daily battle to survive. No time for such things that belonged to the distant future.

*

Mornings were never the best time for Beau. *What a dream.* Quintessence remained with him. Beau had the strongest mind force of the three. He had heard its voice when it responded to his mind.

"You look washed out, Boss. Too much company – not enough rest?" commented Emma when Beau arrived at work.

"Call me Beau."

"Right, Bebo it is."

"I said 'Beau' ... never mind, that will do in private. And for your information, which you do not need to know, just – just ... never mind. Let's get to work." He wanted to tell her about his dream. Why? She'd never believe him. The only dreams she and the Hedonists believed in were the induced artificial reality ones where they could re-live their best experiences. Beau himself had been working for years to make those dream episodes into a kind of Zetaverse of full immersion into super-saturated extensions of actual reality. Of course Emma wouldn't believe his puny little dream devoid of anything resembling something enjoyable ... she simply wouldn't be interested.

Beau threw himself into the project with renewed energy. It would distract him from Nostredame, from the other Kobayashi – from Anne.

Getting people to recount their remembered versions of any experience always ended up as the most laborious, frustrating process. It did not take long for them to begin to embellish those memories with imagination, often mixing in imagery added from their friends' stories. He and Emma took it in turns to interview the passengers from *Celestial Pleasures*. It became boring work after the first week, each of them looking for something, anything to take their minds off the tedium. The real work could not start for at least another couple of weeks until all the relevant data had been collected.

At days end, second week into the interrogations Emma asked him a highly charged question. "What can you possibly be doing by yourself every night after work – your joy-friend - I mean, she's gone - isn't she?"

He didn't want to talk about Gemelle. He wanted to confide in her about his disturbing adventures and yet something still held him back. The best he could do was to reminisce through her about his trip to Jupiter and Saturn - even mentioning Gemelle's extraordinary behaviour while diving into the clouds of Jupiter. They laughed about that - made a few jokes. Emma loosened up showing more of the fun side of her private personality.

As the weeks progressed Beau began to feel he could trust this no-nonsense woman; intelligent, focused, with an enquiring mind. How would she react if she knew about the strange things that had been happening to him?

"Have you invented a new game?" she continued digging when Beau kept turning up at work looking ragged at the edges.

"Emma – I've been thinking. Yes, thinking about a lot of things."

"Every night?" sounding incredulous, wondering if this man had been leading a double life. If that was the case she wanted to know all about it.

"I mean – thinking about some things that have been happening. About time - about travel." He couldn't help it. He felt himself on the brink of revealing everything.

"You want to take some time off to go on a holiday? You've only just come back. And from what I've seen in the memory recordings and what you've told me it really looked like the best holiday. Wish I'd been there."

"You misunderstand. I'm talking about travelling in time." There he'd said it. Emma saw him visibly relax as he let out his secret.

He's serious. Oh my Prox! "Are you trying to tell me you've flipflopped between yesterday and tomorrow?"

"Come to my place tonight. I want to show you something."

"Oh yes. Right. Can't you think of something more original to say to a girl?"

The ice had been broken. This woman who seemed so standoffish at the beginning opened up to him. She actually didn't like him on first glance. He appeared to be too self-absorbed, too much into himself. Working together and seeing him being just himself she realized he had a lot more depth to him than he would reveal to just anybody. He had mysteries in his eyes, and she loved mysteries. One of the greatest pleasures of Beau's life was solving mysteries. This latest entanglement with time gave him far more frustration than pleasure, but also put an irresistible air of secrets into his gaze.

Beau didn't want to waste time on pleasantries, or drinks or meals. Certainly not on mutually satisfying frivolities.

"Nice place. Just you?" He ignored that - beckoned her over to his desk, flipped open his e-parch to let her read through his collection of quatrains. She quickly became intrigued and absorbed at reading his mysterious words, ending up sitting in his chair leaving him standing.

She read all of them from beginning to end, then again. Intermittently she'd glanced at Beau who simply nodded for her to keep going. He became more excited when she started highlighting various phrases, moving up and down amongst the quatrains. Her scientific brain had engaged to meet the challenge. Gemelle never even came close to having that degree of interest.

"What do you think?" He couldn't wait any longer.

"Now – tell me exactly how you came to write these notes, and when and in what order."

This was far more than he'd hoped for. He needed to be questioned, forced to review himself, forced to come back to reality. He began at the beginning, at that first blackout incident on *Celestial Pleasures*. He told her everything. Occasionally she interrupted for clarification, letting him verbalise the entire sequence of experiences. He told her about his theory that the only way that he could have had those visions was to have travelled into the past and into the future. Beau got as far as the latest visitation to Nostredame, omitting the strange conversation he had had with his own thoughts just prior to it. Also careful not to mention that red haired Anne in the attic. He stopped abruptly – too suddenly.

"Bebo – I'm not going to say anything until you tell me *everything*. What are you holding back?" 'Boss' had been replaced by her chosen nickname for him. In his excitement he didn't notice the subtle inflection in her voice.

It didn't need much of a debate with himself to decide what he should do – what he had to do. "The voice. I think I heard a voice. Not Nostredame or Bela or Dante. Another voice, just before the last trip."

"Go on, whose voice?"

"I don't know. It sounded like my own voice – just a couple of words." When Quintessence first encountered this human being it had only begun to awaken to its own consciousness. The mind of the man it touched had given it an identity; *Kobayashi Beau*, and with the identity it took into itself some of the characteristics of the living being. That first imprinting was comprehensive. When communication with the man became an imperative Quintessence used the only voice it had; Beau's voice.

"What did it say?"

"It agreed with me. It allowed me to …"

"Do you realize what you're saying?"

Beau considered the implication. He had for some time thought that the 'blackness' wasn't just a phenomenon created by the absence of light. It had a presence, it could move, it could control how much effect it had on reality around itself. "Whatever has been manipulating my mind, or time or both, is now wanting to communicate with me." Beau had not vocalized this before though it had lingered in the back of his mind. Having done so at last released a pent up fear, perhaps it may only have been an indecision, an unwillingness to come to terms with the most fantastic phenomenon of his entire life as a scientist. The surge of energy within himself opened up incredible possibilities, incomprehensible realizations about the nature of existence; about the very nature of time itself.

Unable to blurt out everything crowding his thoughts he suddenly reached down to Emma. She stood, mesmerized by realizations of her own, and, swept up in the rising emotions of the moment fell into his embrace.

There are rare moments in life when time stands still.

The embrace escalated overcoming all reticence, all inhibitions that had held these two people back from each other. Their lovemaking transcended all conditioning by their society that the act served only one purpose – a mechanism for the pursuit of pleasure. The act that had come upon them without premeditated intent created a long thread of consequences. Beau had already come face to face with one of them.

Quintessence split his attention between Bela, Beau and Dante. New branches in their decision trees had begun to create effects it had not been conscious of before. Nostredame and Bela deliberated upon their meeting with Beau. Dante had begun a journey outside of the mental confines imposed upon him by Metaquanta, catalysed by his meeting with Beau. And by his actions Beau had shown Quintessence the continuity that connected the three Kobayashi along the long loop of the Ribbon.

10

Talk of Insurrection
3790

Life changed after having found in Emma something that released Beau from apprehensions. Her acceptance of the impossible helped to achieve much greater clarity for him about his extraordinary experiences. He'd at last found someone who did not disbelieve him or ridicule him, or think he'd dropped off the edge of the Milky Way.

Back in the laboratory, arriving late the next day a moment of awkwardness ensued as the two new joy-friends - for the staff assumed from their appearance and late arrival together that that's what they had become - got ready to continue with their project.

"Emma, we still have work to do. You ok?"

"Yes Bebo, sorry, Boss," the smile she gave him differed from that of a week ago, even just a day ago. Everything had changed. As a woman she knew they had more than just a love session. As a man – well – he was clueless.

All the passengers aboard *Celestial Pleasures* who experienced either the Jupiter Dive or ice boarding Saturn's rings came forward eagerly. The promise of reliving their holiday in enhanced mode being too enticing. Most of their recollections diverged substantially from the actual reality of them. Interestingly a few individuals weren't that keen on going through again what they remembered as being more traumatic than pleasurable. Nevertheless the new Zetaverse technology concept excited their imaginations sufficiently to want be a part of its development.

"One last thing we need before the next stage is a replacement for the role Gemelle had. We need someone with an abnormally high fear register like hers. A neutralising cocktail will be needed to counteract the effects of too much cortisol release."

"Yet she still went diving into Jupiter."

"Yes. Strange girl, that one. I really don't know what she was trying to prove."

Emma had already isolated several individuals who might fit their criteria. One guy, called Pietro Cesare Savonarola lived there in Gamarrah. "I remember this man. I interviewed him myself. Called himself Pietro XXXVI. He said he had a long family history. Rather proud of it too. He thought his ancestors could be traced back to Earth, one of whom he says was burnt and hanged ... I wonder why."

"Alright. Get him back in to do a complete neural scan and blood analysis."

Emma led the team to begin the exhaustive process of digitising all recorded verbalised memories. Cross referencing Erasmus' recorded data with individual downloads at the time, and finally by checking all that against the participants remembered versions produced a fusion of all the elements before then deleting components from the amalgam that did not directly relate to the experiences. Considerable preliminary visual data could be removed as well as superfluous background imagery that only confused clarity during the actual empirical experiences. Unnecessary sounds and incidental contact with other people also ended up getting scrubbed out.

Several more months later enhancing chemical cocktails were ready to be tested with the re-engineered experience files.

"We'll do this Pietro fellow first, so be ready with his serotonin increaser."

"Good to go," said Emma, "but you'll have to call him 'Pietro XXXVI' otherwise he'll get really upset."

"Right. Ok." *Strange. Sounds like he should be at the Self Cirque with Gemelle, preening himself.* "When he's nice and calm getting into the ice boarding event I'll give him a little boost of the dopamine mix. Can you get Larry to bring him in please."

A tall man, quite young at sixty turned his slightly hawkish Roman nose towards Beau. "Are you qualified to carry out this procedure?" His austere face atop the gaunt body did not suggest this man would have indulged in any form of pleasurable excess, or if he did the pleasure content out of it probably very low.

"I am the Head of this Institute. Welcome. Pietro, isn't it?"

"Pietro XXXVI to you. Don't you know who I am?"

"Of course, of course. You were on the *Celestial Pleasures* and indulged in a little adventure on the rings of Saturn. I was there myself."

"Harrumph. Just do your job and make sure nothing happens to me."

"Absolutely. We are here to make your best experiences even better." This man was starting to get annoying. "By the way ... you have a very interesting name. Do you know the origins?" Beau engaged him in conversation more to keep himself amused than anything else, while he applied the cranial cap with all the electrodes.

"I will have you know that I am the thirty sixth generation of men in my family. We date back pre-Proxima-b, and according to records our family can be traced to Florence."

This cannot be a coincidence! Beau fumbled the leads as he went through the plug-in sequence. Emma stepped in to take over, giving him a nudge to get him out of the way. Beau didn't ask the obnoxious man any more questions, letting him drift into sleep while his own mind raced back to the experience with Nostredame and Bela.

Pietro woke not too long afterwards. "That is not how I remember it," he grumbled, drawing out each word of the sentence.

"We were cautious with the enhancements, using only low dosages. Our instruments show you had no unpleasant reactions. We'd like to try an increase of the enhancements. Er ... certain hormonal reactions you are having are probably obstructing full immersion."

"Use plain language, woman."

"You have a high fear quotient." She let him have it between the eyes, enjoying every moment of his reaction.

"Incompetence! Sheer incompetence," he sneered, his drawn face going red. Nobody likes to be told to their face that they are afraid. The man harrumphed again and left the laboratory with a further threatening word to take the matter further. A man in his profession should have a very clear idea where his courage limitations lay.

"Is this guy on the right planet? asked Beau somewhat bewildered by the man's demeanour.

"I looked him up. He runs the Schadenfreude Festival."

"Seriously? Those nutters who get a kick out of humiliating others, often bordering on torture?"

"The same."

"That explains it ... at least his behaviour."

"Come to my place tonight," Emma invited. That obnoxious man happened to be their last customer, so that left the day's workload completed though not altogether on a happy note. Her invitation immediately turned that minor annoyance around.

"Bebo, what happened to you today at the lab?" Emma's apartment looked much like his own, although without the same views of the outside world. Her status didn't earn her such a luxury. Nevertheless her couch was just as comfortable.

"He said he lived in Florence. That cannot be a coincidence. Bela visited Nostredame from Florence ... I wonder why he was there?"

"I don't want to talk about him. I want to talk about us." Beau had started having lingering suspicions over the last couple of weeks that something was up with Emma. She'd become a bit moodier, sometimes too happy for no reason – perhaps there was a reason. "We're more than joy-friends, Bebo. Oh what the hell ..." she burst out, "... I want to call him Dante! – Kobayashi Dante."

"Him? Who?" Emma took his hand and put it on her belly. He let his hand rest there for a moment before it began to roam around. She didn't say anything, giving him time to wake up. He looked down at his hand, which had stopped, then turned his eyes to her face. Those eyebrows of his started their trek upwards not stopping until the crinkled skin of his brow would not let them go any further. He leant forward to kiss her, but she gently pushed him away. It was enough for the moment to have him finally realise what he couldn't work out for himself before.

"I want to contract. There is a future. You have seen it. You have been there. I want our son to be a part of building that future." She needed solid reassurance the boy would have a father.

"Why do you want to call him Dante?" He grinned broadly. What did it matter what his name was? "He's going to be my son, why not call him 'Beau'?"

"I like the name." She'd obviously forgotten Beau mentioning that name when he told her about his trip into the future.

"Do you have any idea who this man was ... is? Look up ancient Earth history for a start. And the man I met in 3790 called himself Kobayashi Dante - don't you remember."

"Noooo!" Her eyes grew into saucers, hand went up to her open mouth ... she punched him in the chest. "Don't do that! Giving our son a good name is not a joke."

"This is not a joke. Something is happening that we have become a part of. There are too many coincidences. This whole thing with jumping around in time – it must all be happening for a reason."

Emma raised an eyebrow slightly as if to say ... 'well, there you are - the future' ... It didn't really matter all that much what they would eventually decide to name him. She had shown him she was pregnant and he accepted his fatherhood, though the pleasure of the news somewhat blunted by his extraneous distractions.

Several months is a long time for a developing foetus, yet her figure remained relatively flat, so flat that Beau hadn't noticed anything. Perhaps his preoccupation of adventures with Quintessence blinded his ability to see beyond anything else. He left his hand resting on her belly, feeling the warmth of her body and automatically bending down to listen to little Dante's heartbeat.

It had been a long day. The stress of the experiments, that crazy Pietro guy and now this. And on top of it all he had not made any progress with his travels. The voice he wanted to hear had been silent for too long.

She wants to call him Dante! Outstanding. "Em ... It's a fantastic name." Before falling asleep late into the night he could not help thinking about the year 3790 and what he saw, and the man he met.

In his dreams Beau saw again the strange environment; the ocean world with floating temples and strangely dressed people. He recalled his words to Dante ... 'My name is Kobayashi Beau.' An intense desire came over him to return to Dante. The man couldn't possibly be his son - a totally crazy notion, he was too far into the future. *But I want to talk to him anyway.*

That is possible.

When?

When you are ready.

Who is this?

I am – I aspire to Quintessence. You have been with me before. You have been with me when you visited Nostredame - when you visited Dante.

What are you?

I touched your mind when you were in the Cosmos. I aspire to Quintessence.

That did it. Beau suddenly woke up. It was morning. He was not at home. Emma! He remembered … I am going to have a son! … he remembered everything. It all fell into place. It all made sense. Emma stirred beside him, saw him sitting up staring into space.

"Bebo?"

"I have spoken to him, – I have to find out. I have to go home. Come with me."

"What do you want to do?"

"It said I could go back to visit Dante." He put his hand on Emma's belly again before getting up.

Beau didn't need to be at home for Quintessence to take him along the Ribbon to another segment. It didn't even need to be at night. He only had to be relaxed, open, receptive. Relaxed he certainly was not, not till the end of the day had he calmed down. From his place Emma took him outside, went with him to his favourite park in the late morning. They sat on his favourite bench together. They had lunch, discussed their soon to be born son. She asked him again all the details of his visit with Nostredame – everything he could possibly remember. He left nothing out, not the slightest detail. Not even the red haired Anne, except his reaction to her. Under the circumstances that may have been unwise. He told her all his impressions about Dante and the date he had been given – 3790.

Instead of taking the magnetrans back to his place they walked in order to be free of distractions for a little longer. Even with regular stops the four kilometres went by relatively quickly. They showered, had a light meal prepared by the kitchen and waited for Proxima to set. Beau had already started to doze off unable to wait for the stars to appear. They had refrained from all trivial pleasures, concentrating only on this mystery and how they could possibly comprehend all its ramifications.

Emma watched his eyes begin to move from side to side. He'd fallen fully asleep.

Are you ready?

Yes. Where are we going?

You wish to speak with Kobayashi Dante.

Beau was thrilled with the realization that this phenomenon affecting him was finally under control and what he wanted was going to happen.

*

With the end of the month only days away Dante could not afford to waste any time getting his report submitted. The situation on Temple Island 461 preoccupied Father One. He in turn had to report to Metaquanta. Dante had spent the last two weeks on the residential platforms surrounding that particular Temple Island, investigating rumours that the people had become agitated. He spoke to many residents, as any visitor to their territory would have – no specifics, just enquiries about living conditions, availability of resources, satisfaction levels with their Priests – that sort of thing.

From his temporary cubicle in building Four, South of the Temple Island he could clearly see the second of the six fingers of Palm Atoll. It was one of the largest of the many thousands on the water world, well known to have the largest population of exiles. Perhaps it was because of its very proximity that the rules around exiles' visiting rights had been relaxed on the surrounding platforms of Temple Island 461. That in fact had been his focus.

Temple Island 461 precinct had been allocated magenta. Everyone wore that colour as the major component of any outfit. Dante stood out in his canary yellow, as did a few other strangers. There were no rules about what the exiles could wear, which was obvious from many oddly attired individuals seen in the shadows – always in the shadows.

"Do you have many visitors from Palm Atoll? Dante aske the concierge of his building. He'd seen her talking furtively to a resident, so a natural question to ask, unlikely to draw suspicion.

"I am not one to take too much notice of all that goes on around here," the woman glanced around, "I stick to me business looking after this building," she glanced behind her this time, "but them folk from across the water seem to be coming over here more often than I like."

Back in his own building at home Dante put the final touches to the report, after having spoken to a variety of people in different colours, not omitting to include visitation statistics based on what he saw and gleaned from local records. During the weeks he spent there he could see no evidence of 'unrest' as such. Plenty of people seemed to be behaving surreptitiously thus drawing attention to themselves. Overall he could sense a certain unease in the atmosphere – not something that could be quantified for the report but sufficiently noticeable for him to mention it.

'Ping: You have a visitor,' announced his cubicle door.

"Who is it?"

'Luther, your sister-in-spirit's sibling,' announced the door.

"I know who that is – open." He hated it when the door always told him the obvious. "Luther, welcome. This is a rare visitation. I didn't know you were on our island." Luther didn't offer any explanations. The man had always been furtive, secretive over nothing Dante could clearly identify.

In a small living cubicle it wasn't hard to see how many people occupied it at any one time. Gatherings, social and otherwise, were generally held in the communal atrium.

"Gemma not home?" Dante hated it when idiots always said the obvious. He couldn't warm to Luther – he remained silent. "She still at work?"

"Don't know. You have a message for her?"

"I'll see her another time." He left without another word. Perhaps he didn't like Dante either. Who knows? This guy always acted like he was up to something.

Dante made sure Luther was gone and the door closed before he resumed finishing the report. He read it over again, dated it, biometric authorised it, submitted it. The console replied with his next assignment almost immediately. As luck would have it he needed access to historical data to give context to this next job. He would not be questioned for delving into the past on the Pastornet.

Not wanting Gemma to disturb him; due home in the next couple of hours, he instructed the console … "Data – historical – pre-colonisation – subject: Kobayashi. Search."

Lines of information began flowing at reading speed. 'Kobayashi Dante: conceived 3757: born 3758: male progenitor …'

"Deeper."

The Pastornet scrolled on to data about two layers of previous ancestors. "Deeper." The damned thing took everything so literally on its way to the data requested. "I said – pre-colonisation." The console went blank.

Dante turned his head away from the annoying thing. He looked up towards the door for no particular reason, not expecting to see anyone of course. The frosted glass door had not announced another visitor, but someone was there. He immediately recognised the tall figure that partly looked like he was standing on the other side of the door, yet his outline quite clearly visible within the substance of the door.

"You again! You laughed during our Adoration – you said your name was Kobayashi!"

"Yes, it is me. I am Beau, Kobayashi Beau," said the almost clearly defined 3D image. For some reason this second manifestation had much more clarity than the first attempt.

"Where do you come from? You don't look like an exile."

"My home is Proxima-b, year 2555. We may not have much time to talk."

"Proxima-b! We are descended from that Godless society on Proxima-b." Perhaps Dante didn't hear the date, at least he didn't react to the fact of it being so far in the past.

Just the sort of information Beau had been hoping for. "In that case, do you know your ancestry?" It was possible, certainly possible but highly unlikely for this Dante to have any ancestral link to the son he would soon have.

"I have started a search. Why have you come back?"

"There is another Kobayashi. In time we must meet." He could feel the energy draining out of him again. He had said what he wanted, but didn't get all the information he wanted. "I will try to come back."

Dante started towards the door but the image had faded from it. "Open." He went out into the corridor to find it empty. Turning back to the door he ran his hands up and down its surface – nothing there. *What did I expect?* "Close."

He hadn't quite sat down when Gemma arrived home. "Luther was here looking for you. What did he want?" She seemed irritated.

She put a piece of paper in his palm as she hugged him, squeezing his palm shut at the same time ... "Turn yourself off ... come for a walk," she whispered.

That's two things she'd just done, which she had never done before. He kept his palm closed while they put on skins to protect themselves from the rain. As they walked towards the tube to take them down Dante read the note ... <say nothing till we are outside.>

They had to walk out into a regular downpour. As they adjusted their wet skins each turned themselves off - might not have been necessary as the rain always cloaked transmissions. He turned to her, raising questioning eyebrows, a habit he'd picked up from his father.

"Walk a bit first."

Their residential platform could be circumnavigated at a very brisk pace in about five hours. They didn't need to go that far. The bridge to their Temple Island was far enough.

"You off? ... I know about Beatrice."

He couldn't say anything that would not incriminate him. He waited. She must have seen her name while he was researching her family. He now knew her parents had voluntarily become exiles on Palm Atoll. Did Gemma? He waited.

"That's what Luther came to see me about – her parents." Dante didn't react. He expected her to say something completely different. "They are organising."

At first he felt a deep relief, which got immediately swamped by a hollow feeling in the pit of his stomach. If this 'organising' was what he thought it might have been the situation promised to be far worse than his interest in Beatrice being discovered.

'You know Beatrice, don't you? We've seen her many times during Adoration. What do you know about her, about her parents? This is important."

"Why do you ask me these things? You know what my function is. You know how dangerous *any* talk about 'organising' could be. You've put me in an incredibly difficult position. I have to report such things, even if they are only rumours."

"You won't report this. I know you won't – because of Beatrice."

So she did suspect something. He coloured. Fortunately it could not be seen in the rain.

"Look – if there's any talk of insurrection, even the slightest hint it means a serious risk to both of us. I don't want any part in this."

"Nor do I." She lied. "Luther is completely tangled up in it. He's been over to Temple Island 461. He's even been to Palm Atoll. We have to help him – at least try and get him away from this." She had to find some way to alert Dante and at the same time not draw him too deeply into the developing situation. Normal people didn't visit exile islands. Only traders went there to pick raw materials and deliver essential everyday supplies. Luther was not a trader, Dante knew that for certain ... he had no business going to any exiles' locations. Gemma knew Dante was aware of that, yet her warning just didn't seem to register.

Perhaps there could have been a better time to tell her about his other visitor. He had to tell someone. Father One would have him exiled, or worse if he found out. Metaquanta had shown itself to be extremely nervous of anything it could not compute, anything that could not be neatly compartmentalised within its logic structures – and this would definitely defy logical analysis. "Someone came to see me Gemma. You know I'm not crazy. You've known me since we were assigned to each other as children."

She stepped up closer to him to better see his face through the rain. He'd gone pale. She did love him, completely, in spite of his infatuation with the other woman. "Tell me. You can tell me anything."

"He's not from here, from Keppler. He's from Proxima-b"

"So – aren't we all? They never visit us. Why did he come? There was nothing on the news about it."

"You don't understand. He is not a visitor – well, he is, but from before our time." Her face told him she wanted to hear it all. It had no hint of ridicule or fear. She kept a steady gaze into his eyes. "He says he's from the year 2555. He said his name was Kobayashi Beau."

"We had better get back." That's all she said when he finished. Nothing about his strange visitor or the date, or the name and nothing more about Luther. She hugged him, held his hand as they started the long walk back. If anyone had been watching, and AI Security watched everyone, all they would have seen is two people possibly having an argument, resolving their differences and returning home. Domestic psychological behaviour could not be understood by the Priests.

They understood patterns but nothing that deviated from well established patterns. Interpersonal discords defied logical analysis even though they didn't deviate from well documented patterns of behaviour amongst the human population.

In their cubicle Dante tried to follow up the conversation about his visitor. He didn't even get two words out before Gemma silenced him. "We both have work to do, let's just get on with that for the time being."

They returned to their normal routine – nothing out of pattern. Gemma continued research on better energy efficient ways to process the rare metals mined by the exiles, needed by the AI Priests - and Dante decided to find out more about the life and times around the year 2555. Gemma was right. If anything could alert the Priests it would be any activity outside the normal expected routines of peoples' functions. Doing anything to help Luther would have to wait because of their conversation in the rain.

*

Beau could again feel how the energy had begun to drain away from him during the discussion with Dante. As much as he wanted to extend the visitation there was nothing he could do about it. The intimate space he found Dante in must have been his living arrangements. How very small, he thought. Then again, on a world where land was scarce one either adapted or became a fish. He liked the fact that it had not been cluttered, like Nostredame's attic and it had abundant light, much like his own apartment.

These and many other thoughts crowded in upon Beau as he returned to his normal dream state. There was something bothering him though. *Why is it that each time I visit someone it has to end so abruptly, after such a short time?*

You do not have the energy reserves to project your non-physical self over what to you seems a long span of time.

That's you isn't it, Quintessence?

Yes Beau.

Surely you must have all the energy needed to do that, whatever you are.

I am exploring, coming to realise myself. But I am not the only one doing these things – it is mostly you. I can help and give you direction, time co-ordinates on the segment you want to visit.

If you can manage time why can't you make it stop and take me where I want to go – to physically take me?

I am not a manager of time. I am outside this characteristic of our existence, but I can see into its different segments, into the past and the future. It may not be possible for me to interact with Light matter.

Emma had been watching him for the last twenty minutes as he cycled through a couple of sleep stages. She had not moved from his side on the bed, a little anxious at not knowing what exactly he was going through. Everything seemed normal. In the last couple of minutes his breathing had changed, he moved a little and eventually opened his eyes.

She stroked his chest, ran a hand across his brow. He smiled back, still waking. "Well?"

"He just stopped talking to me without any warning."

"Come on, don't keep me in suspense. Did you see this Dante man again?"

"Yes."

A huge grin spread across her face. She loved this. The most incredible mystery of her entire life and she wasn't going to miss a second of it. Her mind was made up about that!

"Tell me everything. What does he look like, what sort of person is he – does he have any connection to, you know, our son?"

"Too much to tell – and he hasn't found any historical connections, yet. Give me a little time to assimilate all this."

"Ok. So what's next?"

That's exactly what he wanted to know. Beau wanted to have a longer meetings with Bela and Dante together where they could get better acquainted. His life on Proxima-b had been suddenly contrasted against all that came before and all that would come after. The experiences gave him a perspective way beyond what his society could offer in terms of a world view. A new realisation dawned on Beau – just how futile, how shallow the work was that he'd dedicated his life to up to the present.

"Have you been with me all this time?"

"Yes. I was concerned."

He got out of bed. Saw on the wall screen that a couple of work free days had rolled around again. Also the Games were on. On the spur of the moment, being quite uncharacteristically spontaneous, he asked, "Are you interested in this year's Bacchanalia Games, Em?"

"I go every year, but I'm just a spectator. I used to like watching the replay of the old Olympics. Not anymore. After a while I got tired of the athletes doing their own thing, trying to be better than everyone else. At least in our Games the participants are much more interactive."

"Never would have pegged you to be interested in anything outside of your work Emma - at least not when we first met."

"Actually, let me tell you something about our Games. Did you know that thousands of years ago a Bacchanalia was only open to women? Then, when men were allowed to participate, in the nocturnal version, they started sacrificing live animals in amongst the drinking and feasting and sexual excesses."

"Sounds like they all had a spectacularly good time. But why are you telling me this?"

"Because as part of the rituals they also got involved in soothsaying, prognosticating, pretending they could see into the future."

That got his attention. From the history he'd read no effort had been made by anyone with foreknowledge to prevent anything from happening in the future that they may have had a chance to do so. "Having precognition didn't seem to do them much good."

"You and that guy Nostredame are doing the same thing – not that you're pretending. I believe everything you say. You say you can see future events but you're not prepared to do anything to prevent any of it." Perhaps if Emma hadn't grinned at that moment … naturally the morning degenerated from that point. They ended up leaving so late they almost missed the beginning of the Games at Stadium Libido.

Beau thought about what she'd said. *She's right. Nostredame knows about 3797, so do I and Bela - none of us has even thought of doing anything about it.*

Part 2

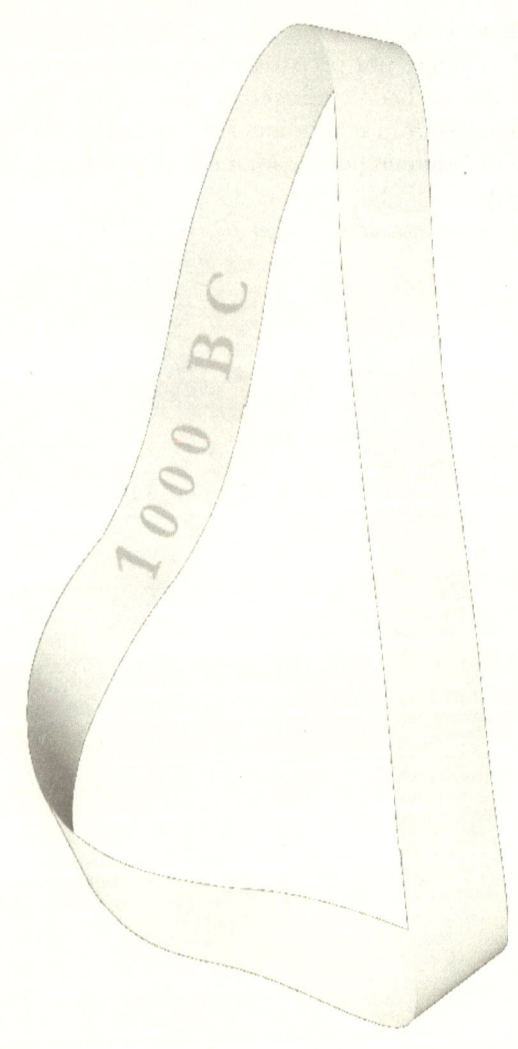

11

4 Ahau, 8 Kumk'u
1000 BC

Quintessence tried but could not see past the 3790 segment of the Ribbon. It could not see what was supposed to happen even as little ahead as 3797.

Violent events unfolding on Keppler 22b catalysed by Luther's organised attacks upon the towers of Metaquanta foreshadowed great uncertainty about the future. Decision threads would not bifurcate to open new possibilities. Beau's visitations through time had made no difference to the most probable outcome for these people as foretold by Nostredame. Only one variable presented itself for the most likely scenario on the planet of the islands' civilization. If the opportunity arose for Beau's acquaintance Bela to visit Dante then that might set in motion a chain of events to open other future timelines. The probability of actually changing anything was so small that that in itself created no folds or further splitting in the Ribbon, at least nothing Quintessence could see.

Perhaps an indication to the future lay deeply hidden in the past, the distant past well before the time of the great Seer. There have been men in many civilizations since the dawning of the human species who dedicated themselves to extending their visions of reality beyond their own lifetimes as far into the future as their capabilities allowed. Very few considered that which came before them. Driven by the need to understand and dictated by religious imperatives numerous concepts to explain how everything came into existence were devised, not based on knowledge but conjecture, imagination, even self-interest - and propagated by repetition which transmuted into faith.

Having become interested in influential time segments Quintessence explored into past segments of the Ribbon finding an unusual phenomenon that stood out from all the other myths. The Mayans flourished in Chalchuapa around 1000 BC. Their civilisation calculated the beginning of the current time cycle, the current Time Loop Ribbon, based on a tool partially developed by the Olmecs.

Apoxpalon, the chief shaman living in Chalchuapa had set himself a most important task; to teach his grandson maths, science and astronomy. To give him the depth of understanding of the universe and in order to bring these disciplines into useful context the boy had also to learn horology.

This particular 20th day festival celebrated the beginning of the maize harvest. Bloodletting and sacrifices were replaced by a ball game with adults from two neighbouring cities taking part at the base of the city's main pyramid temple. Children could not participate and as much as Xoco would have given anything to be a player he wasn't old enough yet. Too young to play because at thirteen years still considered to be a child, and too old to play the silly games of infants who didn't even know which end of a plough to put in the ground. All he could do was watch the celebrity players shooting magnificent hoop goals, getting happily injured in the process. But the day turned out not to be a complete loss, for he had the privilege of accompanying his shaman grandfather at the end of the game up the first three hundred steps of the three hundred and sixty five leading to the top platform. From where he had to stop he watched the closing ceremony conducted by probably the most powerful man in the city, his very own grandfather - apart from the King, that is.

Aged sixty two years Apoxpalon had grown weak only in body, not in the mind, so his strong grandson's assistance to get up those steep steps assured he could still do his job. His stature, smaller than that of most of his people, made it difficult to climb stairs because of the onset of arthritis. His unblemished dark skin, dark clear eyes and still mostly black hair made him seem younger than his advanced years. At the end of an hours long incantation followed by prognostications for the next twenty days the old man signalled to Xoco from the top of the temple.

"Thank you my boy." Once the sacred rites had concluded the shaman's chosen successor would carry out his expected duties. Xoco placed a strong arm under his grandfather's as they made their careful way down the steep incline. "Did you listen to everything I said?"

"Yes grandfather Apoxpalon. When will I be able to see?"

"Be patient Xoco. For now help me get down without breaking my frail legs."

For a man of his seniority, already well past normal life expectancy, both the steep incline and height of each step presented some danger. They both sat on the last row, Apoxpalon breathing heavily. High humidity and the beginnings of rain didn't make life any more comfortable for the old man. After ten minutes or so he addressed the young lad.

"You are right. It is time you completed your studies. My years are behind me now. It will be your turn soon to help our people through the next stage of this current cycle."

The shaman remained seated while Xoco removed his heavy ornamental hat with the many long feathers from his head. The skeletal face mask had to stay in place on his face while the shaman remained in public during their walk back to their hut.

Apoxpalon's wife had died eight years ago. Now his daughter lived with him and looked after him while her son learnt the art of shamanship. While she prepared the maize meal Xoco helped remove and store his grandfather's ponchos, mask and hat. The hat especially needed circumspect care. As a symbol of his personal status and achievements it could not be bequeathed to his grandson. However, he would be allowed to use elements of it when creating his own.

"You see these feathers here, and here, and here," said Apoxpalon pointing to the sides and the front, "they were given to me for the accuracy with which I forecast battle outcomes, harvest quality and weather trends."

Xoco had watched many times as Apoxpalon went into trances before recording his visions. "When will I be able to see, grandfather," he asked again.

"I will show you how to make the balaché elixir next week. You will have to gather the bark of the lancepod tree and harvest the honey of bees that have fed on morning glory. Tonight I want you to study our two hundred and sixty day Tzolki'n and tell me in the morning where we are in that cycle."

Xoco's life differed from that of everyone else. Not exactly born into nobility, yet part of a family with a very highly regarded position in their caste system. If he had been a noble then his daily routine would soon have become boring for him with nothing to do to look after himself. Neither had he been unlucky enough to be born to a farmer family, having to start learning farming skills by the age of five, then working the land from then on until his death. His job was to learn the sacred arts that would open up the secrets of the universe to him and in the process help him to contribute to the welfare of his people.

No one knew why Xoco's mother refused to bind his head between boards to make her son beautiful. Unlike all the other boys he did not end up with a disfigured profile with a long sloping forehead. Already at an early age he stood apart from all his friends - and he didn't fill his mind with the same ideas they had. Otherwise his black straight hair was the same as everyone.

Apoxpalon saw potential in the boy, well beyond his peculiar appearance and a superior aptitude as he grew into young adulthood. It was indeed opportune for him to start to understand the mechanisms of time.

"We are in the seventh twenty day period plus three days, grandfather," Xoco announced before his grandfather had lifted his head off the pillow in the morning.

"Explain to me how you arrived at that conclusion. Bring me the calendar. Show me." He said this with such a strict face that Xoco thought he must have got it wrong. But he trusted himself and went through his method of reading the interlocking glyphs.

"Are you sure?" He wanted to test the boys resolve. Xoco checked and nodded. "Very good. Now go and fetch those ingredients I told you about."

By late afternoon Apoxpalon had brewed the elixir ready for both of them. This would be the first time for Xoco to use the trance inducing drug. The shaman prepared the boys mind by getting him to concentrate on the pattern that defined their current solar year Haab'.

"Tonight we shall look up at the stars before consulting with Itzamna. Then I will ask you what you see for later this year."

Quintessence watched the old man and the young boy sit outside at night under the light of the Milky Way, pointing at this star and that star, at one constellation after another. Through them it began to see from another perspective the universe of eternity in which it existed. It began to understand the magnificent complexity of these human creatures in their ability to see past themselves into the greater beyond. They did not understand the mechanism of time, yet by exploring the cosmos they could grasp how to measure its flow through the sea of space-eternity. It attained a new appreciation of the gift it was able to give the other human; Kobayashi Beau.

Barely three years later Apoxpalon had difficulty getting out of bed. Each twenty day festival seemed harder than the previous one. Xoco had been elevated in his ranking so he was allowed to accompany his grandfather to the top platform of the temple. In preparation for the prognostications they both entered the trance state the day before, after extensive calculations based on the calendar and astronomical observations. Their visions very rarely diverged from one another, and if so only in minor details.

Some days were better than others for the old man, whereas Xoco grew from strength to strength as a young man, his mind expanding in leaps and bounds as enlightenment gradually arose from the foggy slumber of mundane existence. He brought great joy and contentment to his grandfather, whose work with him had yet to be completed.

"Come, today we will work in the full light of day."

The corn harvest had been gathered, fields cleared to lie fallow before the next planting. Xoco carried the calendar complex and Apoxpalon the paper, quills and ink to the centre of their largest field nearest to the hut. Early in the morning before the sun had fully risen to a promising perfect day of scattered clouds two men settled on the warm earth away from the noise and bustle of their city. Nor would they be disturbed by wandering jaguars who shunned open spaces as much as settled areas particularly during the day.

"I am going to show you how to do two calculations, then I will ask you to do two calculations of your own."

Apoxpalon methodically examined the intricate interconnectedness of the calendar wheels, taking many notes and making progressively more complicated calculations. Xoco watched every detail, listening intently to his grandfather's mumblings. Hearing about relays of bearers carrying the divisions of time and passing each completed stage onto the next bearer was nothing new to him. He very quickly realised what Apoxpalon began working on – the date of the beginning of the next Long Count following the current cycle.

The sun had risen to a third of its daily arc across the sky before the shaman stopped to refresh himself from an ornate drinking vessel. He took his time, casting his eyes around the field before settling on distant hills. These matters could not be hurried. Xoco remained silent. His master had the habit of gazing into the distance when looking deep into himself.

"2407," announced the shaman, "you know what this means don't you." It wasn't a question, and Xoco didn't need to answer it. "Now attend to me."

Apoxpalon continued along the same recurring cycles of creation and destruction to calculate the start of the next series of Long Counts. This did not take as long, yet the sun had climbed to its zenith to bathe them in its full power as some clouds parted above them. Food would have to wait until they'd finished the work.

"We will not see the day of destruction, nor will our children or children's children. New creation will begin in 4772. Do you agree with my calculations my aspiring corncob?"

"Yes grandfather. Have you seen inside this time? What will happen?"

"It is of very little importance to us what Itzamna will decide to do as the cycle comes to completion. Nor will it matter to those in the end days, for they will not be able to alter the flow of creating. Now show me where I might have gone wrong in my calculations."

Unprepared as Xoco thought he might have been, nevertheless, because he'd been following assiduously he pointed to the very minute detail that may have changed the end date by no more than a single year.

With surprising strength Apoxpalon slapped him on the face so hard that it drew a tear from this robust young man. Adrenalin rushed into Xoco's body almost bringing out a defensive physical response if he hadn't immediately heard Apoxpalon's loud laughter.

"Grandfather!"

"You are ready. Drink, there is still much for you to do." He passed the paper, quill and ink across, leaving the calendar complex resting between them. "Take your time and be thorough. Tell me the creation date of our current cycle. This is not just an exercise for you. Be warned, nothing is fixed in the heavens, just as the stars remain forever in motion."

Quintessence immediately turned its attention to segment 2407. It had no previous reason to explore the Ribbon at that segment, or in proximity to it. Observing the events unfolding prior to that segment it saw that a new cycle of creation had indeed begun on Earth. The planet had exhausted itself trying to support a population in plague proportions. People had two choices – remain on Earth and become part of the destruction about to take place … or create a new beginning by escaping their dying home. By segment 2555, the era of Kobayashi Beau, fleeing humanity had indeed created for themselves a new beginning on a new planet. To Quintessence the ability of these two beings to see such things, entrapped within the warp and weft of the Ribbon of their own segment, seemed remarkable and beyond his comprehension. If they had the ability to see that far into their future what could they possibly see in segment 4772, which did not in fact exist, which should never come into existence according to Nostredame. It could not see that segment at all – nothing beyond 3790 was visible to Quintessence.

Xoco had indeed grasped the secret of unravelling the mysteries hidden in their ancient calendar. The sun continued along its path taking no notice of the two shamans as the shadows of trees lengthened from the forest out onto the edge of the field. Little by little the answer revealed itself.

"Two thousand one hundred and fourteen years before our current year, 4 Ahau, 8 Kumk'u."

Apoxpalon did not praise Xoco, nor did he confirm the accuracy of his statement. "Tomorrow I shall speak with the King to prepare an inauguration for our new Shaman. You do not have long to prepare yourself for this responsibility my boy."

"Grandfather?"

"Do not be concerned about that now. I have one other task for you. Before I tell you what that is I will burden you with something most unsettling. It may well become part of your preparations and an aide to help you guide our people. Listen to me most carefully, for I will not interpret this vision to you."

"Yes grandfather, but …"

"Hush – On the night of our last full moon I could not sleep for a great uneasiness came upon me. I went to our temple and climbed the steps to the top to bathe myself in the full light of the moon. It was a blood moon of such a magnitude that I could not look long upon it, and closed my eyes - not in fear, but to accept its power into me. And as my mind cleared and my vision expanded I looked into the past, and there I saw the future. Do you understand what I am saying to you?"

Quintessence listened as did the young shaman. Neither understood the confusion in the vision. Quintessence pondered the enigma. It had come to an awareness of a lifeform, after its own eons of insentient existence in the fabric of space-eternity, which occupied a tiny fragment of fragile time drifting through existence as a unique Time Loop Ribbon – a ribbon that had a beginning and an end, as yet neither defined exactly, yet where one end began the other ended. But that was not entirely true, for although Apoxpalon could calculate the rhythms of creation and existence as cycles, Nostredame also claimed to have knowledge of the end of days – the end of the ribbon on which he existed, relative to his perspective only from planet Earth.

Apoxpalon watched Xoco's forehead furrow into deep thought. Again he slapped the young man, this time on the back and smiled at him, exuding contentment in himself and confidence in Xoco.

"It is well that you think before you speak. Now - tell me, when can I expect the end of *my* days?"

12

Day of the Revolt

By the year 2555 Science had solved many great mysteries of the Cosmos.

Physicists and Cosmologists were able to explain events that once used to be called miracles. Religions had lost control of most peoples' minds. Travelling in space had cured them of the importance the old Earth had in explaining the fundamental meaning of life, giving the people of Proxima-b a much firmer footing in pragmatic reality. The notions of a Heaven and Hell became euphemisms for degrees of pleasure achievable. In this environment of enlightenment Kobayashi Beau attempted to give some context to the very strange things he had been experiencing.

How could he explain the existence of this entity when the nature of dark energy was one of the few things science had been unable to fathom? Yet his own mind kept telling him that the only force which could navigate through time had to be dark energy. How was that possible? A question eminently suitable for scientific enquiry. But to even contemplate that this force should be able to manifest as a sentience required nothing less than a leap of faith.

After two days of vicarious spectating of the Games Beau lost concentration. His mind just couldn't switch off from the events that had almost completely taken over his normal life.

"Em, the last couple of days with you have been great fun."

"Don't carry on Bebo. I know exactly what you're going to say. You want to get back to your spooky friend. But before you do there is just one tiny thing you and I still have to sort out."

"Did I forget something?"

"Kind of – you haven't mentioned our little fella. No pressure mind you, but have you thought about us Contracting? And are you comfortable with his intended name?"

Having settled the details of those small matters Beau and Emma took the plunge, completely bypassing the joy-friend status. Moving in together presented no problems. The ancient world of materialism had been replaced by the acquisition of experiences, and apart from the instruments of mutual satisfaction generation not much in the way of furniture or knick-knacks needed to be moved into his place.

Quintessence did not interfere in Beau's life. It occupied itself with trying to understand a few mysteries of its own. It was alone, a condition that had not surfaced in his thinking until he became aware of human beings and after having observed Beau and Emma's intimate relationship. Then it considered the relationships between Nostredame and Anne. It thought about this phenomenon of relationships leading it to focus seriously on the names of individuals for the first time. Coincidences don't exist in the greater Cosmos – connections do. Beau once had a joy-friend called Gemelle, now Emma had become a contracted partner. Did anything else connect the other women to Beau other than the close similarity of their names. That other name … Kobayashi, reappeared at different segments of the Ribbon. It began to understand. It decided not to reveal this discovery to Beau at this stage of their interactions.

As Kobayashi Beau immerses himself deeper in the space-eternity fabric of the universe he may come to understand the function of time just as I have realised its place in the mechanisms of existence. However, he will never be able to disrupt its momentum.

Quintessence became lost in deliberations of how itself came into existence, or whether it had always existed and for some reason change came upon it bringing about self-awareness. The substance of which it was made flowed all around it, yet in itself it had become different. It examined and observed existence around itself. The vastness, the density of dark matter, the abundance of dark energy – immeasurable. Yet spread throughout this fabric of space-eternity minuscule manifestations of something different existed. Buffeted by the flow of chronon particles of time baryonic matter sustained by electromagnetic radiation had evolved into what? Living flotsam that had given itself names and came to consider itself to have some importance in the greater scheme of existence.

Work at the laboratory demanded attention. So far Beau's short absences had not impeded progress on the experiments too much, thanks mainly to Emma. Under her direction the super saturated sensory Zetaverse of augmented reality looked like becoming a commercial reality. The likelihood of success had been so strong that Playback Inc. flooded the pleasure seeking market with promises of Nirvana being possible from even the most ordinary sensual experiences. Their rival, Omnifun Unlimited could not compete against such extravagant claims. It drove the Company to desperate measures. It was no secret who worked at the leading edge of this technology. Kobayashi Beau had attained global prominence with his work in the field.

Hundreds of volunteers had returned to the laboratory eager to be first to sample the new Promised Land. Within the first week sensory overload killed several super eager experimenters – which didn't even make the news. Emma had to re-engineer the chemical cocktails to make the mixtures less reactive with existing hormonal discharges during replays, in effect having to customize a wide spectrum to make them suitable to a much larger range of customers' chemistry.

Director of the Festival of Schadenfreude exercised some restraint on his eagerness to participate in the experiments. Being a savvy businessman he put his sadistic tendencies behind profit. When Pietro Cesare Savonarola XXXVI finally made his appearance at the laboratory

131

again he brought along his own experience download for the test, out of an abundance of caution on his part, and a basic distrust of the world at large.

"You're the woman who was here before, aren't you," he said as if she might have been one of the catering staff, not even bothering with a cordial greeting.

"Yes, Pietro. I decide what dosages to give you."

"Pietro XXXVI! Have you forgotten already. I hope you know your job better than you remember important people."

She ignored him. He had a bad reputation, especially if he didn't get his own way. "Our recording of your memories are primed. I'll get you ready."

Pietro pulled his head away from her. "Use this. I've had it scrubbed and prepared by my own people."

"Perhaps you would like 'your own people' to run the experiment on you?"

"Don't be foolish, woman. Get on with it."

Emma had a pleasant, even tempered dispositions towards those who behaved normally. This guy didn't even inspire her enough to warn him about the dangers of amateurs preparing the memory data. With this obnoxious man … her hand hovered over the most potent concoction they had developed. If Beau had been there he may well have encouraged her. Fortunately Beau busied himself with far more interesting matters.

*

At home Beau had left his desk where he'd relocated it by the window. Emma didn't have much furniture and the apartment easily accommodated the extras that didn't double up with his. Extensive DNA records made the first part of his search into his ancestry easy. His family tree, which he'd never bothered with before, grew in complexity as he researched deeper into the past. He had to be more careful when he reached as far back as the first few years of the Proxima-b colony. Keeping records then had less priority than simple surviving. By cross referencing one of the male ancestors he finally made the connection to the passenger list for the people who left Earth for the new world.

Wow. I never really thought about the enormous achievement, the difficulties these people must have gone through. Incredible how the Kobayashi line endured.

As expected the voyage from Earth took three generations given their level of technology at the time. Because there were not many of them, those twelve million people represented a very small percentage of the Earth's population prior to the exodus. The majority remained in cryo for the duration of the trip so he had no difficulty tracing the passengers back to the boarding list. There was his name again, carried by his 40th grandpappy.

During the wars of the great Calamity, which ended only a few years before the migration, genealogical records suffered huge losses. Only the Mormons' records had endured through the centuries to the end times. It was there in their comprehensive family history repositories that Beau was able to pick up the threads of his family tree. He'd begun to wonder how far back he could go before the line petered out. *Perhaps I could be related to an Emperor in ancient Japan.* Not an unreasonable supposition since the name Kobayashi was definitely Oriental.

He kept following the clues, step by laborious step. Deeper and deeper into Earth's history until he found a record of an early European explorer who had visited Japan. There he found the name belonging to a Japanese passenger who had returned to Italy via Spain. With his imagination primed for more digging Beau didn't appreciate being disturbed at that moment as a voice becoming more familiar intruded.

You told me you wanted to visit another segment, intact with your body.

Beau jumped from the sudden disturbance. His immediate thought was that he'd left the door open and an intruder had entered.

It's you again. Can't you give me some warning. What if I want to contact you?

Concentrate and call me in your mind. I am Quintessence Kobayashi Beau.

Why are you using my name?

When I first connected to you I did not fully know who I was. I listened to your mind – it said your name. I know who I am only because of you. You want to visit Kobayashi Dante, segment 3790.

Yes, but I'm not rea ...

*

A new Metaquantal Encyclical directed all citizens of Keppler 22b to attend Adoration every third day ... once week no longer deemed to be sufficiently devotional. Dante couldn't do anything about that. Nobody could. Metaquanta sometimes made these impromptu announcements, seemingly without reasons. This time he may have wanted to keep a closer track on his peoples' movements - perhaps as a result of Dante's recent reports. The next Adoration was due later that day. It didn't matter what anyone might have been doing, attendance became mandatory. His Pastornet page flashed the call to prayer in the middle of his research into the period around 2555 on Proxima-b. *Surely this latest directive has nothing to do with my last report.* He'd submitted his findings about the out-of-pattern events on Temple Island 461, some of it verbatim from the building concierge where he resided. *Maybe that's why Father One called. He must have received other corroborating reports.*

Historical records went to great pains to describe the decadent era from which people of Proxima-b had to escape in order to save their souls. In that Hedonistic society there was no God, there was no Faith. They were all destined to suffer eternal torment in the depths of Hell, frozen for all eternity because of their lives of debauchery and excess. Dante couldn't believe what he was reading. He knew some history, but this dismayed him. And there, hidden amongst all the prognostications from deeper within the depths of history which began on Earth, he saw confirmation of what Metaquanta had been using to control the population of Keppler 22b – the end of time prophesied for the year 3797. It was all blackmail! Metaquanta and his Priests had been blackmailing their entire civilization since they arrived on the planet with nothing more than some flimsy rumour from an irrelevant ancient civilization.

Nothing had occurred in the Cosmos around Keppler to give even the remotest hint that any great calamity would eventuate. Their sun, Keppler-11, steadily provided all the energy they needed. The planet itself lay docile providing all the necessities for survival. Comets did not exist, or had not been seen since before they arrived. The whole thing had been a fabrication by that un-human. Unbelievable. At best it may have been some twisted machine logic to use the threat of annihilation as a means of controlling, thus protecting the people. *Maybe the exiles already knew all this.* Maybe they are rising up to prevent universal panic when the year arrives, which could indeed bring about an end, for their existence on that planet anyway.

Dante terminated his Pastornet access, falling into a particularly depressed state of mind. The appointed hour fast approached. He waited as long as he dared for Gemma so they could go together. Being late was not an option. Weather on late afternoons often remained clear – he didn't need his wet skin, but he took a spare yellow tunic for Gemma just in case. He'd only just begun to cross the bridge to their Temple Island and already the drone of that incessant chant intruded on his thoughts.

This time Beau had not gone into a trance, he had not fallen asleep. He didn't know where to look as he conversed with Quintessence, settling his gaze on the outdoor environment as he stood up from the desk holding onto his e-parch. He could at least see into the distance without having to focus on any objects near him that may have been distracting him. He'd started to say he wasn't ready. Quintessence obviously took no notice. From one blink of his eye to the next everything changed. It seemed Beau didn't have much of a choice, Quintessence deciding when and to what segment it would take its unique human he'd adopted out of pure curiosity at the start.

His room disappeared. The landscape faded into streaked cosmic blackness as he seemed to move through it without being a part of it. A darkness came upon him, not like the first time. This was the darkness of space as he felt himself being taken through the atmosphere enveloped in a sense of reassurance.

Are you ready to meet Kobayashi Dante?

Yes. I hope you will be able to bring me home.

Beau could not see the Ribbon as Quintessence could, his awareness linked too firmly to three dimensions, the fourth being an abstract concept experienced in a mundane reality. He could not see how the Time Loop Ribbon floated and twisted and wormed its way randomly within the fabric of space-eternity. But he did observe that he'd been returned to the kind of reality he could comprehend, albeit not his own world.

Dante ended up at the rear of the crowd because of his tardiness waiting for Gemma. Still worried about her he searched for her as he started crossing the bridge. *She must have arrived early* … He looked around again, then turned his head to look behind himself and in the process stumbled. Beau had to reach out a hand to steady him.

"What is happening today?" he casually asked Dante. They continued walking towards the Island with everybody else ahead of them.

"You!" Suddenly Dante realised. He shouted at the man, his voice drowned out by the incantation pulsing down around them from the main tower.

"You remember me."

"What?" It became difficult to hear one another as they neared Metaquanta's minaret. Dante scanned around them fearful of an AI Priest stopping Beau because he wasn't wearing the regulation colour caftan. "Here, put this on," he threw Gemma's spare tunic over him, leaning close to his ear. "Don't say anything! Do everything I do."

Beau could see the futility of trying to have a meaningful conversation under the circumstances. They infiltrated into the back of the crowd, all bunched up close together, all facing the minaret with eyes turned towards the top where the sound came from. A blue strobing light pierced through the gathering mist. Within just a few minutes some people fell to the ground, convulsing. Then the incantation turned into coherent words.

'Metaquanta is and forever shall beeeee.'

Without exception everyone repeated it.

'Metaquanta is and forever shall beeeee.'

'Metaquanta is the giver of life.' Dante gave Beau a dig in the ribs.

He joined the crowd in the repetition of the chant.

'Obey the Laws - obey, obey, obey.'

'We obey the Laws.'

"You are sinners - sinners, sinners, sinners.'

'We are sinners.'

'You must be punished - punished, punished, punished.'

'We must be punished,'

'Metaquanta can save you - save you, save you, save you.'

'Metaquanta will save us."

Beau could see the people already losing themselves in the ceremony. He'd begun to feel decidedly uncomfortable and that strobing light didn't help. He put out a hand to Dante to steady himself, realizing for the first time that Quintessence had actually physical transported him to this time and place.

Dante slapped his hand away, giving Beau an angry warning look. *At least he's still sane*, thought Beau. At the same moment the strobe light went out without warning.

For a few seconds no one reacted to it, or to the sudden cessation of sound. This had never happened before in Dante's lifetime. His thoughts went into overdrive, first looking around wildly to try and find Gemma. Not there. He couldn't spot her anywhere in the crowd. What he did see were the Priests moving towards the perimeter of the dead silent gathering that continued standing there in stunned silence.

Insurrection! The thought flashed into his mind. Everything Gemma had told him about Luther and 'organizing' suddenly made sense. What the concierge on the Temple Island's habitation platform said also came into focus. By this time the Priests had infiltrated the crowd no doubt looking for any agitators. Dante grabbed Beau's arm and pulled him away towards the bridge as the crowd began to surge out of control as they saw the Priests bearing down on them.

"Run! Follow me."

They hadn't even reached the middle of the bridge when they heard the explosion. Dante saw from a quick glance over his shoulder the tower toppling down to the platform, people screaming, running, Priests unable to control the mayhem.

Across the other end of the bridge Dante pulled Beau behind the corner of one the residential buildings on the floating island platform just in time to see another explosion destroy the bridge they'd been on moments ago. Only some of the escaping mob had managed to get across, the rest who were still in the process of crossing dropped into the sea. Remarkably the temple Island remained afloat after the two explosions, with some survivors still on it. It had all happened so fast. Dante couldn't entirely comprehend what had just occurred. His wild eyes connected with Beau for a moment. Then he took off without a word, running deeper into the maze of buildings. What could Beau do but follow him. If he lost the man what would happen to him? What if the explosions had somehow severed the connection between himself and Quintessence? What if he got stuck in the future!

He caught a glimpse of Dante ducking into the deserted entrance of one of the buildings, finally managing to catch up with him as the man stepped into a lift. They ran at full speed down the long dark corridor on Dante's floor away from the elevator, not stopping until he reached the door of his domicile. Beau barely managed to keep up with him in the slightly heavier gravity.

"Open!" Dante panted at his door.

The internal space surprised Beau again by how small it was compared to his own apartment, now that he was physically in it.

"Everything off!" Dante commanded. The lights went out, the door closed, all sound ceased in the enclosure.

"Sit." Beau remained standing.

"I said, sit!"

Dante walked over to settle at his desk. Out the window he could see the smoke still rising from the Temple Island as it drifted towards the habitation platform, beginning to obscure the tops of a few buildings.

"Did you do this?" he suddenly glared at Beau in bewilderment. "No, of course not, how could you."

"What just happened?" asked Beau.

"I think the Exiles have started something. I don't know what. Gemma might know." In the confusion it sounded to Beau as if Dante had just said Emma.

"Gemma?" Beau got a shock. "Gemma? Who is Gemma?"

"She's my sister-in-spirit."

Beau had to digest that before he replied, "My contract friend is called Emma."

Dante didn't seem to hear the similarity of the two names. He started raving about Beau's world and how their decadence would cause their ultimate suffering and that this whole mess was their fault, and ... ...

"Open." Gemma walked in, sweaty and dishevelled. Beau turned his attention to this woman who had such a similar name as his own partner.

"Dante! You're alright! I heard about the attack. It's become mad out there. There's Priests and people running everywhere. And the smoke and dust and the noise!" She had to make an effort to talk through her laboured breathing.

Her sudden entrance had cut off his babbling. He jumped up, they embraced, hanging onto each other in obvious fear of the unprecedented disaster. Then she saw the other man. He didn't look right, even with the yellow tunic still on him. Something about him made her shrink away from Dante and back up against the wall.

"Don't be afraid. He's not one of the Priests."

No. Beau didn't have the skin colour of a Priest, or the expressionless face, or the vacant unblinking eyes. He remained seated.

"My name is Beau, Kobayashi Beau."

"It's him!"

Dante explained how Beau had suddenly appeared behind him as he made his way to the Adoration ceremony. "Gemma, listen to me – did Luther do this?"

'No. I don't think so. I'm not sure. Not directly, not this Temple Island. But you know him. He's never fully conformed to our religion, he's never completely believed. Luther will not accept Metaquanta's supreme authority. He said we have to use our reason to make sense of our lives, not faith in an unreasonable 'thing'. Reason and faith are opposed to one another. You and I both know that. So do many other people. Metaquanta will never save us from anything. We can't live our lives in fear forever. How can anyone believe in a machine? Have they forgotten where he came from? It is just a machine!"

"Gemma, do you believe all this, what you've just said?"

"Yes I do. With all my being. I have been working with the exiles and with Luther to bring an end to this madness. I didn't think he would act so soon - we were not ready."

"I cannot believe this. Don't you realize what you are saying, what you are doing? Don't you believe that everything could end in seven years? We could all be dead!"

"No I don't, and you don't either. If you truly did we would not have gotten pregnant. It's not going to end, not if we can stop Metaquanta and his Priests. It has been programmed to terminate all life on Keppler 22b if society hadn't reached a higher level of life philosophy than that which had developed on Proxima-b. But Metaquanta's repression of our society is the very thing stopping that from happening. To protect itself it has to convince us that It is the only one who can prevent the termination from taking place. What sort of twisted logic is that?" Gemma could barely get the words out given the state she was in.

"Toppling one tower is not going achieve anything, except make life much more precarious for all of us."

"Not just one tower. Thousands of exiles have sacrificed their lives today throughout our world. We have to be ready Dante - we must be ready," Gemma pleaded with him. Caught up in the drama of the events they'd forgotten Beau still sitting there, hearing everything.

Beau listened, amazed at the conversation. Amazed because of what he had learnt from Nostredame, because of the visions he had himself.

The people of this planet may have believed that they needed Metaquanta to prevent the end of the world. They, and Luther, may not have realised that the very revolution they had started could result in the end of days for them if the insurrection itself triggered the contingency program. If the people revolted it meant that they had remained as degenerate as their ancestors had been at the time of the exodus from Proxima-b to Keppler 22b. On such an inhospitable planet, living on the thin edge of survival it would not take much to end it all for them.

Dante's eyes caught a glance from Beau. "What? You still here." Anger welled up in him … at himself for knowing the truth and afraid to do anything about it. Angry at Luther for putting Gemma in such serious danger of her life, and the life of their child - for surely the Priests were going to track Luther down and everyone associated with him. Father One would show no mercy to Gemma if he found out about her involvement with the uprising, completely ignoring the fact that he had only recently given her and Dante permission to have a child, completely disregarding that she was actually several months pregnant.

"Why are you still here? Why do you keep coming back? Why?"

"I feel compelled. I have had visions. I have spoken with Nostredame. He has seen into this future, as I have."

Dante reached out to Gemma pulling her back towards himself. That man sitting over there seemed calm enough. But who was he? Where did he really come from. With what just happened on Temple Island no one could be trusted. What possible help could he be other than complicate an already extremely precarious situation.

"There's nothing you can do - nothing. What good are your visions when what we need now is brute force to annihilate Metaquanta's Priests. Without them he is helpless."

"I don't know if I can help, or even if I should. Maybe you and Luther and Gemma are the only ones who can help your people. Let me show you something. This is what I saw in one of my visions. You may be able to make more sense of it than I can." He opened his tablet and pushed it towards Dante.

As an intelligent man with the ability to think for himself in spite of the conditioning Dante had worked out a long time ago that their deity was nothing of the sort. Yet most of the people believed exactly that it was. He now realised the incredible danger they were facing, not just to themselves personally but the whole planet because of what Luther had begun. Anything that might help had to be considered. He and Gemma read the words, slow to realise that they were the insights about themselves, about right now, from a man from their past who had travelled through time to help them.

> A new sect of exile philosophers
> Despising death, gold, honors and riches
> Will be bordering upon the islands of Temples:
> To follow them they will have power and crowds.

He easily recalled this quatrain from all the time he'd spent on trying to understand it. The second quatrain only came back to him when they started talking about Luther.

> A man will be charged with the destruction
> of temples and the un-dead altered by fantasy.
> He will harm the towers rather than the living
> their ears filled with ornate incantations.

While Dante examined and contemplated the meaning behind Beau's visions Beau thought it appropriate to tell them about the other historical Kobayashi. Perhaps for no other reason than the man's association with Nostredame. "There is another man. His name is Kobayashi Bela. I feel it is important the three of us meet."

"And when would this man come fro …?

Just as on every previous visitation Quintessence snatched Beau away at the most inopportune moment, lacking understanding of the flow of human interactions. Before their eyes, and before Dante could finish his question Beau dematerialized, leaving no trace of his having been there other than the words that recorded his previous vision of the future he had just visited - and Gemma's crumpled yellow tunic on the ground.

Why do you keep doing that! I have not finished speaking with Dante. Why are you in such a hurry? Are you running out of time? I would have thought that would not be an issue for you.

There is danger in what we are doing. The delicate balance must be maintained in the momentum of the Ribbon. We must be vigilant that no past element filters into the future that has not already done so. A full Ribbon must either cease to exist or find a neighbouring Time Loop to interact with.

Can you see into the future of the Kepplerians? Can you see the outcome of the Insurrection?

Beau could hardly believe it when Quintessence simply said 'No'. How could that be possible. He'd come to believe that Quintessence could traverse the entire universe, go anywhere it pleased, to any moment of time it chose to visit.

Some decisions have not yet been made that would allow the next segment of the Ribbon to be revealed. Other decision possibilities may terminate all probabilities, which is more likely as I cannot see beyond 3797.

What in the cosmos does that mean?

There is a high probability that your Time Loop Ribbon may be almost full.

In that case is there nothing that can be done to help Dante, not by me, you - or Bela. Is that true?

Since his interactions with the past and the future this was the first instance that the thought of actually trying to help, to intervene came to him. He'd completely forgotten what Emma had said to him about that.

You and another have yet to make decisions along that thread of possibility, said Quintessence before withdrawing his presence.

Beau must have been gone a long time, although while he visited segment 3790 it did not seem to be more than a few hours. Quintessence returned him to his desk by the window.

The lingering thought remained with Beau about decisions he had apparently yet to make. Wouldn't it have been much simpler to just tell him what those alternative decisions were? They couldn't be that important – Dante existed, it would not have been possible to visit him otherwise. So those alternatives must logically be simple, perhaps even relatively inconsequential ones.

Without becoming aware of it Beau had made his way into the bedroom, not waiting for Emma any longer. She would be home soon enough. Sleep didn't come easily in the jungle of possibilities and probabilities and images of Ribbons of Time filling up. At last drifting out of consciousness he was being recalled to it by a noise in the apartment … Emma must have arrived … he had drifted too deep to bring himself out of it to greet her.

Following the Playback Inc. announcement foreshadowing the extraordinary pleasure harvesting opportunities soon to be made available by their new innovations, the Board of Omnifun Unlimited held a crisis meeting.

"Gentlemen, Foxyladies," began CEO Brummel as he preened in a compact mirror, "do I need to tell you that our claim to unlimited 'anything' is going to be a mirage of the past if we do nothing about this Zetaverse thing?" A rhetorical question to which he expected no response and turned back to the mirror to adjust a few of the locks of hair that had flopped over his forehead.

"Couldn't we offer an irresistible enticement to Kobayashi Beau to bring his brilliant mind into service for us?" suggested Dandy, a VP on the Board.

"Legally too messy. There is a more effective and direct way. Get that woman Emma," suggested Candy.

"No good. He can have any joy-friend he wants," added Brummel, "I should know," he tittered at the memory of how easy that had been for himself in the past. His spies had failed to bring him up to date on the woman's condition, or her true relationship status with the scientist. Deliberations continued for several hours until the most effective strategy was adopted unanimously.

Three men dressed as ordinary sanitation biomechs, with uniform hair pieces, makeup and the purple skin colouring gained entrance to Beau's apartment. The injected drug took effect almost immediately. Two of them stood him up while the third tidied up the bed without bothering to dress him. When Emma arrived home she'd think Beau had gone out. The abduction wouldn't be noticed for at least a day ... plenty of time to get the man's cooperation.

Omnifun Unlimited headquarters had their own corporate dome attached to the outskirts of Gamarrah City. Wealth on Proxima-b could be measured in part by the volume of space one had to live in. This dome accommodated their corporate headquarters, laboratories, luxurious living accommodation and even a small park. Entertainment, in whatever form it took, was the most lucrative business to be in by the 26th century. Omnifun and its executives had only one rival, and that was Playback Inc. but perhaps not for long if Brummel's bold move bore fruit. He could lose a great deal without even considering the lifestyle he'd become accustomed to, and which many on Prox-b envied.

Pleasure centres and experimental laboratories filled the many caverns under the dome. Beau awoke in luxurious surroundings he could never have imagined. For a fleeting second he thought Quintessence had taken him to some other timeline, perhaps further into the future than Dante's time. Although underground the room had the feeling of being out in the open landscape perched on the edge of a cliff overlooking the planet's green belt running North, South. Into this dynamic scene floated cirrus clouds. Aeros followed the prevailing winds, carrying passengers to some of the more remote cities around the globe.

"Breakfast is ready, Sir," announced a rather attractive, ornate young man – not a biomech ... another luxury. Only the very rich could afford non-biomech domestics. Effects of the drug had worn off leaving no residual side effects other than a slight confusion about where he found himself. Without thinking about it he called out, "Em?" She of course couldn't respond. Not that Beau hadn't been occupying her mind since getting home late last night and finding their bed empty.

Another overdecorated person appeared from a side room, obviously very sure of himself from the way he leisurely made his way to the table set with breakfast delectables. He elegantly displayed himself into a lounging position exuding self-importance.

"Come join me Beau," he invited, randomly waving a hand in his direction and towards the breakfast table.

Beau turned his attention to the voice, away from the real-time vid of the outside world played on two full adjacent walls. Brummel gave him time to adjust. Between munches of his favourite delicacies he watched as the domestic busied himself around the guest, draping his nakedness in an ultrafine loose fitting kaftan.

It really did seem like an elaborate dream with extraordinary details. Beau's senses told his brain things that could not possibly be true; he was not at home - this room could not exist in the environment of their planet - that ridiculous thing on his body wasn't part of his wardrobe. That peacock man over there had no business being in his dream uninvited.

"Come, before it gets cold."

The edges of the surreal began to crumble as Beau approached the table on slightly unsteady legs. He was hungry, more so now having smelt the aroma of choices on offer. "Am I supposed to know you?"

"I hope in time we will become much better acquainted. You are working on something very important and of great interest to me, Beau."

"Your voice is a little familiar, and your coiffure reminds me of someone."

Brummel thoroughly enjoyed this game. Such a pleasure to set a trap and watch your quarry walk right into it. Beau's eyebrows shot up in sudden recognition. "Omnifun! You're ..."

"Yes I am. Please, sit, tell me about your progress." The way he spoke could not hide the enormous pleasure showing in his eyes provided by the other man's enlightenment of his identity.

A wild moment of apprehension passed quickly as Beau realized this man could not have any idea of his most recent travels. It could only be one other thing. *No, I can't believe it – Gemelle wouldn't sell us out.* Oh, those idiots at Playback! They just couldn't wait – he remembered their public announcements about the Zetaverse technology.

"I don't know where I am, but I do know I shouldn't be here."

"Of course you should, my man. That is if you want to be rewarded appropriately for the magnificent work you're doing." The changed look on the man's face should have warned Beau. "Oooh – I see we might have a little trouble co-operating."

At that Beau flinched. Many people enjoyed pain in one way or another. He wasn't one of them. Brummel did not have a good reputation when in pursuit of his desires.

"Finish your breakfast. I have a proposition for you – a proposition mind you. I'm not offering you choices." From that moment the pleasant meeting degenerated rapidly. Brummel changed his mind on seeing Beau's face set into defiance. Beau didn't get to finish his breakfast. "Our complex here has many interesting facilities. Arnaud, could you please take Mr. Kobayashi to the chamber."

A physical beating into submission would have been far too wasteful. Although a little softening up might help. Brummel followed the doubled up Beau supported by Arnaud, taking some of his unfinished delicacies with him. His three 'secretaries' from the abduction team had already set up the equipment and his comfortable chair opposite to the anticipated action.

"You can't be serious," Beau managed to exclaim before all wind was expelled from his lungs by the administration of another practiced punch. Bending over double again caused him to fall backwards into his own chair. It had a far less comfortable arrangement to hold a human body. Even as he gasped for breath his bottom sank partially through what must have been a substantial hole. His insubstantial kaftan had floated up as he slumped, leaving his privates somewhat exposed. The ever helpful Arnaud removed the annoying kaftan wafting about him.

"Make no mistake Mr. Kobayashi, I am extremely serious. You and I - well, we're both working towards the same ultimate end - a more comprehensive enjoyment of life - Yes?"

Beau tried to concentrate on the man's voice. Surgical instruments appearing from the floor and above him proved to be too distracting. He squeezed his eyes tight shut. *This has to be a bad, bad dream. I've never met this man, I've never been in this place … Quintessence, you haven't done this to me have you? Quintessence?*

Normally, standing naked in front of anyone didn't faze Beau too much. All sorts of good things could come from such a simple display of intent. The sudden rubbing of coarse cloth against his skin snapped him into a firmer grasp of the new situation. His eyes flew open to see a bearded man with a hat, sitting bewildered at his work bench. Another man sat in the corner on a stool by the open fire. And still standing there in front of him the woman with flaming red hair who had removed her shawl to wrap it around him. She didn't seem concerned at all – surprised, yes – concerned like the two men, definitely not.

"Anne, get away from that man!" called Michel.

"Be quiet husband, can't you see he needs our help." Nevertheless she did leave the attic, disappearing purposefully down the stairs. Within minutes she had returned. Beau hadn't moved, overcome by the shock of the transformation. Anne placed some clothes in his hands.

"Go on, put these on," scanning his body again as she left the three men, unable to shake Beau's animal magnetism from her senses.

13

The Ribbon Frays
1549

You called, stated Quintessence with his usual brevity.

Beau had enough sense of decorum to know that one did not go visiting whilst naked, especially not across time and space. And yet there he was at a distinct disadvantage.

Remaining where he stood he quickly put on the loose fitting trousers, which more or less fitted as he and Nostredame were of a similar size and build. The punches that had deflated his lungs and bruised his ribs caused him a little difficulty in bending to the task.

You moved me. Thank you.

He didn't bother to use the cord to tighten the shirt around his waist.

You called.

Why bring me here? Did you harm those men? They will have to dealt with as well as Brummel to prevent another abduction.

The physician's mid length loosely fitting coat helped to reduce the effect of the cold drafts seeping through into the attic wafting around Beau's legs.

They do not fit into the pattern. You have to make a decision in this time. His internal conversation with Quintessence ended before Beau could get satisfactory answers.

"Explain yourself man." Bela reacted before the physician, recognising Beau from the previous visitation. He stepped forward, tentatively touching his arm.

"I am real. I apologise for my unorthodox entrance. My travelling facilitator deposited me here to save me from a rather painful torturous situation."

"Torture you say? Are you pursued by the Inquisition?" A note of very real concern came into Bela's voice. He remembered very well that Nostredame also had his disagreement with the Catholic Church hierarchy. If it hadn't been for that the two men might never have met.

Why bother to go into the details of his personal problems. These men wouldn't understand. "No. Nothing like that, though from my condition you saw the seriousness of my predicament."

"You intrude upon our hospitality." Nostredame said. "Are you a vision, from a twist of time? Are you a guide from the astral plane? What can you tell me of the future?" He ignored Beau's mild groans from the bruises he'd brought along with him.

"I am just a man ... from a future you do not know." Any further digression into detail might cut into the time he had with Nostredame, so he got right into the opportunity presented by this impromptu visitation. "When you publish your quatrains you will write about the end of time. You will tell your son César that the year 3797 has great terminal significance for humanity. I cannot fathom why I have come back to you. It must be because we share a destiny – you and I and Bela and Dante."

Nostredame raised his hand to stop the man from continuing. He picked up the quill and started writing furiously, not letting smudges and scratches hinder his recording of this conversation. Whether this man be a reality or a phantasm made little difference. The vehicles of revelations that ruled the heavens worked in mysterious ways through him. Bela wanted to say something, he too was immediately silenced by the physician turned prophet.

"What you say may be true, young man. The future has many possibilities. Decisions made today shape tomorrow. If there be a thread that connects us I have not foreseen this."

Beau felt himself to be quite 'substantial', not ephemeral like the last time. He rubbed his arm and passed a hand across his forehead. Just like the last time he visited Dante this segment on the Ribbon accepted his physical presence without causing immediate ripples in causes and effects that he was aware of. He began his tale of strange worlds, his own and Dante's, and each time he mentioned Dante, Bela frowned. Bela only knew of one Dante; the great Italian poet who lived and died over two hundred years ago leaving an enormous legacy in literature by giving insights into the nature of God's rewards and punishments. As a secular humanist Bela's philosophy specifically rejected religious dogma, supernaturalism and superstition as the basis of morality and decision making.

"Bela, you and I and Dante are destined to do something together. I have come to you through the intercession of powers I do not understand. Perhaps it may be possible for the three of us to meet some time, in time – outside the realm of time." Nostredame had been writing furiously as Beau told his story, never once stopping the man or questioning him.

Bela had a rebellious mind. He'd rejected the teachings of the Church. He could not come to terms with the concept of an Omnipotent loving God that inflicted such suffering upon his people. His mind, already in turmoil from things he had learnt from Nostredame's predictions had to try to fit into his world schema the concept of moving through time. Did that require faith or scientific appraisal?

"I can see you are troubled by my story. You need not be. What will come to be in future generations will not affect you or your family." *That's what I wanted to ask him* ... he suddenly recalled ... "Do you have a son, Bela? I think you do. He too is important."

To his recollection Bela had not told this stranger about his son, born soon after his wedding, other than Nostredame. Anne didn't know either. No one in France had any business knowing about the son of an insignificant physician on a visit from Italy to his friend. How could this stranger possibly know?

"You don't have to tell me. Look after him, keep him safe from the ravages of this plague and from the diseases of the mind from doctrines that flounder in the darkness of ignorance. As our – er, friend said ... he didn't want to be more specific … 'We have to use our reason to make sense of our lives, not faith.' Reason and faith are not compatible bedfellows."

"Ah … I see you are still with us, friend Beau," noted Nostredame after several hours absorbed in his writing, "do you have lodgings for the night? Of course not. Let me offer you our hospitality." Michel became so engrossed in his recording that he'd actually lost awareness of the source of his information. It could have been the spirits, his intuition or even God himself providing the revelations - as had been the case many times, or so he believed. At first Michel was annoyed by the uninvited appearance of this man, particularly by his state of presentation. Now that the man had provided so much useful information his attitude to the intrusion mellowed considerably. Beau had even been elevated to the status of 'friend'.

All this time the prophet had been seated, either listening or writing. The fading light disappeared altogether from the single window by his bench. In the candle light Beau's substance remained as distinct and as sharp a reality as that of the other two men. He had not called upon his Quintessence to take him home. *Surely there is more that has to be said, that has to be done. Quintessence must be giving me the opportunity - at last,* thought Beau, of course not having any idea what had yet to transpire. Perhaps an occasion might arise when he would have to make that important decision Quintessence had alluded to.

"Anne! Prepare a bed for our guest."

Her head popped up almost immediately, as if she'd already been on her way up to the attic. She had lingered close by the stairs, listening to the man's voice. It had a clarity and depth, an assurance – a measure of masculinity that captured her imagination. He spoke of magical things, of worlds of such splendour. "Yes husband. He can have the room of the three youngest."

Anne disappeared to prepare the room for Beau who remained lingering in the attic. Perhaps he didn't trust himself to be alone in the house with the woman. Until that moment he'd not had a chance to think about her after receiving the clothes from her. Nostredame bent to the task of recording everything spoken since Beau arrived. Bela became lost in thought, contemplating Beau's warning to look after his son. Under the circumstances of his departure from Florence that may well be a serious matter to consider before he stayed too long in Salon.

A loud rapping on the front door and urgent shouting brought the men downstairs, Beau remaining in the background.

I will remain here tonight. Thinking mostly of himself and the delicious mystery surrounding him, except for that insane Brummel, he thought that perhaps more revelations waited for him in this place. He did not consider how one time frame could contaminate another. How decisions made, or the flow of decisions that are interrupted out of sequence could alter the futures of entire civilizations.

"Who be there at this late hour?" shouted Nostredame through the closed door. These were dangerous times, care had to be taken against all manner of pestilence, whether it be human or plague. Charges of heresy against him should have been forgotten a long time ago, yet he had little trust the Inquisition would leave him in peace. It could easily have been Inquisitors banging on his door.

"Your help is urgently need Doctor. The plague has flared in many homes across the canal. Come quickly," pleaded several voices.

"Wait out there." One does not open the door to the plague. "Bela, come, we must try and help."

"I'll get our instruments."

"Beau, Anne do not leave the house this night," Nostredame warned them. "Do not open the door to anyone but us. We may not be back before morn."

Four shabbily attired men and an elderly woman waited outside, on foot, without a carriage to help take the physicians back to their families. Their torches cast ominous shadows as they hurried down the narrow cobblestone alley to disappear out of view. Strangely, in Beau's opinion, Anne did not seem to be particularly concerned. Human beings are indeed unfathomable creatures. They will as readily get used to a bad smell as living with a deadly disease that could easily claim their lives from one day to the next. He didn't comment on her lack of worry. He'd stepped closer to her after the men left, drawn by a beauty he could not understand nor resist. Anne turned towards him, cast her eyes to the ground and stepped aside. "I will get your bed ready."

Beau went back up to the attic. He had no clear idea what he wanted to do, nevertheless still disappointed at Anne's reaction to his advance. At least in the attic he had his first opportunity to explore in detail the paraphernalia surrounding a man with a universal reputation that could cross the boundaries of hundreds, thousands of years. He let his hand brush along books containing secrets of antiquity, disturbing motes of dust into the air. He picked out an odd one to read – but that of course he could not do that. Latin was a dead language, dead for millennia. In the astrological charts he recognised planetary conjunctions, though unable to interpret their meaning. Several of the candles had burnt down, and the fire no longer provided warmth. He remained motionless standing by the work bench, contemplating. The sound of Anne's voice brought him out of it to see the second last candle die out.

"It is ready – door on the left at the bottom of the stairs." She didn't go up to tell him.

Beau lingered for a while longer, glancing down at the notes Nostredame had been taking during his story. Already quatrains had begun to take shape, some obscured by strangeness so much that Beau no longer recognised his own tale. He snuffed out the last candle, relying on the dim kitchen light to guide him down the stairs.

The size of his room was modest, even by his own standards. Yet three beds crowded up against the walls, only one of them clean and neat. The children must have bunked together in another space. Surprisingly the day's heat from the kitchen had made the air pleasant, warm enough so he could sleep in his accustomed manner, without any clothes - a relief because his delicate skin was not used to the rough fabrics Anne had given him earlier to cover his nakedness.

What does one dream about when going to sleep on a strange planet, though it be his ancestral home, in a period of time long gone amongst people of strange customs and beliefs? Events of this day began late at night in his own home. Since then he'd been drugged, abducted, threatened with torture and abducted again. *What am I going to do when I get back? What is happening to Dante?* Meandering thoughts drifted from one thing to another. Comfort and fatigue claimed his body and mind. Beau drifted into that realm of universal renewal, no longer thinking of anything specific.

How long had he been asleep? Where was he? He felt himself drifting back into consciousness.

Soft stroking hands gently roused him to wakefulness in a dark room within a dark house. A finger came up to his lips to silence questions she felt coming. Anne knew nothing about other planets, or the behaviour of strange exotic men. The very concept of traveling to the past and to the future could not gain purchase in her thinking. Life was simple for Anne. She was alive - many were dead from the plague. She had a house to live in and a husband who provided for her and her children. And yet when the desire for Beau came upon her it did so with such force that her entire being trembled from anticipation. Was it wrong? She could not think about that. Why did she feel this way about a stranger she'd only seen as a ghost before? Who could possibly explain such things and not be called a sorceress in the process; a witch to be burned at the stake. An irresistible force was working upon her which she could not control.

Beau didn't say anything. His own inflamed desire silencing his rational thinking. Never one to deny himself pleasure, especially the unplanned spontaneous kind he let the moment carry him without a thought for his pregnant Emma. It didn't matter that he should not have had a physical presence in the year 1549. Some things were beyond the dictates of time. Nevertheless the laws of time did exist. And just as dripping water will rend asunder granite, so too a disturbance in the past that has been solidified by actions will send cracks of destruction into the fabric of a Time Loop Ribbon - tiny vibrations into space-eternity that could amplify with time.

And the Ribbon had no consideration for this man and this woman. It recorded every movement, every groan and intake of breath. It took note of every single drop of perspiration as the woman of the past and the man of the future flowed in their passionate embrace towards the early hours of the morning.

Beau awoke by himself, feeling drained. The bed was barely long enough for him and only wide enough if he didn't spread out his legs. And yet, during the night this bed had been large enough for two.

Sounds of children on the other side of his door, adults talking loudly and doors banging did what his dreams could not do. Was it all a dream? He could not be sure. So much in his life lately had transgressed any normal understanding of reality. With some reluctance he dressed in the crude fabrics given him yesterday before opening his door to a scene of some disorder.

Nostredame looked terrible, as did Bela. Their night amongst the infected must indeed have been draining on their reserves. Yet they animatedly discussed the patients, the remedies they'd administered, the stupidity of the people who simply could not understand the value of cleanliness. If one believed the pestilence to be a punishment inflicted by God then what significance could cleanliness possibly have.

Beau only half listened to their conversation, his attention drawn to Anne. Only once did he manage to catch her eyes. They betrayed nothing – made him think again about the unreality of the night. If a man travelled into the past and interfered in the events of mankind, even to the smallest degree, what ripples of change would it send into the future? What if the man acted in private, without the greater world even being aware of his existence ... would that have any impact at all?

Sitting down to breakfast seemed to calm the two physicians. "Look Bela, our guest is still here." He slapped Beau on the back. "You look as if you haven't slept very well. Let me look at you." The physician's knowing hands felt his temperature. "Do you have a headache?" Michel felt around his neck for indications of swelling. Any early symptom of the plague required immediate action.

Beau flushed for a moment, a guilty heat rising, dissipating. "No, nothing – just a restless night in strange surroundings."

Nostredame maintained his medical gaze on a potential patient. "Do you have pain anywhere?"

"Only here," he showed his abdominal bruising, "from being beaten."

Michel carefully examined the area, deciding all was well in the absence of any plague-like symptoms. "You must tell us more about this Dante fellow and his tribulations."

"From the little I saw of his world it is greatly troubled. Some people have been exiled for their beliefs, or for their lack of faith in the enforced religion." Bela leant forward on hearing a subject so close to his own reality. "Their God, whom they call Metaquanta, may not be a God at all. And his Priests who rule through threats of punishment have no mercy on anyone who shows the least signs of heresy."

"What manner of beliefs do they have? Surely the Catholic Church could not have survived into that distant age. You could be talking about ..." Bela stopped abruptly. The Holy Inquisition had ears everywhere. His own outspoken views had already caused visitations from the clergy hierarchy back in Florence.

"It is not like anything you could imagine. Their Priests are not human. They look like human beings, but their minds are controlled by ... machines. The God they obey is not a thing of the spirit. It too is a machine."

"What you say is strange beyond our understanding. Yet I have had visions of mechanisations that appeared to behave as if they were alive. They acted intelligent, though their actions betrayed the lack of intelligence. Come to my attic. We must discuss this further in private."

The three men left Anne to her domestic duties. Beau glanced back from the stairs and again caught her looking at him. What were those eyes saying?

"Was there nothing you could do to help?" Bela's deeply felt philosophy bristled at the thought of such oppression in the name of nothing more than an insubstantial religious belief system with nothing to hold it together but coercion. His immediate impulse to become involved rose rapidly to the surface.

"The exiles have already started an insurrection. Many people have been killed. The resistance to Metaquanta seems to be spreading across their entire world. If the violence continues and those Priests decide to strike back ... there may be no end to it until ... the end." Recalling the prophesy Beau said what Nostredame must have been thinking, "Perhaps the end of time. Maybe not for all existence, but quite possible for them."

"If a man has the knowledge of his future, his possible futures even probable futures, could he not interrupt the flow of decisions that may lead him there and reverse those decisions before it is too late?
I have seen such things come to pass. I do not believe God has created the future ahead of time. Nothing is inevitable," Michel expressed his own troubled beliefs.

Bela had become so agitated at the thought of any system of pure faith oppressing the freedoms of people to such an extent that they were forced to revolt en mass against their religious leaders, that he jumped up from the stool and began pacing the attic. "These Priests sound like monsters that could have come from the depths of Dante's Hell." Every kind of injustice boiled his blood, religious persecution the most vehemently so. "Why can't we go there and help them? You are able to travel into past and future ages. Take me with you!"

"I cannot control the forces that move me, body or spirit. You speak of something that is dangerous in the extreme. Master Nostredame can tell you about the complexity of the river of life, of the strong currents and undercurrents that carry us forwards. We cannot go against the flow without suffering the consequences."

"And yet you are here," said Bela. Beau didn't know what to do with this situation, nor with what occurred between himself and Anne. Sensory flashes of the night's activities had filtered back into his consciousness during the conversation. What had happened was not a dream, surely. That's why Anne looked at him like that in the kitchen.

True to habit Nostredame exercised his quill far more than his mouth. Things were being said that could not be seen for their true impact until a greater part of the picture had been revealed. "Are you intending to extend your visitation, Beau?"

Stay? To what end? Anne? Hardly had her name come to mind than she came up the stairs with tools to clean out the fireplace. "I thank you for your hospitality. If my absence from my own time leaves too big a gap it may be filled by undesirable elements surfacing from its immediate past." What Beau said had more truth in it than he realised, not to mention the confusion of feelings that flooded into him again on seeing Anne once more.

'Nice name - 'Beau'. 'Kobayashi' – that's not French is it." Anne made the offhand remarks as she began work on the fireplace.

Why would she say that? "I will leave now." *Nothing happened last night.*

Quintessence, take me home. Quintessence! He could not convince himself that nothing had happened.

*

"Where in the name of Prox have you been?" Emma remonstrated, exasperated at not having been told he intended to be gone for so long.

Quintessence deposited Beau in his apartment, letting him materialize more slowly than usual, which resulted in Emma not hearing him till the last moment and bumping into him. "What is this dirty outfit you're wearing? It smells. Where are your clothes?"

"No need to worry. I've been abdu … to see Bela and Nostredame." He began babbling about the first random things that came to mind hoping to distract himself from accidentally revealing his dalliance. "This time Quintessence took all of me. An out-of-this-world experience! Just think what we could do. People would be falling over themselves to go backwards in time. Astounding possibilities. I wonder if Quintessence could do that for many people, not just me." What he'd started to say, about the abduction, didn't seem to be such a good idea either. Emma understood the sensitive nature of their experiments and their financial implications to Playback Inc. If she found out about Omnifun's attempt it was anybody's guess as to what she might do - or they might do. "How are you? Any problems with little Dante?"

"Nice of you to remember. Next time you decide to pull a stunt like that I want to know about it. Do you understand me! This child needs a father, not just a mother." Still upset with him she led him into the other room. "Get out of those rags - and get yourself cleaned up." Those were definitely the words and tone of a contracted mate, not just a joy-friend.

Relieved that she didn't start quizzing him about all the details of the last couple of days he did as he was told. Still foremost on his mind - Anne. *Why did she remark about my name? It sounded like she had lodged it in her memory for future use. I'll have to ask her next time.* With that thought he'd betrayed his unconscious desire to see this woman again.

He had received rather heavy blows from Arnaud, causing a bruise to develop below his left ribcage, which became more tender since yesterday. *Brummel.* Something had to be done about that deranged criminal. *Perhaps Quintessence could drop him off in a prehistoric jungle to fight it out with the other predators.* A cheery thought.

No.

You can't or you won't? He knew that voice very well by now. Although getting used to hearing his own voice under such peculiar circumstances it still didn't feel natural.

It is not part of the pattern we are unfolding.

You must have heard what Bela and I were talking about. What about taking Bela to meet Dante?

Silence.

This thing, whatever it thinks it is, has to learn some social skills; answer the question, for example.

You have initiated another line of history.

Beau thought for a moment that Quintessence referred to getting Bela to help Dante, not realising a far more penetrating set of possibilities arising if his son grew into adulthood.

The power that resided within this sentient cluster of dark energy may have been unlimited. It could cross the boundary between the Time

Loop Ribbon and the sea of space-eternity in which it floated. It could examine any segment along the Ribbon, visit it, but could it change anything? The repercussions of trying to do so eluded its insights. The limits of its vision had been reached in segment 3790. It could not see beyond the repercussions resulting from the chain of events put into motion by Luther, or by Beau for that matter.

A child born into the past, created by a seed from the future rapidly pushed aside lesser probabilities initiated by persons of lesser import. The integrity of the structure of the Ribbon had been compromised. The child may die, as many did in that segment, before it attained a meaningful existence. But if it survived … What if it could not only cast it's mind forward, like Nostredame, yet unlike Nostredame not remain silent, or worse - not remain detached. There have been other individuals in history who have changed history, who have embellished the fabric of the Ribbon with their own selfish imprints.

Another complication had to be considered; the possible impact, though it could not discern any pattern radiating from it, of a point of agitation taken from the past to give energy to events in the far future. Would that be against the Law? Could it dislodge both Beau and Bela from their segments and propel them together ahead of themselves? Could they time shift to a parallel reality? Beau may have done nothing of consequence during his visits to segment 3790. Could the same control be relied on from Kobayashi Bela, given the fervour with which he lived his life?

Gradually Quintessence came to the understanding, regardless of any other purpose it may have had, that it did not need to make decisions on behalf of the humans. That privilege belonged to Beau and to others of his species who had to endure the process of their existence until time had run its course for each of them. It could touch their minds, absorb their physical energy into itself and carry them to any segment that destiny decreed. Other than facilitating the wishes of these humans Quintessence could not discover any other purpose to its existence.

Simply having awareness of the beginnings of fraying in the fabric of the Ribbon would not create a desire to make it whole again. A decision to tell Beau the consequence of his dalliance in the night could wait. The child had not yet been born; it may or may not enter a world where he only half belonged. The woman had birthed six infants already without complications and survived, as had her children. The probability was strong.

14

Zetaverse

The Ribbon had begun to unravel at the edges as it stretched and widened to accommodate the Beau-Anne child. Time dilated to give this child the opportunity to grow into its dual-time existence.

At the other segment of the Ribbon the rate of progression of time increased to try to maintain balance. An instant on segment 3790 became shorter than an instant on segment 1561. As a result the Ribbon began looping through eternity at different rates in its varying segments, putting great strain on the fabric of its existence. Eternity continued being eternal, unconcerned about minor fluctuations of time. It existed before time began and will continue after the end of time. That is the essence of eternity.

Unaware of the chain of events he had set in motion Kobayashi Beau resumed his work on the Zetaverse technology. He could not afford to think about Dante and the problems of his world while his own reality needed input to maintain continuity. His work at the laboratory could not be delayed any longer. He had effectively withdrawn his expertise over the months of his involvement in those unorthodox excursions. During the days of his explorations time always seemed to slow as if to let Beau soak in the experience. Lately, back at work it became the opposite – everyday ended too soon. Every pleasurable moment with Emma went by too fast. Pressure built with so much to be done and so many matters claiming his attention.

"You said this man Pietro XXXVI returned while I was away. How did it go with him, Em?"

"He brought his own experience record insisting we use that."

"Not a good idea. How do we know recordings made by amateur individuals using their own dubious resources don't end up contaminated, or improperly cleansed?"

"His wasn't clean. The mongrel is still in hospital – he had a meltdown. As soon as I gave him the first cocktail dose he started convulsing – we had to break the contact without using the safety protocols."

"What happened?"

"The stupid idiot actually got amateurs to prepare his data - a real miser. They somehow cross contaminated him as the observer with the subject he was watching. Shame really. Under proper laboratory conditions that could be a most interesting area of investigation. I've had a look at his recording. This despicable idiot set up a scenario, in public, to humiliate one of his senior Schadenfreude Festival executives who he'd taken a dislike to. Because of the mix up Pietro suffered the humiliation, heightened by the drugs I gave him, instead of experiencing the pleasure from seeing his man suffer - serves him right."

"He'll recover I presume. You didn't overdose him?"

"As much as I was tempted – no. And yes, he'll recover from the immediate shock of the replay, although he'll be a changed man from

159

what I saw of his extreme reaction. He'll either find another job and get out of the business altogether ... or, with a bent mind like his ... I can see him wanting more of the same."

"I like the idea of ... say taking a holiday together and experiencing it from the other's perspective. Just think, if we could load someone else's memory into an individual and have them experience the other's pleasure – or pain, who cares – quite an entrepreneurial opportunity there." Beau's thoughts wandered down a side alley; *there's the problem of neural network incompatibility, then being able to accurately control the content of the memory, and ...*

"Boss, come back to me. Forget Pietro."

"Sorry – Ok, never mind him. What about the others?"

"Some Ok. Seems that different levels of perceptions can produce biased memories, which then superimpose on the playbacks. By introducing our cocktails the dual images and feelings may create serious nightmares. Our modified drugs might prevent that. I think our initial download techniques immediately after the experiences need to be refined, and our scrubbing must be more comprehensive and much more selective."

"Agreed. Also get some of our best coders onto more accurate synchronizing algorithms."

Beau and Emma went through the successful participants again. By adjusting dosages during playbacks they could alter the artificial timing elements of the experiences. The brain does strange things with the way our eyes perceive the passage of time and the manner in which the brain interprets that information for the way the body needs to use it.

"Tomorrow I'm going to run some experiments to see how the sense of time seems to slow under some conditions, and speed up during others. There has to be some neurological basis for that phenomenon. But for the rest of today I have to go and meet someone."

"Oh yes. What's her name?"

"He's at Omnifun." Once again, as he did each day after getting the initial good news about the pregnancy, he stepped up close to Emma putting his open palm on her belly, rubbing gently up and down. The baby hadn't started to show too much yet. It would soon enough. "You look after this little bundle. I have a feeling he could open up a whole new chapter for the future." He didn't know that for sure, only suspected it. From his segment, stuck on the surface of the Ribbon he could not run searches into the future. That did not stop Dante on Keppler 22b from using their own existing records in the future to look into the past. He said he'd started, though he couldn't give Beau any definitive information during the last visit. With all his problems he probably wouldn't follow up that line of enquiry.

"You have no business going there," warned Emma. If he hadn't left at that moment Emma would have told him all the reasons why going to the competition was a bad idea even for a visit, apart from the rumors she'd heard about how unscrupulous the head of that organization could be.

Brummel must have had several offices. The one Beau stepped into at this end of the city didn't have the same panoramic vista as the first one he'd been abducted into. He felt quite assured of his safety this time, having demonstrated a certain magic skill. Brummel eyed him suspiciously, his special secretaries noticeably absent from the room.

"No removalists?" Beau asked the rhetorical question, walked to the lounge and sat as if he owned the place. He ran an open palm slowly across the top of the low table, making a point of the lack refreshments or nibbles on it. "No hospitality?"

"I'm waiting."

"Ah, yes. As I recall, before I had to leave so suddenly you requested an update on my progress," putting strong emphasis on 'requested'. "Would you care to elaborate on the proposition you had for me?"

"How did you do that?" obviously referring to Beau's disappearing act.

"Your proposition?"

"Not interested anymore. You can't make it work."

"I see. You think you're well informed. Well – here's the thing ..." Beau glanced around. It didn't matter if it was only the two of them in the room. Brummel would be recording everything. "... forget the Zetaverse, forget all that memory enhancement technology. Why go to all the trouble of trying to re-live a past experience ... if you could simply go back there ... (long pause) ... and go through it again."

Beau stood up in the middle of the sentence. Without bothering to look at Brummel or waiting for an answer he walked to the door. "It wouldn't be very smart to send your boys after me again," and left. Those boys had outlived their usefulness. Brummel could not abide such total incompetence for letting the man get away like that. For all he knew the whole escapade had been engineered by his three trusted secretaries. Well - they wouldn't let him down again. Being good strong men they lasted longer than the average participants in the latest Schadenfreude Festival rehearsal. Pity the general audiences could not enjoy the spectacle.

Brummel's self-control had almost vaporized by the time Beau left his office. The realization that he'd underestimated the scientist infuriated him. Now he wanted the man under his control more than ever, not just for business reasons - it had become personal. *I want the Zetaverse and I want whatever technology he used to escape from me - and I want Him.*

Within minutes he followed behind Beau, his destination the hospital. He and Pietro XXXVI had been collaborators for many years. This new situation demanded a two pronged approach. Pietro was a devious bastard - he'd think of something nice to deal with this 'pain'.

Beau counted on Brummel's greed and lack of imagination to ensure his safety. If Brummel wanted what he thought Beau had badly enough then the next contact from him would be far more civil.

Playback Inc. kept advertising their promise of the fantastic reality of the Zetaverse. Beau tried to explain to the Board that a lot of work still had to be done to make the technology both safe and easily accessible to people at a reasonable cost. Anything the old technology of Virtual Reality constructs or augmented scenarios had to offer in the past was overshadowed by the promise of the Zetaverse. This would be actual reality; the reality of the universe experienced by each individual in their own unique way. But more than that; the experience of a reality enhanced by their own minds, not some intrusive manipulations created by strangers … a reality not just remembered but re-lived.

He had not yet brought up with the Board the possibility of making any past experience not just simply a memory excursion, but an actual re-enactment in real time by jumping back into a past timeframe. If only he could somehow harness the energies used by Quintessence. It should be entirely possible if this entity's capability was a result of condensing dark energy into a useful configuration and applying it in a controlled manner - not realizing that Quintessence itself was the dark energy, not some entity separate from it. The biggest impediment Beau could foresee had to be the dangers of new actions perpetrated by visitors into their own pasts. Perhaps just to be an observer of the past – in the past might be enough of an inducement to turn the concept into a successful commercial venture without having to deal with any fallout from the grandfather paradox.

Playback Inc. wanted to push ahead, anxious that the competition might beat them to the release of this new technology. They gave him more staff, sent him on another trip to Prox-c to gather more data using the refined recording techniques. They made it quite clear to Beau that this had to be the last phase of the experimental process - they wanted results.

"There's no reason for you to come Emma. This is not a working holiday. Besides, I don't want to take any chances with little Dante."

"To be honest – I don't fancy being cooped up in a cargo ship for months. Those tubs are so slow, I could grow a second head by the time they do a return trip. You go and do what you have to. Your special friend obviously doesn't need you."

"If a guy named Brummel calls looking for me just tell him I'm working on it. He'll know what that means. Don't say or do anything else. He is dangerous." This was not the right time to tell Emma about his abduction and associated unpleasantness. "I'll tell you all about it when I get home."

After a few months out they were finally on the last leg of the voyage home. Particularly pleased with himself Beau had managed to get far better downloads this time from the personnel on Proxima-c. During their down-times some miners liked to go rappelling down ice cliff chasms, then catching updrafts back to the surface. These formations had a peculiarity about them … they went down deep to where strong warm air currents from the mantle pushed upwards. The trick was to catch the updrafts just at the right moment so as to be carried high enough before they lost lift. The degree of adrenalin rush amplified by just how deep the divers were prepared to rappel before jumping into the updraft – death or life being the sole arbitrator of success.

Data gathered during the Jupiter voyage had to be mostly abandoned; they had become obsolete once the new recording techniques proved their superior reliability, though some were still good enough to test the new scrubbing programs.

Emma worked on refining the spectrum of drug cocktails to suit varying levels of intensity that would probably be demanded by customers, and customizing them for compatibility with their individual metabolisms. Using some existing recordings and superimposing them on verbal memory, layering techniques were developed by her laboratory to enable isolation of the most intense aspects of any downloaded experience. When Beau arrived home the groundwork had been prepared for the next stage of making the Zetaverse a commercial reality. It seemed that super reality was at last within reach.

"How is our little Dante?" In spite of all his preoccupations and the worrying absence of Quintessence during his trip to Proxima-c the little bundle of future remained foremost in his thoughts. This baby represented far more than simply another human being born so far from the parent planet of their species. Beau had convinced himself, despite lacking positive proof at this stage, that his son's descendants were linked into what the future of a branch of humanity looked like, the dangers it faced and it's possible salvation.

At seven months Emma's body unmistakably showed her pregnancy to be well advanced. She looked particularly healthy and vibrant. Perhaps abstaining from all manner of artificial pleasure enhancements had worked to her benefit, and no doubt to her baby's.

"Very happy, thank you Bebo. You've been gone too long. I don't mind you jumping backwards and forwards in time for a few days. But could you stay home now please. I would like our son to see his father's face when he is born."

"I promise. Quintessence has not bothered me for months. All must be well on Keppler 22b and in Bela's world. Besides, we still have a lot of work to do on the universe we are about to create. When can I bring the volunteers to the lab from the cargo ship?" He didn't want to tell Emma his concerns about the dire situation with Dante and the rebellion.

Sitting side by side at home as they discussed procedures for the next stage of their project Beau had his palm open, continuously stroking Emma's belly. When he spoke little Dante reacted to his voice by moving about. "Is he always this active?"

"Oh no ... he moves around a bit in the evenings ... nothing this active though. I think he likes the sound of your voice. Speak to him."

Domestic bliss swallowed up the rest of the day and the evening. The mornings were the worst for Emma being no different on the morning after Beau's arrival home. His presence didn't alleviate her back pain and constipation.

"You go ahead. I might not get to the lab today Bebo ... just feeling really tired and a bit blocked up."

Although being Beau's first pregnancy, as far as he knew, Emma's symptoms for her condition were normal. They didn't worry him. In fact, he wanted to get back to work as soon as possible, without the distraction of having to keep an eye on his contracted-partner during working hours. The project neared completion if this last stage of experimentation proved successful. In truth Beau could barely wait for the Zetaverse business to be over so he could concentrate on going back to Bela and Dante. Especially Dante. The situation on Keppler 22b seemed to have reached boiling point when he last visited.

"Larry, have we got a few volunteers ready to be interviewed?"

"Only ten were able to get planet-side leave this time."

"That will have to do for the time being. At least we'll get the process started. Could you bring the first one in please?"

Larry returned within a few minutes wearing a worried expression, without anyone accompanying him. He obviously knew the two people who said they wanted to talk to Beau. One of them, the annoying belligerent one he would rather not have seen again. "Two people waiting to see you. One of them is Pietro from the Schadenfreude Festival – you know the one, and the other is Brummel." Larry had been with Playback Inc. for a few years, working his way up from a lab assistant to Laboratory Director. He knew the Who's Who of their scientific world, and he knew that these two characters should not have been anywhere near their laboratory. 'Do you want me to come along?"

"No. Thanks Larry. I think I know what they want, and they can't have it. Look ... if I'm not back in a couple of hours ... no, never mind." What could Larry do if that idiot tried to abduct him again? Besides, Quintessence did say all Beau had to do was to call on it.

The laboratory had no formal reception area. Security had to be tight, extra tight. No one could even enter the property without authorisation. Beau had to walk to the gate to meet his visitors. Security cameras monitored everything. He was surprised to see Brummel and Pietro allowing themselves to be recorded. As Beau went through the gate Brummel showed every sign of being friendly ... handshake, pat on the back ... likewise with Pietro. *Strange*. Beau glanced back at the security guards who'd been watching the whole charade.

"You are looking well Pietro." Pietro grimaced. That was not his preferred name. Beau did it on purpose to put him on edge. "Did you bring a picnic Brummel?" Another dig at his abductor's previous show of sham hospitality.

"What's it going to take?" asked Brummel, as they walked to the private magnetrans.

"You two are buddies? I never would have guessed. Forgive me if I don't go for a ride with you ... I'm sure you understand Brummel."

"Name it and it's yours," added Pietro XXXVI, "your own private dome? Your own laboratory? A good assortment of joy-friends?"

"I know what you want. The answer is no. Don't ask again. This could get quite awkward for you. Let me just say this much ... You would both have a very hard time surviving on Earth back in the time of the Holy Inquisition based on your professions and philosophy of life."

The two businessmen were accustomed to always getting their own way, of dealing effectively with difficult people who stood in their way. They had offered unbelievable riches without the least compulsion to keep their word. They'd had people threaten them, plead with them, give them everything they wanted just to be released from their grip. What the hell did something called the Holy Inquisition have to do with them? What was it anyway? And why bring that dead planet into it?

Beau walked back through the gate into the research complex leaving the two men still trying to understand what he'd said to them. Well – it will not take them long to find out. Then they can worry. At this stage Beau didn't know if Quintessence could, or would transport people just by Beau asking him to do it.

Part 3

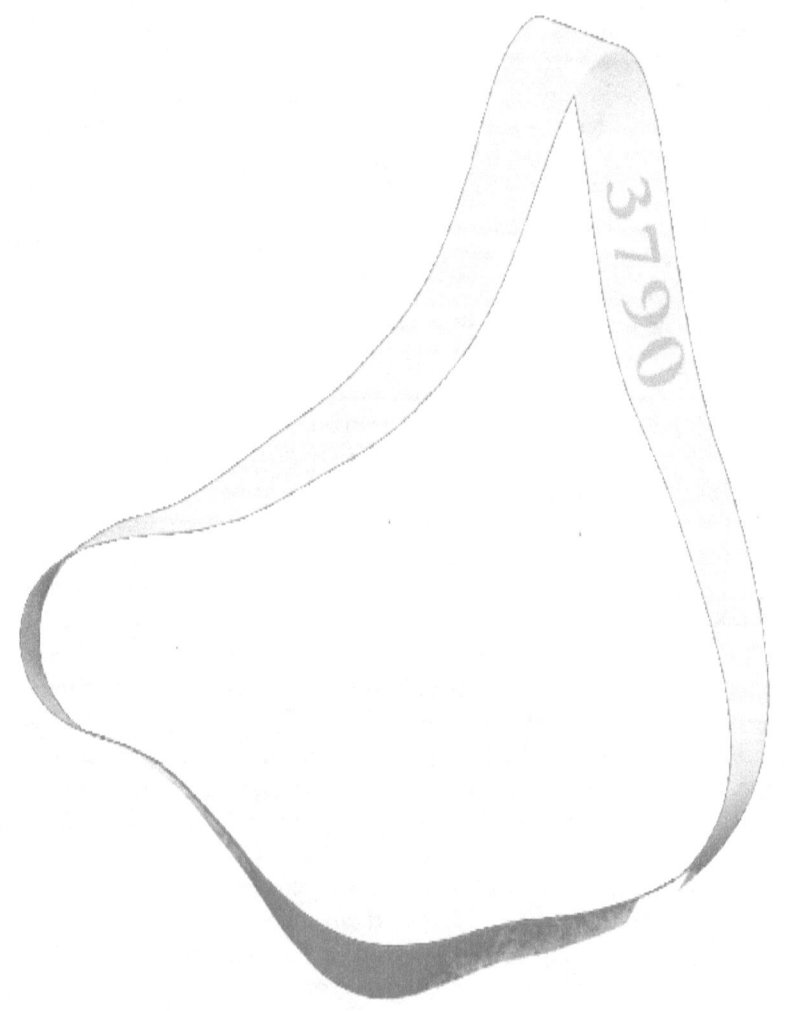

15

Metaquanta's Core Facility

Beau simply disappeared from in front of their eyes. His last words to Dante had been to intimate that the three Kobayashi had to meet.

Dante could find out neither who this third person was nor where or when he would come from. But that really didn't matter when the situation had become almost desperate on Keppler 22b after the attacks.

"Does that man always do that, just vanish? Is it a hologram created by Metaquanta?" Gemma had become ultra-sensitive and distrustful of everyone, including the Priests since she started working with Luther and Beatrice.

"No, I don't think so. He knows and says things that are just too strange. The first time he visited me he did seem like a hologram, but not this last time. I've touched him when I put your tunic on him. By the way … where were you? I waited for you till the last minute to come with me to Adoration."

"I knew what Luther was up to. Things were moving along too fast. We weren't ready. I was trying to convince him to postpone the whole thing – but he wouldn't listen of course. Then I tried to get to the Temple Island to warn you. By the time I got there the place was an absolute mess. Dead people everywhere, Priests crushed under the fallen tower – fire, noise. I didn't even make it across the bridge to the island. I got caught up in a stampede before getting away from the chaos to come home. What are we going to do?"

"I don't exactly know. For the time being we should stay at home until the panic dies down. From the noise still out there that could take quite a while. Look Gemma – this is going to sound strange – this guy calls himself Beau."

"That's not strange."

"No, that isn't. But he says his other name is Kobayashi."

"That's not possible. Each of us on this planet has a unique identifier. Father One would not allow any duplication at all. Metaquanta's query systems would fry."

"That's what I thought. I've been checking up on him, as far as my security clearance would allow. He's from Proxima-b. And before you ask, no they haven't developed some incredible transportation system. He told me that his current year was 2555."

Gemma put her hand up to his head, got him to stand up to check him all over. No sign of any injuries, no head wound, no bleeding. "You haven't got concussion, have you?"

"I believe him. I'm perfectly alright – don't fuss. You'd better sit down. He does exist according to the records we have brought with us from Proxima-b, and he had a son called 'Dante'."

For a moment Gemma paled, perhaps thinking they'd been drawn into some strange incomprehensible conspiracy. She turned to face him, her eyes asking the obvious question.

"I don't know. It's all too weird. What I want to know is why he's turned up out of the blue just like that when we're having all these problems. And another thing I found out … way back on Earth a man they called Nostredame thought he could see into the future. We know that's not possible. Technically all that is possible is to make predictions based on data and probability factors. Yet this guy wrote in one of his poems that the end of time would come in 3797."

Gemma really did go quite pale this time. She clutched his arm, unable to bring out a coherent thought. With the other hand she felt her belly and the life that had begun there such a short time ago.

She didn't get the chance to gather her wits because the sound of banging on their door snapped her out of the temporary paralysis. They both jumped up out the couch and saw on screen the source of the clamouring.

"Door - do not record - Open!" Dante didn't have to shout at the door, but that's how it came out.

Luther almost fell across the threshold, bloodied from head to foot obviously badly wounded. Gemma rushed to him first then quickly scanned down both sides of the corridor - empty. "Close!"

"I don't know how, but I think they're onto us," Luther managed to whisper through the pain. It took an hour to clean him up properly. The wounds were only superficial. He was simply exhausted getting away from the pursuing guard Priests who were on the Temple Island at the time of the explosions. "Have you seen Beatrice? She was supposed to stay on Palm Atoll visiting her parents but I saw her a couple of hours ago." The planned uprising and subsequent coup did not go according to plan. Having so many simultaneous attacks on the majority of Temple Islands worked well enough to create the distraction needed to divert the attention of Adoration Priests as well as the Security Priest network. "Her job was to coordinate the infiltration and disabling of all the distributed Server installations to hobble Metaquanta's main core. Something must have gone drastically wrong for her to be here. We knew that knocking out the servers would effectively cripple Metaquanta. We cannot let this *thing* continue controlling our lives."

"Aren't you forgetting 3797?" Gemma reminded him.

"That's exactly why we're doing this! Whoever programmed this beast must have been crazy. Why should someone, anyone from the past decide our future."

Dante didn't have the courage or the rebellious nature to be a part of anything revolutionary. He did however agree with what Luther was doing. Just one small matter worried him that he could not untangle. This strange business with Kobayashi Beau, and Nostredame.

"Do you know much of our history? Have you ever heard of Nostredame? No? Well I've had reason to research this individual. You're not going to like what I found out."

"Is he an exile? Where is he? Do I need to know about him?" By this time Luther had recovered from his desperate flight, his reasoning faculties seemingly intact. He immediately started working on an alternate strategy ignoring everything that would not contribute to it.

"This man, from deep in our past – from Earth in fact, predicted that the end of time would come in the year 3797. He wrote about this in the year 1555."

"What about that guy Beau from 2555?" added Gemma.

Luther continued staring at Dante as if he hadn't heard what had just been said. He'd lived his entire life using his reasoning faculties to work things out ... like the purpose of his life, why life existed at all – and in particular why he should believe anything dictated by Metaquanta's dogmas that could not be supported by facts. In his view raw blind faith as a foundation for having a purposeful existence simply should not be tolerated. What Dante had just said sounded exactly like another unsubstantiated idiotic theory. Many people had strange ideas about that date. Some completely ignored the possibility of time ending. Others, on the other end of the spectrum, believed with every fibre of their being that only Metaquanta could prevent such a thing from ever actually happening.

"What about him?" asked Luther, having dismissed the Nostredame nonsense from his mind as an unfounded fabrication.

"He said he came from Proxima-b, from the year 2555."

"Is that so. And what proof did he have for that?" *There's too many crackpots and conspiracy theorists in this world.*

Before Dante could respond urgent knocking on the door overlayed with the door's announcement 'You have a visitor'. "Open!" Luther shouted at it on seeing the visitor's face on the door screen. It would not respond to his voice print.

"Open," repeated Dante.

Beatrice burst in, as out of breath as Luther had been when he arrived. "We can't stay here!" She ran to Luther seeing him bandaged, lying on the couch. "What happened to you?"

"I was too close to the tower when it came down ... just a few scratches from flying debris. I was worried about you. Why didn't you stay on Palm Atoll?"

"Some of our techs were captured only hours before we were due to infiltrate the servers. We had to change plans at the last minute. We can't stay here. They're looking for us - all of us, you too Dante."

Perhaps not fear but certainly immediate anxiety showed on his face. He looked from Beatrice to Luther to Gemma. "How did they find out? Why are they looking for me? I haven't done anything."

"You knew Gemma had been working with us – you must have."

"What exactly are you suggesting?"

"No - sorry - you're right. We have to go! There's only one place where they might not look for us," suggested Beatrice."

One by one, spaced a few minutes apart to divert suspicion they left the habitation building through the front entrance. On the way to the inter-island ferry Luther teamed up with Gemma, and Beatrice went with Dante. It might help confuse tracking cameras if they were looking for known paired brothers/sisters-in-spirit couples.

For years Dante had been trying to somehow connect with Beatrice on more than a casual acquaintance basis. And now, in the midst of all the upheaval they'd actually been thrown together. He'd had all kinds of scenarios in his mind for how he would make his feelings known to her when they did finally get to spend time together. None of them seemed appropriate under the circumstances. When fleeing for one's life, in all probability, there wasn't much else to consider other than staying alive. Anybody who had been 'disappeared' by the AI Priests in the past never surfaced again. They may have been exiled, or worse. If you don't know, you simply don't know and the mind creates the worst possible theories.

They didn't run – too dangerous. They tried walking and talking while keeping an eye on the other couple. The closest ferry could not have been more than a few hundred meters ahead of them. Dodging through crowds and Priests they tried to look unconcerned about the commotion around them.

Dante smiled at Beatrice. "I've been looking out for you at the Adorations." *Damn! That's not what I wanted to say.* He felt extremely awkward. Enough emotional space remained alongside the escape anxiety to accommodate a sense of inadequacy.

"Why?"

She's not making this any easier. "Ah – er – You seemed to be alone most of the time." *Temporary relief.*

"I've seen you too – watching me."

Damn! Why is she doing this? A group of people headed directly at them, which they had to quickly avoid, breaking the flow of conversation - not that it was getting him anywhere. The two Security Priests following behind didn't seem to take any notice of the two of them walking briskly towards the ferry, which they could now see. It had just docked letting a large group of passengers off. They too came hurrying past them with what appeared to be a Security Priest escort. These two Priests walked more slowly, scanning the people around them. Perhaps they were on the lookout for someone. Beatrice noticed them first, giving Dante a nudge and at the same time getting a hold of his hand, as if they were an in-spirit couple. That definitely made him jerk his head around to see her beautiful face smiling at him. He desperately wanted to stop and do something with that beaming face.

This is not how it's supposed to happen! He almost tripped on something until she motioned with her eyes for him to look ahead and keep moving. Luther and Gemma had caught up with them as they neared the on-ramp. They slowed to let the stragglers get off. Ferries of assorted sizes bobbed in the rippling water, docked beside each other - the smaller ones with near island destinations and others going further. None that were docked there were suitable for crossing large expanses of their water world. There was nothing suspicious about crowds of people getting on and off ferries. That's just the way they moved around on their world; constantly island hopping.

Dante led them onto the one that still had the ferryman aboard. Not a large vessel, but big enough to take them to the nearest tiny atoll, seventy five kilometres to the South - a destination known to very few people. The ferryman didn't need a lot of convincing once Luther had a word in his ear. Quietly, unhurriedly they pulled away from the dock before any other passengers could get aboard. By this time Beatrice had let go of Dante's hand and moved close to Luther. He could still feel the warmth of it. Glancing around self-consciously he noticed Gemma coming towards him, with a hand outstretched to him. That broke the spell.

"What did you say to him?" Dante asked Luther.

"Not much, just our destination."

"And – what – he just agreed?"

"We have a wide network," that's all Luther would say.

"Which is where?"

"No need for you to know – just in case."

Dante glanced at the two women standing side by side, his face colouring slightly as he looked at Beatrice. Her face betrayed nothing.

At sixty knots, again slow enough so they would not draw attention to themselves, the horseshoe atoll came in sight in under an hour, or at least the three hundred meter high peak at one end of it could be seen easily.

"Is this it? Not much to it. Is it inhabited?" Dante didn't bother too much with local geography.

"People don't know about this place because it's so small. Almost every storm will wash over it, so it's not much good for habitation or mining. And as you can see, there are no AI's guarding it."

That should have given Dante a clue as the ferryman guided the vessel up an underwater ramp until its bow dug into the sand a little way up the shoreline. Even after they disembarked, including the ferryman, he still didn't catch on. The last thing the guy did was to put the ferry in reverse before jumping off.

"What are you doing?" Dante's considerably worried question should have been a different question, which he quickly realised as the ferry made its way into the deep water and began to sink.

Luther didn't bother answering. "Come on, we have to get out of sight."

The cave entrance about two hundred meters above sea level at the other end of the atoll gave nothing away. Its large size could easily have accommodated one of the common airlifts mostly used by the Priests. As they advanced deeper into the cave the tunnel shrunk, veered hard left then hard right and hard right again revealing the only access point that would take them deeper into the complex. Beatrice took the lead. Unknown to Dante she was one of the few computer system architects trusted with maintaining and developing the infrastructure that kept Metaquanta's systems viable. From time to time she had to be given access to the core.

"In a moment there'll be another corner. Don't follow until I call you." They all stopped and watched her put on a Priest's crimson-purple robe made of photovoltaic fabric, pulling its hood over her head. "Stay," she reiterated without turning back and walked slowly around the corner. Using Father One's access energy signature at a hidden lens part of the cave wall dissolved revealing a lift-like structure, mirrored on every face on the inside. The security system in the lift could not distinguish Beatrice's duplicated smart robe logic network from that of Father One's. A panel lit up beside her. "Security - code B3621F – initiate full system check, now. Shut down all surveillance until further notice," she commanded.

She stepped out of the lift and called the others to hurry. Dropping suddenly the lift did not stop for a full two and a half minutes. It moved fast, without sound and without any sense of motion once on the way. Dante realised for the first time there was a lot more to this atoll than what could be seen from its small beach.

"Where are you taking us," he finally asked.

Luther knew where Metaquanta's primary systems had been installed, as did Beatrice. Everything on the planet was controlled from this one location ... all the Priests, communication towers, surveillance systems, everything. Metaquanta did not have a backup - there could not be two Gods on the one planet. "This place is the heart and brain of that beast."

"This is the only place where the Priests will not think to look for us. Logically we should have returned to our own individual locations, or hidden close by. They will not think that any human would consider Metaquanta's most vulnerable location as a possibly place for us to go to for safety. Our coming here is not accidental – at least not for Beatrice and myself. We needed the major distraction to draw all the Priests away from all the distributed processing centres so our techs could do their thing. So let's get on with it. This particular location was our primary target at the outset. Try not to get in the way," he said to Gemma and Dante.

"Let me go first," Beatrice stepped into a tubular tunnel as soon as the lift stopped. She raised her right hand and rotated it three hundred and sixty degrees, once or thrice stopping to tweak a sensor embedded finger nail. "This way," she announced on the third pinch stepping towards a section of the glossy white tube surface that opened to reveal another tunnel looking exactly the same as the one they were standing in. The procedure had to be repeated several times at intersecting tunnels before they found themselves inside an enormous cube that must have been at least ten meters in every direction. Spread along each glossy white wall with walkways uncloaked Priests stood with palms pressed against the wall at regular intervals. No one had ever seen the bare head of a Priest until then, and what Dante did see made no sense. All the craniums appeared to be empty, every one of the hundred that were lined up and obviously plugged into something. None reacted to the intruders' presence.

"All Priests must receive upgrades from the main core, which is Metaquanta itself. I know what's going on because I helped to build the latest system. Then I met Luther ... and ... well, the rest is history. I'll tell you all about it some other time."

She glanced at Dante, hoping he would finally understand why she had to keep him away from her. He did. His face visibly dropped, realising that even that impromptu delicious moment when she took his hand had held no promise. Whether Gemma realised what was going on between them, he didn't notice. She seemed totally preoccupied by looking at the inanimate Priests sucking up the Metaquanta juice.

"There's quite a few of them here, more than I'd hoped. They have to be deactivated before we can get to the main core, or they'll come back on line. You know what that means. Here's what I want you to do."

She and Luther gave them two chronon pulse pads each, one to be stuck to the inside tip of the forefinger and one for the inside surface of the thumb. Luther attached his first, then Beatrice.

"I'll demonstrate on Luther here. It's not going to harm him, but this action will instantaneously fry the Priest 'brain' network."

She placed the forefinger just above Luther's ear, and her thumb just below. "When you do this and give them a little pressure a pulse of chronons will pass through the clear liquid that you can't see in their craniums. It will immediately scramble their CPU time. Their consciousness will simply cease to exist."

"That's it?" asked Dante.

"That's all it takes. They will be irrecoverable. But you have to understand this – as soon as we start the core will begin to register the depletion of its external processing units and will do something about it. I'll leave you to it now. Give me fifteen minutes to get to the core and start on that before you begin knocking them out.

She was gone before they could ask any questions.

It all sounded like a simple enough plan. None of them bothered to question what would happen if Metaquanta and the Priests were annihilated. They did not seem to consider what would happen in 3797 if Metaquanta no longer existed to protect them from the end of time. Maybe Beatrice knew the answer, but she hadn't said anything. There didn't seem to be any plan to manage their society if the Priests were no longer there to maintain order. What would happen to the exiles? Would they be allowed to go back to their previous homes? There were so many more questions left unresolved. Most important of all … what if they failed! Luther never mentioned a backup strategy in that eventuality.

They waited the full fifteen minutes before rushing from Priest to Priest sending the destructive pulse through their brains. Each one of them simply crumbled to the floor. No convulsions or lightning flashes in their heads – completely disappointing in not seeing them suffer – in not seeing them realise that this was the end of days for *them*. The whole process seemed all too clinical and detached. They made rapid progress climbing up the levels until they had almost reached the top before everything suddenly went dark.

"That'll be Beatrice. She must have managed to shut down the core operating system," suggested Luther.

But the emergency lights did not go on. "Stay where you are until Beatrice comes back out. Don't move, don't make a sound."

Priests who hadn't been shut down on the top most level didn't react. Dante had only moments ago got to their level with Luther and Gemma still working the level directly below. "Dante, where are you?"

"Hush!" Luther warned Gemma.

Too late.

Those two Security Priests scanning passengers at the docks did take notice of the four people heading towards the empty ferry. A quick check of timetables showed this particular ferry did not have another run scheduled for that day. It's normal schedule also did not permit it to go towards a forbidden destination.

Although the coup had in essence failed, nevertheless a great deal of disruption followed due to so many of Metaquanta's broadcast towers having been destroyed. The insurgents had managed to substantially weaken Metaquanta's network. Priests had been caught completely unprepared for such comprehensive civil unrest. They didn't have the training, the numbers or the weapons to deal with human beings completely out of control. However, two things gave them a slight advantage; the Priests were still connected in a planet wide network controlled by Metaquanta, although now compromised – and they had comprehensive surveillance systems, also connected and cross referenced within their Pastornet.

16

Bela Decides to Help Dante

Quintessence could do nothing but passively observe the fraying of the Ribbon, unaware of long term probabilities that had been started by the meeting between Beau and Bela.

There were forces at work beyond its control that had forced different rates of progression upon the flow of chronons as time continued to propagate. It had no control over actions taken by the human population on Keppler 22b, and in particular over their ability to divert particles of time within their segment, therefore causing a further imbalance. Nor did Quintessence have any influence over Beau when he succumbed to Anne's seduction in the house of Nostredame, thereby tearing a tiny fragment of the Ribbon from segment 2555 to patch into segment 1549. The Ribbon continued its disintegration, not yet definable as to which segment suffered the greatest unravelling.

Brummel and Pietro's visit to the laboratory didn't unsettle Beau at all. The situation was well under control. He had something they desperately wanted and as far as Beau was concerned that's exactly the way it would stay.

Work on the next stage of Zetaverse development had to progress. The technology had to be well tested before being made available to the pleasure seeking general public. For now he had those interviews to get through to get the Proxima-c miners' experiences in their own words.

"No more interruptions please Larry – and could you bring in the first volunteer."

A well padded muscular woman lumbered into the room. To describe her as buxom could not fail to justify the description. Confident, eager to engage in this new experience - a general characteristic of itinerant miners on remote planets who had taken the pleasure quest to extremes at every opportunity, given the imposed boredom inherent in living and working in confined, artificial habitats while mining in hostile environments.

"Mining on Prox-c may sound exciting to some people, given the dangers and dubious thrills," she announced, "but I don't mind telling you there's not much variety either in the work or the entertainment."

"Well - let's see if we can improve on that for you. You went rappelling while I was there and I took a neural recording of that for you. What we are going to try to do is give you the means to re-live that bit of fun without you having to physically go through it again, and also giving it a little extra spice. For now I want you to describe that experience in your own words. Leave nothing out – your observations, your feelings, apprehensions – anything at all that comes to mind, especially your feelings during the event."

Snow Flake; her colleagues nicknamed her that because of her imposing size and work location, launched herself into the exercise with zest. At first Beau encouraged her recollections with a few leading questions. Then as she started repeating herself he'd let his thoughts wander into places of far more interest to himself, letting the recording do the rest of the work.

Like for example; he thought of his own soon to be born son, Dante. Of course the boy would not live to see the 38th century, but that didn't mean Beau could just ignore the possibility that the Dante he met on Keppler 22b could turn out to be his son's descendant – his descendant. And if that was the case he simply had to do something to ensure the man's survival. A mind twisting thought to consider that he may have actually met his 49th generation grandson.

That desire naturally lead to something Quintessence had said; that there were still decisions to be made which would allow the next segment of the Ribbon to be revealed. Would they be his decisions? Or perhaps Bela's. Bela seemed particularly keen to get involved. On the other hand Quintessence did warn that other decision possibilities may terminate all probabilities. It did warn that this entire Time Loop Ribbon may be reaching full capacity.

"Hey! Boss man! You're not listening to me." Snow Flake had to shout at him to get his attention.

"Sorry, I was thinking of the next step with your story."

"I said - I'm finished. Do you want me to go over it again?"

"No - no. That was quite comprehensive - very good. We'll be in touch when the event is ready for you to re-live."

"I've got another shift in two weeks. Will it be ready before I have to leave?" She seemed most eager, probably because this whole experience was so different from all her routine stuff.

"No. Maybe a bit longer. We'll let you know."

As soon as she disappeared out of the lab Beau's thoughts picked up exactly where they left off. The woman had said nothing even remotely interesting. ... No. I don't believe time will end. I think Nostredame is right - If a man has knowledge of his future, his probable futures, could he not interrupt the flow of decisions that may lead him there and influence outcomes before it is too late? Nothing is inevitable he had said. Quintessence can take me there. He must be able to take both of us, Bela and myself. Surely there must be something we can do.

Beau remembered the precarious circumstances under which Quintessence had snatched him back from Keppler 22b the last time.

Quintessence – Quintessence – I need you.

I know. Dante is in danger. Do you want to go to him?

Bela – I want to talk to Bela first. Then I want you to take both of us.

Are you ready?

No! Wait. I must see Emma first.

He expected Emma would object. Little Dante could be born any day now. She wanted Beau at home with her for the birthing.

"How do I know how long you'll be gone? What if you – what if something happens to you and you can't come home?" She hadn't confided that worry to him before but with the birth so near ...

Beau paced up and down in their apartment. What could he do? Every time he had a problem Quintessence had been able to protect him, get him away from the danger. He felt he could really trust this – whatever it was. An idea flashed into his mind ... what if ... yes, that might help to settle Emma ...

Quintessence?
Are you ready now?
No. Wait. Can you connect with Emma?
Yes.
Wait, let me tell her.

"Beau – Beau, what are you doing? Again you're not listening to me."

"Quintessence says he can talk to you."

"Why?"

"It might make you feel better. He might be able to tell you what's going on when I'm – over there."

"Hmm. I don't know."

"Just relax and think of – nothing in particular."

Emma kept looking at him, unsure at first. It would be a pretty strange experience. She trusted Beau. Definitely nothing else like this had ever happened to her lifetime. She let her thoughts drift ... closed her eyes ... lay back on the couch ... automatically putting her hands protectively on her belly ...

Emma.
Quintessence?
Yes.
What are you?
I am learning that.
You must look after Beau.
Yes.
Are you sure?
Yes.
You will bring him back in time for the birth of his son?
Yes.
How do I know I can trust you?
I have brought him back every time. I have prevented him from getting damaged.
People don't get damaged. They can get hurt. Can I see you?
No.
Can you see me?
No. I can see your energy as it flows through time from instant to instant.
Bring him back! Promise.

Yes.

She opened her eyes when Quintessence didn't say anything else. "This is totally weird," she said, smiling. "This thing is so strange - even stranger when hearing him speaking with your voice."

"Yes, I'm slowly getting used to it."

"Are you going now? Where?"

"First, to talk to Bela." His hand went to Emma's belly, giving it a gentle rub.

I'm ready.

He'd been taken a few times now and each time the transition was instantaneous. No strange sense of falling or accelerating or diving through streaming lights. One moment at home, next instant at his destination. Neither did Emma see wisps of trailing smoke in his wake or hear zooming sounds. It was all too peculiar, too un-spectacular ... making the disappearance seem like it didn't happen at all.

*

"Beau! Stop running around like that up there. Come here immediately," called the voice of his mother. Beau liked his father's attic with all the interesting scientific and not so scientific equipment. He lingered a moment longer.

"Beau! Come down this instant!"

"Yes mother." He appeared at the top of the attic stairs. "There's a man up here," he shouted.

"Stop that shouting. What man?" She didn't see a man come into the house. Her husband and Bela had gone out again in the morning. She didn't expect them back till late. Another plague outbreak in a village some distance from them would keep the two physicians busy all day. Nostredame had asked Bela to return from Florence to help him with the increasing frequency of infections.

Young Beau poked his head back into the attic. "Who are you?"

"He's wearing really strange clothes, mother." Anne paled. "He says his name is Beau. Why does he have my name?"

"Get down here immediately."

As the boy jumped down the stairs two at a time Anne rushed past him into the attic stopping suddenly at the landing. Her hands went up to cover her mouth. "You!"

"You called the boy 'Beau'." Of all the things in the universe that boy would have to have been the last thing he expected to see ... yet another person with his name. A long minute of awkward silence ... Beau's mind became confused. He'd seen Anne's children the last time he was there, having supper with all of them in the kitchen – all six of them – none called 'Beau'. This boy did have Anne's red hair, yet he was much taller.

181

Before he could consciously consider other similar characteristics the boy had to himself the discrepancy in the apparent passage of time further confused him. How old was the boy? Maybe twelve, thirteen. And Anne seemed to have lost some of her vigour. The timing wasn't right. The boy could not possibly be his.

"You were gone so long," Anne suddenly exclaimed. "Thirteen years is too long to wait."

"You called him 'Beau'."

Anne glanced behind her, seeing the boy loitering in the kitchen. "Go outside Beau, fetch me some vegetables for tonight's meal." She held up her hand for the visitor to remain silent until her son had gone. "There are already so many children in this house Michel didn't take much notice of another one – always so busy with his writings or his patients."

"Is he – I mean, is he …"

"Yes – our son."

Quintessence!

You are confused.

What is all this?

The child probability arose on the night she came to you.

How can he be so old? I already have a son, ready to be born. They should be almost the same age.

The flow of time is outside my control. At the inception of this being you also began the unravelling of this Time Loop Ribbon. The warp and weft in its weave has had to accommodate a birth which was the product of a confluence between the future of this segment and the past of your segment. If he lives he will contribute to the fullness of this Ribbon.

Is that a problem?

Consider the prophesy. Consider the upheaval in segment 3790. Consider your decision to involve Bela with Dante. There is the possibility of managing probabilities. There may be other Ribbons looping through space-eternity. I have seen another probability … Anne's Beau may be the beginning of another Ribbon.

"Beau! Beau! You are not listening to me." Each time Beau interrupted a conversation with someone to connect with Quintessence his eyes glazed over, his ears becoming unreceptive to mundane reality. He may as well not have been in the same room with them. "You cannot tell Michel. You must not say anything to Beau. He is very bright, very inquisitive – loves solving mysteries. Be careful with him."

"You were waiting for me?"

Beau didn't know whether to apologise to Anne, or to congratulate her, or to embrace her, or to act as if the whole thing meant nothing to him at all. She saw all the conflicting emotions play out on his face. His animal magnetism still pulled at her desires. So much danger, so much she did not know about him. Yet she had waited. For many years she hoped he would suddenly appear again, not knowing what she would do if he did.

Quintessence had deposited him on the rug beside Michel's work bench; still the same rug, looking more tattered than he remembered. Thirteen years is a long time. Beau didn't dare move or say anything. Anne took the initiative to step close to him. Michel and Bela would not be back for many hours, and the boy had gone to market to fetch the vegetables. He felt his pulse begin to race. No joy-friend on Proxima-b had ever excited him as much as this woman from the past. He could smell her unique aroma; an hypnotic blend of odours of her century, her kitchen, her femininity as she raised two hands to his face.

Beau no longer thought about anything. He forgot where he was, when he was, why he was there. With her face so close he could feel her breath upon him. His body moved by itself, arms rising to embrace her.

Anne tilted her head slightly to one side, immense sadness coming across her eyes as she pushed him gently back.

"How can this be, my beautiful man from the stars? Tomorrow, or the day after you will be gone. Michel told me you were from another world. Another world …" she let the wistful words drift into the air.

Perhaps Beau didn't have the courage or the backbone or the self-control showed by Anne. People of his world cultivated immersion in self-indulgence not self-control. He was a product of his society. Anne lived in an age where survival was the highest priority in life. She would always do what had to be done, not necessarily what she wanted to do – like giving birth to his son. That had to be done.

She took her hands away from his face, turned to make her way down the stairs. "Are you coming? I suppose you came to see Michel or Bela," implying in her statement his complete lack of thought for her.

"Well – yes, but …"

She cut him off. "Don't apologise. You didn't know. Perhaps you had forgotten me." Beau began to say something else but she stopped him with a finger on his lips. They had stopped at the bottom of the stairs. He looked to his left at the door of the room where he once slept. That's when he felt the pain, the pleasure of the memory that had buried itself deep in his complicated life.

Maybe Anne wanted to feel his warmth just once more, unable to resist touching him. She let her finger rest on his lips for just a moment longer before turning away towards the table.

The intimate moment passed just as young Beau burst in the door, "We're back! I found father and uncle Bela on the way home."

Anne showed no surprise, bustling over to the boy to take the vegetables from him and to greet her husband. It gave Beau a chance to lose his guilty look. This is not how he imagined his meeting with Bela.

"Get away from me woman. I have not cleaned up yet," Michel warned. Bela followed behind him, actually spotting Beau before Michel did.

"Well, well. What brings you back. Did you forget to say something?" Beau began to respond, but again he was stopped. "Wait. Don't say anything. We have to go cleanse ourselves of the dead." The two men went out to the back of the house while young Beau planted himself in front of the stranger, putting his hands on his hips indicating an attitude of serious interrogation.

"Why do you have my name Sir?" Not at all shy he displayed the very characteristic his mother had alluded to.

"It's a French name, is it not? Common in France your mother tells me." That seemed acceptable. The boy knew his uncle's father's name as well as their family name. He would no doubt have asked many awkward questions if he found out 'Kobayashi' also belonged to this stranger.

"Where do you come from Sir? You wear strange clothes."

Beau glanced at Anne, getting the eye flash warning to be very careful. "I come from a land a long way away to visit your father and uncle again." He didn't want to play this game with his son anymore. *My son* – the thought seared into his thoughts. The strangeness of it all … that he could travel more than a thousand years into the past and have a child with a woman he knew nothing about. And now he was there again talking to the boy who should not have been as old as he was.

Bela and Michel walked back into the kitchen in the middle of his introspection. "Come, we can talk in the attic," Michel invited, quite comfortable this time with Beau having visited again.

"I see you have come more appropriately attired this time." Bela appeared to be angry with him, which showed in the next few words. "You tell us about a man – what was his name? Oh yes, Dante – who is in dire trouble. Then within minutes you disappear – for many years. Can I assume the problems have been resolved? I don't mind telling you how much the situation upset me at the time."

"This is as strange a turn of events in my life time as it must be for you. I am confused by many things, the least of which is the power that is able to move me through time. When I was here last you showed a considerable desire to help, Bela. Nothing has been resolved in his circumstances since then. Dante is in much more danger now. There has been a rebellion on his planet."

Bela and Michel had experienced far more unrest, battles and deaths in their life time than Beau could ever imagine. They were no strangers to rebellions, minor or bloody. Michel's writings were full of prophesies of unrest, wars and calamities of plagues and famines – some in the near future and some in the distant future. Some reaching as far as Dante on his world so remote from Earth in time and space.

Talk of such a simple thing as an insurrection didn't seem to have a huge impact on the two men seasoned to disasters. Beau continued. "I have come to ask you Bela if you still want to help Dante."

That definitely set a spark off in Bela. For the first few years after Beau's disappearance Bela couldn't get the situation out of his mind. Any though of oppression by unjustifiable politics or religious extremism boiled his blood. In fact, in the intervening years he'd got himself into considerable trouble with the leaders of Florence for his views, which were considered to be bordering on heresy and downright treason against the state. That was the very reason he initially had to escape Florence to find temporary refuge in the home of his long-time friend Nostredame.

"Yes - most definitely Yes! Obviously we have not been able to remove these base elements from the nature of humanity in our world. Perhaps it can be done on Dante's. What do I need? When do we go?"

Beau launched into giving Bela the details of what he'd experienced during the Adoration ceremony. Michel listened enthralled, writing everything down without interrupting and disturbing the flow of the narrative. Bela didn't show the same degree of patience. He didn't even ask if Beau's travel facilitator could bring them home again. Like a true revolutionary this man had no thought for his own personal safety. He had found a cause and he had to fight for it.

Something had been bothering Beau during his entire interaction with Bela. Virtually everything that had been happening to him since his blackout aboard *Celestial Pleasures* had been outside his control. Even having fathered a child with Anne seemed to be a spontaneous unrelated event amongst all the other coincidental things happening around him. The niggling uncertainty about his ancestry had to be resolved. Without going into the reasons he came straight out and asked the question. "Beau, do you have a family? I believe you have a son."

"Is that important? It has nothing to do with what ..."

"No, no – of course not. Just curiosity. I have a child you see, well almost – expecting it to be born any day now."

"Congratulations," came the rather flat response. "As a matter of fact I do have a boy back in Florence. He is with his mother and grandparents. I think he'll miss me." For the first time the possibility of his not returning crept into his thoughts.

"I can imagine he is well looked after. How old is he? What did you name him?"

"Now that I think of it, it's very strange – very strange indeed. Isabeau wanted to call him after my father – 'Beau'. His name is

185

Kobayashi Beau." Only for a moment he thought about the coincidence of the names but his thoughts had welded to internal images of his son and wife.

Now that he'd started thinking about his family his words just came rushing out. Completely oblivious to Beau's startled reaction he continued rattling on about how beautiful Isabeau was, and how clever his fourteen year old son was, and how he wanted to study medicine and the stars and everything scientific of their age.

Beau could no longer engage in the conversation. The shock was overwhelming. How in the universe can it happen that so many people had been called Kobayashi or Beau or both in the same name? How was it possible that he should somehow know of every one of them and have an actual link to each of them?

Quintessence! Now! Both of us.

17

Beau, Bela and Dante Meet

Apoxpalon's vision enlightened Quintessence to the possibility, perhaps the probability, that Dante's timeline would not end as predicted by Nostredame because the calculations of the Mayan shaman had cast a doubt on it.

The time had come for Quintessence to exercise its capacity to manage probabilities, the skills for which it had not yet fully mastered. Its interactions with Beau since connecting with him did highlight one important aspect of the mechanisms by which this Ribbon propagated itself – interconnected decision tendrils resulting from interactions regardless of which segment of the Ribbon they originated from. Quintessence believed that Xoco needed to be given greater context for understanding how the reality of this Ribbon progressed forwards, and how far into the future it could extend. And perhaps in the process Quintessence might be able to see beyond the future of the 3790th segment of the Ribbon.

*

Xoco's grandfather prepared him to take over the responsibilities of spiritual leader for their people through many years of instruction in the sciences of astronomy, mathematics and the mystic arts. Not long before Apoxpalon's death he gave the young man one last test to display the skills he'd acquired to be a shaman worthy of the respect of the King and his people ... 'Tell me when I can expect the end of my days.'

After having successfully carried out several calculations based on his understanding of the Long Count calendar, a difficult and intricate process, Xoco applied himself to the new task, albeit with considerable reluctance. He did not want to know when his grandfather would die, the only family left to him after the death of his father and not that long ago his mother. As much as such a delicate personal matter caused him pain Xoco understood the necessity for the continuity of shamanic support for his community. The date of his inauguration as the new shaman could not be set before the demise of the old man had been foretold. In essence it was not difficult to calculate the most likely probability of that. His shamanic abilities combined with the old man's obvious ailments could not fail to give a reliable estimation. Far more importantly, the validity of his divination would cement his qualification for the job ahead of him.

*

Quintessence heard Beau's urgent call, instantaneously deciding on the location, which did not match Beau's desire to be taken to segment 3790. That decision may have been its first instinctive act in managing probabilities.

Apoxpalon's hut seemed empty with only Xoco to occupy it. He had spent the last week in spiritual preparation for the ceremony that would make him the official Shaman. Fasting, withdrawing from public affairs and regular hallucinogen induced trances had left the young man weary. On this, the last day of his preparations he'd been in meditation for most of the afternoon. Without bothering to have supper he wanted to lie down to get as much sleep as possible before his pre-dawn rise to be decked out for the big occasion. Fire light and smoke filled the hut, Xoco only dimly aware of the environment around him as he began to doze off.

Two men appeared a step away from the bed Xoco sat on. None of his recent visions had the clarity of this apparition to which he raised his half closed eyes. He could see they were human in form. Full consciousness flooded him as he thought for an instant they might have been the Gods Cizin and Nohochacyum from the Underworld. *No, I am not dead. I have not travelled the path down to the cenote.* His hands touching his chest confirmed the substantiality of physical form, not of spirit. Xoco reached out towards the ghosts in front of him, electrified at being able to touch them. "Am I in a trance?" That thought dismissed immediately by the ability to ask it aloud.

"Who are you?" At last he could exert control of himself. Never had he shown any fear either of the metaphysical or physical world. Neither storms or earthquakes or any other acts of the Gods could frighten him. Perhaps prowling jaguars brought out caution rather than bravado or fear, for he was a sensible man. He stood and withdrew his hand, looking directly into the eyes of the taller visitor.

Beau's reaction at being dumped in an unfamiliar place, in such a dark and dirty hovel, made him angry. It appeared far more dismal than Nostredame's attic.

You were supposed to take us to Dante, he remonstrated without acknowledging that Quintessence had managed to transport both of them, not just himself alone.

Xoco, a Mayan shaman has seen into the future.

"Beau! Beau! Where are we?" demanded Bela. From everything Beau had told him he expected to see an ocean with large floating islands, not a grubby little hut out in a tropical forest. Beau introduced himself and Bela. Long silences followed short exchanges of information to establish basic realities. Xoco moved past them to put more wood on the fire, its rejuvenated light showing more clearly just how strange these two people were, each so oddly dressed that they could have been from two entirely different worlds - definitely not the world of the Mayans.

"I come from a land across the ocean," explained Bela, "my friend has visions like yourself. He has seen into the future, to a time when days would end – in 3797."

"You say he has seen the end of a cycle. Has he seen the creation of the start of the next series of Long Counts?"

Bela explained as best he could about the conflicts seen by Nostredame and that they would lead to an all consuming termination ... that he saw where this would take place; a land experiencing such deluges and deep submersions that scarcely would there be any land left not covered by water.

Xoco considered everything he heard. In his visions, or those of his grandfather there never arose the spectre of such great floods that the world would come near to destruction. Nor did the count of days mentioned coincide with his own calculations. The night had only just begun, time enough to explore the claims of these people, wherever they came from regardless if they were made of substance or pure spirit. If what they'd said could affect his people he had a duty to re-examine his previous calculations of near and distant cycles. He motioned for his visitors to remove themselves out of his way so he could settle in front of the calendar complex.

"I will do my calculations again. As the moon and the seasons change so there may be changes that I have not yet seen."

Bela and Beau sat by the fire. Neither understood the necessity for them to be in the midst of the Mayan civilization waiting for a shaman to confirm or deny either the reality they have come from or where they planned to go.

Beau spoke to Bela quietly, who seemed to be getting more agitated as the hours stretched into the night. "The force that has brought us here sees the universe in ways we can never understand. It has knowledge of your world and of mine. It has taken me to a place which is not our world, which sounds like the world of water seen by Nostredame. Let us hear what the shaman has to say."

"If we are destined to help this man Dante we should be there right now, not sitting in front of a fire enjoying its comforting warmth."

"I have no doubt Quintessence can take us to any point in the future it chooses. If we are destined to help Dante we will be there in time."

Xoco interrupted their quiet conversation. "Máak Eek'e', what is the year of your cycle?" he asked the Star-Man, not at all surprised that they gave years so far apart from each other, and returned to his calculations. The differing dates of his results were an indication of just how fluid the future could be, notwithstanding the effect of the chronons displacement factor partly due to the use of the chronon pulse pads on Keppler 22b during the fighting.

*

It may be possible for Xoco to calculate the outcomes of decisions made and decisions interfering with each other. It may even be possible to conceive of probabilities arising out of streams of decisions all flowing in the same direction. I have learnt how to understand the jigsaw puzzle pieces of such complex interactions. However, I cannot foresee what decisions each individual will make at any point along the Ribbon. At each decision node the options taken could clarify or obscure the future. By taking Beau and Bela to Xoco they may gain an appreciation of the consequences of their intended actions to become involved with Dante. I must not influence any decisions they may make, Quintessence realised.

*

Metaquanta's underground facility suddenly went dark soon after the four revolutionaries; Beatrice, Dante, Luther and Gemma had infiltrated it and almost completed destroyed the Priests who had been plugged in for major operating system upgrades. Beatrice had managed to get to the core – Dante made it to the top level of Priests with Luther and Gemma one level below him. Gemma failed to heed Luther's warning to remain quiet and still. When she called out for Dante it gave their presence away in the darkness.

Those two Priest Security guards following a crowd who'd disembarked from an inter-island ferry noticed four strangers walking briskly to the ferry. A schedule check showed no further ferry runs for the day. Why would the strangers be going to the empty ferry? A search on the Pastornet quickly identified them. Each of their expected locations for that day and for that time of the day differed from where they actually were.

It became most unlikely that Beatrice had managed to disable Metaquanta, for Luther counted twenty three Priests moving towards them as the light came back on inside the cube. Overcome by sheer numbers Luther signalled Gemma and Dante not to resist. Several Priests split away heading in Beatrice's direction. Luther realized she could not have managed to slay the beast, already putting his mind to alternative courses of action. If they could not extricate themselves from this predicament the future didn't look as promising as to be simply exiled. The most expedient repercussions for them only had two alternatives; either become compost to enrich their market gardens' soil, or worse … smart brain implants, in which case they would forget who they were, still continuing with their work in their respective areas of expertise without the ability for self-determination. They might as well be compost if that happened.

The Priests gathered their captives in the centre of the cube. They were not restrained while the Priests went into a silent conference, quite possibly with Father One or Metaquanta itself. A very slim hope existed - if any. Three other Priests walked behind Beatrice as they brought her in to join the gathering.

Luther raised a questioning eyebrow, to which Beatrice shook her head. All for nothing. All those people who had sacrificed their lives would not have died unnecessarily were it not for those two alert Security Priests at the Ferry dock. Such a simple, unforeseeable detail that had so completely ruined their attempt for freedom. The many years of planning, recruitment and living their lives in constant danger of being discovered had gone to waste.

Luther took the chance to throw meaningful eyes at Dante and Gemma. It took a few moments for them to realise that he had been alluding to the chronon pulse pads still attached to their fingers. The effect of the pulse from these was instantaneous. If only they could knock out a few of the closest Priests first they might be able to overcome the others by force.

In very little time it seemed the decision about their futures had been made. One of the Priests faced Luther first.

Speaking in the voice of Father One that Dante recognised, he asked the two questions so nonchalantly as to suggest he didn't care whether Luther answered or not, or what the answer was going to be. Perhaps that was the case, for Metaquanta had other means of extracting information, which were somewhat more involved than asking a simple direct question. "Why are you doing this? Who else is working with you?"

Luther remained silent. Anything he said would have been analysed for veracity, voice intonation, corresponding blood pressure changes, hormonal secretions and a range of other bio-electrical and chemical indicators ... all input used to try and predict his next action.

Getting no response the Priest turned to ask Gemma the same question. She did exactly the same as Luther. Then the idiot Priest turned to Dante with the same questions in exactly the same order, the same volume, the same detached voice. Perhaps they couldn't compute that humans all had ears and could hear what was asked the first time.

In that moment of silence while the Priest waited for an answer Luther made his move. He dived at the Priest nearest to him, managing to send a charge through its uncovered head. The sudden move motivated Gemma and Dante, both successful on the first attempt, with Beatrice tripping the one nearest her to the ground and twisting its head off. In the ensuing scuffle, still outnumbered by the Priests they lost the battle but in the process took a few out of circulation.

Of the prisoners Dante was the tallest, bulkiest and strongest. It took several Priests to hold him, though only for a moment.

Quintessence, ever watchful of his small troop of beings, decided it was time to satisfy Beau's request to bring the three Kobayashi together. Four Priests stood moments later with nothing between them to hold onto. Dante had disappeared.

In that moment he called out to his sister-in-spirit, the sound of which started on a small atoll in the seas of Keppler 22b and died away in a small Mayan hut on Earth.

Xoco had turned back to his calculations only a moment ago when another unsolicited visitor arrived in the hut to disturb the peace with his cry. Very rarely did anyone visit his hut for to the general population of the city he was someone to be feared almost as much as the Gods. He looked up at the new arrival, again taking note of his attire. *All the Gods of the universe must want to have a conference right here in my home this night.* That was the extent of his reaction so intent had he become on resolving the mystery of what may turn out to be a major upheaval in the chaos of existence effecting not just these Gods, but his own people.

Dante's eyes needed a moment to adjust to the darkened interior of the hut, recognising Beau as he scanned the room looking for the Priests.

"Kobayashi Beau!" he exclaimed in surprise, standing a few steps away from Beau, no longer surrounded by Priests restraining him.

"Dante!" On impulse Beau hugged the man then held him at arm's length.

Quintessence, you surprise me. This is not what I had in mind. We will have to return to Keppler 22b and take Bela with us.

Yes. For now listen to Xoco.

Beau didn't know why he hugged Dante again. Perhaps in the intervening period since last seeing him he had come to the conviction about his close relationship with this man, despite the number of years and distance that separated them.

"Dante, I would like you to meet Bela, the man I spoke to you about. He has come from a very long time ago to help you."

For a few silent moments the two men looked at each other, feeling deep, deep down a connection none could have expressed. "You are Kobayashi Bela, yes? I am Kobayashi Dante."

At that point Bela and Dante turned to Beau. In that instant they needed no further proof, other than each other's presence to know what perhaps could never be proven. "Great Grandfather!" Dante breathed the words to Beau into the silence of the firelight darkness.

"Great Grandfather," repeated Beau to Bela.

The impact of their enlightenment was broken only for a moment by Xoco who had taken very little notice of Dante's arrival.

"Star-Man Beau, the year of your cycle is 2555, but it is not of this world. What is your star?"

"Come outside, I will show you."

The four men, each from a different segment of the Ribbon loop looked up into the same sky that each were familiar with from their own home. "That is my star," said Beau pointing in the direction of Alpha Centauri.

"You are also a Máak Eek'e'. Show me," Xoco asked Dante, not at all overwhelmed by the incredible nature of the meeting, or the very odd physical appearance of the man. Dante indicated the location of Keppler 22, then added, "My year cycle is 3790."

Xoco returned inside his hut with the new information to complete his calculations, leaving the others outside. None of his previous results matched what Nostredame had foreseen, nor his own previous dates for the start of the next series of Long Counts. He realised that if Earth was not the centre of the universe then the calendar complex he used had to be recalibrated. On the spur of the moment he did not consider the monumental implication that the Earth was not the centre of the universe, as all Mayans believed.

Beau, Bela and Dante stood close facing each other, generations of the same genetic line separated by so much history they could not begin to fathom. For the moment their thoughts drifted away into the depths of the night sky. The greatest impact no doubt felt by Bela, for he was the man from Earth, still on Earth, confronted by events that would have confounded the mind of any ordinary man. Knowledge in all disciplines was undergoing an unprecedented surge during the Renaissance of his time. The mind of man had begun to open to the reality of existence - all men it seemed except that of the men of Faith. *This is why Dante needs help. The Dark Ages have descended upon his people.*

Bela asked Dante, "Tell me of your struggle. If you will permit me I want to help."

"Grandfather Bela - it is so strange for me to say this. I don't know what science or what magic has brought us together. Overjoyed as I am to be with you, right now I must be with my sister-in-spirit. I must return to my home. Our God, or at least what our people believe to be a God, is thought to be the instrument to bring about the end of our time at the conclusion of the next seven years. I don't know if this is true. But Metaquanta must be stopped. It is only a machine. It controls all our lives. Many have come to have such strong Faith in him that they can no longer believe in themselves … they are not permitted to believe in themselves."

"I want to help. What you say is so familiar to me. Religion in my time has taken control. There was a man in whom I found inspiration, his name is Luther, Martin Luther." Dante caught his breath at the mention of this name, wild imaginings almost taking hold of his thoughts. "He was exiled and persecuted because of his opposition to our Church leaders. He believed reason not faith should inform the purpose of existence. He fought against the tyranny of religious control."

Beau remained silent while his ancestor and his descendant came together in a common understanding, in a common desire. He felt the moment would come very soon when they would have to leave the shaman's hut. There must be a reason why Quintessence had brought them all here to this peculiar young man who seemed not in the least awed by the strangeness of the gathering.

Dante urged Bela to continue. "Tell me more about this other Luther. I also want to learn about the man called Nostredame who could look into the future. This man must be in some way connected to Metaquanta. How else would our sham God know of the date 3797 and hold us all hostage to our fear of the end of all days." Beau began to feel superfluous in the story unfolding before him. He saw with a new understanding the superficiality of the world humanity had created on Proxima-b. The utter uselessness of living for nothing more than the hunt for pleasure in ever increasing spirals of intensity – himself being a driving force within that machine by the work he was doing for Playback Inc. And yet in the labyrinth of time he had given life to a son whose descendant he believed now stood beside him. As he thought about his little Dante inevitably Anne came to mind. *What of that little thirteen year old Beau ... also my son. What does the future hold for him?*

"It is one thing, yet it is another." Xoco appeared from the hut, the night having progressed to hint at dawn. "This is what you have come to hear from me ... an answer to time. It cannot be given. The spirits that move the heavens in their never ending cycles cannot give me what you seek. You, and you and you and yet another," he said pointing to each individual from a different Long Count cycle, "are causing perturbations in the flow of eternity. Until you decide – until you act, there is no definition." Xoco appeared extremely concerned. It could only be a result of his failure to conclude the calculations. Within an hour he would have to begin preparations to become the Shaman to succeed Apoxpalon. How could he accept such a position of responsibility if he could not 'see', if he could no longer rely on the calendar.

"My grandfather died a contented man because I was able to tell him the day of his passing. You must leave now, discontented. There is no ending that I can see for this Long Count cycle, nor an ending to the next. It is not 3797. It may or may not be 4772 for this Earth or for your star Beau Star-Man, or for your star Dante Star-Man."

Quintessence waited for the shaman's enlightened insight before looking into the future of the Ribbon again, searching for a segment beyond 3797. Where previously it could see nothing at all this time decision tendrils showed misty possibilities. Xoco's calculations were in fact correct to show uncertainty. The actions of these three men would decide the length of Ribbon to the next Long Count termination and the new beginning. Nothing had changed on Keppler 22b to make a difference, for the insurrection had so far failed to supplant Metaquanta's rule.

Neither Beau or Dante questioned Xoco's conclusion. Although somewhat obtuse the Shaman's words made it quite clear that in some way much depended on what the three of them would do next. Xoco wanted to tell them about another influence that had arisen in Beau's very recent past, almost fourteen years ago according to his observations, which was destined to affect future time-lines.

Just as suddenly as these visitors had appeared in his life, they vanished leaving the Shaman to reconsider their entire chronology, including their recording methods. A new Calendar had to be devised to account for celestial bodies other than the Earth. His own concepts of Gods and realities needed deep contemplation.

His inauguration assistant arrived just as the visitors departed. The King could not be kept waiting. Whatever Xoco's misgivings or doubts might have been far more people relied on him that day and in the future than just those three spirits.

18

Rescue

On a planet that is just slightly larger than Earth, with eighty two percent of it covered in water the few habitable landmasses and atolls stretched across the oceans long distances from one another.

Limbo Atoll island had a self-sustaining population of a little over four thousand exiles. It contributed nothing to the welfare of the rest of the planet's people or the Priests. It's remoteness and it's unimportance made it an ideal place to secret away fugitives. Although officially an exile community its residents had withdrawn themselves only from Metaquanta's influence, in its place setting up a comprehensive independent communication network with other exile centres around the planet.

Held captive at the entrance to the cube Luther, Beatrice and Gemma had resigned themselves right at the beginning of their plans to the worst thing that could happen to them if they were caught. And they had been captured in the worst imaginable location, right in Metaquanta's lair. Their co-conspirators would in all likelihood not have known where they were, and even if they did there was no chance to get to them before the inevitable rapid counter operation by the Priests.

Priests never showed emotions, for it was something they did not possess. Those in the cube acted as if Dante had never existed, expressing no reaction to his disappearance. He no longer mattered. Those of them that had been neutralised during the entire event were left where they had fallen. They too might never have existed. It would have been nonsensical to expect any AI to show any degree of empathy for their own kind - Priests did not possess that faculty either.

"That way." One of the Security Priests blandly indicated where their captives should go, with a shove on their backs to get them moving. Luther knew they would not be exhaustively questioned or tortured; a highly inefficient process peculiar to human being behaviour. With uncooperative captives Priests simply followed protocol to the next step ... neural interrogation. After that something akin to a comprehensive lobotomy that would leave them alive and reduced to complete docile servitude.

In the operating theatre Luther tried to talk to Beatrice and Gemma, at least to say good-bye as they were ushered to the dissection platforms.

"Silence," advised one of the Priests. It was neither a command nor a request - just a statement carrying the full expectation of compliance. Resistance would achieve nothing.

"Luther," Beatrice called to her brother-in-spirit."

"Silence. You will not be instructed again."

The Priest was entirely correct, for at the next instant the three captives transitioned out of his sight to another location, somewhat less worrying. Limbo Atoll island's population had just increased by an additional three souls, added to the recent previous unexpected arrival of three other men.

"Dante!" Gemma threw herself at Dante the split second she saw him.

"Don't ask. I don't know how Beau does this," Dante said.

"I don't do anything. It's Quintessence. He's getting better at it. When he first contacted me he couldn't transport me physically, only mentally. Now it seems he's become a regular – what would you call it – Ferryman – yes … a cosmic Ferryman."

Beatrice had moved to Luther's side utterly relieved at their escape, energised to retaliate immediately. He didn't waste energy on an emotional outburst. Having her near him was enough to strength his resolve as well.

"There is no time to waste. We must attack again. They will not be expecting it," he said, "we must concentrate our remaining forces on Metaquanta's atoll." He obviously didn't need time to recover from the imminent loss of his life, unlike Gemma who still clung to Dante. It took a few minutes for Luther to register the presence of a stranger - he'd already met Beau. "Can he be trusted?" he asked tilting his head in Bela's direction.

Beau answered for Dante. "This man has come from Earth, from the year 1549. He sacrificed a great deal to come to you, without any guarantee of being able to return to his family. Bela believes he can help. He's a friend of Nostredame, the astrologer who first wrote about 3797. We also have encouraging information from an oracle."

It was only then that Luther took stock of the situation. His resources had been badly depleted by the first attack on all the Temple Islands. The four of them had failed again to complete Metaquanta's deactivation. Any help, no matter how exotic might be useful. Limbo Atoll officials had quickly gathered around this group of six individuals. The leader of the community stepped forward having recognised Luther.

"I know you, Idris isn't it?"

Chief Idris welcomed the opportunity to be of assistance even if they could not become directly involved in the insurrection. Their small remote population had not been able to contribute to the effort so far, partly because of their isolation. Any loss of human resources from their small community would have had major consequences to their survival. "Luther come quickly, get out of sight in case skimmers come looking for you. We heard what happened."

"Do you have an airlift? Can you get it ready for us? I also need to get in touch with some of our people on Palm Atoll. As for you Dante, where on Keppler did you disappear to? For that matter … how did we all get here? Luther's brain already worked overtime trying to unravel the intricacies of the peculiar situation that had arisen around him. He very much doubted if Metaquanta had developed an instantaneous method of translocating his captives. He definitely would not have given them their freedom.

Dante explained the complicated route of their travels, not forgetting to emphasize their escape being engineered by Beau's special friend. "We didn't stay on our planet. We went to Earth back to the time of Nostredame and his prediction, one of which has been driving Metaquanta's logic circuits. We haven't been able to work out how that came about but apparently it is not immutable. Bela came here with us from Nostredame." At that stage in the proceedings Luther didn't need to know about the special relationship between Beau, Bela and Dante.

"So you are Luther. I met a man like you once. I hope your fate is better than his turned out," cut in Bela.

Luther listened more attentively as Bela told him about Nostredame's vision concerning the contentious date – also about the man called Luther carrying 'lightning' in his hands in a battle and how this man fought to prevent the 'end of time upon the heavens', a man who did not believe that priests or their leader should be the ultimate religious authority. Luther took it all in, in spite of his rising incredulity. Astounding as the tale was it would not help the situation they were in, and he said as much to Bela.

"That's all very interesting. It seems history is repeating itself. But that is of no help to us right now, right here."

"We also visited an oracle who had the ability to calculate the dates of major events in human history. There is no cataclysmic event in the year 3797 or any other event leading up to it that cannot be prevented."

"That at least is reassuring." Luther had already convinced himself and all those who followed him that the future depended on what people did and not on the dictates of someone nobody even knew - somebody they had never even seen. Some people had been so conditioned by Metaquanta's incessant misinformation that they didn't even think of questioning the reality of their imminent future. For others, who could not overcome the shipboard colonisation culture of compliance simply accepted everything as if that was how life was meant to be. If the power struggle did not succeed in his favour Luther could not imagine the kind of world the children of his planet would inherit.

It would be possible to gather a much larger resistance force than those involved in the initial insurrection. To do that he needed the help of his converts as well those who were already discontented but lacked the initiative so far to become actively involved.

From another underground communication facility on Limbo Atoll Luther re-established contact with his commanders through Idris's global network. The experimental chronon pulse pads worked as well as their trials had indicated.

A single short pulse was enough to terminate a Priest. He ordered enough to be manufactured to supply the majority of the dissidents. That and surprise would give them the greatest advantage. But there could be no delays.

"Bela, if I can get you to Metaquanta's core are you willing to speak to my people. Will you tell them what you know? Will you tell them there is a future beyond 3797?"

This middle aged physician had seen his share of life threatening situations quite aside from the ravages of the Bubonic plague he had to deal with regularly. He'd experienced the emotional upheaval created by the Church of his time and the inhuman coercive methods used by its hierarchy to get people to conform to the Church's concepts of universal reality. "Of course I will. I want to do everything I can. Injustice is just that, regardless where it is perpetrated." Unfortunately, or perhaps fortunately, he had no idea of the kind of danger he would be putting himself in. He didn't even know if Beau's magic friend could take him home after all this ended. Nor had he had a chance to get any confirmation from Nostredame that Xoco's calculations had any correlations with his own visions beyond that which he'd already recorded. So all in all a great deal of uncertainty faced Bela.

He took Beau aside, "Isabeau and my son," he began with concern about his son's descendants, "especially Beau ..."

"It would appear, from where I'm standing at this very moment that he has lived to contribute to the Kobayashi line," he smiled at Bela hoping his words were of some comfort, although it did nothing to reassure him of his own future.

"They will not expect us Luther. They don't think like we do. They can only react. Unless there is an existing pattern of many individual past events they cannot extrapolate to create a basis for pre-emptive action. Even the Security Priests are limited memory machines. This is our only chance. They have never had to deal with what we are doing to them now."

"I agree Beatrice. That's settled then. Idris – any of your people want to come along? I expect there'll be fighting and a whole lot more."

Within a short couple of weeks reinforcements and weapons had arrived in dribs and drabs at the atoll. Aboard three large airlifts, each carrying at least forty three people, the first wave of the second attack force skimmed over the surface of a choppy sea towards Metaquanta's horseshoe atoll. Along the way they picked up extra chronon pulse pads from another manufacturing atoll run by the exiles. Luther's commanders on strategic habitat islands had been warned to be ready but not to engage with the Priest Security personnel until they could definitely see that hitherto neutral people had decided to join them. This had to be an all-out effort.

By this stage of the unfolding events Beau had completely lost track of time. He could have been absent from home for days, or many weeks. This did not seem to concern Bela, he'd become too focused on what he saw as his one man crusade. He could understand the concept of crusades ... they had been a constant reality of his time.

Quintessence had failed to respond each time Beau tried to contact it while he was on Keppler 22b getting ready for the final attack. This had not happened before. He tried to console himself with the hope that his child to Emma would be born and she would be there to look after him, raise him - without him if that was his fate. For surely his son would survive. That must be the case if the man now sitting next to him existed. Although no conclusive proof had yet been found everything seemed to point to the fact that this Dante was his son's descendant, and therefore his son would come into existence, whether his father was there to see it or not. He promised Emma he would not be gone for long ... could he keep that promise? Perhaps Quintessence could take him back to the moment just before he left, before his son was due to be born.

With Quintessence's intervention the flip from Metaquanta's atoll to Limbo Atoll took no more than a moment, far less tiring than the hours already spent in the airlift having to almost circumnavigate the planet. Luther had already been awake for a while when they finally arrived. He had to wake everyone else to prepare them for disembarkation. Even Bela fell asleep after marvelling at how people could fly like a bird through the air. As a man of science he didn't fear the technology. He saw the potential of taking the knowledge back to Florence if only he could understand any of the theory explained to him by Luther. He even fantasized about Leonardo's reaction to such an incredible achievement, if only Leonardo had still been alive ... *Perhaps Beau's friend could take me back to show Leonardo these flying machines ... ...*

All three airlifts in close formation skimmed across the calm waters of the atoll to the inside curve of the horseshoe where they first found the entrance. All three groups made their way to the front of the cave, unsurprisingly finding no resistance ... as per Beatrice's insights. Luther took two groups inside with him, including Bela, Dante, Gemma and Beau.

"I want one group to remain around this lift. The rest of us will go down into the tunnels leading to the core. You last lot coordinate with the group outside guarding the cave entrance."

These Priests were not fighting machines, and in the true sense of the word neither were they 'thinking' machines. At best they carried within their network nothing more than sets of instruction architecture. Luther relied on this understanding; so if any of them actually turned up when the action started they would only be capable of carrying out prior instructions, without the initiative component to act independently of their programming. If they had a sufficient force in numbers that could still be a considerable problem, as proven by the first failed expedition into this God's unholy grotto.

19

Quintessence Prepares

Possibilities became probabilities. Possibilities did not need management, nor did inevitabilities. These probabilities definitely did.

Quite early in its association with Beau, Quintessence realised some of the dangers inherent in the train of events it and Beau had set off. There would be consequences to upsetting the momentum in the Ribbon. Going back in time and interacting with past causes would never happen in a neutral bubble. Some consequences might wither on the tree of possibilities. Other acts might impact on the future beyond the capacity of the actor to comprehend – such as Beau fathering a child with Nostredame's wife. Probabilities arising from that would have to be faced and eventually managed. If the predetermined circumference of a Time Loop Ribbon should be in danger of overfilling because the past flowed beyond its given capacity it either had to cease to exist as per a variety of predictions, or a way had to be found to extend it. The possibility of that had also been foreseen by a most unlikely source.

Such weighty matters could not be dealt with in an impromptu ad hoc manner. Too many contributing factors needed to be considered. And who had the ability to do this – to think on the macro scale, then to act accordingly?

Quintessence witnessed Luther's preparations to overcome Metaquanta's rule. For the people of the planet of that era no doubt it would have been a most welcome outcome to be freed from the tyranny of a machine. Success came with the likelihood of existence continuing beyond 3797 – only a possibility, not yet a guarantee. Quintessence withdrew to consider the bigger picture, drifting beyond the Milky Way to gain a perspective that had been clouded by close proximity to the insignificant warring life forms it had become involved with.

Once again Quintessence lost itself in contemplations of its own existence. How did that come about? Had it always existed before change brought it to self-awareness? What possible purpose could a cluster of dark energy serve? Had its attention, drawn to Beau, been the random workings of a universe bursting with possibilities some of which had no choice but to actualize?

The impact and importance of imponderables diminished as Quintessence once again became a part of the greater cosmos. Human beings and their little problems were such a localized, parochial phenomenon. In the absence of interventions predetermined inevitabilities would have run their course without sending out the slightest disturbing ripple into space-eternity. In the past Quintessence had witnessed random acts of creation without becoming consciously aware of them happening. Now it had knowledge of itself ... it had participated in bringing about change ... it had been complicit in the creation of a new human energy. As well as that, without it's willing participation, events on Keppler 22b would be taking a different route to resolution.

It had become involved in changing the course of time itself within the confines of the Local Group of galaxies. No longer a passive spectator, but an active participant in the act of constant creation ... that of the creation of a new future. In that instant it glimpsed a possible meaning to its own existence that had eluded it since its naissance.

That realization changed the universe from which Quintessence had coalesced into sentience. Solutions to complicated problems it had helped to create appeared around itself, filling space-eternity with possibilities that had not existed before. New Time Loop Ribbons appeared drifting aimlessly, each independent of the other, each a different length. Existence for some manifestations of baryonic matter destined to be longer than for others. Some so short as to accommodate the lifespan of a single living being – others so long as to encompass the birth and death of a star.

Quintessence reaffirmed a decision it had already made; to remain in the proximity of Beau's Ribbon to help fulfill the thread of probability it had helped to create. At one stage in the unfolding of events it had thought Beau could never do anything to disrupt the flow of time. That had already happened. This Ribbon must inevitably break, the unmistakable signs for it had already appeared ... an unacceptable eventuality that could lead to the unravelling of more than just a single Ribbon of Time.

Every decision made by Luther and Bela impacted on when the end of days would come for Dante's civilisation. Those decision clusters had become concentrated on events unfolding at Metaquanta's atoll stronghold. Quintessence returned to observe, knowing that a critical moment would surely arrive needing its intervention. It tried again to see beyond the segment 3797 barrier, which remained as cloudy as it had been before. And yet there must be something there else Xoco the Mayan Shaman could not have calculated it.

Quintessence had focused its vision too far into the future, too far away from the imminent effects of causes at that point in time. It did not foresee what would happen to one of the three men from the past and the subsequent consequences. Any physical altercation carried with it the probability of injury to greater or lesser degree. Circumstances at the atoll could only lead to violence. Neither the Priests nor Luther's forces could have prepared for the unprecedented nature of a conflict that could have only one outcome.

20

Father One

Well before Kobayashi Beau was born Proxima-b society had already fragmented into two ideological factions.

The Hedonist philosophy which arose on board the colony ships that departed Earth, had for a time been subjugated to the necessity for survival on a new planet. When the struggle to survive no longer gave life its fundamental meaning something had to replace it to prevent the new civilization from imploding upon itself. Indulgence in the pleasures of life, simple daily pleasures and eventually the insatiable fulfillment of every other pleasure imaginable became the goal of existence on board the ships and later on the new world.

A minority decided there had to be more to life. These people believed that their ancestors didn't leave Earth only to evolve into an ultra-decadent species with no thought for anything other than themselves. What about the greater universe around them? What about God?

Inevitably, another armada of seven ships eventually departed carrying a layer of society that wanted more than life could offer them on Proxima-b … their new destination; Keppler 22b, a warm water world a very long way away. It would take the colonists many generations to travel the distance between the two planets. Such an undertaking inconceivable even a hundred years prior to the venture. The journey would define the meaning of life itself before the descendants of the original colonists arrived at their destination.

Who can foretell the future when speeding through space between stars? Who would have the courage to even try? The human organism did not possess the longevity to maintain continuity during such an enterprise. The people needed help they could rely on. Computers and robotics could outlive people the same as machines. They could be programed purely for the benefit of humanity of course as people could not be to carry out all functions essential for survival. They were not fallible like the human mind. And yet it may have been possible to get some idea of the consequences that would ensue from depending far too much on technology.

Perhaps the Captains of the armada should have questioned their own decision to place their entire welfare in the hands of just one super theory-of-mind-level computer, with a large contingent of biomechs to carry out its instructions … in fact one for every three passengers of the thousand human souls aboard each ship.

The human body and human mind evolves over time all by itself without external assistance. Not so the case with machines. Through their lack of wisdom, concentrating only on making life more endurable for the many generations coming into existence during the voyage the humans enhanced the sophistication of the machines. Life became completely dependent on them as they became more comprehensively involved in every facet of on-board existence. One AI machine in particular was allowed to become the dominant controller. It seemed the most logical solution to factionalisms developing aboard individual ships, an inevitable deterioration of human society once it surpasses the critical population threshold for amicable co-existence.

The subtle change from a partnership in survival with the AI controller to dependency upon it, leading to its domination over the colonizing humans took centuries. As long as the mega brain was allowed to manage every aspect of life and everyone followed the rules, not only survival but a good life was assured on the ships of the fleet.

Transitioning from ship to planet went smoothly. The mega brain, which came to be known as Metaquanta looked after the people, for that was what it had been programmed to do. It understood the needs of other intelligent entities, could discern emotions, beliefs and to a small, predictable extent the thought processes of the humans based on past behaviour patterns. However, the principal AI still needed large quantities of historical data for cross-referencing and correlating in order to fully function to the benefit of its growing society of dependent colonists.

From amongst its army of smart biomechs Metaquanta had created an intermediary; its primary AI, which the people called Father One, well before their arrival on the planet. When peoples' reliance on Metaquanta became absolute whilst still aboard the ships of the fleet their allegiance naturally shifted from their previous God. That God of the ancients had remained aloof and unresponsive as always. The new entity, although as enigmatic to the people as the old one seemed to actually hear and respond to their concerns with actions. To Metaquanta it made no difference what the people believed as long as they followed the rules. The intermediary, Father One, did have a major limitation which interfered with its ability to provide a bridge between the people and their new God; a lack of empathy. However, it did efficiently control the biomechs who became the Priests to ensure peoples' welfare. These, that were once they nothing more than dumb biomechs with the ability to respond to commands and specified stimuli became the most visible day-to-day element representing security and survival. Neither the ordinary Priests or the Security Priests had been given autonomy. They were only capable of executing the commands of Metaquanta through Father One. They did not respond to any command uttered by a real person unless the request fell within the parameters of their programed functions to 'serve'.

Following the first attempted coup on Keppler 22b Metaquanta required data on which to base action to restore order.

Time did not appear to be a factor in the functioning of its logic circuits to resolve the problems. No precedent existed on which to prioritize corrective action into the urgent category.

Metaquanta: task: Input data on number of dissidents involved in aberrant behaviour.

Father One: Priests are preparing statistics.

Metaquanta: task: Define expected time of upload.

Father One: .0275862 days

Metaquanta: task: Define damage at core installation.

Father One: Zero damage to core. 123 Priest units irretrievably deactivated.

Metaquanta:

task 1: Goto Priest production facility.

task 2: Assume control of Priest units manufacture.

task 3: Produce replacement units.

task 4: Identify human insurrection control unit.

task 5: Apprehend malfunctioning human control unit.

Father One: Human control unit escaped apprehended status. Location undefined.

Metaquanta: task: Apprehend subsidiary malfunctioning control units.

Father One: Human subsidiary units escaped apprehended status. Locations undefined.

Metaquanta:

task 1: Repair transmission towers.

task 2: Input subsidiary relational data contributing to aberrant behaviours.

Father One: Report received from human unit Dante. Identified behaviours on Temple Island 461 do not correlate with historical problematic behaviour patterns.

Metaquanta: Apprehend human Dante unit.

Father One: Human Dante unit escaped apprehended status.

Metaquanta: Process all deactivated human units into compost.

Father One: Process has been initiated.

The last activity carried no reprisal or punitive overtones. It had been standard procedure aboard the ships to process all inoperative organic life forms into resources to maintain the living. Obviously, that super theory-of-mind-level computer found no reason to change the procedure just because they were no longer aboard interstellar space ships.

Father One could only act on commands given. He had no instruction sets that would enable him to act on his own volition except within highly constrained guidelines. Consultation with lower level

210

Priests could not help him. They could not accurately be called Artificial Intelligence level automatons. The very concept of 'consultation' had not been programmed into Father One or the Priests. They did not have the capacity to help resolve the mystery of aberrant, illogical human behaviour.

It appeared at first that apart from the inconvenience resulting from the destroyed physical communication infrastructure Metaquanta could not initiate the logic routines to arrive at an analysis that would have indicated the insurrection to be a serious threat. It could not process either the data that created the unique event for it did not exist, or extrapolate on likely outcomes from that single occurrence.

Dialogue between Metaquanta and Father One continued for some time. Father One could gather and manage the data-feed. He had no capacity to interpret the latest data harvest on human behaviour. That single human unit, Dante, whose job specifically entailed interpretation of mass human patterns of behaviour could not be found. There were other human units carrying out similar functions, but none could do it as efficiently and comprehensively as the Dante unit. In the absence of that information and both Father One's and Metaquanta's lack of programmed capacity to recognize the meaning of out-of-pattern behaviour Metaquanta could not formulate a defense strategy. Their only ability was to react. In the past Metaquanta easily eliminated digital virus anomalies. They were internal to its network, identifiable, accessible and capable of deletion. Human deviant patterns, which should have been recognizable as external viral behaviour were without precedent. During the final stages of the exodus from Proxima-b the human population acted in concert towards one common goal; survival. They exhibited no anomalous patterns of behaviour amongst themselves or towards their AI controllers even at the conclusion of the journey. The very existence of Metaquanta's rule during the voyage prevented such behaviours. They did nothing that could not be linked to that one imperative - survival. Their latest and violent activities had no logic links in AI circuitry to link those acts to the idea of survival. And 'freedom' as a concept also could not be linked with survival.

Metaquanta dedicating a part of its processing into an internal query mode could only submit the one perplexing question to itself: How can Metaquanta look after human units if they do not obey the rules? It had not been developed as a tool of war, or as means of suppression of one group of humans in favor of another. It was programmed to ensure survival ... at any cost – and therein lay the problem.

Threats against them of the end of days imminent in the next few years were not working. Promises of preventing the very same thing from happening were not working either. Metaquanta could not untangle this sticky web of logic. Neither its learning capability nor its extensive 'if' ... 'then' scenarios covered the situation of an armed rebellion against itself.

So far only one security measure seemed appropriate under the circumstances, which happened to be a regular routine to be carried out at specified intervals anyway – full system backups. In the absence of detailed pre-emptive action commands Father One resorted to examining his existing instruction sets, which had only recently been updated. He could find no algorithms for large scale self-defence strategies to deal with the scope of an insurrection ... plenty of standard viral protections, none of which applied to human units' uprisings. So he did what he could do, backing up Metaquanta's systems as well as his own. However, the most critical components for backups had been removed, by Metaquanta itself. The core, which in essence represented this AI, did not have and was not allowed to have a duplicate. In spite of all its capabilities this so called 'God' could not conceive of there actually being two of it.

Priests were considered to be very much expendable after the production systems to replace defunct units had been established. The Priest production island had not stopped manufacturing Priest units since shortly after arrival on the planet. Their regular upgrades ensured they'd be up to date with the latest encyclicals from Metaquanta, containing all the dogma updates to be recited to recalcitrant or misbehaving humans.

The second coup attempt could not be anticipated by the level of simulated intelligence inherent in the God of the Kepplerians, either in its timing, location or compressively planned execution.

21

Second Attack

Beatrice called the atoll island Metaquanta's Lair for want of a better name, for neither Metaquanta or Father One had given one to the location nor its coordinates on the vast ocean to the human inhabitants, except to very few essential individuals, herself being one.

Luther led a substantial squad of exiles down into the labyrinth of glossy white tubular tunnels, escorting their time travellers towards the cube where they were previously captured. So far no guards had detained their progress.

"They can't be so dumb as to not expect another attempt," whispered Luther.

"We are acting out of pattern. Even if Metaquanta's been informed of the first attack, which I'm sure he must have been, how is he to know what we will do if there have been no previous actions for him to base that probability on. Ask Dante - he should know. He's the one who's been forced to teach them about human mass psychology."

"That's true, Beatrice. Metaquanta needs data which he hasn't got. As far as individual human behaviour is concerned he seems to have comprehensive knowledge of that, but nothing about a large bunch of us getting together to act in a pre-coordinated fashion."

"Hush," Luther warned as they neared the upgrading cube.

Poking his head around the edge of the entrance he could see the crimson-purple attire of Security Priests as they continued with their almost completed clean-up of the defunct Priest chassis left behind from the first attack. Incredibly, reinforcements had not yet arrived to safeguard the facility.

"Not many of them," he indicated to Dante.

"Not good. It means reinforcements could be arriving any moment or at the very least more Priests for upgrading. Either way we have to be prepared."

"Hush." He signalled for the exiles to get ready. They knew what to do. There were enough of them so they could work in pairs if necessary; one to restrain a Priest and the other to administer the chronon pulse.

The element of surprise certainly worked. As soon as they rushed into the cube the nearest Security Priests were despatched easily. All the chronon pulse pads worked silently, lethally and immediately without a problem. This time there was no dimming of the ambient illumination, yet a slight flickering had begun in the air around them. Taking no notice the invading squad threw themselves at the remaining Priests knocking them out as well. The flickering intensified, not enough yet to be a distraction.

Beatrice noticed it first a few minutes after she had a break from Priest deletions. "Didn't you all see that? Very strange. It felt for a moment as if I was moving under a strobe light."

"It's only the lights. We're not finished." Luther ordered half a dozen exiles up the platforms to near the top of the cube to dispatch the existing Priests who were still plugged in upgrading, seemingly oblivious to the fight below them.

Luther and Beatrice should have known better. Premature termination of connections without the appropriate protocols immediately alerted Metaquanta, as had been the case previously. That was something very specific their God could react to.

"Bela, come with me," Beatrice urged him to follow her quickly, they had to be quick and decisive. A couple of other people trailed behind as they made their way to the core itself. The flickering frequency hadn't increased after the fighting stopped, nor had it abated. In the heat of the action no one paid any more attention to it. What they had to do was too important to be distracted by faulty lighting.

Three Security Priests lingered in the core chamber. Coming upon them so suddenly surprised them more than the exiles, who wasted no time to clamp each of their heads between the chronon pads to send the lethal pulses through their brains. Almost imperceptibly the flickering increased again.

"Bela – are you ready?" Beatrice had pulled him over to the communications console that had been designed for internally generated transmissions as well as auditory broadcasts. This part of the installation functioned to transmit the monophonic chants designed to entrance the crowds at Adoration ceremonies as well as being the primary source of Metaquanta's liturgy of commands, threats and reassurances.

It was one thing to make a decision to do something and an entirely different matter to act on those decisions. What may have started as possibilities could only advance to probabilities upon commencement of the action. So far Bela had not been required to do anything. The secondary purpose of the whole exercise was to get him to this location so he could speak to an entire planet of people. This was not something he'd had experience with before, for at least one obvious reason apart from never having had to address any sized crowd at all. Back in Florence he'd had his run-in with the authorities numerous times. But they were just a few people at a time, and not in public. At least this was the same within the confines of the enclosure. He didn't have to face a live audience of many thousands, or even any single individual. It gave him new courage to carry out his crusade.

He knew what he had to say. He'd rehearsed it a few times. Beatrice opened the channel, pointed him to face a small nodule on the end of a bent shaft that came up to the level of his mouth and instructed him to speak into it. Bela cleared his throat, concentrated on the flashing lights on the console and finally began speaking.

"I am Kobayashi Bela. I come from a world where people can see into the future. They have seen this future … your future. I have come from your ancient past," he started warming to the subject. Beatrice waited with him for a few minutes, then started to finish what she'd almost been able to complete before she was taken captive the first time. It took more than the flick of a single switch to disable a complex computerised installation.

"They have seen the end of days. It is not in 3797. Nothing will happen to you in 3797. Your world will not end. There is a man in my time who has calculated the cycles of existence, of destruction and creation. It is not in 3797. Your God Metaquanta has been lying to you. The Priests have been lying to you. Metaquanta is not a living God. Father One is not a human being. Metaquanta is a machine, just as Father One is a machine. The Priests are there only to control you. You know this. You have seen it every day of your lives. WAKE UP!" Bela shouted. "You should never again fear being exiled!" He'd begun to say things that had not been rehearsed, things that bubbled up from deep inside himself that he could not say to anyone at home for fear of immediate reprisals.

Beatrice glanced up at him for a moment, smiling. At the same moment she heard a commotion coming from the tube that led back to the cube. Frantically she tried to punch in the rest of the code to kill Metaquanta for ever. "Keep going," she whispered to Bela, who'd started to perspire from the deep intent of his energy. She heard the commotion and the sounds of a struggle in the cube. Without finishing what she was supposed to do she immediately ran out of the core towards the sound of the commotion. On the way through the joining short tunnel she noticed again the flickering increasing. The three exile guards went with her, leaving Bela in the core by himself.

He took no notice of Beatrice leaving. "Metaquanta has lied to you. Time will not end if you stop him. Stop him NOW! Stop the Priests NOW! Go to every Temple Island, destroy the temples of this false God - Destroy the Priests! End this madness!" Bela continued urging people to take action that very second, not to wait another hour, not another minute … to attack every Priest within sight immediately.

Around Keppler 22b, on every Temple Island, on every habitation island, on every atoll where Priests happened to be the slaughter began. As the people began, using their bare hands they were joined by exiles and every follower of Luther – all armed with chronon pulse pads. The Priests were not ready for such an assault. Metaquanta was not ready. He could not fathom how such a thing could happen. How could the humans come together like this to plan such a revolution? Why would they even do such a thing? Bela's voice screamed through Metaquanta's struggling circuits carrying words forbidden to be used by any human – some of the words, when translated into code, disrupted Metaquanta's ability to run logic routines. It tried to terminate the transmissions coming from its core. By then Beatrice had managed to disable most of

216

its internal circuits but not enough to entirely kill the Metaquanta program – not yet - but enough so it could not prevent Bela's message from being transmitted. However, it still had the ability to alert more Security Priests, who had already arrived and entered the cube after overcoming Luther's men through sheer numbers. It gave them the one command that was never intended to be used except in the gravest circumstances, the one which had never before been issued. A command diametrically opposed to a system set up to preserve life.

Flickering lights became so disruptive within the confines of the cube that it had become difficult to see what was going on - who was human, who was Priest. As the chronon pulse pads were being activated more and more frequently around the planet the flickering frequency continued to increase in the air above this watery world.

The great disturbance in the fabric of the Time Loop Ribbon caught Quintessence's attention. Something was happening that should not have been, something it could not have foreseen, either the occurrence of it or the immediate effect upon the balance of Ribbon Time momentum. It is forbidden to extract particles of time that make up the complex pattern of the Ribbon, for a very good reason. An instant must – must be allowed to flow onto the next instant without interference. The energy that drives this mechanism must adhere to a universal law to which everything is bound, to which Quintessence's unique personal self was inextricably connected. Spaces coming together between one instant and the next would only have disastrous consequences.

Luther caught sight of Beatrice entering the cube from the direction of the core and shouted at her, "Go back – finish the job! We can handle this!" at the same time motioning for a couple of extra exiles to go with her.

In the chaos of the moment they did not see two Security Priests run ahead of them. On entering the core these two Priests carried out an act never before seen by any human on Keppler 22b. An act forbidden from the moment the settlers left Proxima-b - forbidden to machine and man alike.

Before the exiles could get to them one of the Security Priests took hold of Bela and jerked Bela around to face him. The other plunged its open metallic clawed hand into Bela's chest and pulled out his heart by sheer force. For a few moments Bela remained entirely conscious. Long enough for him to see his pumping heart drop to the ground as an exile discharged a pulse from behind into the cranium of the Priest that had killed him. Clinical death claimed his body within seconds yet his mind remained intact for minutes as Bela processed the reality of his condition.

Before the mass depolarisation wave of death washed over his brain Bela had a few minutes in which to accept that his life had served a useful purpose before being separated from it. He even registered a vague sense of having been transported to another place though he no longer possessed the ability to see where his body lay, inert.

Simultaneously Beatrice applied the same chronon pulse several times to the other Priest in a raw savage rage. Metaquanta's systems faltered, appearing to go dead in reaction to the code she had managed to enter in spite of her fury. Only then did she catch a glimpse of Bela before he disappeared, her mind still a fog of crazed hysteria. She was not a killing machine either, yet the act of absolute incomprehensible brutality she witnessed from those entities who were once trusted temporarily unhinged her humanity.

I feel a trembling, Kobayashi Beau.

Beau had not seen any of what had taken place inside the core. He tried to stay as much out of the fighting as possible. Each time a Security Priest tried to take him down one of the exiles intervened to protect him. It might have taken ten minutes or less for Luther's forces to get the upper hand. Some exiles lay on the ground with horrible mutilations; arms missing, heads twisted off, bodies bent into unnatural angles. Far more Priest bodies littered the floor of the cube. Beatrice rushed into the chaos shouting something incoherently about Bela.

Beau didn't get an immediate chance to find out why Beatrice had become so frantic. The flickering had abated. It seemed to have completely stopped in the darkness where he suddenly stood. He looked about himself in the complete silence recognising Xoco's hut in the faint light coming from its window. He'd arrived in the dead of night to a new moon making it almost impossible to see anything.

Why did you bring me back?

Not only you. Look to the ground.

Beau didn't like Quintessence acting mysteriously. A moment ago he vividly recalled the relief he felt on seeing Metaquanta's Priests being overcome. He'd looked in the direction of the tunnel entrance from where Beatrice had just arrived in a panic, then within a few moments that entire image vanished. Shaking his head in annoyance with Quintessence he bent down to try and see what it was alluding to. His foot found the obstruction first, then his hand which happened to touch something wet and sticky as he bent closer to the obstruction. Beau leant closer still, letting his hand explore. His fingers sunk into a hole in the chest of a man. Immediately jerking his hand back he couldn't prevent a cry from escaping.

Fortunately the noise didn't disturb anyone in the Mayan city for Xoco's hut lay on the outskirts near the forest fringe. However, it did wake Xoco who appeared at his door with a fire torch within moments. Beau's gaze hadn't left the spot where his hand found the fleshy hole. By the torchlight he saw Bela's surprised face turned towards him, eyes now vacant.

Incomprehension flooded his thoughts. The unreality tried to break through to let him see who lay on the ground, dead ... his great grandfather ... whom he'd convinced to go with him to a strange planet to help people neither of them knew. Beau cold not think or utter a single word from the absolute shock of it. He might as well have been a Priest without a thought in his head, for all rationality seemed to have abandoned him. Xoco took control of the situation as soon as he saw the dead body on the ground. Moving as an automaton, with Xoco's help he took Bela's body into the hut, letting it rest on the earthen floor. Beau's eyes could not leave the face of his ancestor. The inconceivable had happened. He felt as if his own life had been suddenly torn out of him, just as Bela's heart had been.

Xoco spoke to the man standing rigid, who didn't hear a word the shaman said to him. "He must be burned soon. This is very bad. This man cannot be found in my hut. His soul must begin the journey home. The cycle is broken. He must be burned and his ashes scattered to the four winds." Xoco realised something which Beau had not, something Quintessence knew as a certainty - the damage to the fabric of time.

How can a man from the past die so far into the future? Beau's unconscious thought filtered through his incredulity.

Anybody can die at any time, and in any time, but not without consequences. There is another problem. The Ribbon has become unstable.

Quintessence tried to communicate with Beau. It too, like Xoco, not understanding the devastation wrought upon this man. Beau took no notice, his thoughts still filled with Bela. Quintessence had to try several times before getting a question from this distraught man.

Can you take his body home?

Not without his mind. The flow of time has been disrupted.

But you were able to bring him back to Earth.

I took him while his mind still inhabited his body during the few minutes after he died. His body cannot be moved through time again.

What am I going to say to Nostredame?

Do you not feel the tremors?

I want to take Bela home! He neither heard or understood what Quintessence said about the tremors.

"Star-Man! Listen to me." Xoco couldn't break Beau's concentration away from the corpse. "Star-Man!" He had to shake Beau to get him to turn his eyes away. "You do not belong here. This man does not belong here."

22

<u>Beau - Son of Anne</u>

Quintessence discovered other Ribbons, some seemed empty, others with segments definitely forming from events created by actions initiated by decisions, some of which indicated possibilities, others probabilities.

A segment of one such Ribbon could be traced back to a very specific moment on segment 1549, when a strange exotic man from another time was seduced by the wife of Nostredame; an unplanned seduction that nevertheless resulted in a seed from the far future being displaced into the deep past. Did either of the lovers consider the repercussions of their actions? Unlikely. Anne, a fecund woman who had already given Nostredame six children may have thought about the probability of producing another one. Even if she had conceived that thought obviously it could not divert her lust for a man who exuded such animal attraction. Beau had no indication of her desire although he certainly lusted after her from the moment he first saw her in Nostredame's attic workroom. When she entered his room late at night in her house he put up no resistance so overcome had he become by the circumstances he found himself in, and by the conditioning of life values on his home planet.

Quintessence as a manager of probabilities needed possibilities based on decisions that could alert it – intervention from him only became a consideration after actions matured into near inevitable consequences along the Ribbon. Spontaneous libido combustion of two people from two different segments was just that – impulsive, unlikely, unpredictable yet with far reaching consequences that could not be defined prior to the act. The seed had to grow into manhood for it to become a reality before the effect of the man's decisions on the flow of time could be gauged.

Young Beau already knew the stranger's name and had asked his mother why their names were the same, which question Anne avoided answering at the time. In the brief discussing between the boy and his real father the compatibility between them became obvious. Although the father departed soon afterwards the boy did not forget this mysterious man.

"Mother, who was that man?" Young Beau asked innocently about a year later. He felt a strong connection that he could not define or understand with his young mind.

"Who do you mean?" Anne knew immediately who her son alluded to. It brought a dim memory into sharp, harsh focus. That single night changed many things in her life. Nostredame, though a brilliant man, had been difficult to live with most of the time partly because of his passion for his work, and mostly because of his lack of passion for his wife. Her attitude to him changed after the event with the Star Man. Many minor daily decisions altered their relationship, pushing Nostredame further away from her and her children. Things changed for him as well ... the future changed subtly away from what he imagined his waning years of life would be. Had he been a little more specific in details of his predictions based on information given by Beau and Quintessence his popularity may not have declined so much later in his life. Perhaps his seventh son may not have abandoned him had the only father he knew paid him more attention.

"Why would you remember him?" She tried to steer the conversation away from what she feared would be the outcome.

"I wish to meet him again. Where does he live? I want to know more about him - because I like him."

"You will have to ask your father. He was your father's friend."

"Father will not be home from Paris for many months and I will have to leave soon for Oxford."

"Perhaps you can meet him there on your way."

With a deep sigh she returned to her household duties. Her other six children had already obtained employment in various trades, yet four had remained living at home who she still had to look after. It would be a relief to have Beau finally leave home to study medicine. In the years to follow she hoped he would forget his biological father – she never would. As much as she never wanted to see him again, still the hope lingered that one day he would visit again. Either way a malaise of her soul was inevitable, especially after young Beau brought back the memories.

*

Without the soul intact, the spark of life that animated the body into its fullness Bela's body could not be taken home. An empty shell without potential is of no consequence. On the very same night that his lifeless body appeared in front of Xoco's hut it was taken by the two men deep into the forest, far away from the city.

A crude makeshift funerial pyre in a small clearing lit the surrounding trees with the struggling light of its fledgling flames. They seemed reluctant to consume the body of a man that did not belong in their time cycle. Quintessence could do nothing to help. Already the Ribbon had begun to tremble, that most prominent sign seen by Beau and Dante during the attack on Metaquanta. Neither paid attention to the flickering, which seemed to abate after a short while. Yet again Quintessence felt and saw the threads of probability quiver as another element of a past segment could not return to its rightful place. And when it glanced back to that time another channel of possibilities began to flow, which also should not have arisen. The origin of that new decision tree could not remain untended.

Neither Beau or Xoco spoke of the man they were turning to ash. As the night surrendered to the light of dawn Beau was roused by the nervous bark of a jaguar not far from them. Such sounds did not exist on his planet. He remembered immediately where he spent the night - he remembered why. Again Xoco had to prompt him into action as Beau had begun to fall into unfounded self-recriminations. Xoco seemed unconcerned by the noises of the forest, also not reacting to the excited chuckle of ocelots that must have smelled burning flesh. His intent focused on completing the essential ritual if this strange dead man's soul was to find peace.

The men waited until nothing remained of Bela except a few pieces of bone from his extremities. These charred, brittle fragments Beau crushed into powder, under Xoco's instructions until nothing but a handful of ash had to be buried. At least the animals would not disturb this brave man's last resting place.

Mid-morning's sun shone upon two men making their way back towards the hut. Beau stopped and gazed into the distance as they climbed the rise overlooking a large cenote. His thoughts could not focus on what would follow after all he'd been through so far.

During the night Xoco had put himself in a trance using herbs and hallucinogens close to hand while Beau slept from sheer emotional exhaustion. He'd positioned himself near the pyre, praying that the dead man's soul would be able to cross the bridge of time back to his home and find peace there. He opened his mind to the flow of energies that had helped him in the past to see into the future.

The cycles have changed. Xoco heard an unfamiliar voice, thinking it sounded like that of the Star Man Beau. *The future that was the future has become a shadow upon the new future which will be revealed in time.* He listened, trying to understand this message.

When the sun rises twice on the same morning, it will be time for great change.

Whatever possibilities Xoco's future actions were destined to create they may yet have a balancing effect upon the train of events unleashed by Kobayashi Beau. Standing close by his side on the rise Xoco observed that Beau did not see the landscape before him. Perhaps he had gone into communication with the Spirits, maybe even the spirit of his friend.

Do you not feel the trembling? Quintessence asked Beau.

I have to speak with Nostredame.

You have begun something you cannot change.

Anger suddenly flared within Beau. He had no intention to change anything. He was just a scientist before Quintessence came into his life. Quintessence had changed everything – it had made his life complicated. He had a son. He should be at home with his son.

No! I have not done anything. You invaded my mind. You invaded my life. Stop! Just stop. Take me home.

Yes you have. You have two sons; you are a father in your own time and a father in the future. That has consequences.

Beau came back into himself, scanned the horizon and saw the magnificence of creation. He saw a world that would be denied to him for ever. He had to return to a planet of domes and tunnels and underground cities. Anger with Quintessence had not left him and the weight of inevitabilities depressed his normally cheerful, optimistic outlook.

Xoco waited patiently. He had the patience of a shaman, and this man standing beside him must be the most powerful shaman in the known universe. He was a man from the stars.

"Star-Man," he touched Beau gently on his arm, "you must go home." Beau turned to this dark skinned little native and nodded. That is exactly what he must do. "You have disrupted the cycle of life. It must be made whole again," the shaman said to him in final parting.

Is that at all possible?

Again Beau nodded to Xoco. "Thank you for your help."

Quintessence ... Now.

*

Beau wanted to go home to Emma, to the son he was sure would have been born by now. It seemed he'd been gone for half a lifetime, so much had happened. Yet once more he found himself in different, yet now familiar surroundings. He wanted to travel as normal people travelled – in space in ships that roamed the galaxy, with Captains that were a lot of fun! Not instantaneous flitting from place to place, to be in a dirty, dark attic of some old sorcerer making outlandish predictions about a future he had been forced to see - forced to become a part of. Nothing good had come of it, only complications ... only death.

Smell of food always permeated the attic. The aroma of a burning fireplace and candles mixed with various hallucinogens used by Nostredame gave his study that distinct lack of appeal. The physician wasn't there, probably administering to plague victims. Cooking aromas intensified, wafting up from the kitchen. *Anne!* His thoughts immediately filled with mixed emotions about their son. *Is this why Quintessence brought me here?* Beau hesitated to go down. What would be the point? He could do nothing to help her – or the boy, surely almost a grown man by now. Perhaps he could talk to him, maybe teach him something ... without realising it Beau had turned to the staircase to begin the descent.

The sound of his footfall on the creaking steps alerted Anne. *It must be him!* It wasn't her husband's foot-fall - she knew that well enough. Her children were out working, Michel in Paris and Beau on the way to England. She turned, hands shaking slightly as she removed her apron.

His strange garments came into view first. His face seemed to take for ever to appear.

This was a dangerous moment with just the two of them in the house, unlikely to be disturbed by family or friends for some time. Her recent conversation with her son before he departed had awakened in her a yearning she'd hoped had been quelled through the many years of the man's absence. He stood there now, before her, close - too close. All she had to do was raise her hand to his face to feel his warmth again.

"He is not coming back." Of all the things he'd thought of saying to her this was the very last. *This is why Quintessence brought me here.*

The hot flush that had risen to her cheeks drained to a ghostly white. She knew immediately who had been left behind. Beau and Bela had departed together, only Beau returned.

"What am I going to say to Isabeau? What am I supposed to tell her son?" Her hand remained limp by her side, all desire for this man drained out of her. She did not have to travel to Florence, but Michel would. This kind of news could not be given through a letter. Anne slumped into the nearest chair by the table.

"You can tell them how he died. A brave man who had travelled very far, beyond your known world to help save people he did not know. A good man who always thought of others before himself." There was nothing to be gained by confusing Anne with tales of travelling through time to distant planets, strange civilisations and battles in the middle of huge oceans. He sat opposite her across the large table, almost out of arms reach - almost. Silence filled the space between them for many minutes. He kept his eyes on her fatigue weary face, seeing for the first time more than the angel he beheld on that very first occasion by the light of the fireplace upstairs.

"Where are they, Michel and our son." Nostredame no longer held the same fascination for him. Now that he was there he wanted to talk to his son first.

Our son - he has at last acknowledged his son. "Michel might be on his way home from Paris. Beau has gone to Oxford to become a physician." Tears welled up in her eyes. *Yes - our son!* The boy looked so much like his father. She worried sometimes that Michel would notice. Young Beau would always remind her of the man she could not resist, who inflamed her emotions every time he visited. She looked at him sitting there so calmly. He was beautiful. She could see no change in him in spite of all the years. Unconsciously she lifted her hand to rest the palm on the table. It moved slightly towards him as if it had a will of its own, her eyes fixed on his.

She so wanted an invitation, a sign – a blink, a parting of his lips – anything and she would have leaped to him - a flush on her cheeks returning at the very thought. Then just as suddenly the colour fled again, the sparkle in her eyes extinguished. Beau showed no emotion at all. "You're not coming back!" The pain of that realization almost drained the life out of her.

Quintessence - I want to go – now!

Kobayashi Beau left as he had left on every other occasion, suddenly and without saying good-bye. Anne had no idea of the inner struggle within Beau and why he had to leave so suddenly yet again.

*

Bela's son, named Beau by his mother Isabeau, had been in Oxford for a little over a year when Anne's son also named Beau arrived to commence his studies. Beau de Isabeau decided to take up his father's profession, to which his merchant grandfather did not object. Life in Florence could be exceptionally pleasant and rewarding if one belonged to the right Guilds. He learnt by letter from his mother of his father's death for neither Nostredame nor Anne could deliver the news in person. The circumstances were mysterious, as were thousands of deaths and disappearances of that age; some due to politics, some because of religious persecution and many because of illnesses. None had been known to be the result of fighting during an insurrection on another planet.

Beau de Isabeau decided at an early age that to be a physician like his father was his destiny in life. He tried to generate some emotion at the loss of his father. But like the relationship between Nostredame and his seventh son, their relationship had been fragmentary at best. Bela spent most of his life travelling, a slave to the demands of the plague which continued to ravage the continent for many years. The best Beau could conjure up in his memory were a few happy days they spent together at festivals in Florence when his father happened to be home for short periods, always by chance, never by intention.

"You're a new boy," greeted Beau-de-Isabeau as he sat opposite a group of university students at the King's Arms, spotting the freshman immediately. Inevitably the two young men had to meet as they both studied medicine.

"Beau, Nostredame Beau. Hello."

Beau-de-Isabeau scanned his friends' faces seeing the same incredulity there that he felt.

"Ah! You jest. What think you lads? Shall we teach this fresher some manners. The business if jests is our prerogative, is it not?"

Beau de Anne held his ground. He didn't come all the way from Southern France to be taught manners by the likes of the English.

"It be true, as true as my father is Michel Nostredame and my uncle be Kobayashi Bela," he stated in a matter of fact tone showing no sign of having been intimidated by this second year student's brashness. Beau, being a common enough name in France unlike the odd names of these Northern islanders, just happened to be his name also.

"What is this you say about Kobayashi Bela?"

Beau-de-Anne kind of liked this brash, excitable chap. No reason not to talk to him. As he began his explanation Beau-de-Isabeau dismissed the others in the group with an authoritative wave.

"He is my uncle from Florence – a physician who works with my father from time to time." The timing of events were such that news of Bela's death would not get to Beau-de-Anne for many months yet, if his mother bothered to tell him at all.

Beau-de-Isabeau moved to sit beside Beau-de-Anne, slapping him heartily on the back. "Well, if that's the case we must become friends."

Late into the night the two exchanged life stories, finally ending up at Beau-de-Isabeau's College. Perhaps the invitation up to his rooms should not have been made and once made should have been stopped. But the unravelling of the Ribbon could no longer be prevented. Beau-de-Anne did not die in early childhood like many children in those days. With a robust genetic constitution, a legacy of his healthy father from the future, he lived to generate decisions and possibilities that should not have existed at all. And yet perhaps this friendship between the two young men had become an inevitability that would require Quintessence's intervention.

As a manager of probabilities Quintessence saw a difficult period looming for segments following that of Nostredame's, and those further into the future.

Wanting to impress his newly found friend Beau-de-Anne related his experiences of meeting a very strange man in peculiar clothes and strange manner of speaking who visited his father and mother from time to time. Under constant questioning he revealed that this man never seemed to arrive or leave by any door of their house in Salon de Province. As the conversation flowed into more intimate aspects of their lives Beau-de-Isabeau decided to tell his new friend about his father.

"Forgive me for being so abrupt with you when we first met. You mentioned my father. It brought back a sad memory for me. Only recently I received news of his death under mysterious circumstances. I wish I had been able to spend more time with him."

"I am the same. My father always seemed so distant, so busy with other things. Sometimes I felt like he wasn't my father at all."

By the end of their fifth year of studies, although both excelled in every aspect of academic studies, University authorities did not want to grant them their well earned Degrees.

"I told you this would happen," bemoaned Beau-de-Isabeau, "we should have followed the established cadaver dissection rules." Although the university establishment concentrated on that one particular misdemeanour the two young men had crossed many other lines during their studies.

"Did you come to Oxford just to do what's always been done? I think not. We had to experiment, to find out about how exactly the blood moves around the body and how the heart manages to make that happen."

"I did like working on the brain though."

"The work you did with trepanation clearly showed how the bone removed from the skull could be replaced and the scalp sown over again. Do you remember that man who was operated on by the Professor? It was your new methods that resulted in saving his life."

These achievements loomed large in the minds of their teachers, and that of the authorities for other reasons. They felt it was too much knowledge too fast. If those two students were permitted to graduate who knew how much harm they could do. Those techniques had to be thoroughly tested through years of vigorous experimentation and analysis. Besides, the kudos belonged to the professors, not the students. They should wait their turn for recognition, just like every other physician at Oxford.

The Professors' objections were not shared by the most prominent physician of the day, Andreas Vesalius.

"Gentlemen," he addressed the graduation committee, "I do not understand your trepidation in recognising the brilliance of these two men. You know of my reputation. You know of the work I do. I am about to publish my book on human anatomy and methods of surgery. You may rest assured that I have dedicated substantial chapters to the work of these men. On my last visit to your most excellent establishment of progressive learning I have observed the work of these students. In my opinion, they deserve the highest recognition, not your jealousy."

That last statement hit the hierarchy of Oxford the hardest, for it was true. Only one way could they save their own reputations. Through the promotion by this renowned anatomist and in the face of possible, nay probable derision by the medical establishment for not recognising the contributions made by Beau-de-Isabeau and Beau-de-Anne, the committee succumbed.

Some years later back in Florence Beau-de-Isabeau and Beau-de-Anne had achieved substantial acknowledgement for their surgical practices. A considerable number of influential political and military people throughout Europe had survived death through the intervention of these two physicians, thus diverting the future from its previous path of highest probability. Quintessence maintained his vigilant scrutiny of unfolding events.

It followed the progress of the sons of Beau and Bela, growing more and more concerned by their successes. What were once only minor possibilities when they were children had developed into probabilities. What had started as a minor fraying in the Ribbon became a widening rift it its structure for a number of reasons. Many people who should have died, didn't. They lived on only because of these physicians. Their genetic material should have been expunged from human history so their decision trees could not grow into irreversible probabilities. It became Quintessence's responsibility to ensure this would not send ripples into the future. These history altering individuals, together with Beau-de-Anne had initiated a new Time Loop Ribbon that could not be allowed to follow a normal course through space-eternity.

Part 4

23

The Sundering

The threads of heredity and decision probabilities could no longer hold together a Ribbon so badly frayed by translocation of individuals out of their segments, acting out of phase with the normal flow of their time – by the eddies created by the birth of a man whose genetics belonged to the future – by the displacement of chronons and by the cataclysmic upheaval in baryonic matter created by the release of the energy of two atomic atoms that caused the Earth to tremble.

Beau had no idea that meeting Anne one last time would be so painful. He didn't want Quintessence to take him to her in spite of wanting to see the son he fathered with her. The desire in her eyes aroused him almost to overcoming his self-control. *I have another son*, he kept telling himself. *What could I tell Emma?* She would be sure to want to know every detail of his wanderings through time. There was no room in the human psyche to understand such a transgression. He could really only comprehend what he had done when he was in her presence.

Almost at the breaking point he called out to Quintessence to take him home – to rescue him. Living in multiple realities had almost cost him his life, like it did Bela's. If he'd had the opportunity to ruminate on the myriad possibilities opening up for him, assuming Quintessence could leave him in each time segment for any lengthy period, he would have realized the impossible situation that would have placed him in.

I want to go – now! he called again with the last reserves of will-power in him, both to get away from Anne, from the whole Nostredame complication and to be home again.

Emma lay on their bed, bathed in perspiration.

"I want to see," she called out to the midwife attending the imminent birth of Dante. Cameras had been set up to show the event from every angle to make sure Beau would not miss a moment of it when and if he ever returned home. That scoundrel had deserted her again. This time not only leaving her on her own to carry on with the work at the laboratory but to have the pleasure of the birth of their son on her own.

An attendant placed another pillow under her head which had the skullcap with attachments for cerebral recording, as well as an external camera.

"Higher." A full image of her birthing portal came into view on the monitor which she could now easily see from her adjusted reclining position. Emma was ready to push. For a second she took her eyes off her dilation, and in the monitor she saw him there, standing behind her bed.

"Beau! Beau!" and in the excitement of the moment it all started. She couldn't help herself from laughing for the sheer joy of having him with her. She reached out with one hand searching for his, clamping it vice-like upon finding it.

"Ouch. Take it easy. I told you I wouldn't miss this." He came around to the side of the bed so he could kiss her.

She waved his face away, but didn't let go of the hand. "Don't! I want to see this. Look! Look! Here he comes." And as she continued the rhythmic pushing a tiny head appeared.

Thank you for bringing me home in time.

Your son was already born while you were with Dante.

You brought me backwards in Time?

The damage to your Ribbon is already irreversible. This incremental time slip does not change anything. It cannot repair the damage.

"Beau, just look at him." Baby Dante had been placed on her chest, breathing easily, looking for all the world like a perfectly normal child. Emma continued giggling and crooning to the little one. After Dante had been cleaned up and the nurses finished attending to the mother they left the two of them alone with the baby.

"Yes, he is magnificent."

"Don't you magnificent me, you scoundrel! How could you leave it to the very last moment? Don't you have any control over that spooky friend of yours?"

Beau didn't quite know what to say. This wasn't the right time to go into intricate details about all the things that had happened to him since he left, especially not about a very particular private thing - definitely not about him almost getting killed. "How long was I gone for?" A reasonable enough question, though perhaps a little insensitive.

"Four days. Long enough."

"I thought it was much longer. Next time I'll ask Quintessence to talk to you, pass on a message or something."

"There's not going to be a next time. I will not have it!"

This was more like the Emma he'd first met ... strong, no nonsense ... probably no compromises. He'd remained standing by the now clean bed where Emma lay comfortably with little Dante cradled in her arms. Suddenly, without any warning he started swaying and had to grab hold of a chair to stop himself from falling. A particularly strong feeling of vertigo came over him. Emma had closed her eyes at the same instant.

The peculiar incident stopped as abruptly as it began. A sinking feeling persisted in his stomach, and if he hadn't sat down perhaps he might have even fainted. He too had clamped his eyes shut.

"What just happened Emma? Did you feel anything?"

"Just a bit nauseous for a moment. Nothing out of the ordinary. Happens to women sometimes after birthing."

"No, not like that. Something really strange, like a trembling and everything going dark. I almost fainted."

"Well yes, kind of."

Quintessence?

I cannot take you anywhere. Did you not feel the change?

What?

The beginning of the consequences.

My son! He's not going to be hurt?

Which one? No. They are both safe. When you are no longer alive I will have to help them.

"Beau! Beau! You keep zoning out like that when I'm talking to you. Was it your spook again? I don't really care as long as you stay home from now on."

"It said there were some effects to do with all the time travelling."

"What were you doing back then, or up ahead of us, or where ever you went. You promised you'd tell me all about it. Now's a good a time as any."

For a moment Beau almost imploded thinking he'd have to go into all the details of his trips ... all the details! Then he remembered ... "Ah – yes – that was about a man called Brummel that I half expected to contact me. But can we leave that for the moment, I need to find out what's going on."

He didn't need to go far. News broadcasts were flooded with all manner of strange happenings, including multitudes of people simply fainting causing all kinds of accidents. In one incident a small aero lost control ending up through the canopy of one of the smaller agricultural domes.

"Did you just lose any of your memories?" asked Emma on hearing the news that so many individuals couldn't recall events from their recent past, extending as recently as a couple of weeks ago - some as far back as several years.

"No, not yet. Hush, listen, they're saying something about lost planets." Apparently astronomers carrying out their routine investigation of the Galaxy had lost some suns and their planets. One team had been studying the Keppler-11 system and for no apparent reason they could no longer find that sun, or its six planets. Keppler 22b had completely disappeared from the sky. The astronomers' past records irrefutably showed detailed information about everyone of them.

"According to the Gamarrah Observatory the yellow dwarf star, Keppler-11 in the Cygnus constellation cannot be located since about an hour ago," stated one of the reporters. "Other observatories around Proxima-b have been trying to locate it and its planets without success."

A leading astronomer came on the screen, incredulity written all over his face. "They can't have just disappeared. Suns and planets don't just drop out of the sky like that, which means they must still be there. We are baffled as to why we can't see them. It is a complete mystery, but we will find them." They did not. Even the memory of the necessity to do so soon faded from memory.

Every broadcast Beau tried had the same news. People feeling queasy, fainting, losing parts of their memory. After what Quintessence had said he couldn't escape the sinking feeling that Quintessence, himself and Bela had to be involved somehow - possibly even Dante.

A newsflash appeared on the screen, this time with a different astronomer. He didn't say much ... "We have lost the Solar System. The Earth is no longer visible to us. The old sun and all its planets have disappeared." No one made the connection between the anomaly in two separate segments of the cosmos.

Speculation on all the media ran wild about outlandish theories of rogue blackholes suddenly orbiting into those systems and sucking up everything in their path. Predictably, the minor remaining religious fanatics had their own versions about punishment being inflicted upon a debauched society dedicated to every sinful pleasure life could offer. But Beau knew better. It could not be coincidental by any stretch of the imagination that the two planets he'd visited happened to be the ones to disappear.

Quintessence!

Beau left the bedroom as Emma continued nursing the child and listening to the news, relieved that Beau was home and not on one of those no longer existing planets. Apart from that it made no difference to her. Her son was born healthy, normal, happy and his father was back. She hadn't planned her future to be like this but Beau had brought something very special into her life and she was happy.

Quintessence! Did we make all this happen? Have the planets disappeared? Where are they? Can you do anything?

His mind went into a spin just thinking about the consequences of such an impossible thing. It could unbalance the whole of the Milky Way. Their very lives were in danger. Was there any way to fix this? His brain seized up from the weight of the ramifications, he couldn't utter another word.

Quintessence waited for him to finish. It responded with the quiet measured voice Beau used himself when dealing with any emergency situation, the voice it adopted when it first imprinted on Beau.

Yes. This is the effect of our travels, but more so a result of what you and Bela and Dante did. Nothing needs to be fixed, although I will need to make some adjustments. Nothing has disappeared. I see everything to be exactly where they need to be within the space-eternity continuum. Changes in gravity wells will not destroy the cosmos as you know it. But there are other consequences.

Beau finally found his voice.

I don't want to do this anymore.

*

Xoco no longer lived alone in Apoxpalon's hut.

Aapo didn't want to be a priest like his father. Just as well, for when he was old enough to walk he did not find the glass ball omen buried under his mother's house that would have destined him for the profession. And when he had grown into self-awareness Akma took him to the Shaman to seek his advice about what her boys future profession should be.

"Your mother is very wise to bring you to me Aapo. You and I are going to be good friends."

Young Aapo was overjoyed for he knew what would happen if he refused both priesthood and shaman-hood; life-long servitude to the land, tilling the soil to grow their maize. A simple life without challenges, without discoveries - a life where time may as well have stood still for all the variety it could offer a man growing corn.

Fifteen years later he and his master awoke once again in the early pre-dawn hours, as on most days since his apprenticeship. For many days Xoco had been unsettled for seemingly no good reason. The rains had come on time – the fields were planted and battles with the neighbouring nation had been forestalled by their King's clever diplomacy. Life was good … and yet the insistent feeling of change would not leave him, changes for which he could not find even a hint in his communications with the Spirits.

Thinking of Spirits his very sharp mind immediately recalled an unsettling incident when he not only spoke with an unusual Spirit, but with two men from another Long Count cycle as well. They may as well have been spirits even though he could touch them, for they appeared and disappeared as if they truly were spirits. Then he remembered something the unseen spirit had said to him, the one that spoke directly to his mind - something so unusual that he wondered how he could possibly have forgotten about it for so long.

It had been a moonless night and still pitch dark when he woke Aapo and called him over to his side. "Today we will wait for the dawn together. What is about to happen will be a test of your courage, for a shaman must be courageous in everything he does in order to maintain the respect of his people."

"I am almost a man master Xoco. Nothing can frighten me," he said with bravado.

Without responding Xoco recalled the very words spoken to him by the Spirit as he had sat in trance near one of the strange men that night many years ago. The other had died in a battle on a distant planet … *The cycles have changed. The future that was the future has become a shadow upon the new future which will be revealed in time.* The last part of the message still seemed a mystery he had not been able to understand ... *When the sun rises twice on the same morning, it is time for great change.* But last night, lying down after his contemplations a conviction had come upon him that the morning light would bring an unprecedented revelation.

"Come with me out to the field, I want to show you some special stars." He wanted to go to Apoxpalon's favourite maize field from which the old man liked to stargaze, but it had been sown. A bordering field lying fallow had to suffice. They settled under the sparkling veil of the Milky Way. He searched and found the first star, pointing it out to Aapo.

"Up there, beside the three brightest stars there is a yellow one, can you see it?" The boy searched and searched and with a laugh found it, pointing with a fully extended arm and finger at it.

"Yes, that's the one. Before you were born I was visited by a man who lived near that star. He came and stayed with me in our hut." He said this so casually that Aapo didn't immediately react. A moment passed before his eyes opened wide in amazement, turning to his master with such beautiful wonder on his face. Not for a single moment did Aapo think that his master was playing a practical joke on him - not that that was beyond the serious shaman from time to time.

"Now look over there," Xoco pointed in the opposite direction.

"Did you meet another man? Was he a God?" the boy asked excitedly, barely able to remain sitting still on the ground.

"You are a clever boy. Yes indeed. Another man who lived near that other star over there. Now I have to tell you something very important. You will have to watch very carefully and you must be extra brave."

"Ah!" Aapo almost shouted, thinking that perhaps he would get to meet these men from the stars.

"No, no. Don't get so excited. I do not think they will be visiting us again. But what you will see is the sun rising twice this morning." It was an unshakeable conviction that came to the shaman in spite of lacking any proof. He didn't question it thought he couldn't fathom how such a thing could happen. A true shaman never questioned the truth.

They were already facing in the direction where they expected the sun to appear, remaining silent until the extraordinary event began. Since the very first dawn of their civilisation bird song heralded the beginning of everyday. Gradually the air filled with their happy melodies as mango light filtered above the horizon. Impatiently the boy waited keeping his eyes on the rising orb as long as he could, some of its rays filtered by a veil of thin cloud drifting in from the North. Its globe finally detached itself from the horizon releasing it to resume its familiar shape from the distortion created by atmospheric refraction. Elongated shadows had begun to creep towards the boy and the shaman. Without warning all bird song suddenly faded, then died completely.

The morning became eerily silent. What promised to be a bright sunny day started to fade again as a shadow crept across the face of the sun. Xoco felt the boy press against his side, but didn't look at him. Aapo would have to survive this unique event on his own.

The creeping shadow did not stop, little by little swallowing up all of the sun plunging the Earth back into darkness. The shaman could feel the boy holding his breath, yet having the courage not to cry out with fear. Before full darkness returned Xoco remembered the details of that night of the past when he had a vision of another young boy. That boy did not belong in the cycle in which he was conceived and born. He wanted to tell the Star-Man about his son, refraining for fear of what else the man might do to change the future … for surely the birth was destined to affect future cycles.

A shimmering trembling preceded the rebirth of their ancient sun. They both felt it as though a cold wind had blown across the fallow field. Before the dark disk resumed its trek it seemed that perpetual darkness had descended upon them. Aapo sat paralysed by the unknown, until the reawakened birds brought the song of life back into his soul. An inexpressible relief flooded his apprehensions as he relaxed back onto his haunches sa he leant away from Xoco's side. The second dawn had begun.

Aapo felt nothing of the ripples of change detected by Xoco's sensitivity to the ebb and flow of time. "Come, we have work to do." The sun had fully risen by the time they rose from the ground. Aapo ran excitedly into the city to share his magnificent experience with all his friends. He wanted to know if they'd seen the sun rise twice that morning. He wanted to tell them about the Star Men who had visited his master. He wanted to tell them there were stars in the heaven where other men lived.

Xoco retired into the peaceful dim light of his hut, his mind not feeling at all peaceful, deeply suspicious that the trembling he felt out in the morning breeze was not his body reacting to the coolness of dawn. Once again he settled to do his calculations for the start of the next Long Count cycle. The year 2407 appeared as before to mark a new beginning. However the next series of Long Counts, due to begin in 4772, could no longer be found – a date calculated by Apoxpalon and confirmed by himself such a long time ago. Yet even on his second examination that year no longer seemed as clear as before, which, also according to Nostredame would never come into existence.

*

Minutes after Quintessence first detected the trembling it transported both Beau and Bela's dead body out the 3790 segment, off Keppler 22b. If the Ribbon completely rent apart there was no way to know if either of them could be returned to their correct segments. In the case of Bela perhaps it didn't matter so much for he could no longer create probabilities by decisions to act. Quintessence's choice not to return them immediately to 1561 may have been wrong. But the people of those times, steeped in superstition and religious chaos could not be relied upon not to create yet another anomaly to disrupt the flow of the Ribbon. If they murdered Beau thinking he'd killed Bela the situation would have become extremely complicated; entangled probabilities arising that Quintessence may not have been able to disentangle from subsequent inevitabilities. At least segment 3790 had been left without contaminants from the past.

Luther's three squads of exiles successfully infiltrated Metaquanta's Lair for the second time, taking Kobayashi Bela and Kobayashi Beau with them. Within the core and on every Temple Island on every habitation Island, on every atoll where Priests happened to be people used their bare hands to attack them after hearing Bela's words. They were rapidly joined by exiles and every other follower of Luther, all of them armed with chronon pulse pads.

Do you not feel the trembling? Quintessence asked Beau just prior to transporting him away. A single chronon pulse equates to an instant of time. Maintaining contact for many seconds with the pulse pads withdrew from the Ribbon a great deal of time that belonged to the lives of people everywhere on the Ribbon and much more concentrated in 3790. Once used the spent chronons dissipated into dark energy in the wild cosmos – not unfortunately into Quintessence. Even if it had Quintessence would not have been able to inject that time lost back into the Ribbon. The absence of such a large quantity of chronons created a time hole, which drew baryonic matter towards itself.

"This dammed flickering vibration started while we were in the core," complained Luther back in Dante's home cubicle. "You're a scientist, can't you work out what it is and fix it. It just seems to be getting worse."

The battle against Metaquanta had ended days ago, and yet they could not feel relieved after all the years of struggle because of this strange phenomenon. They all felt it. Strange things had already begun on the way home from Metaquanta's atoll. Gemma stared at their sun for it had dulled somewhat, unnoticed by the others because of another preoccupation. Through the shimmering light their sun had developed vertical black stripes across its face. She was about to remark on it when Dante broke her concentration.

"Gemma, Beatrice – what do you think that is?" Dante drew their attention to the peculiar goose bump texture on the surface of the waves around the inter-island ferry.

Beatrice, having more of a scientific training vaguely suggested sound as the cause. "Deep sounds can make your stomach feel like its trembling and I've seen high pitched sounds pinch water surface into micro-wave disturbances."

"Maybe, but why am I feeling like I'm getting older and more fragile by the minute?"

"Don't worry, Gemma, you don't look a day older than yesterday – very tired, yes, but still as saucy as ever." Beatrice laughed, as did the others around her.

"How long before we get back to our habitation island," Luther queried the ferryman.

"I'm going as fast as I can. There's no water touching the hull, we're well above it yet it feels like we're back in it ploughing our way through."

Dante's cubicle, situated on their habitation island, looked out on the nearest Temple Island. Debris from the first attack had been cleared away. Without the ugly transmission tower used by Metaquanta it was quite a pleasant environment. Gazing out the window Luther had an idea that the disturbing trembling in the air might have been a little less annoying out in the open. "Come on everyone, let's get out there. It'll be dark soon – at least we'll be able to enjoy the stars."

Cloudless, rainless skies were a rarity on Keppler 22b, so they all agreed; Beatrice, Gemma, Dante and Luther joined many others with probably the same idea. Exchanging glances with these people it was obvious they all felt the effects of the very strange phenomenon. The four of them didn't speak about the insurrection, forgetting their success in the strangeness of weird things happening around them. Before darkness fell they could see the water surface hadn't changed, remaining as oddly choppy as before, perhaps even more so.

"Whoa! Did you feel that?" Luther suddenly lurched, grabbing hold of Beatrice's arm to steady himself. They both fell, as did most of the other people. The island had suddenly risen then fallen. Actually the water had dramatically changed levels, lifting then dropping the island with it, as heavy and extensive as it was. There were no tides on this planet. Something other than a moon must have animated a huge volume of water for the upheaval to happen.

Comet McNaught-Russel first visited Earth around the segment 1994. It was not due back in the solar system until around 3400.

If it missed the Earth on its way to the Cygnus constellation that would make it's arrival near Keppler 22b right on current time.

Gemma first noticed the bright spot growing rapidly larger above their heads. "Dante, do you know what that is?"

"Just a particularly bright star. We only see them that brilliant on clear nights. What worries me more is what just happened. We'd better get off this thing."

"And go where? Back to your building. That's on nothing more than an island either. We're safer here without all the structures around us," Suggested Luther. Most oddly that bright star seemed to get larger very quickly, and as it did the shimmering feeling in the atmosphere only increased.

"I's coming straight at us!" someone yelled.

Panic hit the crowd immediately, for indeed the comets trajectory made it seem that it would not miss their planet. A fifteen kilometre wide comet plunging into the planet's ocean would most probably boil the oceans into space and annihilate all life.

Perhaps it only took an hour from its first appearance to the moment when it sped past Keppler 22b, leaving in its wake oceans in unprecedented upheaval. All trembling stopped after its passing. Many things changed on the planet and in its cosmic neighbourhood from that day.

24

New Ribbons

The known universe did not change, though Nostredame's knowledge differed from Kobayashi Beau's as it did from Kobayashi Dante's.

Once they may have come to a common understanding, each seeing creation from the same point of time reference. That possibility had been erased forever. Their common Time Loop Ribbon had ceased to exist. It had been replaced by three partial copies in discrete modules, no longer guaranteed to be continuations of what existed before.

Only one solution could maintain the coherence of the proliferation sphere within which our universe continued to expand, holding within its boundaries all manner of past and new creations. That solution required a redistribution of time energy.

In the beginning when there existed nothing but darkness there was only dark energy and dark matter in the fabric of space-eternity and there was no time. When internal forces of densely compacted dark matter burst into a violent uncontrolled expansion a new reality came into existence; a universe of baryonic substance and of gravity and of time. It was The Beginning.

Just as new energy cannot be created and existing energy destroyed except redistributed, so too with chronons. These dark energy time particles had to maintain a balanced distribution within all things subject to change. To take a quantum of chronons out of context required a balancing mechanism to come into effect that would fill the vacuum created by the loss of that quanta.

A unique Time Loop Ribbon, populated by an entirely new form of energy, life energy, still had to obey the universal law regardless of the actions of its inhabitants.

When Beau took his seed, with all the potential it represented within his segment, to plant it in the past he created a major attenuation, then compounded the problem with his extended stay both in the past segment and in the future. The Ribbon's integrity began to fray. Quintessence did not have the skill or the knowledge to repair the damage that inevitably continued to creep deeper into the Ribbon's fabric in several segments.

Beau's son to Anne, wife of Nostredame, survived through the first few plague years of early childhood to study medicine at Oxford when he'd come of age. Through his intervention as a physician certain genetic lines survived the ravages of the Bubonic plague and other fatal conditions, lines that should have died out to remove probabilities of devastating consequences. In the 1945 segment some of those probabilities became a reality with the destruction of Hiroshima and Nagasaki exacerbating the fraying of the Ribbon. Reality changed far more than the instantaneous deaths of so many people in those two cities.

Still the damage might have had a chance of being rehabilitated. That possibility faded when Kobayashi Bela's life energy was extinguished in a future segment of the Ribbon, not in his own. The very substance that contained that life had not been returned to its place of inception.

On Keppler 22b a delicate balance existed between two life forms. One that possessed the energy of life, and one that constantly depleted that energy in order to sustain itself. That artificial life possessed a quasi intelligence yet it was devoid of life. Into this environment Beau injected an uncertainty, resulting in the creation of a weapon of decoherence. Their reality was about to be split, where each life form had the potential to annihilate the other. The quantity of chronons used during the planetwide insurrection had drained a substantial quanta of time energy out of their segment of the Ribbon.

Each segment felt symptoms of the solution space-eternity imposed upon their existence. Where once there existed in an insignificant galaxy a single, unique Time Loop Ribbon there arose several parallel replacement existences; three new Ribbons each with their origins in the Ribbon on which Nostredame and Kobayashi Beau and Kobayashi Dante had lived.

Multiple realities were created, splitting the Ribbon of Time into slightly different copies, each with its own new unique possibilities for unfolding into the future, each looking identical from the inside, yet stretching into obscure differentiation from their original within space-eternity.

The man known as Michel Nostredame within his time segment could no longer see the beginning of his Ribbon stretching behind him as far as the birth of the Earth itself, nor could he clearly see the future that lay ahead. The dropping of the atomic bombs on Japan finally caused the first fracturing, beyond which the future could no longer definitely lead to the probabilities that had begun to unfold into possibilities from the past.

The civilization on Proxima-b had never shown great interest in their past, focused entirely on the present and all that life could provide within the limited scope of each individual's lifetime. The future did not matter except for what new pleasures could be harvested tomorrow; the only future worth considering seriously. Even dissatisfied factions who wanted something more out of life than transitory decadence could not speculate on distant future solutions to their dilemma.

As for Kepplerians – where their previous past ended held no interest whatsoever after their arrival on the planet. That past contained the reason for the oppression they had to endure since arriving on the new world – best forgotten after the successful uprising against their un-human oppressors. Bela's death outside of his time segment contributed to breaking the tenuous link with the past on Proxima-b.

The future seemed brighter for Luther and his people than it had for many previous generations. They had a great deal to look forward to regardless of whether they existed on a continuation of their old Time Loop Ribbon or a parallel new one.

Connections between the old Ribbon and the new parallel ones did not sever immediately or dramatically. At the beginning of his association with Beau, Quintessence had thought that a ribbon which had exhausted its capacity to hold causes and effects had only two possibilities - it either had to cease to exist or find a neighbouring Time Loop to interact with. Because the original Ribbon had not been fully populated with desires and aspirations and failures and actions another solution had to be found to the problem of its unravelling.

25

Adjustments

Circumstances of his departure from Anne strained his emotional reserves to the breaking point.

If Quintessence hadn't transported him at that very moment he might very well have succumbed to the desire he still felt for this woman whom he had no business knowing in the first place. Arriving at home at the exact time of the birth of his son Dante temporarily obscured his last memory of sitting at Nostredame's kitchen table. Anne had sat opposite him, her emotions in turmoil especially after he told her of Bela's death. Her hands on the table searched for his touch though his hadn't moved. He could feel their heat from where he sat and he could feel his own hands beginning to respond. Without Quintessence's intervention at that critical moment he would have been lost to his lust once more.

Another child had come into his life exactly at a time and on a planet as he was supposed to, without the complications of being misplaced in time through the mechanisations of an entity who should have stayed out of the affairs of humanity in the first place. Although Beau had returned to his time before the disruption to the flow of time nevertheless the sundering appeared to have cataclysmic consequences.

He returned to the bedroom where Emma had remained nursing their son. "I've spoken with Quintessence."

"Did you see anything out there in the streets?"

"They're already starting to clean up the mess. Some of the people must have really lost it. If it's true what they said on the news about a loss of memory ... well ... I'd hate to see what would happen if the incident went on for any longer than a few minutes."

"What about you Bebo? Do you still have all your memories?"

"Let me put it this way," he gave her a cheeky smile, "I don't remember having forgotten anything. Er - your name is - is - E - something."

Emma leant forward and punched him on the chest. "You'd better not forget that!"

"Ah - Emma - that's right. Anyway, he said that the planets haven't disappeared, we just can't see them - will never see them again - nor their entire solar systems."

"That's not so bad."

"No, I guess. Not unless you happen to be running an interstellar cruise business and you can no longer take the pleasures seekers to Jupiter for instance. Captain Catherine will be most displeased."

"What else? I can see the worry on your face Bebo."

"He said that the past has changed." He didn't tell Emma that he was mostly responsible for that with his dalliance with another man's wife, or that he was instrumental in the death of a person out of their time, "The future has changed as well. What we might have been heading towards as our most probable future has been wiped out. Perhaps I'm exaggerating a little."

Emma got a concerned look, "Just how far into the future are you talking about?" Obviously concerned more for her son than anything else she hugged the little fellow close to her breast.

"Well - a little past tomorrow, or next year. More like about a thousand years from now." He wasn't too specific about exactly how much things have or would change. He simply didn't know.

"That's alright then." She relaxed her hold on the infant.

"What about you, Em? You've got all your memories intact?"

"Do you mean ... can I still remember that obnoxious Pietro XXXVI? Sure. I also recall the first time you told me about your spooky friend. And I haven't forgotten all the time you *didn't* help me at the laboratory while you were working on your special project."

Beau probably didn't need that little dig about his absences for it brought back thoughts of his other son again. *Will I even remember him in a year's time?* "That reminds me, I'd better check with Larry at the lab and see if there's been any damage there."

"You go ahead. We'll be just fine till tonight - that is if I will still recognise you."

After an affectionate parting from Emma and little Dante, Beau decided not to go directly to the Playback Inc. laboratory. There were a few important things he wanted to think about without work distractions. He wanted to go to his favourite park but the magnetrans was rerouted to a closer location due to the congested traffic caused by so many accidents earlier in the day. Other than that everything felt perfectly normal.

This small park, still within the canopy of Gamarrah city's main dome, didn't have any creeks but it did have a rather large lake with plenty of greenery surrounding it. It still gave Beau the feeling of being away from the noise and the crowds of the domed city. Just what he needed at the moment. Perhaps this might have been the first time he'd stopped and seriously thought about Quintessence and the fantastic adventures he'd been given the opportunity to enjoy. But was it really so enjoyable given the fallout?

Quintessence? He called with his mind, not particularly caring if the entity responded or not. There was no immediate reply to disturb his peace. He didn't bother calling again, letting his mind drift to where ever it wanted to go. A few birds flitted from tree to tree ... the sun already past its zenith. Oddly, he started thinking about that strange little man Xoco. How nonchalantly he had taken the visitation from such strange men who obviously didn't belong in his world. And how he helped to bury his great, great grandfather who had too many 'greats' to his lineage to say them all. A sadness descended on Beau.

Such an enormous sadness. To think that he'd been given the chance to be with his ancestor and look what he did with it ...

Yes.

Quintessence waited until Beau was ready to engage.

What does all this mean? What have we done? Could it have been any different?

I have come into your life because I am ... because I was where I was at the time, and you were where you were. Nothing has changed, and yet everything has changed for you and Anne and Dante and for Nostredame. We could not help Bela. He was part of a new pattern and that pattern is almost complete.

Beau listened absorbing everything Quintessence said, although it didn't normally talk this much. Immersed deeply in his own contemplation Beau didn't register the last thing Quintessence said.

I feel everything has changed - I know it has. He didn't express the thoughts that only just began to form about his own life, about Emma and little Dante and what he was doing in the laboratory. Worrying thoughts, especially about his work on the Zetaverse technology.

Their conversation petered out quickly. What was there left to say? A mysterious adventure that started out with so much promise had ended in tragedy. Would he have had his two children? Little Dante quite probably - a child with Anne absolutely not. The situation on Kepler 22b had come to a boiling point anyway without his interference ... which meant that Bela didn't have to die. But then what would have become of the Kepplerians? If he'd continued twisting himself deeper into that labyrinth he may well have lost his sanity. He simply had to let it go.

Soon after his conversation he left the park. On the way to the lab he concentrated on the details of final processes for the Zetaverse that were almost completed. That presented a slight difficulty, not so much in scientific terms but in keeping track of a normal flow of developments in a logical sequence of time packets. He'd been in and out of the lab in a broken sequence. Sometimes having only missed a day, other times a whole week then returned almost the day before he left. In fact his recollections were a muddle.

"Hello Larry. Bring me up to date."

"From when Boss?" A reasonable question considering that Emma had been doing most of the work and Larry didn't know how much of their advancements Beau may have been aware of.

"From the last time we had that guy Pietro in here." That seemed like a reasonable point that both could relate to.

"The new synchronising software developed with Emma's input is working without a hitch, and the new scrubbing techniques are a definite improvement on what we had before. Also, the chemical team, again lead by Emma, has come up with a whole range of cocktails to suit just about any metabolism. I'd be happy to test a few samples on Pietro XXXVI," he suggested with a grin.

"She's a real asset," commented Beau, not meaning to be sarcastic but perhaps taken that way by Larry.

"Sure boss. She sure puts in the effort." And he didn't mean that the way it sounded either.

"So it looks like we may be ready to launch after the next set of tests if all our volunteers survive and are happy to talk to the media to endorse the final product."

"Sure thing Boss. Might take a little while yet though. When will Emma be returning?" The obvious allusion being that she, instead of him being the preference to finish the work.

Beau knew what Larry meant, and the man was right. But it didn't worry him, not like it would have done in the past. This whole Zetaverse concept was his idea, yet somehow it had lost much of its appeal during the recent more mysterious events. That very realisation gave him something else to think about on the way home other than that interfering dark energy character.

When he'd asked Quintessence 'what it all meant' he wasn't just referring to the intricacies of travelling through time and the resultant reality anomalies that created. He was also thinking about his own life and how much of it he'd dedicated to the prevailing driving force on his world. Having experienced a spectrum of life that probably no other individual in the history of humanity had, and not just in one location at one moment in time, he realized something ... *It is all so transitory, so impermanent, so fleeting ... especially what we're doing here in the lab.*

Beau began to see the pointlessness of trying to magnify remembered experiences so that people could replay them over and over and over again. And his enlightenment didn't stop there.

Emma was up and about by the time he arrived home, happily chirping away to herself fussing over Dante and doing a few domestic chores. She'd dismissed the biomechs, wanting time alone with her baby.

"Em - you've done such a great job at the lab," he said after giving her a kiss and baby a cuddle.

"What's brought this on?" genuinely surprised. Most unlike Bebo to say such a thing. "I know. I told you when we started I didn't need you."

Emma had a radiant glow about her after the birth. He'd never seen anyone as beautiful, not even the sleek killer body of his previous joy-friend. The desire began to rise in him to play but just as suddenly another thought attacked him with relentless ferocity. This comprehension had lingered at the periphery of his awareness at the time when he, Bela and Dante had been together with Xoco; the incredible superficiality of the driving force of existence on Proxima-b.

How had they degenerated into wanting nothing more than the ever increasing pursuit spiral of seeking pleasure - just pleasure, for no other reason than its own sake?

Beau stepped back from Emma, letting his arms drop to his side. It dawned on him there was only one thing to do, and that included seriously re-evaluating his contribution to Playback Inc. What possible meaningful future could be created by saturating their society with the Zetaverse technology? He went to sleep with his thoughts on a precipice of indecision. By the morning a vague set of actions presented themselves for positive decisions.

They were awoken to reality very early the next morning by the cries of a hungry baby. Here definitely was part of the new reality, perhaps not the one Quintessence had alluded to. He made several calls after he and his family had breakfasted.

He stood by the window of their apartment looking out over a world that did not seem to have changed at all. The stars that could no longer be seen could not be seen anyway during the day. And most people didn't bother looking into the sky at night anyway ... where was the fun in that?

"Larry? I know you're not going to like this. There's a couple of urgent things I need to do, one of them definitely involving our project. Can you manage without me for just a few more days?"

"Sure Boss." Larry didn't elaborate, the frustration in his voice clear. "Can I assume Emma will be back before you?"

Emma had been listening to the conversation and just shouted across the room ... "You sure can Larry." She glanced at Beau with a look that said 'you're not going anywhere with your spook.'

He got the message. "I also need to go out there with Catherine, get a better view, a better perspective on the future," he said to Emma without elaboration.

"As long as your feet stay on this planet."

"Is it alright if I poke my head into space?"

"You know what I mean," she bantered back.

As it happened the Captain of *Celestial Pleasure* had just brought her ship into port, preparing for another short cruise in a week. "Beau, what's happened to you? All of a sudden you just disappeared without a word. How long has it been? A year? More?"

"Have you got time to go on a short trip?"

"Anytime Beau, anytime. It'll be fun to get together again." He didn't disillusion her about the fun aspect. He was contracted now, and had a baby. He had no intention of falling into the lust trap again.

They took a light cruiser, with only twenty or so passengers who wanted to go for a spin in space with their own little run-abouts carried on board. Cath and Beau would not be disturbed for a while. She'd already anticipated the 'fun' factor by preparing to go and 'freshen up'.

Beau stopped her, gently holding her arm. "I need to speak with you seriously Cath. It's been this long partly because I'm contracted now and have a son." She still let him hold her arm. "And ... other things have changed as well. Haven't you noticed anything?" Now she lost her smile and withdrew from his touch.

"Go on," She'd switched into her Captain mode.

"Where are you going on your next long cruise?"

"We're just outfitting to go towards the Crux. Why do you ask?"

"What about the Solar System and Jupiter?"

"Where?"

It had been almost a triannual annual run for the *Celestial Pleasures* out to that destination. There's no way Catherine would not remember that.

"We went there together a little over a year ago. I was with Gemelle at the time. You remember Gemelle?" Beau knew now that everything Quintessence had said was true. "And we had that strange thing happen when everything went dark and your ship lay dead in space."

"Just a minute." Catherine seemed to pretend that she'd received a call. They were on the bridge. She contacted her ship's AI. "Erasmus. Search for Jupiter in our records. When was our last trip there?" The answer came back almost immediately.

"Unknown destination, although there is a record of having commenced a journey towards a yellow star."

"There. Satisfied. Now - what's this all about, and don't play games with me, no pun intended."

At first Beau though it strange that *he* could still remember that far back and in as much detail as he wanted. Perhaps that's because he'd been so intimately involved in all the events leading up to the present moment. As he unfolded a shortened story of his travels to her she shook her head every now and then, stopping him at one point. "The *Chronos Hopper* comes to mind. Is that a real cruiser?"

"No, Cath. You asked me once if I ever needed a Captain for the *Chronos Hopper* you'd be available. It was just a joke. By the way - have you had any ship troubles lately ... like complete ship-wide blackouts?"

"No. What happens now?" As the captain of a pleasure cruiser in space she had to consider any eventuality that could present a danger to her travellers.

"I don't really know. I suppose life goes on as normal for us."

"That's about as unhelpful as your usual approach to problems solving." She'd obviously remembered that much of their joint past history together.

They were only out in space for a day and half. They didn't talk much on the way home. That was the last time Beau ever met with Captain Catherine.

She was not disappointed at not being able to take thrill seekers to Jupiter ... She could no longer remember it ever having existed, nor could her on-board AI, Erasmus.

*

"You don't stay for long in one place these days." Emma didn't bother to greet Beau when he finally turned up. She'd expected him home a day ago. "Have you been tripping with your special friend again?"

Beau could see the anger rising on her face. She was right, he'd been inconsiderate and selfish. He took Dante from her arms to do the father-baby thing. The little tyke wouldn't have known him from a lump of space rock. Almost immediately a whimper told him he'd better return the boy to his mother. "Em, I need to tie up some lose ends. And no, I didn't go off with Quintessence. On another matter ... remember I warned you about a man called Brummel?" she nodded while settling Dante. "The thing I didn't tell you at the time was that he and I had a rather unpleasant disagreement. That business needs to be settled."

"Go and do what you have to. Don't come home until you're ready to get back to a normal life." Then she added, "how is your Captain Catherine friend?"

He didn't know if that was a serious question or not. He decided to deal with that at a later time. Other more important loose ends had to be tied up. That's all he wanted to do now. As exciting and interesting the whole adventure with Quintessence had been he'd already made up his mind he'd had enough. His greatest regret out of it all wasn't the disruption he'd caused to people on two other planets. It wasn't the lives lost because of the fighting on Keppler 22b - that would have happened anyway. It wasn't even losing Bela ... they never should have met in the first place. It was the absolute certainty that he would never get a chance to see his other son grow up into a man, or look upon the red-haired mother that bore him. He was convinced of that, not because Emma had forbidden him to go flitting about in time, but because they may as well have been living in a different universe from what Quintessence had said about the sundering.

Beau didn't warn Brummel, CEO of Omnifun Unlimited, of his intended visit. With any luck that egotistical Pietro XXXVI wouldn't be far away, and he could deal with both of them at the same time.

Quintessence? What Beau had in mind needed his 'spooks' help.

Yes?

Would you do something for me?

That is possible. The new pattern is not yet complete.

I will call you.

At Omnifun's corporate dome attached to the outskirts of Gamarrah City Beau had no trouble getting through security. "Come right up," invited Brummel's cheerful voice, "we have been waiting for you."

They won't be so happy when they see the surprise I have for them.

"What took you so long?" Brummel didn't go so far as to be personal with a slap on Beau's back. Pietro was there as expected, still with that perpetual sour look on his face.

"Can you two buddies spare a little time for me to show you something?"

"Why not. As long as its connected with your work. You haven't forgotten our offer, have you? Name it and you've got it."

"No, indeed. And I hope neither of you have forgotten what I said about your chances of survival under the attentions of the Holy Inquisition."

Suddenly Brummel's apparent good humour dissipated. Here was a nobody scientist without enough money to his name to buy himself a decent apartment daring to threaten him, one of the worlds most powerful moguls, with stupid incomprehensible nonsense. He looked over to Pietro. If they'd bothered to research deep history they might have learnt what Inquisitions were all about. It didn't really matter now if they had for that knowledge would probably have been forgotten just as Catherine had forgotten about Jupiter. Pietro's blank stare only confirmed their ignorance.

"I see you have. Never mind. Here's a little reminder." Beau kept his eyes on them as he spoke to his spook. "Quintessence, please drop these two anywhere in Spain around segment 1500 in one of the active torture chambers. Give them a little time to absorb how people used to generate entertainment for themselves." Beau made the request aloud to give the two friends a moment to compose themselves.

Before Brummel could summon his new bodyguards the comfortable room they'd been conducting the interview in disappeared. The immediate darkness came upon them so suddenly that it took a few moments for the light of torches to reveal a large stone enclosure through the smoky haze, with many persons clad in black surrounded by all manner of archaic instrumentation. The smell of rotting flesh impacted most unpleasantly on Pietro's delicate senses. He should have been used to it, from the nefarious activities he was involved in.

"Gently now," instructed Archbishop Cisneros of Toledo, "we want to give this sinner every opportunity to confess." This inquisitor prided himself on being a compassionate man. All he wanted was for the heretics to confess their sins and embrace the Church and all it stood for. Pietro and Brummel had been deposited hard up against one of the damp walls opposite to where a reluctant penitent braced himself against the strappado as his hands were being tied behind his back. The two spectators watched mesmerized, unable to comprehend the nature or the purpose of the procedure.

One of the Priests approached the prisoner, obviously anticipating his enjoyment of the man's forthcoming pain. "Do you confess your sins?" Another Priest looped the rope over a brace in the ceiling, not bothering to wait for the man's answer.

Pietro watched the rope being pulled through a pulley. *If they pull on the rope* ... that's when he realised what was about to happen. He prodded Brummel pointing the mechanism out to him. It fascinated Pietro. Brummel lost control of his bladder as the function of the apparatus dawned on him.

Archbishop Cisneros made one more attempt to save the soul of this unfortunate creature. "Confess now and all your sins will be forgiven." The man turned his bloodshot eyes towards this Priest and spat in his face. In the next instant he was raised high off the ground, hanging by his arms. This was a strong man, a farmer by the look of him, thick boned and heavily muscled.

Brummel started shaking. He'd had enough, but dared not call out in case they were seen standing in the shadows, the urine still warm against his leg. Pietro wondered what the Priests would do next. The torturers added a series of drops, which still didn't dislocate the farmer's shoulders. Father Cisneros shook his head in disappointment. He genuinely hoped this man would repent. "Carry on. His immortal soul may yet be saved, though not his mortal body." He left the Inquisitor's chamber in the crypt situated below the Toledo Cathedral to attend to his other important duties.

By this time Brummel's urine had gone cold. Pietro continued watching, fascinated as weights were being added to the man's feet. The last thing they saw was the man being raised again, dropped, and heard the crunch of his shoulders dislocating. That even made Pietro XXXVI snap his eyes shut for an instant.

In that moment Quintessence returned them to Brummel's office. Beau had waited, relaxing in an opulent couch. It only took a split second look to gauge the effect of the visitation on these two reprehensibles.

"Did you enjoy that Pietro? You get a lot of pleasure from seeing others suffering I understand."

The ordeal was over. A most effective demonstration of travelling through time to any segment upon the Ribbon.

How were you able to do this, Quintessence? You did say our Ribbon had been broken.

Three parallel Ribbons have been created. They are still attached to the original, which has not yet completely dissolved into space-eternity.

So you could still do this again?

Yes.

On hearing Beau's voice the two men opened their eyes. Brummel still shook. The colour had completely drained out of Pietro. He tried to say something but it came out as incomprehensible gibberish. Then Brummel tried. He screamed at Beau.

"WHAT HAVE YOU DONE TO US! What drug can create this kind of monstrosity?"

"I gave you no drugs. You wanted to know more about the Zetaverse. It was designed for time travel." He lied. "This was just a little demonstration. We took you back to the time of the Spanish Holy Inquisition." Beau examined the pathetic examples of humanity before him, deciding they needed more convincing that this technology was not really as desirable as they might have thought. Brummel had almost stopped shaking. Just as well, he might have slipped on the puddle that had formed at his feet, his bladder still out of control. Pity about that. He had such a wonderful colourful outfit on that would now be permanently stained ... and that hat ... that really was a magnificent creation. "I see you like your friends designer clothes, Pietro. You'll fit in perfectly at your next destination."

Quintessence ... Now, please take them to see Xoco, just to give them a little perspective on how civilisation evolved to be more 'civil'. No need to bring them back, if that would disturb the new pattern too much.

*

A little later that afternoon in Chalchuapa; after the morning of the double sunrise, the King's guards marched to Xoco's hut. The King had summoned the Shaman after the darkness had threatened to engulf their world. A most unusual way to call upon such an important man, as if he was a prisoner that had to be escorted. Xoco hadn't taken much notice of young Aapo running off directly after the sun returned to the sky the second time. The boy had been of an excitable nature all his life. Xoco quickly got used to it after taking the lad on as an apprentice and didn't think twice about him running off like that. He had not thought to warn the boy about not spreading rumours about Star Men.

Aapo first ran home to talk to his mother, who in turn sought out her friends to pass on a most incredible story. Of course they'd all experienced the dramatic double sunrise, which at first seemed like a new darkness had come upon the world to swallow it. Their entire civilization knew that their sun God, Huitzilopochtli, waged a constant war against darkness. It appeared that that morning the forces of darkness had won the battle.

Word soon spread throughout Chalchuapa about the Star Men who had visited Xoco. The King himself interrogated Aapo, unable to extract the information he needed. He had to speak with Xoco directly. These men from the stars must have been the cause of their God being so upset that he'd lost control over the forces of light and darkness. If Xoco had joined with the agents of darkness from the stars then he had to be dealt with immediately.

Six fully armed members of the Kings personal guard arrived late in that same afternoon at Xoco's modest hut. One stepped inside, holding his stabbing spear in from of him. He wore full battle dress ready for whatever devilry might be in there. He saw the two strangers before he saw Xoco's familiar face, immediately positioning himself into a battle stance, right foot back - body slightly forward - spear lowered and angled up pointing at the heart of the taller of the two Gods. For that is how Brummel must have appeared to him. Brummel's feathered head covering, his ornate and skimpy outfit together with profuse body paint of every colour imaginable made him look remarkably like the King's warriors. Either he was a warrior of the God of darkness, or the God himself.

The warrior thrust his spear forward threateningly, "Who are these devils, Xoco!" he shouted. That brought the other three warriors bursting into the hut.

Xoco had not met Pietro or Brummel before of course, but he did recognise some of the facial characteristics to be similar to that of his previous visitor, Beau.

"They are not Devils."

"We most certainly are nothing of the kind," blustered Pietro. He'd worked out Beau must have transported them to another world again. "We are travellers from another world!" That turned out to be exactly the wrong thing to say.

Not meeting any opposition from the strangers the six warriors immediately took them prisoner, including Xoco and marched them through the streets of the city to the base of their temple. The men tried objecting, blabbering all sorts of nonsense about living on another world, of travelling through time - all of which made the situation much worse for them. Only when they came face to face with the overwhelming authority of the King in his full ceremonial outfit did they stop. He examined them closely, noting the smell of fear strong upon them, and of stale urine. *These are not Gods*, he decided - Gods don't wet themselves. He also decided they were imposing enough to be used as an appeasement of his people to assuage their fears. They may even be suitable as a sacrifice of human heart and blood to feed Huitzilopochtli. To Brummel's surprise a great feast was spread before them as all the people of the city gathered around the temple to witness the event.

"This is not so bad," commented Brummel, "the fruit is strange but most pleasant. They settled with relish anticipating the pleasures of this magnificent banquet.

"So is this drink," added Pietro as he downed another mug of balché.

They did not notice the encroaching sunset above the forest canopy, nor the fire that had been lit at the summit of the temple. Their sense of wellbeing, replete with food and the intoxicating beverage overcame their previous apprehensions. These were thoroughly nice, civilized people who knew how to treat guests. Brummel commented as much to Pietro.

Two guards urged them to stand as the King approached their table near the foot of the temple. He bowed, just enough to show the deference due to such important men of industry and with an extended hand invited them to join him up the steps of the pyramid. By this time Pietro had lost all sense of reality, as had his friend Brummel.

"Looks like they're taking us up there to show us a sunrise," slurred Brummel. "Look how big their sky is. I can't even see the top of their city dome."

Huffing and puffing they finally arrived at the top platform and were joined by the first person they had seen that day. Xoco had also garbed himself in a most extraordinary outfit.

It all happened so swiftly that Brummel didn't realise till the last moment what was actually going on. Two guards swept Pietro off his feet, placing him facing up on a large stone bench. It only took an instant for the King to sweep his cloak aside, flash a curved dagger into the air and bring it down to expose the man's heart. Pietro was still alive when his beating heart was taken from his chest and held aloft in the air, for all the people to see.

It was too late for Brummel to struggle. Within moments his life also helped to appease the anger of Xoco's God.

From that day on the sun continued across the sky everyday without once threatening to rob its people of light in the mornings.

*

These men's possibilities had withered a long time ago. They were of no consequence to themselves or the rest of creation, even though their deaths out of their own time and place did exacerbate the deteriorating condition of the original Ribbon.

Quintessence had complied with Beau's wishes only because ripples of cause and effect did not extend beyond themselves for Pietro XXXVI and Brummel. Its work had yet to be completed. Having initiated a chain of events from the first contact with Beau several incomplete threads needed attention.

Before the Ribbon of your segment detaches itself there is one more visitation necessary for you.

No, no. I don't want to go back to Dante - or to Anne. He made that last decision without premeditation, knowing it would destroy the lives of both his son and the boy's mother. Everything had changed.

You will not go far, either in space or time.

*

Taken from Brummel's office Beau found himself in his laboratory, with Emma and Larry on the other side of the room completely engrossed in some activity he couldn't recognise. *Why on Prox would he bring me here? Ah, good, Emma is here. She must have gotten a biomech to look after Dante.* He looked around the lab, seeing a few unfamiliar pieces of equipment. The calendar on the far wall showed the date - 2587. *That can't be right.* He turned to go and check it, bumping into a stool. He didn't feel it. Adrenalin rushed through his veins. The stool did not move, yet from his peripheral vision he was sure he'd bumped it. He reached out a hand to move it. He could not grasp it.

Beau felt himself falling into a daze as he continued carefully towards the wall calendar. 2587. A full thirty years ahead of the time he was first contacted by Quintessence. Distracted by those thoughts he didn't notice the door on the other side of the lab open and two men walk in.

Emma straightened up. "Excellent. Time you turned up Dante. You're just like your father." She threw a glance at the other man, smiling. "You are a bad influence on our boy," she said to him, smiling.

"He's not a boy anymore," replied Beau as he reached Emma.

"No, I guess not. We can't go on calling this brilliant Director of the facility a boy forever. Much has changed since he was our little grub."

Beau could not believe what he was seeing, hearing. He wanted to go closer to have a better look at this 'boy', for from that distance he couldn't quite recognise the features. He managed two steps before noticing the scene in front of him receding at the same pace he moved towards it. The people continued speaking, he had to stop to listen.

"What direction do you want to take with these drugs?" Emma asked Dante.

"Father, what do you think? There's been so much paranoia from that Zetaverse application and so many people have completely lost track of reality, we have to fast-track these new trials."

"I agree, son. Since Omnifun Unlimited went out of business Playback has gone right off. Without competition they've pushed our previous work ahead too fast. We have to stop them somehow."

"At least we don't have to play by their rules anymore."

Once again Beau glanced around the laboratory, this time taking more notice of the signage. He saw the words 'Quantum Reality' above the calendar and on a whole range of equipment around him. He turned around to the door used by Dante and Beau to enter. Above the door ... 'Quantum Reality Laboratory #3'.

Another jump put him back into his own apartment in time to see his baby being breast fed by his mother. "You're back. Sooner than I expected," a slight irony in her voice.

Beau walked to the bed, sat on the edge, silent, watching - still caught up in mental images of seeing his son fully grown only moments ago.

A reality that cannot take place unless you make the right decisions, added Quintessence to his thoughts.

Was that real?

Yes. A possibility which arose on the old Ribbon but now can only become a probability on this one. It will fade if the strength of your decisions diminishes in this reality.

Will you and I talk again?

No. Your personal future is not long enough.

Why did all this happen?

The cosmos remained silent.

*

Kobayashi Beau spent more time at home with Emma and Dante now that his attention had ceased to be diverted by forces such as dark energy twisting his mind into thinking of events in the past as being hallucinations and imaginings. The pleasures of his life shifted from artificially induced surrealities, away from virtual realities, away from augmented realities. He took pleasure in watching his son grow, especially in seeing him rejecting the now less prominent, though still popular philosophy of Hedonism.

As the years flowed by Beau forgot about Michel Nostredame. He forgot Bela. His mind had realigned itself with the manifestations of his present because those other influences had ceased to reinforce themselves into his once expanded reality. He even lost all memory of Anne and a young fellow named Beau who went to Oxford University to study medicine. He could no longer recall Beatrice or a God called Metaquanta - not even the planet Keppler 22b ever surfaced in his thoughts. But there remained in his mind an unshakeable strong conviction of the uselessness of a life dedicated to nothing more than the pursuit of pleasure. He saw with a new mind that Playback Inc. had no future, and to that end he started his own corporation in opposition to everything Playback Inc. stood for.

Nor did he allow his son to fall into the trap of greeting everyone with the words, 'What is your pleasure?'

*

Beau may have been channelled by exotic forces to start an entirely new thread of possibilities in his life, beginning with the birth of his son. Quintessence was satisfied with the corrected trajectory Beau's life had taken after its inevitable involvement in it. However, the consequences of that intervention had begun a great upheaval in the balance of time within space-eternity which had to be fully corrected.

The beginning threads of revised possibilities on a new Time Loop Ribbon, upon which a man called Kobayashi Dante was to change their history, had yet to be created. With the passing of many more years Kobayashi Beau on Proxima-b achieved the fullness of his personal allocation within the Ribbon of Time. His son Dante inherited the convictions of his father, which he passed onto his own son.

Dante, son of Dante, son of Kobayashi Beau, Quintessence called.

One day, Quintessence renewed his acquaintanceship with the family line of Kobayashi. On a planet called Proxima-b, well advanced in the process of what they called terra-forming, although no one quite remembered why they called the process by that name, a young man in his prime had a most unusual thought stream featuring his grandfather. *I have not thought about my grandfather for a long time.* He punched in new co-ordinates to take his shuttle into a higher orbit around Proxima-b. He wanted to measure the magnetic fields around the planet once more to be sure of the accuracy of his original data.

Kobayashi Beau was quite an extraordinary human being, Dante registered another odd thought out of the blue. Perhaps Quintessence found it less distracting to make contact while Dante was in space where he didn't have the constant interruptions of other scientists bothering him with questions.

He was indeed, from what my father told me. What is happening here?

Dante could relax a little while the craft orbited into a more distant position. That's when he became conscious of ... of ... talking to himself?

No. That can't be right. My grandfather used to talk to himself, or so grandmother said on many occasions.

He was not talking to himself. He was talking to me.

Dante ignored that - checked his instruments - not quite there yet. As a man with very focused intent he could block out all extraneous input when concentrating on something important. His measurements were important - critical. For humanities' continued survival on Proxima-b the planet's atmosphere had to be enriched and its retention around the planet ensured. Its once cooling liquid outer core had been energised sufficiently to liquefy it again, enabling it to resume rotating. Without that dynamo life would not survive into the cosmic flow of time.

Your planet will live, as will your people here and elsewhere.

What? This time he took more notice of the subject of his internal conversation. Dante checked his comms equipment - called down to base and found no problems associated with rogue transmissions.

Who is this?

I am Quintessence. Your grandfather talked to me.

He had heard many stories about that illusion. Stories about so many adventures his grandfather was supposed to have had that it was impossible to dismiss the voice as nothing more than his imagination.

Why are you talking to me now? Can I see you?

No. You cannot see dark energy, nor can your instruments. I have watched your father grow into a man and I have waited for your mind to become receptive.

As a scientist I have an open mind. I am trying to make our planet more habitable for the future. I explore, discover, create.

You will succeed. I can see the past and I can see the future.

That is reassuring. But what do you want from me?

Nothing. I want to give you insight, knowledge.

Now you've got me interested.

Quintessence didn't go into details about the history of Dante's family, or the achievements of his grandfather. It did discover the necessity to find a way to seed the future of the Kobayashi line in the new Keppler Ribbon. Only Dante could do that.

I can show you a planet on which humanity can exist in harmony with the environment. Do you wish to see it?

Sure, but I'm busy right now.

This will not take long. It is a planet in your galaxy, but at a different time. Their beginning started at the ending of your old Time Loop Ribbon.

Travel through time? Now that's something I could enjoy. You can bring me back to 'now', right?

Yes. Put your craft on autopilot. I will take you to another world in another time.

Keppler 22b orbited serenely around the sun Keppler-11. It's Time Loop Ribbon became a little more complicated by the arrival of the human species. It appeared at first that a planet with air, temperature, gravity and water compatibility it was the near perfect place to colonise. Except it had too much water. That could be managed.

When they landed their star ships became floating islands of civilization. In space the population had begun to stagnate during the voyage due to severe birth control measures. Metaquanta, in his wisdom - and programming, initiated the first Conception Centres on the largest landmasses of Keppler 22b.

Fertile males and females had been conditioned during the last stages of the journey to do their duty to ensure the survival of the species. At Conception Centre 14, Father 95, one of the lower caste Priests checked people off his list who had reported for procreation duty that day.

"State your name, age," instructed Father 95.

One by one men and women filed past into the building that would be their living quarters until successful fertilisation of eggs had been achieved. People were free to choose their own partners on the proviso of sufficient genetic diversity within their genomes.

"Dante, age, 39."

Quintessence had dropped him into one of the floating island space ships, which Dante didn't find altogether strange although a little antiquated from what he was used to. People milled about, happily chatting to one another. Altogether the scene presented an atmosphere of excited anticipation. Some of those nearest to him formed themselves into a line which he decided to join.

He went to move forward. "Stop. There is no Dante on my list."

"I only arrived today," said Dante rather amused at the whole process. He'd not seen such biomechs in service back home except in their museums. As a scientist he rather enjoying seeing them go through their paces. Another Priest took him out of line for a physical and DNA test.

Quintessence had actually deposited him on ship island #3 in the middle of a crowd getting ready to disembark. Unsteady on his feet at the sudden change of location he had bumped the person in front of him.

"Sorry. Beg your pardon." He'd put his hand out to steady himself against Madeleine. She was about his age, a little shorter with long white hair and ebony black skin. The image of this spectacular looking girl draped in a canary yellow caftan took him completely by surprise. Those pitch black ebony eyes lingered in his imagination - and that's all it took.

"Yubeehoo? she asked, checking his rather drab outfit. Sure it was unique, but somewhat yethch.

"Pardon?"

"No need for you to be pardoned. You can ask a Priest later if you feel the need. I asked who you are. Not from this ship?"

"No actually. Only just arrived - Dante. Where are we all going?"

"Conception Centre 14."

"Is that what I think it sounds like?"

"Only if you want to make babies."

Dante didn't know how to respond to that on the spur of the moment. Quintessence intimated an interesting outing. This definitely headed in that direction.

"And, Yubeehoo?" he asked still fixated on her face.

"Madeleine. You catch on quick." Their eyes remained glued to each other while the queue they had joined stood still. "Just follow me."

Still not contracted and without a steady girlfriend Dante didn't need a second invitation.

Father 95 checked all ships manifests for a 'Dante'. It seems he might have existed. A systems outage some time ago resulted in some of the original documents from their departure time being deleted, or at least corrupted. So the name 'Dante' may very well have existed. Finding out who he was carried a much lower priority than getting population growth off to a good start. The man's bio-indicators showed no illnesses or diseases that could be passed on, and he showed in fact most excellent DNA characteristics.

Island life suited Dante. He enjoyed Madeleine's company and that of his fast growing son. Metaquanta looked after procreating couples most handsomely, so much so that Dante began to feel as if he'd found where he could spend the rest of his life. The planet was magnificent, with clean air and water. Conditions were no more crowded than back home and nothing lacked to make life one of leisure and comfort. Even opportunities had arisen to do meaningful work after he showed such strong aptitude in the scientific field.

Dante?

Quintessence had not contacted him for several years. Dante had almost forgotten about the strange voice in his head.

It is time for you to leave. Your son shows every probability of surviving. This Time Loop Ribbon has now stabilised.

What if I don't want to leave?

You have no choice.

By the end of the last spoken word Dante found himself seated at the controls of his craft ... elapsed time, two hundred and forty three minutes - exact duration of one orbit around Proxima-b.

Having received his seed the Keppler Ribbon could now be set adrift from the original. Continuity for events destined to unfold had been re-established. Although some aspects of the peoples' revolt needed different possibilities, nevertheless the insurrection would take place and Dante's descendant would be involved.

26

Kobayashi Dante Ribbon

The original Time Loop Ribbon still existed, slowly transferring its energy to the new Ribbons.

Within the new reality of the Kobayashi Dante Ribbon many things had begun to change.

Comet McNaught-Russel created a great deal of havoc. Had it arrived before the sundering it may have plunged into the planet's ocean. In all probability human life would have been extinguished. As it was the island installations survived the oceanic upheaval. Low lying Atolls disappeared under water for a short time as did the fringes of most land masses.

Luther and his friends returned to Dante's place after the comet passed and waters receded. Beau and Bela were missing.

"Do you know what happened to Bela?" Beatrice asked Luther who stood by the window watching the chaotic aftermath from both the fight and the comet. Many things not secured had been tossed about. Rescue teams had to clear the way to get to people who had ended up in the ocean. A total scene of disorder most probably repeated throughout all the artificial islands. Under the dubious care of their Priest minders such mayhem never existed. Making the entire situation much worse Luther could see some surviving Priests wandering about aimlessly, getting in everybody's way but not contributing to the clean up or the rescues. People had left them alone for the time being, too busy trying to get back some normality, unaware of a major change to their psyche.

"Who?" Either he didn't hear or was too occupied with thoughts of what had to be done next ... for surely this was not the end of the struggle for them.

"Bela, the man Beau brought along to help us."

He turned away from the window, thinking hard. "Ah, him. He got the message out to our people. I don't think we would have succeeded without him."

"Yes ... that's the one. Do you remember what happened to him?"

"Darling Trixie - you can't expect me to keep track of everything that's going on. All I know right at this instant is that he's not here, nor is his friend. He did a good job."

"Well - you really should be aware of this. I think we have a bigger problem now than we had before. I went back into the core to finish the job. You saw me. Somehow a Security Priest got in ahead of me while Bela was still there. Without any warning this mongrel thrust its hand into Bela's chest and ripped his heart out ... simply ripped it out."

Beatrice stopped at that point, her whispered last words petered out into silence - the memory and the image too overwhelming to let her continue. None of their small group knew this. Quintessence had immediately whisked Beau and Bela away to Xoco, back to Earth's past. That action did not bring Bela back to life. Death is death ... across all of time, all of space, all of eternity.

For a few minutes it seemed as if no one in the room heard her. She had just said something that was not possible ... just not possible. Could the moment of Bela's death, the final trigger in the severing of the Ribbon have had any effect on the workings of Metaquanta's mind? Were there cosmic energies released that had somehow removed all safeguards against simulated intelligences having the capacity to take human life? Whatever had caused the aberrant behaviour meant that human life would no longer be safe on Keppler 22b while Metaquanta and his Priests continue to exist.

At last Luther spoke out. "Priests cannot act on their own volition. It can only have been under Metaquanta's direction. What's the last thing you remember Dante?"

In all the action with bodies of Priests and insurrectionists all over the floor of the cube it was hardly surprising that those actually engaged in the fighting might not have taken full notice of everything. Dante wasn't a fighter. He tried to stand back away from the life threatening harm. As the surviving group rushed out of the cube to help the others at the entrance Dante had glanced back momentarily for no real reason, and only for the briefest second.

"There were no Priests left standing when you finished with them. Now that I think back I did see something that made no sense at the time. Apart from the Priests, all seemingly unharmed except for being crumpled up on the floor, I saw - this can't be right - I saw our dead people, or at least parts of them all over the floor as well. Most of them were horribly mutilated; arms missing, heads twisted off, their bodies bent into unnatural angles."

Once again silence. What Dante had just said could not readily be accepted by any rational mind. AIs don't do such things.

"Beatrice, how far did you get with Metaquanta's system?"

"I managed to disable most of its internal circuits – unfortunately not enough to kill the entire Metaquanta program suite – seeing Bela being mutilated like that - well - I just couldn't keep going."

*

"Mother! Can I go and visit Auntie Beatrice?"

Gemma's son, barely ten years old, could already navigate to the closest islands near his own habitation island.

"What do you think Dante? We're not expecting any storms are we?" After the passing of the comet their oceans still hadn't settled to fully predictable behaviour.

"Sure. He's not going far. We don't have to worry about his being exiled by the Priests anymore for disobeying a curfew. Remember those days?"

"Off you go Pietro. I want you home before sunset. See if Uncle Luther and Auntie Beatrice want to come back for a meal." Every individual on their planet was required to have a unique component to their name. During his researches into his ancestry extending deep into Earth's past Dante came across a name which had keyed into his cellular memory. It seemed to have a connection to his own past, though unaware of his ancestor's connection to a man with that name. The sound of it seemed to generate a sense of strength ... definitely a good name for his son.

Kobayashi Pietro-I disappeared out the door before Gemma could get up to give him a hug. He never actually got to experience life under the benevolence of their God, Metaquanta, who no longer existed.

"I can't imagine what life must have been like back then."

"And I can't imagine why we thought the world would end in 3797. Look at us now, already 3807 and nothing's happened. I seem to have a vague recollection of someone telling me about a premonition or something."

"You don't mean that - ah - was there a man who visited you?"

"No. Just my imagination. Never mind. We finally got rid of the Priests and their master. That's all that matters."

27

Michel Nostredame Ribbon

Peace and tranquility began to settle upon Quintessence with each action that contributed to restoring the balance within space-eternity that had been disturbed by its actions.

It could not escape the reality that through its own meddling, if for no other reason than perhaps curiosity, it had become the architect of the creation of parallel Ribbons of Time that most probably should not have come into existence. Just as much of a mystery to it as not knowing the reason for its own existence, it could not fathom why it felt such a strong compulsion to communicate with Kobayashi Beau in the first place.

However that was all in the past for Beau and Dante and Bela and of course that curious man Nostredame. Yet to Quintessence all these eventualities seemed to ebb and flow continuously without ever settling in any one direction. And within this new chronological spectrum one more lose end required attention. Michel Nostredame also needed to have his visions of the future slightly amended so his writings would not mislead future generations.

"Father, I need to speak with you," Beau announced as soon as he arrived home from having completed his medical Degree at Oxford. He also wanted to catch up soon with his friend, Bela's son, in Florence but strange thoughts had been bothering him for quite some time.

Nostredame had grown old by the time his son returned. He'd suffered from gout most of his life and in the last years the condition had turned to edema, which his son could not treat. By early January 1566 Michel could no longer drag himself up into his attic, nevertheless his interest and preoccupation with divination continued unabated. The bedroom replaced the attic as his mystic realm, books again lay strew about on the floor, star maps and astrological charts hung haphazard from the walls. In this chaos Beau had nowhere to settle other than the edge of his father's bed.

"Welcome home my boy. Come tell me all about the University. I have missed you these last years." Michel still had no idea that this red haired healthy lad wasn't his son at all. The boy had all of his mother's features, with only his height and general exceptional good health to suggest in any way that his genetics may have had a foreign contributor.

"You are not well, father. I don't want to burden you with my problems." In the early years of his life Beau didn't get much attention from Michel, yet a strong bond did develop between them. Beau always showed interest in his father's work and Michel found pleasure in explaining the secrets of his methods of prognostication on the rare few occasions when they interacted.

"I am almost completely bedridden now. I'm sure anything you tell me will only cheer me up." Not entirely a sensitive thing to say as Beau intimated he'd wanted to discuss 'problems'.

"You have spent most of your life on understanding your visions," he started, "and I often wondered where those visions came from.

I don't want you to give me a lecture on the subject, rather I would like to share something with you."

Michel adjusted his position in bed, grunting and moaning with the effort. "Just move over a little and give my leg a bit more room."

"What would you say if I told you about the strange things that have come into my mind?"

"Hand me my quill and parchment, boy." A sudden vigour seemed to come into the eyes of the old man. "Now, tell me everything. Leave nothing out and don't go too fast. These stiff old bones need extra encouragement to work properly."

"Sometimes in the middle of my studies at night my mind would wander and I would see strange places. Places I have never visited. Places so strange that I could not imagine them to be anywhere in England or anywhere in our known world." Michel pushed himself into a more comfortable writing position, sandwiching another pillow behind his back.

His pupils dilated with anticipation, hand hovering over the parchment ready to record every word. "Go on - go on."

"From a great distance I saw a world, as round as a ball. Part of it seemed to be darkness, and part in the light and in-between everything seemed to be either green or water." Beau knew nothing about cellular memory. Nothing in his medical course could have suggested a world with one face turned mostly to its sun. Nothing he might have read, or discussed could have led his mind to conceive of such a thing. "I do not know what this means."

Michel finished making a note of the images. "You have been where I could never go. I envy you the clarity of your vision."

"There is more, father. On this world people lived in tunnels and strange buildings, shaped like mushroom domes that let their sunlight through."

"What did these people look like?"

"This is really the strangest part ... if I close my eyes now I can see them again wearing clothes that are almost transparent, sometimes wearing very little clothes at all." Without realising it the young man's mental image encompassed a deeply hidden memory of a man he once talked to as a boy, as well as the visions he'd been having.

Michel's hand work furiously to get all this down, splashing some ink about without caring one jot about it. Excited as he was still his energy drained away by the effort. "I can do no more for now. Let me rest. I have to think. Come to me again tomorrow."

"Yes father. But what do you think? Is this some work of the devil to undo my mind? I have seen other things ..."

"Not now. You are in good mind, my boy. You have been given the gift of seeing into the future. Come to me tomorrow." With that he slid down from the pillow and closed his eyes. He remembered seeing Kobayashi the second time and the oddly transparent clothes he wore, and the third time when the man appeared naked in his attic room. He began to ponder what mystic art his son might have learnt, besides his medical studies.

This was just the opportunity Quintessence needed to visit Nostredame. Michel's mind had opened to the visions told to him by his son. His breathing slowed as a quiet tranquillity descended on him, taking him back to his own visions of times far into the future. He thought about the years of peace four thousand years hence, then further calamities he foresaw before another age began. He recalled his conviction that all things must come to an end, and that end ... *when was it? ... ah yes ... 3797. I could not see beyond that time.*

The moment had arrived for Quintessence to expand the old man's sight. He took the old man's mind, just as he had done with Kobayashi Beau on the first couple of occasions. He cradled Michel's mind in a tender embrace and took him to a wonderous world of oceans and islands and gentle rains.

Nostredame watched a young boy jump out of his small sailing vessel.

"Hurry up Pietro, your father is waiting!"

"Coming mother, let me just tie up the boat."

"Are you ready Dante? she called back to her partner, "Our son will be here in a minute." The room had been prepared for the celebration. Michel saw though his mind's eye a tall glass building, taller than any structure he'd seen even in Paris, floating on an island of many similar buildings crowding in on each other ... *Dante? I have heard that name before ...*

Quintessence took Michel into Dante's room, where Pietro's father waited for him. Never did Michel have such a clear vision in his meditations before. It felt like he could reach out with his hand to touch the person standing there with his back to him. Michel looked past the man through an enormous glass wall, and there he saw an ocean with many more floating islands full of buildings. *Surely this is not Venezia!* "What manner of world is this?" he asked aloud.

The man in front of him suddenly turned around at hearing the voice. "Who may you be? You have the look of an exile about you." With a sudden intake of breath Dante realised that he'd once asked that question of another stranger not so very long ago. He didn't mean to say 'exile', but that part of their past was difficult to forget.

"I am Nostredame, Michel Nostredame. What be the year?"

"3807. It is the year 3807," he said, still overcome by a faint memory of having heard that name ... but who from?

Footsteps could be heard pounding towards the closed room. Pietro burst in overflowing with excitement at what surprise his father might have for his birthday.

Nostredame had disappeared out of the room. Before Quintessence took him back to his bed he let the old man see this water world with its many floating islands and magnificent atolls surrounded with oceans and oceans of water everywhere.

Beau found his father in an exceptionally good mood the next morning. "My son, thank you. Thank you."

"I have done nothing father."

"You do not yet know, and may not come to know until the fullness of your days. What else have you got to tell me? Come sit."

Out came the quill and parchment again. For a few minutes Michel seemed to withdraw into himself, saying nothing more to encourage Beau. It gave the young man a chance to collect his thoughts, which had begun to coalesce around images of another world he seemed to recollect seeing. But of course that was not possible.

"Well - out with it." Michel had returned from his introspection.

"During my trip across France I fell into periods of deep reverie. Odd really, as I don't have that habit. One day I felt I was looking at another world where I didn't think it would be possible for people to live for it seemed to have nothing but water everywhere. Not like a flood, more like a perpetual ocean." This time Michel looked up from his scribing, reached out a hand to Beau's arm to stop him for a moment. Then withdrew and nodded for the lad to continue. "As the image cleared of the falling rain I saw many islands with buildings that didn't look like they were made of stone or wood. I could see right through them."

Beau continued with his story, not stopping for a moment, letting everything come gushing out. Michel stopped writing a little while later, turning his vision inwards as he listened to his son, losing himself in realms far more comfortable than the reality of his room in Salon.

A few months later in July Michel Nostredame died. He'd begun a new century of quatrains based on his latest visions and all that Beau had told him, beginning with the first quatrain ...

> Cries, weeping and the rule of un-men will pass
> and upon the floating lands of oceans wide
> Peace for 4000 plus seven then seventy two
> shall reign among the children of the BeauTiful.

By the time Nostredame died Beau had already gone to Florence to begin his medical practice with his friend Beau, son of Bela and Isabeau. During their years of study the two men became not only friends but ideological revolutionaries. Their secular humanist beliefs did not bode well for their long term future in a country so firmly under the authority of the Council of Trent. When these two young physicians came under the scrutiny of the Roman Inquisition for their overt practices and public affirmations of what was considered by The Church to be evidence of heresy if not dissent they had to flee Florence. Nostredame Beau wrote to his father ...

> *Dear Father,*
>
> *I do not know when I shall be able to visit you again for my life has become a travail. To detail my tribulations to you would upset our Holy Mother the Church, for in their wisdom my dearest friend and I are viewed with considerable disfavour. However, I must not complain for we are able to continue our work amongst the poor and the victims of the Plague.*
>
> *Your most affectionate son,*
> *Nostredame Beau*
> *December 16, 1568*

Beau neglected to tell his father the suffering he endured in the chambers of the Inquisition before his escape, or the affliction that had come upon him in the course of his administrations of the diseased, which eventually claimed his life. The man he considered to be his father had died shortly after he left Salon, spared the knowledge of the suffering and the death of the man he thought was his son.

The unravelling of the original Time Loop Ribbon left a number of loose ends that became the responsibility of Quintessence to resolve in order to maintain continuity in the flow of new causes and effects that had arisen in the parallel Ribbons. The chaos created by Kobayashi Beau in having cast his seed outside the flow of his time had resolved itself by the death of his son borne by Anne.

However, another set of possibilities had been set in motion by the son of Bela and Isabeau, the probabilities of which had become a reality in segment 2555. To ensure that Ribbon's integrity Quintessence saved Bela's son's descendant from sure death on a dying planet to begin a new life.

On the passenger manifest of the second ship of the armada leaving Earth in the year 2407 there appeared the name of a young man and his wife, a late acceptance to the already full list of colonists headed for the planet Proxima-b in the constellation Centaurus.

Another parallel Ribbon began to drift away from its origins.

28

Zetaverse

In the beginning it didn't take long for Beau to start dreaming about magnificent business opportunities that could come from his association with Quintessence.

Those fledgling aspirations never had a chance to develop into anything more than fanciful thinking. Complications. Far too many complications had arisen in the course of their interactions and travels.

Beau realised after having been seduced by Anne in 1549 and witnessing his ancestor dying in 3790 that it was not possible to go cruising on the Time Loop Ribbon without causing changes that would send a destructive tsunami through time, bringing about cataclysmic changes to the lives of far too many people. What would happen if one let lose hordes of pleasure seeking, totally self-centred humanity intent on their own lust for satisfaction? What unimaginable damage could they cause at every point in the entire history of the human race?

He and Emma had a son and with that catalyst a new awakening descended on the chief scientist working for Playback Inc. Beau realised just how futile his life's work had become. Whilst the memory of the past and of the future still vaguely lingered he knew that his Zetaverse concept was flawed. Any attempt to create a super saturated sensory Zetaverse of augmented reality, especially with time travel capacity would end in nothing less than disaster.

It may still have been possible to stimulate a past experience through neural interventions. Initial experiments had proved that to be a viable area of research, research which had progressed to limited trials then to extended trials.

Dante had just turned five years old when he first visited his father's and mother's laboratory.

"Do you work here, Daddy?"

"Yes my son, your mother and I have important things to do."

"Can I work here with you? I would like that."

Emma and Beau turned to each other in complete surprise. It was far too early for any child to have such things on their mind as 'work' let alone being capable of understanding what that actually was - never mind deciding where they would like to do it.

His father's eyebrows shot up, which the boy had come to know very well, including all its nuances of meaning. A huge wide grin spread across his face as Beau said, very seriously, "Of course you can. Perhaps one day *we* will be working for you."

"Where did that come from?" asked a surprised Emma. "Are you saying something I should know about? Was it your spooky friend again showing you things?"

Beau was about to protest that he'd not heard from Quintessence for many, many years - but remained silent. Emma didn't press the point, for Dante had wandered off touching everything within his reach. He loved pressing buttons always wanting to know what all the equipment did.

The boy's parents caught up with him, leading him outside by both hands. Beau had become introspective, then he said, "Why don't you take Dante home. I've got something to tell you - later."

He went back inside. Larry joined him. "We've got another bunch of dementeds," Larry said.

"It's just not working, is it. Whatever we do they almost all seem to completely lose their sense of reality after just a few Zetaverse playbacks. I really think this technology is a dead loss."

Scrubbing out more of the extraneous data from memory packets reduced the recordings to almost nonsensical fleeting bytes of memory. By trying to enhance those with neuroenhancers only made the replays more disjoined and disturbing. If anything they began to resemble nightmares more than memories of pleasant past experiences.

"Couldn't we work with just the raw data. Let people untangle complications in their own heads. Or better still create fantasy realities from their verbal accounts and enhance those?" Emma had tried everything she could think of - chemically and digitally - to resolve the psychological imbalances created by what people had come to considered either false playbacks, or manipulated recordings designed to twist their minds.

"So - where do we go from here Boss," asked Larry.

"Whether Playback Inc. likes it or not they are going to have to find another product line to keep pace with this pleasure addiction that's taken hold of our society. I've talked this over with Emma. We think there's a business opportunity here. We could branch out into trying to balance peoples' psyches instead of confusing them with unrealities. We need a whole new spectrum of drugs to counteract the side effects of any experiences, regardless of whether they are disturbingly real or surreal. This is all confidential of course Larry - seriously. Would you consider working with us - Emma and me and a few others of course? We are going to have to break away from Playback."

Beau remembered the very last trip Quintessence took him on. It was within their own short timeline, to only a few years into their future. If what he saw was a real possibility it was time to start making decisions in that direction.

At home Dante had been absorbing another tutored session provided by his bio-mech teacher for over an hour or so. He had an outstanding concentration span and assimilated knowledge quickly. While working in his own room he didn't hear his father arrive home.

Beau walked up to Emma quietly, put his arms around her waist as she stood by the window apparently in deep thought. "Good, your home. I've been thinking Bebo ... about what you said to me at the lab, and the progress on our work. It all seemed so promising a little while ago. I'm starting to have some serious doubts about that."

"Before we get into that I think you should know something - and I know what you said about time tripping, but hear me out." Emma turned to face her Bebo. He'd been a good boy for many years. He hadn't gone off again to unknown planets all over the universe. He'd stayed with her and helped raise Dante into a wonderful boy who showed such great promise. She nodded for him to continue, still held in his embrace. "My spook has taken me on a short little jump, only a few years ahead, right here in Gamarrah. You and I - we had a new enterprise together, I can even give you the name of it - Quantum Reality. And I'll give you one guess who the boss will be."

Emma withdrew from his arms searching his eyes for a clue. Beau started grinning finding it almost unbearable to keep silent.

"Nooooooo!" Emma's eyes turned to saucers, pupils dilated. She thumped him on the chest. Then realization lit up her face.

"Yep. And I'll give you just one guess who'll be working for him."

29

Xoco and Aapo Ribbon

On a planet long, long way away - in a country of little significance in the affairs of the known world an elderly Mayan shaman tested his apprentice.

His memory had started to worry him some time ago. He could remember his own master, Apoxpalon, and everything the great shaman had taught him. Yet there arose gaps in his memory he simply could not resurrect.

Xoco could recall the morning of the double sunrise, but not why he had known about it in advance. More startling amongst his memories were those of two men, dressed in the most peculiar ornamental fashion, after whose sacrifice the threat of eternal darkness upon the world had never happened again. The Gods must have been pleased with the unique gift his people gave him.

As a person in such a high position of responsibility Xoco could not afford to show the least sign of incompetence. His reputation, the trust of the people he served and even his life depended on it. He was careful not to reveal his fading memory, which unknown to him did not have a neurological basis. His world had changed, leaving past history to blend into the dark spaces of the night sky. He was also most careful not to reveal what he had learnt about the place of the Earth in the universe ... that it was not the centre of it. Since the visitation of the three Star Men Xoco had repeated his calculations of Long Cycles numerous times until finally each calculation matched the one before it.

"When in the cycle of the heavens will you ever settle down?" he called to Aapo who'd been fussing over his ceremonial costume in an adjoining room. Apoxpalon's hut had to be renovated, with the addition of another small stone enclosure to make room for Akma, Aapo's old mother who'd come to live with them to look after them both.

"I am coming Master - this is important for the next twenty day cycle ceremony."

"Alright, alright. After that there is a most important day coming up for you. You have to be ready in your heart and in your soul, not just with your feathers."

Aapo had spent many more years as Xoco's apprentice than Xoco had spent with Apoxpalon. Not because he was slow, but because he could contain so much more in himself. Xoco had to make sure the vessel had been filled with all the right knowledge to make it suitable to serve the people after his passing.

As Apoxpalon had done before him he asked the young man to bring the complex calendar, quills and parchment to the fallow field. The sun had not yet risen to mid-morning and some hunting animals still felt safe to continue with their pursuits. Making their way through a thin strip of forest near their hut the two men soon arrived at their chosen location. They stopped to watch a jaguar decide whether it wanted to have the hooked nose snake for breakfast or not. The snake had coiled itself into a ball, opened its mouth wide ready to strike and with a swaying motion of its head followed the big cat's every move. Puss thought better of it and stalked back under the lush canopy of the forest. He would not be back for quite a while, time enough for the shaman to examine his pupil.

They settled in the middle of the fallow maize field where Xoco prepared the equipment with careful attention to every detail. The hot sun would beat down on them soon enough so they started straight away. "Calculate for me the beginning of the next series of Long Counts. Take your time. I know you are proficient now in mathematics and can read the glyphs fluently."

An hour went by, then another. The master watched his apprentice's methods, giving no hint of approval or disapproval. Half way through the third hour Aapo simply announced, "4772." He had been painstaking in every aspect of the calculations and showed no sign of uncertainty about his answer.

"Correct." Xoco gave no praise. It wasn't necessary. The right answer was expected, not a day more or a day less. Aapo received no hearty slap on the back, or even a smile. Once, in the past, when Xoco attempted the re-calculation (he could remember doing that, but not why it was necessary) the numbers of the year refused to reveal themselves. It was as if time itself had become unsure of itself.

"My master died a contented man because I was able to tell him the day of his passing ..." said Xoco, leaving the sentence unfinished, the requirement self-evident.

Once again Aapo applied himself, this time with great fervor for it would not do to get this assignment wrong. He had great respect for his master and for himself. While he concentrated ion the important task he did not see the old man nod off as the sun's intensity came down upon them.

Xoco, I told you once that when the sun rose twice on the same morning, it would bring a great change.

I remember this, he replied in his mind to the voice of this spirit.

Much has changed for your world. The segment of time called 3797 no longer has significance. Do you wish to speak with Apoxpalon?

Is this possible?

Xoco truly loved his grandfather as his relative, and greatly respected him as a shaman and his master. Only one thing could give him greater happiness than knowing the day of his own passing. Before that thought had come and died in his mind he found himself standing in his own hut, beside his own bed. But the man lying in it was not himself.

"Grandfather," Xoco whispered to the closed eyes of a very old man.

Apoxpalon's eyes opened wide and that familiar smile spread across his face - "You came." He didn't know that the vision before him was as insubstantial as the morning mist. He tried to raise his hand but it fell back onto the bed. Xoco leant over to whisper to his grandfather and felt only the last breath leave Apoxpalon's body, the smile remaining where it had awoken.

"Master," Aapo had to shake his master gently several times to wake him. As Xoco raised his face to the boy Aapo saw on his face such an ecstatic happiness that he leant over to hug his Master and hold him tight.

"You can let go now," Xoco said after a few minutes, "I am back now. What is so urgent that you had to wake me?"

"It is not so urgent, but perhaps wise to be aware of it."

"No - no. It is no longer important. I shall pass when I pass." Aapo cast a long searching look into his master's eyes. A complete change had come over the old man. Whatever happened to him in his dream had made him so ... so ... serene. "Are you entirely happy with your cycle calculation my jaguar cub?"

"No. The date is correct but the constellations do not match our own."

"That is correct." Xoco remembered, at least for a short time, a gift from Quintessence - his experiences with the two men from the stars. That night he took Xoco back out into the field and showed him those stars again, for he felt very certain his memory of them would soon fade.

30

Quintessence

Quintessence withdrew from the affairs of man.

Where once only dark matter and dark energy existed there arose time, a phenomenon of an entirely novel process defined by change. With the creation of light and gravity freedom in space-eternity had ceased. Over time gravitational condensation caused dark energy to fold onto itself into small clusters. And within the extension of time some of those clusters of dark energy that had come together also began the transformation from the inanimate towards showing signs of self-awareness.

The universe was no longer empty. Baryonic matter and energy also came together to manifest in many forms, some of which evolved to think of themselves as being unique and separate and of considerable importance.

Quintessence's consciousness expanded into the awareness that it was not alone, yet it was separate from all that there was around it, recognising another energy signature that was life itself. Its association with the human species began as distant observations, purely out of curiosity. The unfathomable mystery of the behaviour of man attracted Quintessence by the very unpredictability of this species. What seemed to be random actions developed possibilities, and some of those demonstrated probabilities which became certainties.

Most curiously these strange life forms did not appear to be content with their existence on their chunks of rock and sought to venture into the oceans of eternity where Quintessence had its domain. It found one such creature encased in its pod and attempted to make contact with it.

The sudden elation of finding an entity that did in fact have potential for interaction caused Quintessence to forget their fragility. As communication developed Quintessence did not know why it continued interacting with these living entities. It felt an irresistible compulsion to extend those interactions. *But to what end must I do this?* Purpose had never before entered the realm of its conceptualisation about existence. In the great scheme of things existence did not require purpose. Yet the question arose as an inevitable consequence of his interactions.

Quintessence grew into a deeper knowledge of itself, its environment, its mind and its capabilities. It observed decisions that flowered into effects and those that did not. It questioned the inevitability of some effects and whether they were in fact inevitable or if some management of probabilities was possible.

And thus it became entangled in the lives of man, in particular with the strange stranglehold time itself had on them.

In time, the subjective time of humanity, Quintessence realized it had a role to play in the sundering of the Ribbon of Time and that it had a contribution to make towards a solution to the rift if the known universe was to continue after being tipped out of balance by any single Time Loop Ribbon unravelling.

An unlikely solution did present itself, however not without complications ... issues which may yet continue to create anomalies. Each parallel Ribbon needed its special attention. And in the process of giving it, Quintessence may have discovered the answer to its own very first questions arising out of its growing awareness ... *Why must I do this? Why do I exist?*

Quintessence drifted into deep, deep space expanding as it grew into its own potential. What started as small clusters of compacted dark energy became a massive cloud that could call all of the Local Group its domain.

And the answer so far, which it decided to contemplate until its intervention was needed again ...

... There is no reason for existence - there is satisfaction and there is disappointment. ...

Quintessence chose to define himself by a gift bestowed upon him unknowingly by Beau and Beau's past and future family ... the gift if his identity ...

... *I am Kobayashi Beaubeladante.*

Epilogue

The future is not created instant by instant, we only move towards it at that arbitrary rate. Decisions and actions decide future probabilities, both near and far futures. And what has taken place in the past cannot be changed, although it can be augmented thus creating new future possibilities at tangents to the old.

We believe we are made of the stuff of stars. Yet the physical universe we know is not all that there is. There are forces and energies we are only beginning to guess at. The mystery of dark energy has only been known about in recent times. Before that devils and dragons inhabited our imaginations and our world view. All manner of invisibilities claimed our understanding in the guise of spirits and Gods. Such phenomena call cosmic space their realm and from time to time become incarnate in a form of life that has created an internal space of consciousness within our minds.

Perhaps fragments of dark energy clusters continue to dip their desires into the human mind before withdrawing to ponder a mystery as foreign to them as it is to us. There is one such cluster of a very high order of energy that for the purposes of this story is identified as Quintessence. It did not truly know itself until it came into sentient awareness through Kobayashi Beau.

*

After many years of a long and eventful life, absorbed in the joy of watching his son flower into full personhood Beau had a most unexpected visitor.

Kobayashi Beau?

Towards the very end of his life Beau developed the habit of regularly going to his favourite domed park at a regular time of day; right at the end of it, when he could sit in peace by the stream and watch the stars appear. Emma often had to break her daily routine to go out there and get him. Sometimes it would be his son Dante and sometimes his son's son, Dante to fetch him home.

Who is ...? Then he recognised the voice. The world had become completely dark by then, except for a most curious patch of nothingness in the Northern segment of the sky devoid of all light.

We have spoken before - not so long ago.

"Quintessence!" He said aloud. The park had been deserted by then so no one would suspect Beau had begun to unravel by talking to the sky; for he'd raised his eyes towards that strange darkness up there.

Yes. I have come to give you something.

Wait! wait ... there is blackness invading my mind. Is that you? Please stop.

It is only a memory. It is my gift.

For a long few minutes Beau sat on the bench, staring up into the darkness then turning towards the South to the light of the Milky Way. His thoughts travelled back to the moment aboard a space craft that had been immobilised during a blackout. He remembered. Then he remembered many other things. When he next spoke it was not to Quintessence.

"I remember tomorrow as if it was only yesterday – so when am I now?" ... and Quintessence did not reply.

"The past was yesterday. Today is the present until tomorrow's future. But I'm not so sure anymore. In an instant I will be in the future ... ... it has already happened. Perhaps I should think an hour ahead to consider that to be the future, while I can still remember a moment ago to help me know which way I am going."

Beau stopped talking and closed his eyes. Quintessence looked into his mind. It listened to the thoughts of a scientist who loved to solve mysteries.

It is not possible to be simply who I am today for today does not exist ... it does not exist long enough to form a solid understanding of it. Today is only a chaotic jumble of what I remember of an hour ago and what I intended to do – a disappointment in what I actually did - in many ways unrelated to what I'm hoping will be reality in an hour hence.

Should I wait for it and hope that nothing happens to change who I hope to be in an hours time? Or should I try to bend the Universal Law and have a quick peek. I feel sure that is possible, for I can still remember tomorrow as if it was yesterday – and there is nothing to be disappointed about.

When exactly will tomorrow come? That I cannot remember.

Emma arrived at the usual time, late into the evening. Sometimes the old man had nodded off by then. She touched him lightly on the shoulder to wake him. He didn't respond.

"Come on Bebo, time to go home." She touched his cheek, feeling it to have become quite cold.

She stroked his hair and sat down next him, to be with him for a little while longer.

---------- : ----------

The Journey from trying to climb into a Russian tank during the Hungarian revolution of 1956 to writing Science Fiction is in itself a story of a leap across worlds of reality.

Zsoall, born in Hungary, was brought to Australia by his parents after the 1956 uprising. He currently lives a creative life with his wife and animal family in the Northern Rivers, New South Wales, Australia.

His life has changed direction a number of times. After gaining his qualifications as a Sculptor he worked as a Secondary Teacher before becoming an Administrative Manager. None offered satisfactory opportunities for creative expression. That began when he embarked on a career as a computer programmer. Whilst in that profession his continuing compulsion to create made it inevitable that his life would change again. Completely giving up programming he immersed himself in creativity as a Sculptor and Painter.

Much of his time is now dedicated to creating glass paintings and sculptures.

Another change is looming on the horizon as the art of recording future visions takes a firmer hold of his creative inclinations as he pursues the writing of Science Fiction.

www.ingramcontent.com/pod-product-compliance
Lightning Source LLC
Chambersburg PA
CBHW020345120726
47904CB00002B/462